MASQUERADE

William X. Kienzle

BALLANTINE BOOKS • NEW YORK

Library of Congress Catalog Card Number: 89-77890

ISBN 0-345-36620-4

This edition published by arrangement with Andrews and McMeel, a Universal Press Syndicate Company.

Manufactured in the United States of America

First Ballantine Books Edition: April 1991

FOR JAVAN

"And, after all, what is a lie?
'Tis but the truth in masquerade."

—"Don Juan"
Canto XI, St. 37
Lord Byron

ACKNOWLEDGMENTS

Gratitude for technical advice to:

Ramon Betanzos, Ph.D., Professor of Humanities, Wayne State University

Father William Dowell, Pastor, Prince of Peace Parish, West Bloomfield, Michigan

Jim Grace, Detective, Kalamazoo Police Department

Sister Bernadelle Grimm, R.S.M., Samaritan Health Care Center, Detroit

Timothy Kenny, attorney-at-law, Larson, Harms & Wright, P.C.

Sister Patricia Lamb, R.S.M., Pastoral Associate, St. Joseph the Worker Parish, Grand Rapids, Michigan

Irma Macy, Religious Education Coordinator, Prince of Peace Parish, West Bloomfield, Michigan

Gerald P. Maloney, Chief Substance Abuse Therapist, Heritage Hospital, Taylor, Michigan

Sergeant Mary Marcantonio, Office of Executive Deputy Chief, Detroit Police Department

Donna Martin, Vice President and Editorial Director, Andrews and McMeel

Thomas J. Petinga, Jr., D.O., FACEP, Chairman, Department of Emergency Medicine, Mt. Carmel Mercy Hospital, Detroit

Walter D. Pool, M.D., Medical Consultant

Noreen Rooney, TV Book Editor, *Detroit Free Press* (Retired)

Joseph G. Schulte, Executive Vice President, Ross Roy Communications

John E. Shay, Jr., Ph.D., President, Marygrove College

Sister Jan Soleau, I.H.M., Director, Alumni Relations, Marygrove College

John Sommerfeldt, Ph.D., Professor of History, University of Dallas

Werner U. Spitz, M.D., Professor of Forensic Pathology, Wayne State University

Inspector Barbara Weide, Youth Section, Detroit Police Department

Rabbi and Mrs. R.W. Weiss

The Reverend Canon and Mrs. C. George Widdifield, Pastoral Associate, Christ Church Cranbrook, Bloomfield Hills, Michigan

Any technical error is the author's.

Marygrove College   Detroit, Michigan

The Subject Is Murder

"Men never do evil so completely and cheerfully as
when they do it from religious conviction."—Pascal

A Seminar Workshop on the Role of
Religion in Murder Mysteries

Marygrove College   Sept. 4–8, 1989

Mystery novels are currently enjoying a renaissance unmatched in history. Add to mystery the element of religion and we have a match made in heaven
(or hell). The root word for mystery means "that
which is hidden." St. Thomas Aquinas says there are
two absolute mysteries in Christianity: the mystery
of the Incarnation and the mystery of the Trinity.

None of our faculty would dispute St. Thomas regarding the possibility of an absolute mystery. But
they will lead us through mysteries that have solu-
tions, with sleuths (albeit fictional) who unravel the
puzzles of murder most foul. Depending on which of
our faculty is writing, the sleuth may be a priest, a
monk, a rabbi, or a nun. But with a religious background and motif, the mystery, in a certain sense,
has "come home."

Our goals are the same as they have been for all our
previous workshops: to provide information, inspiration, instruction, and encouragement for all writers—published or unpublished.

Our featured speaker is the noted televangelist and
successful publisher, Klaus Krieg. Our four faculty
members are all published mystery authors.

Whether or not your field is the religious mystery
novel, you cannot help gaining valuable insight into
the publishing world from those already successful
in this field.

Learn how to attract an agent, find a publisher,

write the query letter; how to recognize "boilerplate" pitfalls in contractual language; the dangers in self-publishing; the vagaries of pub dates, and how to promote the finished product.

All this in addition to an introduction to the religious mystery novel by those who understand it inside and out.

Featured Speakers:

Klaus Krieg, Founder of P.G. Press, and internationally famous evangelist of the P.G. Television Network.

Rev. David Benbow, Rector of St. Andrew's Episcopal Church, Chicago, Illinois, and author of three novels. The latest: Father Emrich and the Reluctant Convert.

Sister Marie Monahan, IHM, Director of Continuing Education for the Archdiocese of Miami, Florida, and author of Behind the Veil.

Rev. Augustine May, OCSO, Trappist of St. Francis Abbey, Wellesley, Massachusetts, and author of A Rose by Any Other Name, as well as many articles in monastic publications.

Irving Winter, Rabbi of Congregation Beth Shalom, Windsor, Ontario, Canada, author of a series of mystery novels from which the popular "Rabbi" television series has been adapted.

1

"WHAT THE HELL is this doing here?"

Father Ed Sklarski glanced around the large room, but got no answer from the sprinkling of relaxing priests. No response forthcoming, he tried a slightly different tack. "Who brought this here?"

Father Jim Tracy looked up from the book he was reading. "What is it?"

Sklarski rattled the heavy stock paper. "I don't know. I just found it on the table here. Some sort of brochure. From Marygrove. A writers' conference or something. Something about religion and murder mysteries."

"If it's about religion, it's in the right place here." Tracy smiled and returned to his book.

Sklarski, with nothing better to do at the moment, read on silently from the artsy pamphlet.

Sklarski, feeling a little mid-afternoon numbness, decided to make himself a drink. He glanced at the bar. Plenty of scotch; no hurry. He studied the brochure more carefully. To no one in particular he said, "Who are those people, anyway? I don't recognize anybody but that jerk, Krieg. Does more damage than an army of goddam devils."

Tracy had been paying only marginal attention. At that, it

was more advertence than anyone else in the room was giving
Sklarski. "Krieg? The television producer? What about
him?" Tracy asked.

Sklarski pointed to the name, a useless gesture. "Says he's
going to be featured at this workshop at Marygrove."

"Really!" Tracy lowered the book and removed his bifocals. "That's odd, even for a relevant place like Marygrove. Who else is on the list?" Sklarski focused with some
difficulty. "Um . . . David Benbow, Anglican . . ."

"Mystery writer," Tracy identified.

"Marie Monahan, a nun . . ."

"Mystery writer."

"Huh! Augustine May, a Trappist . . ."

"All of them, eh?"

"And Irving Winer. A rabbi, would you believe?"

"You must know him," Tracy said. "That TV series on
Sunday nights is based on his books."

"The one about the rabbi?"

"Uh-huh."

"Now that you mention it. But . . . you know all these
people?"

"They're all mystery writers. They all have religious
sleuths that correspond to themselves. The priest has a priest
sleuth, the nun, a nun; the Trappist, a monk, the rabbi, a
rabbi. It's quite a good idea, really, if you want to follow the
dictum, 'Go with what you know.' "

Incredulity was evident in Sklarski's expression. "You
mean you've read them all?"

Tracy smiled. "I haven't read Monahan yet. But the others? Yes."

Sklarski slowly shook his head. "What is it with you? All

you ever do is read books. God! How many books can you read? There're only twenty-six letters in the alphabet!''

Tracy chuckled and returned to his present book.

Sklarski, while continuing to read the brochure, moved to the bar, where he selected the one glass that, by common consent, was reserved for his use and his alone. It was never washed.

"Aha!" There was triumph in Sklarski's voice.

The other priests gave him their startled attention. It was at this moment that Sklarski blew the cobwebs out of his glass and splashed in a bit of scotch. Sklarski's routine constituted an act of faith in the antiseptic powers of alcohol.

"Aha!" Sklarski repeated. "Now we have it. Here's the reason. That's why this pamphlet is here." No one asked what that reason might be, so Sklarski, pointing at the revelatory line, continued. "See here? It says: Resource person: Father Robert Koesler, whose religious background and periodic contact with the Homicide Division of Detroit's Police Department will provide valuable authentication to our workshop.

"Where is he?" Sklarski bellowed. "I saw Koesler a little while ago. He must have brought this thing with him. Where is he?"

Actually, if Father Robert Koesler had been closer to the Paternoster clubhouse, he could have heard Sklarski easily. But, as it was, Koesler was communing with nature close by on the Lake St. Clair shoreline.

For some time, Koesler, albeit somewhat absently, studied the ground. At length, he selected a flat stone, then skipped it over the barely undulating water.

Six skips. Not bad, but hardly championship caliber.

He inhaled deeply. The air was undoubtedly polluted; wasn't everything? But, somehow, with no factory or other industrial complex in sight, on a clear brisk September afternoon, at the shore of this pleasant adjunct of the majestic Great Lakes, everything seemed salubrious.

However, as pleasant as it was here, he had no intention of joining the Paternoster Club. His duties, as well as his priorities, were too demanding to make practical such an investment of time and money. He was there this day as a guest of his friend and classmate Father Patrick McNiff, whom a parishioner had once accurately described as "somewhat stuffy but never uninteresting."

Founded in the early fifties by and for priests, the club was intended as a facility for R, R & R: rest, relaxation, and reflection—to which could be added retreat. In the early sixties, the membership had peaked at sixty. Now, thanks to the clergy shortage, it was approximately half that.

Located in Ontario, northeast of Windsor near Stoney Point, the club's spacious cabin sits on ten acres of land at the tip of a peninsula embraced on three sides by Lake St. Clair and a man-made canal.

Koesler selected a thinner, flatter stone. Four skips. He would not be entering any competition.

If I shot an arrow, thought Koesler, it wouldn't go very far. But if it were to hit U.S. land on the other side of the lake—out of sight of this spot—it most likely would hit Harsens Island. That was home to Ed Sklarski, now retired—or who, in popular parlance, had achieved Senior Priest status.

Koesler shook his head. Senior Priest status was one of the many fruits of the Second Vatican Council. Before Vatican II, in the early sixties, priests just did not retire. They died, like as not, on a Saturday afternoon while hearing kids' confessions, halfway through an absolution, bored to death. Somehow, it all seemed more appropriate—dying in the saddle, as it were.

Now there was mandatory retirement at age seventy. Retirement to what? The priest had no wife to live out with him "the Golden Years." No family with whom to visit or to invite home. Today's Senior Priest might move to a warmer climate, there to vegetate. Or hang in there doing whatever parish chores he chose. What with the vocations crisis, priestly retirement was a luxury the Church could ill afford.

Koesler hunched his shoulders. Was it getting cold?

He was beginning to develop a philosophy that "nothing is as good as it was." Not the music, not the movies, not the newspapers; not entertainment, not cars, not pride in workmanship, not anything. Well, if he was developing into a full-fledged curmudgeon, he was of an age at which it seemed appropriate.

He walked along the beach, almost mesmerized by the rhythmic lapping of the waves.

On another, brighter aspect, he reflected, this was just about his favorite season, autumn. And it was just beginning now, a bit ahead of time, on the second day of September. The sun had already begun to tilt from its directly overhead summertime course. There was a nip in the air. Footballs were flying. Baseball was nearing the home stretch. Soon the leaves would display their breathtaking colors.

The only fly he could discern in the present ointment was the commitment he had made to that blasted writers' workshop.

Bob Koesler was forever repeating that same blunder: accepting invitations to events many months in the future. In analyzing his own pattern, it seemed that when invited to participate in something in the distant future, he would convince himself that it was so far off that it would never happen. Or that perhaps in the meantime he would die.

In any case, there was no getting around this one. The panel of experts (or "faculty" as they were called) would assemble tomorrow at Marygrove. And he would be there with them.

Apart from having become a conscientious reader of mystery novels, he could think of no reason why he should be a "resource person." True, he had had some small contact with Detroit's Homicide Department. But that had been quite fortuitous. The Fickle Finger of Fate, as the late lamented TV program, "Laugh-In" put it. It was a case of his being at the right—or wrong—place at the right—or wrong—time, depending on how one looked at it.

He had been of some small help in solving a few cases in the past. But that had not been due to any native expertise in crime detection on his part. No, all the cases he'd been involved with had a religious, mostly Catholic, element. So he had been able to supply the missing church ingredient needed in the resolution of such investigation. Now that he considered his present involvement, he could not imagine why he had ever accepted this invitation.

The only consolation—and it was not inconsiderable—was the prospect of his meeting the four authors.

Koesler had a special regard for writers. He had read at least one offering of each author on the panel. It was something like experiencing a Dick Francis novel. Francis had been a successful jockey. And, regularly, the race track provided the background for his plots. Thus, in addition to providing a pleasant diversion, a Francis book was more than likely to give one added insight into the racing game.

So it was with the present four. And it wasn't only that theirs was a religious background, but that their backgrounds were so diverse. Besides the entertainment and the mystery, the reader got an insight into the specialized world of an Episcopal (and married) priest, or the drastically changed nun's world, or life in a cloistered world, or the world of the Jewish culture, so filled with tradition and law.

Koesler was, of course, steeped in the unique lifestyle of the Roman Catholic priest. With his express interest in religion, he found fulfilling the revelations the others provided. He was eager to meet them.

He was less than enthusiastic about being made available as a "resource person." Especially since he sincerely felt he had little to offer. But he had agreed to do it. So, ready or not, here he came.

Koesler realized that he was shivering ever so slightly. He checked his watch. It was getting late. The imminence of sundown, plus the breeze from the lake, must have lowered the temperature.

Quiet, undisturbed moments were rare and such time passed quickly. He would have to collect McNiff and head home. Both of them had Saturday evening, as well as Sunday, liturgies to offer.

He turned and walked toward the cabin.

Around this time tomorrow he would be preparing to go to Marygrove and meet his fellow participants in the workshop. His final thought on the matter concerned Klaus Krieg. The one who, in Koesler's view, did not fit.

Krieg was a publisher, not an author. That part was all right; writers would be pretty lonely people without publishers. It wasn't that a publisher, as such, was out of place at such a conference. It was the stuff that Krieg published. In

Koesler's view. P.G.'s publications were simply not in the same literary league as the material turned out by these authors.

It was obvious that P.G. Press made money—lots of it. But then, someone once said that no one had ever gone broke by underestimating the taste of the American public. Klaus Krieg might not have been the original author of that aphorism, but he certainly seemed to bear it out. In all honesty, Koesler had to admit that his knowledge of the quality of Krieg's entrepreneurial empire was largely secondhand. Koesler had read only one book published by P.G. Press. The setting had been New York's Catholic Church. And if the story had been anywhere near true, most New York parishes would have been forced to close: There wouldn't have been any priests around to say Mass or hear confessions, let alone administer a parish. According to that book, most New York priests were in bed pretty much around the clock, and hardly alone.

It wasn't just that the book needlessly and gratuitously debased the priesthood—although that was bad enough. Women, in the book, were depicted as kittenish creatures curled in sacerdotal arms, and grateful in a depraved way for the macho favors they had been granted.

Once he was sure the book could not possibly have been salvaged by a single redeeming feature, Koesler had put it—and all future P.G. books—aside forever. From reports he'd received from others, and from reviews and news articles he'd read, he had concluded that his experience with P.G. was by no means isolated.

P.G. Press was giving both religious and romance novels a very bad name. But from all indications, P.G. Press was making money—lots of it.

And that was not even the half of it. The greater money-making venture, by far, was the Praise God Network. Klaus Krieg was among the foremost of the current crop of tele-vangelists—once again, as far as Koesler was concerned, giving religion a very bad reputation.

All in all, he was not yearning to meet Klaus Krieg. Or, as he was sometimes disrespectfully referred to by some of the media, "Blitz" Krieg—German for "lightning war."

Nor could Koesler guess what had motivated the organizers of this workshop to include Krieg. Those writers who had such an evident respect and reverence for religion really had nothing in common with Krieg except the most tenuous connection with some sort of religious expression. How would or could they relate to such a person?

Koesler did not fancy confrontations. And he had the clear premonition he was walking right into a classic showdown.

But here he was at the cabin. He entered to find almost everyone in helpless laughter. The only one who seemed not to be getting the joke was Koesler's host, Patrick McNiff. McNiff seemed bewildered.

Sklarski, the first to show signs of recovery, gasped, "Tell him . . . tell Koesler what you just said."

"What's so funny about it?" McNiff was obviously flustered. "I don't see anything so funny about it."

"Tell him," Sklarski urged.

"Wait," Tracy interrupted, "we've got to set it up. It's no good without the setup."

Sensing he was the butt of a joke, a joke he didn't get, McNiff showed clear signs of increasing anger.

"I woke him up just before you came in," Sklarski said to Koesler. "I asked him why he bothered coming all the way over to Canada just to sleep all afternoon. Then . . ."

he turned back to the baffled man, "what did you say, McNiff?"

McNiff was gathering his belongings—a book, a couple of magazines, an electric shaver—and slamming them into a duffel bag. "I don't remember." He was turning defensive.

"Come on, why did you sleep all afternoon?"

"Because I've got a cold," McNiff tried tentatively. He wasn't sure whether it was this statement that the others had found humorous. It was something he'd said, he just wasn't sure what. No one laughed. This wasn't it.

"So," Sklarski pursued, "what do you do when you've got a cold?"

"Actually, I haven't got a cold. I'm coming down with one."

"Okay," Sklarski was getting impatient, "what do you do when you're coming down with a cold?"

"Go to bed."

"That's not what you said."

By process of elimination, McNiff concluded, the second part of his statement had to be it. "I don't remember." He would not play the fool. Not knowingly, at any rate.

Koesler looked inquiringly at Sklarski. It was evident McNiff was not about to cooperate. It was also evident that Sklarski would not let him off the hook.

"You said," Sklarski supplied, "that whenever you were coming down with a cold, you always tried to curl up on a couch for a few hours with an African."

Laughter renewed.

McNiff's eyes darted confusedly from one to another of his confreres. "It helps," he explained in bewilderment.

"I'll bet." Sklarski guffawed, and spilled his drink.

"C'mon," Koesler said, "it's getting late." On the way

home, he would explain the difference between African and afghan and hope that McNiff did not become so testy he would get flip with an officer at the border. Koesler did not want to spend this night justifying his existence to customs officials.

Koesler was positive that at any given moment, customs officials could out-testy even McNiff.

2

THEY DID NOT appear to be nuns, certainly not in the traditional sense.

One carried a large suitcase. She was dressed in a beige summerweight business suit. The clothing neither accentuated nor disguised her figure, which, while mature and full, was firm and feminine.

She was Sister Marie Monahan, a member of the Sisters, Servants of the Immaculate Heart of Mary religious order, and a graduate of Marygrove College. She was also author of *Behind the Veil*, a recently published and fairly successful mystery novel.

Her companion, Sister Janet Schultes, also a member of the IHM order, was coordinator of the writers' workshop that would begin tomorrow. Shorter and slimmer than Marie, Janet wore a light topcoat over her dress uniform. Both dress and coat were the deep shade recognizable to the practiced eye as IHM blue.

She also wore what was known as a modified veil, which sat well back on her head, revealing her nearly white hair. Sister Janet carried a black attaché case that contained Sister Marie's conference papers.

Since Janet had met Marie's plane at Metro Airport, the

two nuns had been chatting nonstop. Classmates and best of friends, they had been separated by many miles for many years now.

The two were about to enter the Madame Cadillac building at the center of Marygrove's campus. Before climbing the steps, they paused to study the cornerstone.

Marie read the words aloud. " *'Arbor Una Nobilis'*—the one and only noble tree. Remember, Jan, from the Good Friday Mass—the hymn?'' She recited from memory. " 'Faithful cross, among all others/One and only noble tree/ Not a grove on earth can show/Such leaf and flower as grow on thee.' ''

Janet joined in with the original Latin, " *'Crux fidelis/ Inter omnes/Arbor una nobilis/Nulla silva talem profert/ Fronde, flore, germine.'* ''

"You remembered! The Latin!''

"It's a meditation for me,'' Jan replied. "I try to recite it each time I enter the building.''

Marie shook her head. "Good Friday, the Mass of the Presanctified—a little bit of history.''

"It is history, Marie. The toothpaste is out of the tube. We'll never get it back in. That era, that liturgy, that hymn, that language—all gone!''

"Yes, I fear we've thrown the baby out with the bath water.'' As she said it, Marie winced inwardly, but, other than a slight shudder, gave no indication of what she felt.

"Come on,'' Janet urged, "let's get inside. You're not dressed for this weather. You've forgotten what autumn's like in Michigan.''

They hurried up the stone steps into the building, and headed toward the elevator.

"Seem familiar?'' Janet pushed the third-floor button.

"Frighteningly. Of course I wouldn't have expected these immortal and sanctified stones to change. They built this place for the ages."

Janet smiled. "The stones are about all that hasn't changed. You and I certainly have . . . let's see, how long has it been now?"

"Oh, dear . . ." Marie grimaced. "I've been gone from Detroit for . . . what? Almost fifteen years. Add another five to that and I'll have been gone from Marygrove for about twenty years!" She smiled. "At our age one does not want to total up the years too frequently."

"Remember when we went coed?"

"Barely. The first young men were arriving on campus just about the time I left. And now you've got . . . what?"

"Actually still not all that many." Janet held open the elevator door as they exited on the third floor. "Our enrollment is about 80 percent female."

"So your football team is not headed for the Rose Bowl." They laughed.

"Nor are the pickup teams of volleyball and basketball players going to post-season playoffs. The major interest of Marygrove is still study and learning," Janet added.

"Good," Marie said emphatically. "But . . ." She hesitated. "How do you attract them? I mean, I may have been away from Detroit for a bunch of years, but it's still near and dear to my heart. And I've bled for the city. I read about it almost every week. The drugs, the violence, the murders, the children killing and being killed! I would have assumed any student would have to think several times before enrolling here. After all, Marygrove is smack in the middle of Detroit almost."

"Marie, what did you expect—an armed camp?"

They entered the private residence wing.

"Is it much further? This bag is getting heavy."

"Just down the hall."

"What did I expect?" Marie picked up the thread of their conversation. "Some security. I haven't seen any security people. If you've got some, I'd like to know where they are."

"Well, there are four or five on duty nearly all the time."

"Four or five? For all these buildings? For all these—what is it—sixty-eight acres, isn't it? Mostly woods, just the way God made it. Why, we drove right in here off McNichols Road. There wasn't anyone at the gate to screen or challenge us. Anybody could drive in here."

"There was talk of putting up a gatehouse," Janet sounded apologetic, "but it was deemed too expensive. Besides, just as you said, the campus is heavily wooded. Even if there were a gatehouse and a guard at the entrance, there's nothing to stop someone from climbing the fence at some secluded spot and getting in here."

Janet indicated they'd arrived at Marie's room. They entered. Marie looked around before setting down her suitcase. "Quite nice. You do it?"

"Uh-huh. There's so much of the college that isn't used anymore, it's fun making something out of nothing. This used to be dormitory space."

"I remember."

"I had it remodeled. Six private rooms. Just enough for the workshop faculty."

Marie began to unpack. Janet sat on the one, single bed.

"So," Marie said, "no one at the gate, and the whole place accessible to anyone who can climb the fence: Is all that supposed to make me rest easy?"

Janet frowned. "I said there was security. You didn't see

him, but there is a guard in the main parking lot. There's one in here, too. He must be making his rounds. Then there's one in the Liberal Arts Building, the Theater, and the Residence Hall''

''That's it?''

''Well, there's more. But it's sort of intangible.''

''Intangible?''

''Marie, Marygrove has changed. Not just the coed thing. We're in a mostly black, mostly poor city. Once you get away from the riverfront section of downtown and a few isolated neighborhoods, you'll find neighborhoods that are near death. But even in those neighborhoods, there are people who want something fine for themselves and their families. A goodly percentage of our students are from those families.

''Marie, this place has become a haven for poor black women—many of them older women—who want an education. This may be hard for you to understand, but these women have declared Marygrove off-limits to hoodlums.''

''And that keeps them out?''

''For the most part, yes.''

''It works?''

''Seems to.''

Marie smiled. ''I don't know. This conference is all about murder, isn't it?''

''Fiction, Marie, fiction.''

''Sometimes there's only a thin line between fiction and fact.''

Janet laughed. ''Stick to your field, Marie: fiction. Just think,'' she added, with a smile of wonderment, ''an author—a published author. When we were students here together, who would have thunk it?''

''Not I.''

"How'd you get into it?"

"By accident, mostly, I guess." Marie sat on the room's only chair. "I was thinking about all the things that have changed in our lives. Oh, not only the changes in the Church. More the changes in our order."

Janet nodded. "Almost as day and night. In the beginning, we were teachers—almost all of us in parochial schools."

"Exactly. If it hadn't been for teaching nuns, there would never have been a parochial school system. All those parishes could never have afforded lay teachers. Parochial schools almost certainly would never have even been considered without our coolie labor. Some of the religious orders were founded to train nuns as nurses and hospital personnel. Some orders trained nurses and teachers. But, by and large, they mass-produced teachers."

"That's right," Janet agreed. "And so we were. Except for the few who were cooks or domestics, or the few who served the order in management or health care, we were all teachers. And so it was into the fifties and early sixties, and—"

"And then," Marie broke in, "the roof collapsed."

"The candidate supply dried up. So many of the Sisters left us. And so many more decided to enter other educational fields—adult ed, continuing ed."

"As in my case," Marie said.

"In charge of continuing education for the entire Archdiocese of Miami."

"Yes, the archbishop himself bestowed on me the freedom to draw up the entire program and set the budget." Marie laughed. "Then he gave me the freedom to raise all the money for the budget."

"I wasn't aware your job was that big. I didn't know they expected you to be a fundraiser too!"

"I didn't know that either in the beginning. But then the archbishop said, 'Welcome to the world, Sister.' "

Janet looked concerned. "How were you able to do it? I mean with all that responsibility, where did you find time to write? I mean, write a book!"

"It wasn't easy. And I wouldn't recommend it. But, as I was saying, I got to thinking of how our lives have changed so drastically over the years. And I thought: Why not? I'd always found a lot of fulfillment in writing."

"Yes, I remember that. But, a book!"

"It was the best way I could think of to tell our story. To create a nun who had lived through all the things we've experienced. Life in the old convent, the tightly knit community. Life today, an entirely new ball game."

"In a murder mystery?"

"Why not? Mystery is no stranger to the Church. You might even say the Church is built on mysteries. Besides, there's something neat and finished about mystery stories. I've always liked how all the loose ends get tied up. I find it very satisfying.

"The biggest problem is finding time. A few evenings, a few early mornings; every once in a while a weekend. It's a long process under the best of circumstances."

"I'll bet!" Janet moved about the room, touching pictures, draperies, fixtures, almost compulsively. "And now? Another one?"

"I don't know about that. Not right away, that's for sure. For one thing, the publisher's got me doing a bit of promotion."

Janet grew animated. "That sounds exciting. Do you travel much?"

"Not a lot. Some telephone interviews. A bit of radio and television. You know: 'Why is a holy nun of God writing about murder?' 'What does a nun know about murder?' '. . . about the world?' '. . . about anything—other than how to say the rosary?' "

Janet laughed. "Really! That bad?"

"That bad!"

"I'm embarrassed. I haven't checked, and I should have: Is *Behind the Veil* on the *New York Times* best-seller list?"

It was Marie's turn to laugh. "Heavens, no! I'm what's called a mid-list author. On a few best-seller lists, but not for any length of time. A soft-cover sale. A book-club offering. It did get reviewed in the *Times*, but it was sort of negative: 'The characters in Sister Monahan's first novel talk like nuns' . . . that sort of thing."

"That's not fair. I read your book. The only thing missing was America's favorite 'F' word. And not everyone in the country stoops to *that*."

"I know. But that's the way it goes. Actually, I think all the other authors in this writers' workshop are in the same boat I'm in—mid-list authors." Marie wandered to the open door in the rear of the room. "Nice bathroom. All for me?"

"All for you. Father Benbow and his wife have their own bathroom. Rabbi Winer's wife didn't come with him, so he's sharing a bathroom with Father Augustine and Father Koesler. And Mr. Krieg has his own facility."

"No one would wash from the same bowl as he, eh?"

Janet snickered. "Just the way it worked out."

Marie glanced at her watch. "Just five o'clock. How long do we have before dinner?"

"About an hour."

"How 'bout a walk? I'd like to see the place again. Besides, I'm a little keyed-up."

"Sure." Janet slipped into her topcoat. "Want to borrow one of my coats? It's getting really chilly out there."

Marie took a windbreaker from her suitcase. "I haven't forgotten Michigan weather entirely. Particularly how it changes from hour to hour. Come on; maybe we can find some of those elusive security guards you've been bragging about."

Janet showed her surprise. "Why this obsession with security?"

Marie's laugh was tinged with nervousness. "Oh, I don't know. You just never know when a gal's going to need some security. Call it a premonition."

"I don't like to hear you say that. I remember your premonitions. What I remember mostly about them is their accuracy."

"Forget it, Jan. Let's just enjoy our walk."

They struck out briskly across the campus. Neither spoke for some minutes.

It was Marie who broke the silence. "Who invited that guy anyway?"

The question startled Janet. "Guy? What guy?"

"Klaus Krieg."

"Oh. My predecessor. The former director of development."

"Why?"

"I'm not sure. I didn't get to know Jack Regan very well. He resigned to take a job at UCLA, and I was named director just before he left. We had only a few meetings. He handed me this conference as a fait accompli. And when I saw your name as one of the participants, I paid no attention to the rest. I was just so happy we would be able to get together again." Janet paused a moment. "What's the matter with the Reverend Krieg anyway?"

"Please don't debase the title 'Reverend' by bestowing it on that creep!"

Janet giggled. "Creep? He is an evangelist, after all."

"Come on, Jan; you know better."

"All right, so he's a creep. But Jack Regan seemed to think he'd draw a crowd. And—no offense intended—but wouldn't you agree that Klaus Krieg is the major drawing card of this workshop? I don't mean to take anything from you or the other writers," she added hastily. "The students undoubtedly will learn a lot from all of you. But their prime objective is to get published. And Krieg *is* a publisher."

Marie smiled fleetingly. "And he's rich."

"Very."

Still, Marie thought to herself, Krieg must have had a motive for accepting. Why exactly is he here?

3 HE HEARD THEIR voices. Although he had met her only once, he recognized one of them as belonging to Sister Janet Schultes.

He was good at that. At one time in his history, Rabbi Irving Winer had sustained the thin strand of his life by honing his every resource and faculty, not the least of these his five senses.

He had tabbed them the instant they exited the elevator. Clearly, they were making no effort to keep their voices down. But he had made every effort to be silent, hoping they would not accost him.

He assumed, correctly, that the other female voice belonged to the nun-author, Sister Marie Monahan. Janet was serving as, for want of a better title, hostess of this workshop. Earlier this afternoon, she had welcomed him, shown him to his room, given him a map of the campus and a schedule for the workshop, and answered the few questions he'd had. She'd suggested he might be tired and want to rest. Eagerly, he'd assented as a way of assuring seclusion.

He had no idea that Janet and Marie were long-lost friends, wanted to be together, and had no intention of invading his privacy. So he made no sound.

In time they left, again taking the elevator. Once more a gladly received silence pervaded the third floor's private residence wing.

Rabbi Winer gazed out the window. The immediate scene seemed downright bucolic. There were about as many trees as God allowed to grow in one place. Beyond the woods, he could make out the city in brick and neon, and pedestrians and homeowners and muggers and apartment dwellers and hope and despair. If he consciously tried, he could hear the city's sounds. But he preferred not to hear. It was easy to block out the far-off noises.

Although the room's temperature was pleasant, even a bit on the coolish side, the rabbi was perspiring. The window revealed his present reality. But his mind, his memory, continued to invade the present with the past. Even as he tried to suppress the ancient images, he knew from experience he would not succeed. Little by little, the unwanted but vivid whispers from the past grew until they blotted out the present.

It was November 9, 1938, not September 3, 1989. And it was Munich, not Detroit. God! Dear God! He did not want to live it again, but a perverse power decreed that he must.

Earlier in November, Ernst von Rath, the German Embassy attaché in Paris, had been assassinated by a young Polish Jew, Herschel Grynszpan.

Although at the time Irving was only twelve, he knew things were changing radically and rapidly. More and more Germans were wearing the Nazi uniform. His parents and older sister grew more secretive, as if trying to shield him from what he sensed was happening. It seemed the Nazis were eager for an event they could designate as the "final straw'' calling for what would eventually be termed the ''final solution.'' As it happened, the von Rath incident was it. And November 9, 1938, would forevermore be known as Kristallnacht, the Night of Crystal, or the Night of Shattered Glass.

And that was precisely how young Irving Winer was introduced to Kristallnacht. Heavy-booted feet tramped up the stairs, followed by pounding on the door, followed by orders shouted in imperious German. Then the sound of glass shattering, furniture splintering, voices pleading, voices commanding.

In bed, covers pulled over his head, young Irving never saw the Nazis who destroyed his home, the precious musical instruments, the heirlooms, the works of art. He never saw the Nazis who seized and dragged his father from their house that night. But he knew; somehow he sensed, as he cowered beneath the covers, that his boyhood, his youth, was ending prematurely that night.

In the days and weeks that followed, his mother determined to stay in Munich and await her husband's return. She was equally determined to get her children out of, and as far away from, Germany as possible. In both resolves she failed. Never again would they see her husband, their father. He was among the earliest to be cut down in the brutal resolution of Hitler's ''problem.''

In his first twelve years, as a member of a traditional, loving Orthodox family, Irving Winer could never have guessed or imagined the depth of cruelty to which humans could descend. This brutal phase of his education began immediately after Kristallnacht.

The synagogues were burned, repeatedly if necessary, to destroy them utterly. Jewish-owned stores and businesses were vandalized. Jewish people—men, women, and children—were insulted, publicly humiliated, and abused. They were forced to wear the Star of David as a mark of degradation.

Finally, in a seemingly random choice, Jews were rounded up like animals and taken away to a secret fate.

By the time the three remaining Winers were packed into a cattle car and started on their train trip to Dachau, Irving had already learned what it was to be treated as subhuman refuse. He was about to learn that there was nothing he would not do, no service he would not perform just to stay barely alive. Dachau taught him that.

On their arrival at the concentration camp, decisions were made. Olga Winer was transported to Hartheim, where the ovens worked overtime. Her ashes were indistinguishable from thousands of others. Olga's daughter, Helen, became a subject for experimentation before following her mother.

Irving's young, strong body was judged useful for the moment.

He slept whenever they let him. He ate whatever they gave him. The rest of the time, he labored. He did whatever he was told to do. And, unlike almost every other inmate of the camp, he survived.

When, toward war's end, the beasts who ruled him told him they needed him to betray his fellow prisoners—God help him! God forgive him!—he did so.

He survived.

After the Allies liberated his camp and he began slowly, tentatively, to become accustomed to a far more human existence, the enormity of his experience began to trouble, then torture him. Chronologically, he was nineteen. In every other way, he was older—much, much older.

As soon as he could, he emigrated to the United States.

He tried to lose his very identity in a series of enterprises. Religion came closest to giving him a certain small measure of absolution. And so he became rabbi of a Reform congregation, two steps removed from his strict Orthodox upbringing.

His motives for embracing the Reform branch of Judaism were unclear even to him. But it was conceivable they had something to do with his experience with the strictness of Nazi discipline that had controlled so much of his life.

He married. They had no children. Tests indicated he was sterile, made so by illnesses he had contracted at Dachau. His wife was understanding and supportive.

She was patient, as well, with the dark moods that engulfed him with some regularity. His problems stayed hidden within the privacy of their home. His congregation knew him only as one who had survived the Holocaust and was a wise and good rabbi.

And now, in addition, the congregation gloried in Rabbi Winer's literary accomplishments. They boasted of their rabbi, the author. "Yes, that's right; our rabbi is the one who writes the books. Yes, he's just a regular guy. His door is always open to us. We wouldn't trade him for anyone."

Although it was generally known that he had been subjected to the horrors of Dachau, that fact alone was all anyone knew of his past. He made it clear to everyone that the subject of Dachau was, as they would say in the land of his birth, verboten. With his wife alone did he share—and that with much reluctance—the details of his captivity. Even then he could not bring himself to tell her how, near the end of his time in the camp, he had become a traitor. It was his ultimate secret.

No matter how he tried, he could not forgive himself for betraying his fellow prisoners. If his sin were ever to be revealed, it would, he felt, mean the end of everything. The end of his rabbinate; the end of his marriage; the end of his last shred of self-respect; the end, of course, of his writing career; the end of his life.

But one person knew. Irving Winer had no clue as to how this person had discovered the secret. Those limited few in the camp who had known, only two of the guards and one prisoner, were long dead. Yet, still, one person knew.

Klaus Krieg knew. And he had hinted that the secret might not be safe. In the oblique warning that was issued, it was evident that Krieg knew he was toying with dynamite and that the thread alone was enough to turn Winer toward desperate means.

The implied and manifest threats on either side had produced a tenuous Mexican standoff. But it was, at best, a delicate balance.

And now, this very evening, Winer was about to meet his enemy face to face. He was unsure how to handle this meeting. It was for this reason that he had argued with his wife and finally convinced her not to accompany him. Somehow, Rabbi Winer would have to resolve this matter alone. One on one.

The prospect put him on edge. Too much so, it seemed. He was aware that his pulse rate had quickened and that, even though this was a cool evening, he was now perspiring freely. As he had on similar occasions, he turned to prayer.

He removed from his suitcase his siddur, the Jewish prayerbook. The rabbi prayed that God would have a special word for him. One that would show him the proper course of action.

After a brief prayer for guidance from the daily liturgy, Winer opened the prayerbook at random. His hope was that God would direct his hands to find the special message.

It gave him added consolation to read in the book's original Hebrew. This was Tehillim, the Book of Psalms. A good omen. The powerful prayer of Psalms was Winer's favorite in the Bible. The index finger of his right hand was touching the numerical identification of Psalm 109, one of the "cursing Psalms." Just what the doctor ordered. His attention wandered up and down and through the Psalms, snatching at phrases that seemed particularly appropriate.

They have opened wicked and treacherous mouths against me. They have spoken to me . . . with words of hatred . . . and attacked me without cause.

When [my accuser] is judged, let him go forth condemned, and may his plea be in vain. May his days be few. May his children be fatherless and his wife a widow. May his children be roaming vagrants and beggars; may they be cast out of the ruins of their homes. May the usurer ensnare all his belongings and strangers plunder the fruit of his labors. May there be no one to do him a kindness, nor anyone to pity his orphans. May his posterity meet with destruction. Because he remembered not to show kindness, but persecuted the wretched and poor and the brokenhearted to do them to death. He loved cursing; may it come upon him; he took no delight in blessing; may it be far from him. And may he be clothed with cursing as with a robe; may it penetrate into his entrails like water and like oil into his bones; may it be for him like a garment which covers him like a girdle which is always about him.

*But do you, O God, my Lord, deal kindly with me for Your
name's sake; in Your generous kindness rescue me; for I am
wretched and poor, and my heart is pierced within me. Help
me, O Lord, my God; save me, in Your kindness.*

Winer sat back. He closed his eyes. In the silence that
engulfed him he contemplated the words he'd just read. The
words of the Psalm seemed to describe his ''enemy'' quite
well. Klaus Krieg, completely devoid of pity or kindness. On
the contrary, quite capable of cursing, indeed, causing the
destruction of, the defenseless.

Of course, in this day and age, one does not expect God
personally to right the wrongs of this evil person. The time
has passed when a recalcitrant Pharaoh is sent reeling by ten
plagues imposed directly by God. In those days, Moses could
threaten the Egyptians confident that the Ribono Shel Olom,
the Master of the Universe, would act in miraculous and
destructive punishments.

God was not going to do Winer's work for him. That
was not the message of the Psalm to which God had led
the rabbi. The message, clearly, was that Krieg must be
stopped, must be punished. *''May his days be few.''*
Capital punishment. What on earth could be a more appropriate sentence?

As Winer continued to muse over the Psalm, he grew more
calm, more self-assured. He was aware that his pulse rate
had slowed and regulated. Far from continuing to perspire,
he now felt cool. As usual, he had found his strength in
prayer.

He continued to pray. He continued to think.

''May his days be few.''

On the other hand, maybe there was, indeed a fate worse

than death. What was it? In Shakespeare? "The evil that men do lives after them. The good is oft interred with their bones."

Wasn't that the thrust of the Psalm? To reward evil with evil?

Then, let it be done.

4 "YOU'RE NOT GOING to wear that, are you?"

The Reverend and Mrs. David Benbow were dressing for dinner. She, in slip, seated at the vanity, was applying light makeup.

"What's the matter with it?" Benbow studied himself in the mirror.

Tall, with a suggestion of a natural wave in his blond hair, David Benbow had nearly maintained his athletic figure of earlier days. The beginning of a paunch was about all that hinted at his mid-forties age. There was not a mature line in his face.

"The tie," Martha said.

"What's the matter with the tie? It goes with this suit, doesn't it?"

"Well, now that you mention it, not really. But that's not the point."

"Well, then . . ."

"The point," Martha stopped brushing her eyelashes, "is that the participants in this workshop are clergymen or religious. I should think you'd be expected to wear your clerical collar."

"You think so?"

"Definitely."

"It's a bit uncomfortable for that, you know. Unless you think it's really necessary."

"I think so. You wouldn't want to pop into dinner to find you're the only one not in uniform."

"Oh . . . I suppose." Benbow removed the tie and shirt, rummaged through a drawer and came up with a black, collarless shirt. He slipped into the shirt and affixed the plain white clerical collar that was peculiar to, but not exclusive to, the Episcopal and Anglican priesthood. When, eventually, he would don a jacket, he would be wearing a black worsted suit with a red pinstripe and a clerical collar. Proper.

Martha resumed her adornment process. In her early forties, she betrayed her age to a far greater extent than her husband. She did not find this sporting or even fair, but there was little she could do about it. The lines that were absent from David's face could be found abundantly in hers. Her once svelte figure now was more relaxed. However, she had earned every wrinkle, every pound.

They had met when he was a senior, she a freshman, at Northwestern University. They married after his graduation. During his three years in the seminary, she left the university and worked as a realtor.

He was ordained and found a position as an associate in a Chicago parish. His $12,000 salary was barely enough for them. She, in real estate, was earning considerably more than he. They agreed they needed the second income, which, in reality, was his. So they decided against having children, at least for then.

As their individual incomes increased so did their standard of living. No longer was there even talk of children. She had become a broker, he a pastor and, over the past seven years, the author of three mystery novels. By almost anyone's measure, they were a successful couple.

Neither would have given consideration to asking the other to give up anything the other was doing. By this time, they had relinquished most of the perks of rectory life: the rectory itself, a car allowance, utilities, and the housekeeper (whom they now employed personally), instead of having the parish provide all these goods and services.

In their situation it made sense to them. They were building equity in their own home. And they were beholden to no one in the parish.

David busied himself with the contents of a small black carrying case. When he turned he was holding two cocktail glasses filled to the brim with a clear liquid.

Martha smiled at his reflection in the mirror. "What have we there?"

"May I interest you in a martini, love?" He walked toward her with great care, intent on not spilling a drop. No mean feat with glasses so full.

Martha shook her head. "Aren't hors d'oeuvres and drinks on the schedule before dinner tonight?" But even as she spoke, she accepted one of the glasses. She turned back to the mirror and placed the glass on the vanity. Neither spilled a drop. If either had an anxious nerve, it was not discernible.

He sipped from his glass, thus raising the odds against spillage. "Look at it this way, love: maybe yes, maybe no. The young lady who showed us to this room did not appear to have both oars in the water. There very well may not be any hors d'oeuvres, let alone drinks. And wouldn't it be frightful to have to face this group cold sober?"

Martha frowned. "You'd think the one in charge of this

conference would have been here to greet us. What's her name—Sister Janet or something?''

''Indeed. Off somewhere, leaving a child to do the job!''

The Benbows had no way of knowing that Janet and Marie were at this moment extending their walk through the grounds, catching up with each other's history, and either solving or shelving most of the Church's problems.

''All I have to say,'' Martha said, ''is, This is not a good beginning. It augurs a long week.''

''Five days, actually, love. Sorry you came? Miss the business?''

''Not really. You and I were long overdue to spend some time together. We haven't had a vacation in God knows how long.''

''We're busy people.'' He held his drink to the light as if examining its contents. ''Just like Nick and Nora.''

''Who?''

''Charles—Nick and Nora Charles. The *Thin Man* series. Bill Powell and Myrna Loy . . . you remember.''

''I remember, all right. I remember a time when you'd be quoting Scripture instead of alluding to murder mystery movies.''

''Can't help it, love; Nick and Nora appreciated their martinis. We are following in prestigious footsteps.''

Martha dove into a light blue dress with lace at the high neck and sleeves. David smirked as he watched her wiggle into the dress. ''How very modest of you. I believe the Romans refer to that as a 'Mary-like' outfit.''

She giggled. ''The least I could do. After all, if memory serves, I'll be the only spouse here, won't I?''

''Uh-huh. Of course the nun is single and presumably a virgin to boot. The Roman priests remain celibate.''

"Priests? I thought there was only one Roman—the monk. Father . . . uh . . . Augustine."

"They brought in another one, at the last hour as it were. A Father Koesler."

"Koesler? Never heard of him. What did he write?"

"Nothing that I know of. He's somewhat of an amateur detective on the local scene, I take it."

"Extraordinary."

"Yes. Then there's the rabbi. Although he's married, his wife isn't accompanying him. He's here by himself."

"Leaving Krieg."

"Leaving Krieg." An unmistakably bitter tone crept into David's voice.

"Dear, dear . . ." Martha finished applying lipstick. "What is there about Krieg that upsets you so?"

"He's corrupt."

"So are lots of people. No, there's something specific about Klaus Krieg, isn't there? I can tell; I can read you like a book."

"Really!" He smiled sardonically. "Well, as a priest one comes to tolerate a vast array of personalities. Saints are nice. I don't even mind sinners at all. But hypocrites are quite another thing. It's just that Krieg gives hypocrisy a bad name. In Krieg's pantheon, Jesus Christ is a nice guy, but the messiah is Klaus Krieg. And the pitiful part is that millions of trusting souls have bought him. And in buying him, they are paying for him."

Martha smoothed her skirt and sat down across from her husband. She sipped her drink. "There's something more. I sense it."

"What more is necessary?" There was a tinge of anger in his voice.

"No matter. In any case, he's not bringing his wife?"

"No. As I understand it, at no time did he have any intention of bringing her." David grew thoughtful. "It is as if he came deliberately unencumbered. As if he wants to have something settled once and for all," he added, almost as if to himself. His face hardened. "If so, I'm sure he'll get his wish."

What a strange thing for David to say, thought Martha.

She shrugged and finished her drink. David was distancing himself from her. It was by no means the first time he had kept his real feelings from her. They were not as close as they once had been.

Yet she was confident that, in time, she would understand.

In those early days when they were relatively poor, terribly dependent on each other, things had seemed better. Odd; she would have expected that things would improve as their lives became more comfortable and free of financial worry. She wondered if things went that way with all couples. Maybe it was youth, common problems, and shared concerns that drew married couples close. Maybe it was unrealistic to expect things to remain unchanged let alone get better.

Maybe, maybe, maybe.

She hoped no drinks would be served before dinner. That martini had been quite enough.

5 FEW PEOPLE HAD ever heard of the Trappist Order. Even fewer would know who the Trappists are had it not been for Thomas Merton.

Merton joined the Trappists in 1941 and he wrote *The Seven Storey Mountain*, a book that sold over a million copies and is read even to this day.

As a Trappist, Merton wrote many books, articles, and poems extolling the importance of silence, solitude, and prayer. In 1968, he met a tragic, almost ludicrous, accidental death—electrocuted by a defective fan. He lies buried in characteristic simplicity at Our Lady of Gethsemani Abbey in central Kentucky. His grave is marked with a plain cross bearing his Trappist name, Father Louis.

Father Augustine May, OCSO, was thinking about that as he sat in the modest room assigned him in the Madame Cadillac Building.

Tom Merton, he thought, as he slowly swirled a water glass one-quarter filled with Jack Daniel's Kentucky whiskey, Tom Merton did an awful lot for us Trappists. He brought in a lot of dough and a lot of vocations.

In the 1950s, a bumper crop of young applicants came to the Trappists, many of them attracted by the writings of one monk, Father Louis. At the peak there were more than two hundred at Gethsemani Abbey alone. Father Augustine knew the statistics well. Entering in the early sixties, he had been among the last of that bumper crop. Now, hell, the Kentucky abbey would be lucky to have eighty monks. And his own monastery in Wellesley, Massachusetts, would feel successful if it had half that number.

Father Augustine—Gus, as he was known to his confreres—hoped he wasn't being too vain in thinking he could make a difference. He was convinced the world was more than ready for another Thomas Merton. Was it just possible the next Merton could be himself?

He swished the whiskey around in his mouth. The familiar tart taste made him grimace. Somehow he found the pungency pleasant.

He had tried the Merton approach—writing for scholarly and, mostly, contemplative periodicals. But the articles brought in little money and, as far as anyone could tell, no appreciable vocations. Then came the mystery novel, *A Rose by Any Other Name*. The money was better, appreciably better. Of course, it all went to his abbey; that was taken for granted. What had caught his abbot off guard was the publisher's insistence on an author tour to a few major cities, for TV, radio, and newspaper interviews. Only with the greatest reluctance did the abbot grant permission.

Father Augustine had to agree that such trips were not what Benedict, Bernard or, especially, Rancé had had in mind.

Benedict, of course, started the whole thing in the sixth century. He was not the first, but he surely was one of the founders of Western monasticism. The key to it all was the community of men living together with vows designed by Saint Benedict's rule of life.

In the ninth and tenth centuries, reforms were made as monasticism grew away from Benedict's concept. But these reforms at the Synod of Auchen and at Cluny were overshadowed by those of Saint Bernard in the twelfth century and the beginning of the Cistercian order.

Bernard's interpretation of the monastic ideal endured virtually unchanged for five hundred years. Then, in 1664, at the monastery of La Trappe in Normandy, Abbot Rancé made an extremely tight right turn, and the Trappists emerged with a negative appreciation of mankind and an emphasis on penance unknown to the earlier reformers.

Throughout fourteen centuries, then, one might view the rule of life set down by Saint Benedict as an inspired document. Even now, it remains the foundation of Western civilization's monastic life.

That way of life was, perhaps, perfected by Saint Bernard at the beginning of the Cistercian order. Then Rancé added a spartan rigidity to his reorganization of the Trappists.

It was into the Trappist religious order according to Rancé that Thomas Merton and Augustine May entered. But it was not Rancé's version of the Cistercians that Father Louis left when he died. As was the case with so much else in Catholicism, the Second Vatican Council helped change all that.

The religious order that Merton and May entered, among many other stiff structures, forbade talking at any time to anyone but one's superiors without explicit permission from the abbot. Of course, communication was necessary, so a sign language peculiar to the Trappists evolved. Stories are still told illustrating the inflexibility of the "Trappist way of life," such as that of the monk who ran from cell to cell rousing the other monks and giving the sign for fire because the abbey was burning down around their ears.

Benedict's rule called for "ora et labora"—prayer and work. The preconciliar Trappists interpreted that so inflexibly that at any given time when they were neither sleeping nor eating, they were either chanting prayers in chapel, or working, usually in the fields. Which led to the expression, "either in the [choir] stalls or the stables."

One of the demands made of religious orders by Vatican II was that the orders reexamine their present status against the purpose for which they had been founded and that they return to those roots.

For the Trappists, that meant erasing much of what Rancé had introduced and restoring the monastic precepts of Benedict and Bernard.

No longer are monasteries carbon copies of one another. The Trappists—the Order of Cistercians of the Strict Observance—have found unity in diversity. Sign language is gone. And, in an order founded for the contemplative life, finally, time has been allocated for contemplation.

Almost thirty years ago, Harold May had abandoned a promising advertising career and entered what he considered to be a little bit of heaven on earth—Our Lady of Gethsemani Abbey. Rigorous but heavenly. And then, with the overwhelming changes—resisted at first—Father Augustine May, ocso, found a more profound and sensible heaven. This was what he was eager to share with today's men, young and old.

He looked at the glass he was holding as if he had never seen it before. Was this his second or third drink? He couldn't remember. Amazing how one could build a tolerance for the stuff. But, whichever number this was, it would be his last.

For now. In a few minutes, he'd be going down to dinner. Food would take the edge off the alcohol.

He had arrived at the college wearing a business suit, but of course he had packed his Cistercian habit. Now he took it from the closet. The white tunic covered its wearer from neck to foot. A black scapular, much like a burial shroud, fitted over the head, falling to the floor fore and aft. A hood was attached to the scapular, but was pulled over the head only at specified times. Finally, a wide, heavy leather belt. This simple, ancient habit he wanted to share with others.

He knew he could not hope for enormous numbers of new applicants. Monasticism never had been attractive to a multitude. Always it had been a very specialized vocation. But it certainly ought to be more appealing now.

He began to don his habit.

Look at all those gurus roaming the country, advocating Transcendental Meditation, Zen Buddhism; there were the Maharishi, the Baghwan, Moonies. The East evangelizing, as it were, the West. The first time in history. Augustine recalled Saint Francis Xavier, who brought the Gospel to India and Japan, and died on his way to China. And the thousands of Christian missionaries who had followed Xavier. Always the West to the East.

Until now.

Augustine May was only one of many who were concerned about and wondered at this present phenomenon. Neither he nor his colleagues had much doubt concerning the motives of these largely successful gurus. Most of them became far more financially secure here than they could be in their respective homelands. And, while some undoubtedly were sincere, one could not ignore the economic rewards.

The larger question concerned their followers. Charges of

brainwashing led to the innovative reaction called depro-
gramming.

But beyond the fringe groups and their immature needs
that responded to the blandishments of the mystic East, there
were quite normal young adults who recognized in themselves something missing, a psychic glue that could hold
together the varied facets of their lives.

These, Augustine and his colleagues realized, were legitimate needs that were being met at least partially by the gurus
with their versions of ancient Oriental religions. The hypothesis was that these seekers, completely beyond their power
to change things, were products of Western civilization. Thus,
whatever they might discover in the East, they would always
remain foreigners to that culture.

The idea, then, was to introduce them to the contemplative
heritage of Western civilization. For it existed, to be sure.
The West would not have survived without it. Only at about
the time of the Enlightenment and the Industrial Revolution,
did this contemplative approach to reality begin to fade, to
eventually be ground under and virtually disappear in retreat
from materialism and capitalism.

It was here, at this point, that Augustine May saw himself
stepping into the picture. In mystery he had found a popular
genre. *Rose* would be only the first of many novels he would
write. His abbot had almost no alternative but to permit—
nay, encourage—him to write. Each monastery had to be
independently financially solvent. God, and the abbot, knew
that Saint Francis Abbey, an expansion abbey to which he'd
been assigned, regularly moved from thin ice to open water.
Gethsemani, for example, did very well with cheese and
fruitcakes. But Gethsemani was not about to bail out Saint
Francis. Nothing personal, just against the rules.

With his expected success, no bailout would be necessary: Augustine May would singlehandedly save Saint Francis Abbey. He would then become the toast of the Trappists. Coincidentally—and perhaps of equal or greater importance—his fame would spread and redound throughout this country and—why not?—the world.

This, Augustine assured himself, was not idle pride. He would accomplish all this for God and the Cistercian Order. Was there all that much difference between the two?

His problem, to this point, was that he had gotten it all backwards. Merton had written his magnum opus, the classic *Seven Storey Mountain*, first. After gaining popular fame, he had gone on to write more substantial religious wisdom. Merton's contemplative work scarcely would have achieved the acceptance it had without that best seller. *Seven Storey Mountain* had given Merton entrée to the mass public. A goodly number of that vast readership had stayed with Merton throughout the rest of his life. So he had been the cause—not merely the instrument—of a large proportion of popularity that the Trappists enjoy to this day.

Granted Augustine had published—no mean accomplishment in this day and age. But who had read him? A few monks, even fewer erudite professors of arcane subjects. By no means the reading public Merton had attracted.

Augustine counted on *A Rose by Any Other Name* to turn things around. Of course, it was no *Seven Storey Mountain*. How many books are? But Merton had written one—and only one—million-seller. Augustine would make up in quantity what was lacking in quality. *Rose* would be but the first of a series of popular novels with monastic settings. He was certain he could achieve this goal. Then, after having made a solid name for himself, he would produce the scholarly, profound, contemplative, Mertonesque writings.

And there it was: Augustine's formula for his personal—and the order's corporate—success.

He checked his reflection in a full-length mirror. Nice. The habit gave him the immediate cachet of poverty, antiquity, simplicity, cleanliness, and yes, even holiness.

He finished his drink, set the glass firmly on the dressertop and headed for downstairs, where he would meet the others in this workshop.

He gave momentary thought to taking the elevator but decided on the stairs. He could use the exercise. It would clear his mind.

He would need a clear mind, and everything else he could muster, including God's providence and presence, to deal with Klaus Krieg.

Funny, before the publication of *A Rose by Any Other Name*, Augustine had never heard of Klaus Krieg. Or at least he'd paid so little attention to the televangelist/publisher as to be completely unmindful of his celebrity. No Krieg-type book would be found in the monastery, nor did Saint Francis Abbey have television.

Of course, Augustine did not spend his entire life behind cloister doors. Oh, he had in the beginning, when he would blow on his finger and wiggle his hand to indicate air conditioning. But after Vatican II and his move to Massachusetts, he was sent outside the monastery with some regularity. He was a better than average speaker and what with the priest shortage, pastors frequently were desperate for weekend help. Supply and demand. He was sent to these parishes on condition that he be allowed to address issues at the core of Cistercian existence: solitude, silence, self-denial, the centering prayer, the contemplative life and, occasionally, donations to the order.

Still, even on the "outside," he had been spared exposure to Krieg and the Praise God Network. To a man, priests loathed televangelists—and at the very top of their aversion list was the "Reverend" Klaus Krieg. Thus, with no exposure to Krieg whatsoever, not even having been afforded the luxury of selecting what he and the pastor would watch on TV of an evening, Augustine could not have picked Krieg out of a lineup of two people.

Until Augustine's book was published.

Shortly thereafter, he was bombarded by mailings and phone messages from P.G. Press proposing contract talks.

At first, the abbot leaned toward looking into the Krieg propositions. However, not for nothing had Augustine spent years in the advertising business. He smelled a con.

On a mission to Framingham, he stopped in a large bookstore, browsed and searched until he found several books bearing the P.G. logo, all in the religion section of the store, as he had expected. The title and dust jacket of one book promised a monastic setting. A few scanned pages confirmed his initial diagnosis: It had something to do with a monastery. And there was something peculiar about it. He bought the book.

Later that evening, eschewing the pastor's offer of before-bed drinks and the TV news, Augustine retired. He propped himself in bed and opened *Their Secret Solitude*. It was bad, but he persevered. He forced himself to finish the book. Actually, after about page 25, he had to force himself to read each page. It was that bad.

The fictional "Monastery of the Blessed Spirit"—fictional

to the extreme; it resembled no monastery he'd ever heard of—was replete with spurious monks.

The story began almost innocently with Brother Gregory fighting vainly an overwhelming urge to masturbate. In no time, the reader learned that the procurator, Brother Louis, had no sooner hired a young village maiden as cook than he raped her, several times in several ways. Throughout the book, he periodically found new occasions and new ways to rape her. Naturally, Abbot Rufus, by this time, was found to be a sadistic homosexual. The sex was kinky, kinkier, and kinkiest.

And so it went. It was almost an afterthought that the local antediluvian archbishop had been swindling everyone in and out of sight for years.

Augustine, revolted by this raunchy insult to legitimate monastic life, had a difficult time getting to sleep that night.

When he returned from Framingham, he told his shocked abbot what he had discovered. He then had to caution Father Abbot, who was close to hyperventilating at the thought of what P.G. Press might perpetrate against Saint Francis Abbey, that, just as a book should not be judged by its cover, so a publishing house should not necessarily be judged by one book. Even a book this execrable. So, Augustine received permission to make several long distance calls.

The third call hit pay dirt. It was to Dick Ryan, with whom Augustine had once worked in a New York advertising firm. Ryan was still at the same firm, but had risen to a position in management.

It took a few moments for Ryan to place him. It wouldn't have taken that long had the caller not identified himself as Augustine. Realizing the problem, he immediately gave the befuddled Ryan the name Harold May, and the connection was made.

Ryan was unaware that Harold had had a book published. Then, as the conversation proceeded, Ryan recalled having heard about *A Rose by Any Other Name*. But he hadn't linked Harold to the Father Augustine who had authored it. "Well, congratulations, Harold. Son of a gun, I didn't know that was you. Yeah, sincere congratulations."

"Thanks. Yes, it was I." After the two exchanged small talk bringing each other up-to-date on their separate and very different lives, Augustine recounted his past publishing experience, the bombardment by the P.G. empire, and his grossly negative reaction to the one and only P.G. book he had read or was likely to read.

Ryan whistled softly. "So Krieg wants you, eh? Well—how is it you monks put it?—resist him, strong in the faith."

"*Tu autem, Domine, miserere nobis.* I'm surprised you know that antiphon, Dick. You must be a better Catholic now than when I knew you."

"That's true. But then, you're a better Catholic now, yourself."

Augustine chuckled. "It's good to know we're both working at it.

"But Dick, I didn't really call to ask your opinion about my linking up with Krieg. My question is: What is he up to? Why in God's green world would he want me? What possible interest could he have in me?"

"Authenticity."

"Authenticity?"

"You're a real, live monk, my friend," Ryan replied. "I must admit I've never had the misfortune of reading anything put out by P.G. Press. But I know their reputation. Everybody in the business knows what Krieg is doing.''

''Well, I'm no longer 'in the business,' Dick. Could you fill me in?''

There was a pause marked by the sound of deep inhaling. Ryan had just lit a cigarette. Instantaneously, Augustine recalled the pressure-packed days in the advertising world. He himself had smoked like a chimney; with few exceptions, they all had. It got so one could not imagine having a phone at one's ear without the attendant cigarette between one's lips.

''Okay,'' Ryan said. ''I won't get into the TV scam for the moment. That's a long story all by itself. But Krieg didn't ask you to fake a miracle for his TV viewers. He wants your pen, not your crutches.''

Augustine snorted.

''Part of it works this way,'' Ryan said. ''Krieg maintains offices in Los Angeles for budding writers. Haven't you ever seen the ads in magazines, trade papers?''

'' 'Fraid not.''

''Damn, that's right; you don't read the trades any more.''

Augustine shook his head, a motion that could not be heard over the phone. Reading the trades was just one of many, many things he no longer did.

Ryan continued. ''Say you're an amateur writer, know in your heart you're good, and that sooner or later you'll get published. All you need is a chance, a break.''

Millions of them, thought Augustine.

''Well,'' Ryan said, ''you look at the ad from P.G. Press—''

''Excuse, Dick: What in hell does P.G. stand for?''

" 'Praise God,' P.G.—get it?'' It was Ryan's turn to snort. "Krieg is doing God no favor.

"Anyway, you see this ad. It says, 'You haven't been published? Not to worry. Send us your manuscript. Either we'll publish you or we'll tell you what little more you need to get published. Of course this uses up a lot of our time, and time is money. So if you want us to read you, help you, publish you, counsel you, it only stands to reason that you should reimburse us for our time. Depending on the length and complexity of the script, $100 and $500 for a reading. A guaranteed response. This is your big chance. Don't let it slip by.' ''

Augustine interrupted. ''Don't tell me: The writers don't have a chance. It's stacked against them.''

"You got it. Krieg maintains a large office full of people who read these manuscripts. They've got one job and one job alone: to reject and return every manuscript they get. No exceptions.''

"Then why do they have to read the scripts? They're just going to turn them down anyway.''

"They've got a boilerplate introduction and conclusion for their rejects. The opening theme is: 'You've come so close. You're not far from best-seller fame.' Stuff like that goes on for maybe three, four pages. The conclusion goes: ''We are genuinely interested in your talent. We want to see your work again. So make sure you keep in touch and should you turn out another manuscript . . .' But the middle of the rejection has to evidence that they actually read your script. The reader has to get specific about some of the things in the script. That's the only reason anyone there reads the submission.''

It was Augustine's turn to whistle softly. ''Is that legal?''

"Legal? Yeah, I think so. And definitely not unique. They

said they'd read your submission and they did. They didn't promise they'd do anymore than read and critique. They didn't say they had no plan other than to reject your work. Moral? Hardly. Legal? I think so. One thing you learn quickly when you study Krieg: Morality has nothing to do with his entire operation.''

"Amazing! Frightening, really. But what's it got to do with me? Why is he so interested in me? I'm published. Just once, so far, but published anyway.''

"Like I said in the beginning, old buddy: authenticity. Anybody can write that crap that Krieg publishes. Anybody. It's formula. They give the writer a plot—some of those writers can think up their own, some can't—anyway, P.G. sets the pace: After the plot, the publisher sets a frequency of moral turpitude. Every three pages, straight sex; every ten pages, kinky sex; every seven pages, group sex. If the background is a convent, you get lesbians. If it's a parish or a diocese—or, in your case, a monastery—you get every kind of sex imaginable. If your imagination needs help, they'll help you.''

"Am I getting thick in my moderate age?'' Augustine asked. "I still don't get it. Why me?''

"I was getting to that. As I said, anybody can write this stuff. And it sells pretty good. Actually, it sells damn good. The thing is, it would sell one helluva lot better even than it does now if the author were on the inside. Nothing titillates the reader like having the genuine article tell the story: 'How can an innocent, celebate monk like Father Augustine know so much about forbidden sex?' ''

"I'm beginning to get it.''

"Uh-huh. I'm not surprised that Krieg's laying on you to

climb aboard. I'd be surprised if he weren't leaning on every man or woman of the cloth who writes to join his stable."

"Still," Augustine objected, "it doesn't make sense. I wouldn't write that stuff."

"He's willing to take the gamble. But not till he narrows the odds."

"Pardon?"

"I haven't seen his pitch personally. But I'll bet the first wave of persuasion is lots and lots of assurance that he'll keep all the annoyances out of your quiet life. P.G. Press will shield you from all the mess attendant on publication of a book. Leaving you to quiet contemplation within the secure walls of your monastery."

"He's already mentioned that."

"I was right then. The next step I'm pretty sure about. He'll offer you a contract with a very handsome advance. That's what all those readers of his are working for: The money those poor suckers shell out to have their scripts read goes in part to pay the meager salary of the readers, but mostly it goes to offer people like you a sizable advance . . . sound good so far?"

Augustine thought for a few moments. "Well, yes . . . I suppose. But what good does all that do him? I'm still not going to write the kind of junk he wants."

"Wait. You get a lot of money on signing, but if P.G. doesn't find your manuscript acceptable—which they inevitably won't—you'll have to pay it back. And they tie you up in an option on your *next* book. Most authors—who've already spent the money just to live on—eventually capitulate—either to writing the kind of trash they want, or letting them do it."

"But . . ." Augustine was puzzled. "Is one lousy book by me worth all the trouble they're going to?"

"Oh, yeah, Harold; if they could get a real live monk, religious habit and all, belonging to the Trappists—one of the biggies; if they could get you to write one of the T&A books—don't ask what that stands for . . ."

Augustine hadn't been out of the world that long. He remembered tits and ass.

". . . if they could get you, they'd make a quantum leap out of and above their regular sales level. Might even garner a little bit of respectability. And as far as getting one book and one book alone from you, they'd figure you; you and your abbot; you, your abbot and your order would be so overwhelmed with the royalties that you'd write some more garbage for them."

"Fat chance!"

"Harold, it's a gamble. The whole thing is a gamble. The table stakes are just the dollars they offer you as an advance for signing the contract. If you didn't produce, or if you produced what in their lexicon was an unacceptable manuscript, they'd demand the advance back. It's well worth their time and money."

Augustine grimaced. "I think I've got the whole picture, Dick. I thank you mightily. Now that you've shown me the pitfalls so clearly, I'll be careful where I step."

"Okay, buddy. Just watch very carefully where you step. Krieg does not give up easily. He'll use everything he's got, everything he can get. So, cover your a—uh, watch out behind you."

Augustine smiled now, recalling his conversation with Dick Ryan. Funny how when one becomes a monk, erstwhile acquaintances feel they must clean up a language that once you shared.

But his smile quickly faded. Dick Ryan had been more prophetic than he possibly could have suspected. In a little while Augustine would meet Krieg again face to face. They would sup together. Then, in the words of John F. Kennedy, they would see who ate what.

Koesler was running late. Not like him. But his tardiness truly was due to unforeseeable circumstances.

He'd taken care of the Saturday evening and Sunday morning liturgies. After which he had been bone-tired—his usual state of a Sunday afternoon. It wasn't offering Mass that was so draining. It was preaching. The three Masses he said over the weekend were no particular problem. But trying to deliver a meaty, thoughtful, and thought-provoking homily was quite another thing.

There had been a Detroit Tigers game on TV that afternoon. Surrounding himself with the Sunday newspapers, he'd settled into an easy chair. In no time he'd drifted off to sleep. Nothing wrong with the Tigers; baseball was such a slow game of odds and percentages that, in his exhausted state, it pitched him into dreamland.

He'd awakened with a start. It was 3:30 and he was supposed to be at Marygrove at 5:00. The Jesuit who was to cover for him during the coming week had not arrived. A call to the University of Detroit revealed that the Jesuits had forgotten, but would send a man right over.

Koesler gave brief consideration to calling Mary O'Connor, the parish secretary and general factotum, to greet and brief the pinch-hitting priest. God knew Mary could easily take good care of the parish by herself. But Rome was not into ordaining women just yet. And in addition to the transfer of keys, the substitute would have to be apprised of the minimum obligations that would require his attention during the week.

In the end, he decided to wait for the visiting priest. If nothing else, protocol dictated that the keys of the kingdom be passed from one sacerdotal hand to another.

By the time the Jesuit had arrived, keys were entrusted, and necessary instructions given, it was 4:30. Koesler drove posthaste to Marygrove, and was shown to his room. It was too late to bother unpacking. The few things he'd brought could wait for a more leisurely time to be put away.

It was almost 5:15 as Father Koesler took the stairs toward the main floor.

When would he ever learn, he wondered, as he hurried down the stairs; when would he ever learn to say no to invitations he did not really wish to accept. To begin, he should have refused—politely, of course—the overture to participate in this writers' workshop. Although he enjoyed reading mystery novels, particularly those with a religious milieu, he was sure he was not qualified to contribute to this conference.

Secondly, having failed to turn down the initial invitation, he surely should have declined the added proposal that he stay at the college during the conference. He easily could have commuted the few miles between his parish and Marygrove. But Sister Janet had been so unrelentingly and respectfully insistent that he had accepted.

At that point the commitment had been made and there was no getting around it. When would he ever learn? Reluctantly, he had to admit that at his age and with his track record, probably never.

There were several dining rooms on the main floor. The

end of the corridor resembled a Saint Andrews Cross. At the end of the building was the large kitchen. The wing to the right of the kitchen was a large cafeteria, the wing to the left was the main dining room. As he walked down the hall, his eye caught a note taped to the door of a smaller dining room on the left.

The note read, "Conference Faculty Dining Room."

This, thought Koesler, had to be it. As he put his hand on the doorknob, the thought crossed his mind that no matter how distasteful this week might prove, at least he would not be dragged into an investigation of a real murder.

He turned the knob and entered the room.

6

WELL, NOW THIS was awkward.

Koesler stuck his head through the partially opened doorway. This, indeed, seemed to be the place where he was supposed to be. But if there had been conversation going on, it very definitely had halted with his appearance.

The small group in the dining room stood looking at him. Expectantly? It appeared they hoped he would do something, anything, to get this show on the road. If that was what they were expecting, they were about to be sadly disappointed.

More rapidly than it takes to tell, he took stock of each person in the group. There was no real need for ''Hello, I'm . . .'' badges. A simple process of elimination disclosed who was who.

He knew the nun in the modified habit. Sister Janet Schultes. The one who'd gotten him into this mess. Standing next to her, also in a modified habit, also wearing the telltale IHM blue . . . that must be Sister Marie Monahan. He could see her Irish ancestry in her fair complexion, ruddy cheeks, luxuriant eyebrows, and dancing eyes. She and Janet could be sisters. Not only were they dressed alike, they evidently were of the same vintage—although Marie had obviously had a few extra desserts, something that in the traditional habit wouldn't have made much difference. Actually, it didn't make that much difference now, it merely contributed to her matronly appearance. In any case, she exuded friendliness and warmth.

The next one was the easiest. In the traditional full habit of the Order of the Cistercians of the Strict Observance, he had to be Father Augustine May. Of medium height and build, he had inquisitive eyes behind thick glasses, a rather prominent nose—and no need for the carefully cut monastic tonsure: He was almost completely bald. The remaining hair, around his ears and circling at the back of his head, was trimmed close.

Another easy one was the gentleman in the stark clerical collar. Roman Catholic priests occasionally wore such an unadorned collar. But usually their clerical collars were all but completely hidden by a rabbat, an extension of the black vest. This specific collar, plus the fact that one of the participants was an Episcopal priest, made it more than likely that this was the Reverend David Benbow. Koesler reminded himself that Episcopal and Anglican priests were also addressed as "Father." He didn't want to offend, particularly over something as inconsequential as a title.

Father Benbow somewhat resembled the actor Michael Caine. The thinning, wavy blond hair, the slightly amused, almost supercilious smile. He was fairly tall, slender, and of a rather ordinary rectangular build. And there was something else: He was holding a half-full martini glass complete with an olive on a toothpick. That was noteworthy only in that the woman standing beside him was holding an identical half-filled-with-olive martini glass. It put Koesler in mind of . . . oh, who? Bill Powell and Myrna Loy, Nick and Nora Charles.

Except that as far as Koesler could recall, Nick Charles had never posed as a priest—Episcopal or Roman Catholic.

No matter.

As to the woman standing next to Reverend . . . uh, *Father* Benbow, that was open to debate. She was not one of the authors. There was only one woman author, Sister Marie, and he had already identified her. This woman was somebody's wife. Rabbi Winer, Father Benbow, or Klaus Krieg? Time for a guess. Standing next to Benbow, holding the identical drink—voila! Mrs. Benbow.

The only contrary argument might be that she seemed a bit older than Benbow, but that happens. She, like Sister Marie, had put on a few extra pounds that undoubtedly were unwelcome. Something else: She seemed almost to err on the side of modesty. What did they used to call that in the good old days? A Mary-like dress. Long sleeves, high neckline, below-the-knees length and some winsome lace at collar and cuffs. Koesler doubted that she dressed like this ordinarily, but, all in all, he liked it. The modesty was a refreshing change from what one too often encountered at affairs such as this.

The final person to be identified—there were a few obvious students waiting tables—was more of a challenge. He was standing apart from the others, although he, like the others, was holding a partially filled glass.

The problem was that he could be one of two people. If Koesler was correct in guessing the identity of the others, this final character in the drama was either Rabbi Irving Winer or Klaus Krieg.

He couldn't have been more than five-foot-six or -seven inches tall. At 150 to 170 pounds, he was a bit rotund. Wisps of hair reached across the top of his balding head. Koesler had never met the rabbi and, at best, had only seen photos of Krieg in ads for his TV show. Koesler had never seen the show. In the ads Krieg might have borne some faint resemblance to this man.

But the tipoff was the clothing. It bordered on the nondescript. A blue pinstripe suit, vested, unpressed; a gold watch chain across the round tummy; and scuffed black oxfords. All in all, not the garb of one as reputedly wealthy as Klaus Krieg.

So, Koesler concluded in a tentative way, this man is Rabbi Irving Winer.

Or, not.

In any case, it seemed time to test his skill at amateur detection. He approached the least certain of his guesses. "Rabbi Winer?"

"You must be Father Koesler." The rabbi took the priest's outstretched hand.

Success.

Now Koesler moved from one to the other with far greater assurance. "Father Benbow."

"Father Koesler."

"Mrs. Benbow."

"Please, call me Martha."

"Certainly.

"Father May."

"Father Augustine, really."

"Certainly.

"Sister Marie."

"Father Koesler."

"And last but not least, our hostess, as it were, Sister Janet."

"So glad you are here, Father Koesler. I was beginning to worry."

Sister Marie glanced at her watch. "Jan, for goodness sake, it's only 5:20!"

"You don't understand, Marie. Father Koesler has a reputation for being early, not to mention on time."

Koesler smiled as he reddened. "I'm afraid that's true. Today was the exception that proves the rule." He wasn't going to go into his Tigers-induced nap nor even the forgetful Jesuits.

In response to Janet's invitation, Koesler requested tonic water. It was delivered on the rocks with a thin slice of lemon. He scanned the sideboard containing the liquor bottles. Ordinary selection; none of the various bottles bore an expensive label. In keeping, he thought, with Marygrove: never really wealthy and now leaning toward serving the poor.

Koesler turned back to the assembled group. Everyone seemed ill at ease. Strangers to one another, none appeared confident enough to get the verbal ball rolling. Well, at least everyone had a drink. But . . . "Uh, isn't someone missing?" Koesler gave voice to the obvious, something at which he excelled.

"The Reverend Krieg," Sister Janet said. "He'll be here shortly, I'm sure."

The mention of Krieg seemed to unplug the floodgates. "With any luck," Benbow remarked, "his plane went down."

"David!" Martha Benbow exclaimed. "What a dreadful thing to say! That's not very Christian."

"Nonetheless—" Benbow began.

"Nonetheless," Augustine interrupted, "I'd have to agree, with one proviso. I'm sure none of us would want it to cost the lives of innocent people, but I certainly would not mourn the demise of that man."

"Of course, no innocent lives . . ." Benbow corrected himself.

"Life is precious," Winer stated. "That is why we salute 'L'chayim.' But I will join you two gentlemen: If there is one person on this earth today who would do the world a favor by leaving, it is Klaus Krieg."

"My God! I can't believe it!" Sister Marie exclaimed. "Is it possible we've all had the same experience with that man?"

"Why, Sister," Martha said, "you mean you feel the same as the men?"

"It comes in the form of a confession, I'm afraid—but, yes, I do. Even though each of us writes murder mysteries, I have no doubt we all have a special reverence for life. So it comes as a shock to face up to the truth. And the truth, it seems evident, is that we all have been touched by Klaus Krieg and we all have concluded that the world would be better off without him. And I cannot think of another single human being I feel that way about."

Though Sister Janet appeared troubled by this outpouring, she said nothing.

It was Koesler who spoke. "This is impressive. I'm on the outside looking in. I'm no writer. I have no idea what you've gone through with this man. I've never even seen his TV program, and I've just read one book his company published."

"Which one?" Benbow asked.

Koesler was at a loss. "For the life of me, I can't recall the title. It had something to do with priests." He glanced at Benbow and was reminded that there was more than one variety of priest at this conference. "Roman Catholic priests," he added.

"Celibates!" Winer exclaimed. "That would mean they were all in bed with uncounted numbers of women."

"How did you . . . ?"

"No, I haven't read the book," Winer quickly declared. "The literary—if one can use that term in connection with Krieg's efforts—the literary device is unvarying. The parish priest—the celibate—is in his rectory all day. Meanwhile, all those housewives are in their homes all day. Everyone is bored, so . . . If it had been about a rabbi, he likely would be charging usurious interest, indulging in 'creative' book-keeping, and carrying on with the wife of the president of the synagogue—just for spite." Winer shook his head.

There was a pause, as if no one had anything to add.

Father Augustine cleared his throat hesitantly. "Did any of you . . ."

Koesler noted a slight slur in his speech.

Augustine began again. "Have any of you been contacted by P.G. Press to write for them?"

Now the floodgates were opened wide. In reinforcing testimony, each of the writers told of Krieg's invitation, the persistent pursuit—unrelenting assault, really—that Krieg's organization had engaged in. There was no particular order in their narratives. Details spilled out as one's experiences reminded another of a similar ordeal. Each had been romanced with extravagant promises.

Fortunately, in each instance, the writer had bothered to check into P.G.'s publication history. The sleaze factor was so obvious it was unmistakable. In keeping with Father Augustine's information from his friend in the ad agency, each writer had received the good advice from one or another source to have nothing to do with P.G. Press.

And yet, even with the effusiveness of their testimony, Koesler got a nebulous impression that something was being held back.

It was as if these writers were eager to share their individual dealings with Krieg, that they experienced some relief, some catharsis in getting off their chest what had been a miserable episode in each of their lives. Yet each seemed to stop short of complete revelation.

Koesler could not in any way testify to this impression he harbored. He could not substantiate it.

His ponderings were interrupted by Sister Janet's announcement that dinner was ready and all should take their places at the table. The announcement was almost a command—less an invitation to dine than a direction to cease this trend in the conversation.

Koesler found Sister's attitude understandable. After all, even though she hadn't planned or instigated this event—that had been the brain child of her predecessor—she was the hostess for this workshop. If all did not go smoothly, the buck would stop at her desk. And things were not unruffled when four members of the "faculty" wished the fifth speaker dead.

But, willy-nilly, dinner was going to be served. So the writers who had been so animated in describing their battles with Krieg now filed passively to the table. Koesler noticed that Augustine and Benbow freshened their drinks before being seated.

Sister Janet led a traditional before-meal blessing.

There was no particular seating arrangement; each took a place at random. The Benbows sat together. Sister Janet took a place next to Martha Benbow; Sister Marie sat next to Janet. This left the four men together. No boy-girl-boy-girl at this table. There was, of course, one unoccupied seat.

"We're not going to wait?" Martha Benbow asked.

"For what?" her husband responded.

"For the Reverend Krieg."

In view of the just concluded detailed excoriation of Krieg and his communications empire by nearly everyone in the group, this brought a moment of shocked surprise. Then someone snickered. That broke the ice; everyone roared with laughter. They weren't laughing at or about Krieg; having done everything short of hanging him in effigy, they all found the idea of waiting dinner for him the height of irony.

When the laughter came under more individual control, the group took note that soup and salad had been served. Somewhat more relaxed, they began to eat.

"I have some little experience with writers . . ." Sister Janet spoke rather forcefully. She did not want the conversation to revert to Klaus Krieg again; that would be counterproductive to the harmony and good humor she'd hoped would mark this conference. Thus, the effort to steer the table talk along less controversial lines. "So . . ." she proceeded, having gained everyone's attention, "I feel I'm safe in assuming that none of you has a lot of time for reading. In my experience, this seems to be a common complaint of writers."

She paused, looking around the table. Her guests, spooning soup or passing salad dressing, nodded agreement and/or facially reflected the futility of finding time, particularly for light reading, while pursuing a writing career.

Sister Janet, having established her premise, pushed on. "Well, I enjoy a little more luxury in this than you do. I've been able to read some of all your work." She turned to Father Benbow. "I haven't read all your books, Father Benbow. You have been productive. But I have read a couple.

"I think it's marvelous that you all have been able to communicate an authentic religious experience."

Sister Marie moved her empty soup bowl aside. "You're right, of course, Sister. I've wanted to read something by each of you. Especially since I knew we all would be getting together for this conference. I just haven't had the time. But I did learn enough about all of you to know that you all did the very same thing I did. It seems we all followed that sage advice to 'go with what you know.' Many of the characters in my book, along with the main character, are nuns. And no one needs to tell me about nuns.

"I'm aware that the protagonist in your books, Father Benbow, is an Episcopal priest; in your book, Father Augustine, a Trappist monk; and in yours, Rabbi Winer, the main character is a rabbi and the setting is a synagogue.

"That's what you had in mind, wasn't it, Sister Jan? The authentic religious experience?"

"Exactly. And, as I read your books, I marveled at how each of you was able to invite your readers into your particular religious framework. The interesting thing to me was how you all seemed to accomplish so much with anecdotes.

"And this is what I was getting to: I think it would be interesting if each of you would recount an anecdote from one of your books. The ones that you use all seem to have a purpose in the plot."

Koesler, feeling more completely left out than he had in a very long time, considered this to be a rather elite exercise in show-and-tell.

"Why don't we start with you, Sister Marie? Would you tell the story of the nun on the train?"

Marie was reluctant to chance having the just-served beef Stroganoff cool off. Nonetheless, it seemed time to sing for her supper.

"It's not a perfect example by any means," Marie began, "but, okay, here goes.

"The story involves a nun on a train. It doesn't matter

where the train is going, say, Chicago to Los Angeles. It's dinnertime the second day out and the nun goes to the dining car. All the seats are taken except one at a table where two well-dressed men are seated. They invite her to join them. The trio have a pleasant time, and, after dinner, the nun makes to return to her stateroom. But the two men urge her to stay. They contend that since they've enjoyed each other's company at dinner, and since the evening is still young, she should accompany them to the club car.

"Reluctantly, she agrees. So they go to the club car. The waiter asks if they'd like to order drinks. The men each order a Manhattan. They ask if she'd like a drink. She declines politely but firmly. They urge that she join them in a drink. She finally agrees, but she must see to it that no scandal is given: She'll have a martini, but asks that it be served in a coffee cup.

"The waiter tells the bartender, 'Two Manhattans up, and a martini in a coffee cup.'

"The bartender looks up and says, 'Is that damn nun still on this train?' "

While the others were laughing at the story, Sister Marie was able to down a couple of bites of dinner. It was delicious, but definitely cooling.

After the laughter died, Marie added, "That story was helpful in my book because after the nun tells it, she is able to point out the flaws. And they are, of course, anachronistic errors. If the nun was wearing a habit which was that easily recognizable, she undoubtedly would belong to the pre-Vatican II Church—which would date the story sometime no later than the early sixties or any time before that. However, if a nun was traveling anywhere in that era, she would certainly be accompanied by another nun. Nuns simply did not travel alone back then.

"On the other hand, if she was traveling alone, it would place her in the post-Conciliar Church and in all probability she would be wearing ordinary lay clothing with probably no more than a small gold cross to denote her religious status, so that it would be unnecessary for her to worry about taking a martini in a coffee cup for appearance sake.

"And when my fictional nun gets done explaining all this, the reader has an added insight into the differences between the pre- and post-Conciliar Church."

"Now, if that incident had been contained in a P.G. book," Father Benbow said, "there wouldn't have been that much time spent in the dining car and the threesome would not have repaired to the club car. All three would have . . ." He let his thought drift off unuttered. After all that had been said about the P.G. Press, nothing more need be added.

"Your turn, Father Augustine." Sister Janet did not want the group's attention to revert to Krieg. Indeed, she was becoming more grateful that the Reverend Krieg had not yet arrived. "Why don't you tell us that delightful story you have in *A Rose by Any Other Name*—the one about the Trappist and the bishop?"

Augustine continued to cut his food and eat it. Koesler noticed that the monk's hand trembled ever so slightly and his enunciation seemed determinedly articulate. Koesler thought the pattern might be described as overspeak.

"Well," Augustine said finally, "all right; if you wish. It's an apocryphal story, you see. In it, a group of monks are working in the field. Being of the Strict Order, they are forbidden to speak to each other—or to anyone, for that matter.

So they work all day in complete silence. No one can tell what they're thinking.

"One day, as it happens, a bishop visits the abbey." He looked around the table. "Now comes time to explain that while the rule forbids the monks from speaking to each other, they are permitted to speak to their Father Abbot or to a ranking prelate—which would have to be at least a bishop.

"Anyway, this one day, a bishop visits the monastery. The monks are working in the fields as usual. The bishop goes for a walk in the field, ostensibly for exercise, though mostly to see what the monks are up to.

"He comes up to one monk who is digging away at the potato crop. Now the bishop considers himself a better-than-average amateur psychologist. So he says to the monk, 'Brother, you look very, very sad.'

"The monk stops digging and looks at the speaker. He sees the pectoral cross, recognizes him as a bishop, and realizes they may speak to each other. 'You're right, bishop,' he says, 'I don't feel at all happy. Not at all, at all.'

"I guess," Augustine threw in as an aside, "I guess the monk must've been Irish."

The others chuckled their appreciation.

"Anyway," Augustine continued, "the bishop becomes interested in the monk and decides to analyze him and free him of his depression. 'Don't tell me, brother; let me guess,' he says to the monk, 'it's the hours you keep. In bed by 6:00 or 7:00 in the evening, up at 2:00 or 3:00 to sing Matins. Up again at 6:00 for Lauds. Those hours could wear anyone out in time. That's it, eh, Brother—the hours?'

"The monk thought that over and said, 'Not really, bishop. I couldn't say that was it. No, not really.'

"Undaunted, the bishop tried again. 'Well, Brother, if it's

not the hours, it's probably your vehicle of sleep. After all, a lumpy straw mattress on bare boards. I meant to mention that to Father Abbot; how can anyone expect you to function when you have to try to get your rest on such a machine of torture? It's the mattress, isn't it, Brother?' The monk thought about that for a while and finally he said, 'No, bishop. No, I don't think it's the mattress.'

"The bishop considered this for a while. It was unlike him to take two straight strikes. So he said, 'Brother, I think I have it. It's the food. No meat, no eggs, strictly vegetarian diet, day in and day out. All the while preparing meat from scratch on your farm and serving dandy cuts of meat to your guests. That's an exquisite kind of torture. It's like the forbidden fruit: You can't have it and yet it's dangled before you. No one could take that endlessly. I don't blame you for your depression. It's the meals, isn't it?'

"The monk leaned on his shovel and thought quite seriously. Then he said, 'Sorry, bishop, but I don't think so. You have a good point, but—no, I don't think it's the menu.'

"Now the bishop has had his three guesses and he has struck out. But bishops get to play by their own rules. So he gave the matter some deep critical thought. After all, no one was going anywhere; they had all the time in the world. At length, he snapped his fingers; he'd solved the question.

" 'I have it, Brother'—the bishop fairly bounced—'how could I have been so blind? It's right here before me. I've been walking around in the middle of it all this time and haven't paid the slightest bit of attention to it. It's the silence! Here you are, working, praying, eating, living shoulder to shoulder with your fellow monks, and you don't even know what their speaking voices sound like. How can anyone expect a man to live so close to his fellow man—probably, all things considered, his closest friends on earth. Men you will bury. Men who will bury you. And you never speak to them. That's it, isn't it? It's the silence!'

"The monk started to nod as a small smile began to form. But gradually his expression changed to one of doubt and then disagreement. He shook his head. 'Gee, I'm sorry, bishop, but that isn't it, either.'

"The bishop was completely baffled. He didn't mind swinging at this puzzle all day long; it didn't matter how many strikes he took. The problem now was he couldn't think of any more afflictions the Trappists faced. Yet this poor monk was clearly troubled. The bishop had set out to free him of his psychological dilemma, whatever it was, but had failed. It wasn't the hours of sleep and prayer, it wasn't the impossible mattress, it wasn't the strictly limited diet, it wasn't the pervasive silence.

" 'Brother,' the bishop said finally, 'I give up. I can't figure out what's depressing you.'

"The monk thought a bit more and then said, 'Well, bishop, I'll tell you: It's the whole damn thing.' "

It was a funny story well told, and Augustine's audience appreciated it, even if at least one of them had heard it before. Still, all including Father Koesler, enjoyed it.

Koesler himself was known for his anecdotal homilies. Many of his friends thought of him as a "story man." A few of his confreres occasionally referred to him as "Inspector Frank Luger, NYPD," an allusion to a character in the "Barney Miller" TV sitcom, who virtually lived in the past and constantly told stories about "the good old days with Foster and Brownie and Kleiner."

And, Koesler thought, why not? It starts when one is a child and discovers that one of life's greatest pleasures is to listen to adults tell stories. Skilled raconteurs were so generally appreciated that not only did audiences want to hear the same stories over and over—but without having a single cherished word changed. Finally, the Gospels demonstrate that Jesus Himself was an inveterate storyteller. Nearly everything He taught was couched in a parable.

Koesler noted that even as Augustine told his story, the monk continued to eat his dinner. And, as he did so, his hand shook less and his speech became more steady. Though there had not been all that much amiss to begin with in any case.

Koesler was the only one in the gathering who gave such attention to detail. From long experience, he did not expect the others to notice what was obvious and of possible interest to him.

As the laughter died down, Augustine raised his fork to quiet the group, and added, "Don't anyone bother telling me what P.G. Press would have done with that story. I read one of their books, *Ignosce mihi, Domine*. I know that if Krieg had had anything to do with it, the monk and his abbot would have had more than words together. And the bishop probably would have been establishing a special relationship with the sheep on the farm."

Another round of laughter.

Sister Janet tapped her glass with a knife.

A startled Koesler was put in mind of that most gauche of all customs at wedding banquets, when repeatedly tapped glasses urge spousal kisses, over and over. Such was not the case here. For one, the seating arrangement isolated the girls from the boys. For another, one woman was married and the other two were nuns. Some things deserved to remain sacred.

"Thank you, Father Augustine," Sister Janet said. "Now, Rabbi Winer. There were so many homey stories in your books, Rabbi. Maybe you could tell the one about the lady who was giving birth for the first time.''

Now that his attention had been drawn to Winer, Koesler noticed that the rabbi had only toyed with the Stroganoff. Perhaps he was not feeling well. If that was the case, Winer might have been wiser not to consent to this five-day-long conference. However, with the invitation to contribute his anecdote, the rabbi brightened noticeably.

Winer chuckled. ''All right,'' he said. ''The story takes place in Paris and involves a married couple. The husband is French, his wife is Jewish, and they have a Jewish obstetrician.

''She has been pregnant a little more than nine months, by someone's count. And all she and her husband know is that it says in the book that nine months is term. Something should happen now, but they're unclear as to what. The only one who is calm about this is the doctor. This very definitely is not his first delivery.

''Suddenly one sunny afternoon, she begins to have pains, severe pains. Her husband remembers reading in the Bible that in pain shall women bring forth children. This pain seems to qualify.

''So the husband calls the doctor and tells him that his wife is in pain. Should they all meet at the hospital forthwith?

'' 'What is your wife saying?' the doctor asks.

'' 'Wait!' the husband says, 'I didn't know I was supposed to pay attention to that.'

''He leaves the phone, listens to his wife for a minute, then returns to the phone. 'Doctor,' he says, 'she is saying, "Mon Dieu!" '

'' 'Not quite time yet,' the doctor advises.

''Time passes, but the pain doesn't let up. In fact, it gets worse. The husband does not want to become a pest, but feels he has to do something. The only thing he can think of is to call again.

" 'Doctor,' he says, 'it's worse, much worse. Is it time to go to the hospital yet?'

"Patiently, the doctor asks again, 'What is she saying?' Once more the husband checks. 'Doctor,' he says, 'she's saying, "sacre bleu!" '

"With a smile in his voice, the doctor says, 'Not quite yet, my friend.'

"In no time, the man is back on the phone. 'Doctor, I'm sure this must be it. I've never seen anyone in such pain.'

" 'What is your wife saying now?'

" 'She's saying—'

" 'Oy, gevalt!' " A strong voice from the dining room door completed the sentence.

In a suddenly flat voice, the rabbi concluded his story: " 'It's time,' the doctor said."

"Praise God!" the newcomer proclaimed.

While it was a funny story, only the stranger in the doorway laughed. And he laughed heartily, completely oblivious to the fact that he laughed alone. Anyone else, thought Koesler, might well have been embarrassed.

Again relying on the process of elimination, Koesler identified the newcomer as Klaus Krieg. Amazing how much Krieg physically resembled Rabbi Winer. They were approximately the same height and build. And yet how different their physiognomy. Winer was nearly bald while Krieg had a full head of dark sculpted hair . . . or was it a toupee? Koesler leaned toward the rug hypothesis. Though if it were, it would be one of the better, more expensive ones. Also, Krieg's attire appeared to be many times more expensive than Winer's.

But by far the greatest difference between the two men was in their facial expression.

There really wasn't much to say about Winer's visage. Not only did his features constitute what some would consider a typical Jewish face, but there was an aspect of sadness that never seemed to leave him, even when, as he had just done, relating a humorous anecdote.

Krieg, on the other hand, exuded nothing less than complete confidence and self-satisfaction. When Koesler first saw him, Krieg, having stolen Winer's thunder, was laughing at Winer's joke, which he, Krieg, had just completed. Now he had stopped laughing, but a smug smile still played at his mouth—a smile that put Koesler in mind of all the ads he had seen for any of the televangelists. They, as well as their entire entourage, always oozed that same smug, self-satisfied smile. The only exceptions Koesler could think of offhand were the Jimmies—Bakker and Swaggart—when caught at good old moral turpitude. When you came right down to it, a tearful televangelist was refreshing if rare.

Sister Janet almost knocked over the chair in her haste to greet the newcomer. "Reverend Krieg," she said, "welcome to Marygrove. I hope you don't mind that we started without you."

"Not at all, Sister." Krieg spoke without looking at her. He was keenly and confidently studying the others at table. "We'll just make ourselves at home."

With that, Krieg nodded to a companion Koesler had not hitherto noticed. The man, evidently an assistant, responded immediately to his employer's casual gesture. He went directly to one of the waitresses and quietly conferred with her. The young women seemed cowed as the man shook his head vigorously. The two then left the dining area, presumably headed for the kitchen.

For no reason Koesler could imagine, Sister Janet seemed embarrassed. "I'm sure you know the other participants in the workshop, Reverend," she said, after a slight hesitation.

"I have met Father Benbow . . . and Father Augustine"— he inclined his head in each cleric's respective direction— "but, my loss I'm sure"—with a smiling hint of a bow—"I've never met the other authors in person. However, I'm well aware of who they all are and what they've done." He emphasized the final few words, seeming to invest them with a meaning that eluded Koesler.

The empty chair obviously was his, so Krieg made his way to it. As he did so, he greeted each of the others without introduction, correctly as it turned out.

Martha greeted him politely. The others' response was stony silence. At most there was an almost imperceptible nod. Father Koesler was puzzled by the measure of animosity that seemed to be projected toward Krieg. It struck Koesler as inordinate, even from people with a basic difference of opinion over religion. True, their differences were radical. Still, he was surprised at the intensity of their reaction.

Krieg then caught Koesler off guard by recognizing him. "And last, but by no means least," Krieg said, "we have the formidable Father Koesler."

It was one of those rare occasions where Koesler was at a loss for words. He did not share in whatever it was that the others felt with regard to Krieg. Until this moment, Koesler had been enjoying his spectator role.

"Well, really, I . . ." Koesler faltered.

"No false modesty now, Father," said Krieg. "You may think that only Detroiters are aware of your amazingly successful periodic forays into murder cases. But your reputation extends far outside this city, I assure you.''

''Thank you.'' It was not a particularly apt sequitur, but it was all Koesler could come up with in response.

As Krieg seated himself, Sister Janet spoke. ''Reverend Krieg, before you came, we were in the midst of having each of our writers share with us a favorite anecdote. I think it was proving an excellent means of getting acquainted. I was just about to ask Father Benbow to tell us a story. Father, why don't you tell us the one about the bishop and confirmation?''

Benbow hesitated, then said, ''I think it's gone. I'm afraid I'm going to have to beg off. The atmosphere just isn't right for any more funny little stories.''

From their silence, the others seemed to concur. But not Krieg. ''Well,'' he said, ''I'm sure we regret your decision, Father Benbow. I've read all your books—in point of fact, I've read all of all your books,'' he said, regarding each of the others, ''but''—returning to Benbow—''I agree with Sister: The story of the bishop at confirmation is a masterpiece, a little gem. Sorry you don't feel up to it. I'll just recommend it to everyone here just in case any of you don't know the story. And''—Krieg began to chuckle—''I'm not going to tell which of Father Benbow's books has that particular story. You'll have to read them all and find it for yourselves. But I will say this: You'll have a fine time hunting it down.''

Koesler could not get over Krieg's ebullience. It was as if there were an underlying joke at the funeral and Krieg was the only one who was getting the point.

Followed by Krieg's assistant, the young waitress reentered the dining room bearing a tray containing Krieg's delayed dinner. Nervously, she set the dishes before him. He glanced at each, smiled, and nodded to his aide, who then positioned himself alongside a cabinet near the door. His stance was one the military would term "at ease."

As Krieg began toying with his food—it was steaming hot—Sister Janet said as genially as possible, "We'll forgive you, Father Benbow, just this once. But how about you, Reverend Krieg: Would you honor us with an anecdote?"

Krieg waved a forkful of food. It seemed a means of cooling the food, as much as a gesture of response. "Now, Sister, I'm not as talented as these good writers. I'm just a minor publisher who preaches some."

Everything about the man belied that statement, from the cut and quality of his attire, to the manservant who anticipated every need, to the immediate preparation of an alternate dinner. Koesler took note of what had been served Krieg. The salad and vegetable seemed identical to that which had been served the others. The major substitution was the pièce de résistance, which appeared to be a cheese omelet and milk, along with coffee and cream. Koesler wondered if the substitution and the fuss and bother it caused was not just another statement Krieg used to reinforce his own importance.

Sister Janet was nearly pleading as she implored Krieg for a story from his vast reservoir of experience as publisher and preacher.

Krieg granted her plea, while continuing to pick at his food. "Far as I know," he began, "this is a true story. Billy Graham tells it. Seems Billy was preaching in one of those humongous cathedrals in England. He was up in a high, ornate pulpit, goin' after sin and the sinner, Praise God!

"Well, Billy was gettin' pretty worked up, in that way of his. He started hammerin' on the pulpit and swayin' to and fro and shoutin' and yellin' and wavin' his fists in the air. About the time he had the crowd as scared as they were ever gonna be, he stopped dead—just froze. You could have heard a pin drop. He had that bunch of sinners in the palm of his hand.

"Just at that moment, a small child in the front row said, just loud enough to be heard in that vast, silent church, he said, 'Mama, what are we gonna do if he gets out of that cage?'"

Krieg threw his head back and roared. "Praise God!" he shouted through the laughter that he shared with Sister Janet, Martha Benbow, the man at the cupboard, and Father Koesler, who cut short his mirth when he saw the four writers accord the story no more than a brief smile. However, their near deadpan response to a genuinely funny anecdote did nothing to faze Krieg's appreciation of his own joke. He was still wiping tears from his eyes after all other laughter ceased. At the end of it all, once again, he proclaimed, "Praise God!"

Koesler concluded that the phrase could become a bit wearisome.

Krieg touched napkin to lips. He'd finished his meal without a touch of dessert. He'd eaten very little. Koesler wondered how, if this were a representative meal, Krieg maintained his roly-poly shape. No exercise, probably—and undoubtedly this was not a typical intake.

At a nod from Krieg, his assistant unlocked and opened the cabinet, whence he extracted a variety of bottles, which he placed on the serving ledge.

Koesler took note. These were not the inexpensive liquors served before the meal. Even a casual glance at the labels revealed these to be among the highest quality and cost.

"I'd like to invite you all to join me in an after-dinner drink, if you would. It would be a nice ending to a delicious meal, and a pleasant warming for the evening ahead."

It was one of life's embarrassing moments. No one did or said anything.

Whatever chemistry was going on here, a goodly portion of it was escaping Koesler. Yet he thought it uncivil, if not ungodly or un-Christian, to give no response whatsoever to an invitation that, to all appearances, seemed sincerely offered.

So Koesler responded. And in doing so, he thawed the antipathy of the others. He was followed to the array of liquors and liqueurs by Janet and Martha, then by Benbow, Winer, Augustine, and Marie. Last came Krieg, looking pleased that the logjam of opposition was at least showing some movement.

Koesler, first to arrive at the cupboard, inspected the display. None of the bottles was small. In some cases the booze was in full gallon containers. There were no price tags, but a gallon of Chivas Regal, twelve years old, did not come cheap. The same could be said for Cutty Sark, Dewar's White Label, Glenmorangie ten years old, Canadian Club, Jack Daniel's Old Number 7 Tennessee, Bushmills, and Bombay Dry Gin. Then there were the liqueurs: Solignac Cognac, Frangelico, Grand Marnier, Galliano, Benedictine, B and B, Amaretto di Saronno, Chartreuse, and E & J Brandy.

The quantity and variety were overwhelming.

In honor of that half of his heritage which was Irish, Koesler poured a shot of Bushmills into a snifter. He rolled the amber liquid around the base of the glass, occasionally inhaling the sweet-smelling bouquet.

Standing off to one side, Koesler, between occasional sips, checked out what the others were doing. Krieg's assistant/companion stood nearby. At six-foot-three he and Koesler were of equal height. There the comparison pretty much ended. The associate was built like a brick armory, with no discernible neck, just a granite-like head that melded into massive shoulders.

Extending his hand, the priest introduced himself. "Hi. Father Koesler."

The associate snorted, looked impassively at the priest, and said, "No. Guido Taliafero."

Hand still extended, Koesler hesitated. Then he understood. "No, *I'm* Father Koesler."

"Oh." Guido nodded and took the outstretched hand. Koesler was prepared; he slipped his hand as deeply into Taliafero's as possible. Koesler knew, from the school of hard handshakes, that the greeting would hurt less if his palm were wrung than if his fingers were squeezed. Still, there was pain. Koesler swallowed it. "Worked for Reverend Krieg long?" he said, finally.

"No."

"Oh . . . uh . . . what did you do before you came to work for Reverend Krieg?"

"Played football."

"That figures. But I don't place the name. Wait a minute; yes, I do. There was a Taliafero. But wasn't he a quarterback?"

"Not NFL. Canadian League."

"Oh . . . uh . . . well, nice meeting you, Guido."

"Same here."

And that was that. Taliafero remained at his post, in an "at ease" stance. Koesler felt awkward trying to continue this monosyllabic conversation; he moved off to a vantage whence he could more easily observe the others. As their drinks were poured, he noted their choices: Janet, Amaretto; Marie, Benedictine; Martha, Galliano; Benbow, E & J Brandy; Winer, Frangelico; Augustine, Chartreuse and then Grand Marnier; Krieg, Frangelico.

Neither the drinks nor the momentary lull in hostilities appeared to have healed the situation. Janet and Marie were off by themselves. Benbow, Winer, and Augustine seemed to have found some common ground; at least they were talking among themselves. Augustine gave some indication that he was not feeling all that well. Martha was talking to Krieg. Whatever her husband's problem with the publisher, Martha did not seem to share it.

Krieg, catching sight of Koesler standing by himself, motioned him over. Koesler joined him and Martha.

"So, Father," said Krieg, "did you know that Martha here is in real estate? Very successfully, too."

"No, I had no idea."

"Not only that," Krieg continued, "but she's been thinking of doing some writing. She's been telling me some of her ideas. Promising. Very promising."

"Reverend Krieg has been most encouraging," Martha said. "It certainly motivates a person when a publisher says he's willing to read your work. I don't think I would consider taking time from my schedule to write unless I were sure the completed version would be read. But now . . ."

"Praise God!" Krieg said.

"You're thinking of writing for P.G. Press?" Koesler asked Martha.

"At least tentatively," Martha said.

"Have you ever read any of the books the Reverend's house publishes?" Koesler asked.

"Not yet. But I surely will. First chance I get."

Lady, thought Koesler, are you in for a surprise.

At that point, Sister Janet spoke loudly. "If I may have your attention, everyone . . ." She got it. "According to our schedule, those of you who will be conducting seminars tomorrow—namely, Fathers Benbow and Augustine, Rabbi Winer and Sister Marie—should go to your conference rooms on the second floor at this time. The locations are in the folders you will find''—she gestured—''on the table near the door. There will be facilitators in the conference rooms to brief you on the students you may expect tomorrow.

''Martha Benbow, Father Koesler, and I are to go to the Denk Chapman room here on the first floor.'' She addressed the two named directly. ''There are some last-minute details that I could use your help with.

''Reverend Krieg, your conference room is not quite ready. So, if you would, please, remain here in the faculty dining room for a brief while longer. One of our facilitators will come to get you in just a short while.

''Shall we go now?''

Koesler noticed Krieg nodding to Guido Taliafero. The guard acknowledged the signal, then left the dining room, disappearing in the direction of the building's front door.

Glasses were deposited on the table, folders located, and the group began to disperse.

As Koesler left the dining room, he saw Taliafero's massive form silhouetted against the front door. Beyond that, just outside the entrance, was a white stretch limo, standing in what Koesler knew was a no-parking zone.

Indicating the limousine-in-violation, Koesler asked, ''Krieg's?''

''Yes.'' Janet sighed. ''I'm afraid so.''

The man has ways of impressing others, thought Koesler, with his celebrity, his wealth, his importance. His clothing—the finest cut; the most expensive material. Guido Taliafero—a lackey, present whenever needed; performs tasks, even leaves, with only the slightest signal to indicate the com-

mand. The liquor—the finest labels in more than adequate
supply. And now, a stretch limo—two people in a vehicle
easily large enough for an entire wedding party. What next,
Koesler wondered.

The trio walked along the corridor. As they entered the
Denk Chapman room, Martha Benbow spoke. "You know,"
she confided, "I thought Reverend Krieg rather charming."

"But then," Koesler said, "you really don't know much
about the man, do you?"

"You mean watching his program on TV, or reading any
of his publications." She was a bit defensive. "No, I don't
know all that much about him."

"Judging from the reaction of the others, to know him is
not necessarily to love him." Koesler wondered how much
Martha's opinion of Krieg was predicated upon his professed
interest in publishing her work sight unseen. "But I must
admit that I can't quite fathom the intensity of feeling I sensed
in the dining room. Do you have any clue?"

She thought for a moment. "No, I can't say I have. But I
must admit I'm troubled by it. It's not like David to think or
speak that way. I mean, I've seen him in ecumenical and like
groups. He's always been the very model of a most understanding Christian gentleman. The type whose bottom line
is, 'Well, I guess we agree to disagree.' " Her brow fur-
rowed further. "But not with Reverend Krieg.

"I must agree with you, Father Koesler. It's not only
David; the others seem to manifest the same inexplicable
animosity toward the Reverend Krieg. I simply don't understand it. And it troubles me."

A sudden roaring clap resounded.

"Good God!" Martha exclaimed. "What was that?"

"An automobile?" Koesler hoped it was, but knew it wasn't. "A backfire?"

"A gun!" Sister Janet shuddered. "Gunfire! It's on this floor! The dining room!"

They turned and raced back toward the dining room.

It was the dining room, no doubt about that; high-pitched screams were emanating from within.

As Janet, Martha, and Koesler entered the room, a hysterical waitress was being calmed by another waitress.

Koesler saw the body immediately. Crumpled on the floor, it looked like a pile of laundry that had been carelessly dropped. That is, if you could believe a laundry bag of expensive pin-striped blue silk.

In seconds the first three were joined by Benbow and Winer and then Marie, who dashed breathlessly into the room. She gasped at the sight of the inert figure. Almost prayerfully, she breathed, "Oh, my God!"

Koesler was first to approach the body. Krieg's white-on-white shirt was now almost completely red. Koesler could discern what appeared to be a small dark hole on the upper chest. Blood was trickling from Krieg's mouth and nostrils. The priest stood frozen.

Not so Janet. Quickly she knelt next to Krieg and placed her fingers against his carotid artery. She looked up at the others and said, wonderingly, "He's dead! My God, he's dead!"

At that moment, a young woman burst into the dining room. "It's Father Augustine," she gasped. "He's dead!"

7

"SHE COULDN'T HELP it; she thought he was dead," Sister Janet said.

It had been only about fifteen minutes since seemingly everyone in the building had heard the single shot. Almost simultaneously, the student facilitator assigned to Father Augustine had entered his classroom to find him slumped in a chair, mouth hanging open grotesquely, face ashen. It had all happened so quickly, she assumed he'd had a heart attack. She thought he was dead.

She ran to the dining room and blurted out her news before she realized that something catastrophic had happened here also.

Coming only moments after Krieg had been pronounced dead, the announcement brought a second wave of shock to the participants. Everyone followed the all-but-hysterical facilitator upstairs to the classroom to see if Augustine was beyond all possible aid.

They found Augustine just as the young woman had described him. They were as shocked as she had been.

Then Augustine snored. One outrageously loud snore.

They roused him. He became extremely sick to his stomach. They had no way of knowing that between the drinks in his room and the free-wheeling mixture of drinks he'd had before and after dinner, he had ingested a significant amount of alcohol.

All they really knew was that, for one reason or another, he was not well.

Several students who appeared on the scene volunteered to mop up, get Father to his room, and summon a doctor.

Unsure what to do next and bewildered by all that had happened in so brief a time, the room's other occupants moved, or, rather, were led by Sister Janet, into an adjoining classroom. None seemed eager to return to the scene in the dining room. Some sat, some stood; all were stunned.

Janet was first to speak. "We were together," she said. "Father Koesler, Martha, and I were together when we heard the shot."

Her statement hung in the ensuing silence. Evidently she intended to exclude the three of them from any possible suspicion of involvement in the death of Klaus Krieg.

Sister Marie was the first to grasp her implication. "What did you mean by that?" she demanded, obviously appalled.

"Nothing." Janet was apologetic. "Only that the three of us were together when it happened."

"So none of you could have done it!" Marie charged.

"Well, yes: None of us could have done it."

"Meaning one of us did do it?" Clearly, Benbow was angered.

"Oh, David, I'm sure the Sister didn't mean to imply—"

"On the contrary, Mrs. Benbow, I'm afraid Sister Janet meant precisely that," interrupted Winer.

"Janet," said Marie, "how could you!"

"Marie, I'm not accusing anyone," Janet protested. "How could I? After all, we *are* religious people. But *somebody* shot Reverend Krieg. And whoever it was, it couldn't have been Father Koesler, Martha, or me. We were together."

"So you have an alibi . . ." Benbow was becoming angrier.

"Just a minute, Father Benbow," said Winer, "the Sister has a point."

"Oh, yeah?"

"Think," said Winer. "We, the four of us—" He interrupted himself: "Make that the three of us; Augustine is out of this entirely since he was unconscious at the time of the shooting." He returned to his premise. "—we were united by two things: We are writers and we hated Klaus Krieg."

"Hate might be too strong a word," Marie protested.

Winer shook his head. "I hesitated initially to use the word, Sister," he said. "As Sister Janet noted, we are people given to religion and hatred should not be part of our makeup—"

"But it is," Benbow cut in. "It just flat out is. Think back on our conversation earlier this evening. Think of what each of us had to say about Krieg. It wasn't a case of 'not a kind word was said'; we were . . . taken in by an unscrupulous charlatan and we were angry about it. I can't see that 'hatred' is too strong a word for how we felt about Klaus Krieg."

"You actually think that one of *us* killed him?" Marie was incredulous.

Benbow responded simply. "Somebody did."

"Somebody who had a motive," Janet added.

"I guess we all had that," Benbow said.

"This is preposterous," Martha Benbow cut in. "Perhaps—just perhaps—all of you had reason to dislike the man. But anger and murder are not the same. All of us are angry at people from time to time. That's no more than human. We get angry all day long at checkout clerks, at other drivers, at parking, at bureaucracies, at government. We get angry at relatives, coworkers, spouses. Some of this anger comes and goes momentarily. Some of it lasts a lifetime. But just because we get angry with people doesn't mean we're going to kill them. Good heavens!''

''That's all very true, Mrs. Benbow,'' said Winer. ''But there is one indisputable fact that must be faced: Klaus Krieg is dead. In all truth, I must confess I am not sorry. God forgive me, but I am almost relieved. I never thought I would be completely unmoved by another person's death, but I am. I'll say it, and I think in our hearts we will not deny it: The world is a better place without Klaus Krieg.''

''And somebody killed him,'' Benbow said.

''And somebody killed him,'' Winer repeated. ''Not likely one of the student waitresses or one of the facilitators. Then, who?''

''An outsider,'' Martha suggested. ''Somebody who hated him and was physically and emotionally capable of killing him. That must be it! Surely not one of you. Someone none of us knows.''

''I think not,'' Sister Janet said. ''Since this is the only building on campus in use just now until the workshop students check in, we were able to pull in the security guards, sort of circle the wagons more closely. Actually, this building is quite secure now. I don't think an outsider could have gotten through without being detected.''

''That pretty much—inevitably—brings us back to us, doesn't it?'' Benbow said.

''The three of us,'' Marie said. She seemed almost in a trance. As if this were a stage production and she were in the audience instead of being one of the participants. ''Father

Augustine was unconscious—or so it seems.'' She was un-willing to dismiss any possibility no matter how remote. ''And Martha, Janet, and Father Koesler were together. None of them could have returned to the dining area without the others knowing it. That leaves Rabbi Winer, Father Benbow, and . . . me.''

Silence.

Everyone knew what the next consideration must be, but no one wanted to consider it.

Finally, Benbow enunciated it. ''Given we had motive, which of us had the opportunity?''

The three self-consciously considered each other.

Benbow sighed. ''Okay, I'll begin. I didn't see either of you after we left the dining room until we returned after he'd been killed.''

''And,'' Winer said, ''I didn't see either of you.''

''This is ridiculous,'' Marie said, ''but I did see Father Benbow and Augustine, though only briefly.''

''All right then,'' Benbow said, ''where were we? We were all headed for the same general location. How did we get separated? Why didn't we, except for Sister here, see each other? As far as I'm concerned, I started up the front staircase to the second floor. Father Augustine was with me, but he was walking sort of unsteadily, weaving a bit. I asked him if he needed any help, but he just shook his head and mumbled something. I didn't realize he was not well. So I walked ahead of him. Lost him at the turn of the staircase. Then I went to my classroom.''

''Was the facilitator there?'' Winer asked.

''What kind of question is that?'' Benbow bridled.

''A very ordinary sort of question,'' Winer replied gently, spreading his hands to signify its innocence. ''If there was anyone in your classroom, you would have a witness to testify that you were with someone else when the shot was fired."

"Well . . . well . . . in fact there wasn't anyone else in the classroom," Benbow stated. "But there's nothing odd about that. The facilitator wasn't in Augustine's room when he got there. And he must have arrived there after I got to my room: I left him staggering around behind me on the staircase. His facilitator didn't get to his room until just about the moment the gun was fired. She found him unconscious— or so it seemed.

"So there was no one in my room to provide an alibi: so what?" His tone was challenging.

"So nothing," Winer said. "It's a natural consideration to want to know where everyone was at the time of a crime."

There was an awkward pause.

Then Sister Marie spoke. "The reason neither of you saw me was that I took the elevator. I saw Father Benbow and Father Augustine start up the stairs. It was as Father Benbow said: Father Augustine was quite unsteady. I thought of offering to help him, but I knew that Father Benbow would be more capable of helping him in every way . . . you know, man to man.

"I had to wait for the elevator for quite a few moments; it is very slow." She looked to Janet for corroboration.

Janet nodded vigorously.

Marie continued. "Finally, when the elevator arrived, I got on alone. The door had just opened at the second floor when I heard the shot. I immediately pushed the first-floor button. When I got off the elevator, I heard the commotion in the dining area and I hurried there. That's why I was the last to arrive. But I didn't see anybody from the time the two men took the stairs until I returned to the dining room. I have no way of knowing whether Father Benbow continued up the stairs or doubled back.''

''That, Sister, is a cheap shot!'' Father Benbow was nearly shouting. ''What right have you to suggest that things did not happen exactly as I described them? What right have you to imply that I might be the killer?''

''I didn't—''

''For that matter,'' Benbow cut in, ''how do we know you actually took that elevator? When I turned to go up the stairs, I saw you standing at the elevator. I didn't see you get on the elevator. How do we know you actually took the elevator? You were alone, as you yourself testified. What if you—''

''I beg your pardon, sir!'' Marie shot back.

''Please,'' Sister Janet broke in, ''before this goes too far, let's hear from Rabbi Winer.''

''As it so happens,'' Winer began, ''after we left the dining room, I was going to go up to the classroom, but I stopped first to go into the kitchen and compliment the cooks on the meal.''

''But I saw you,'' Benbow said. ''I watched you at dinner. You hardly touched your food. Why would you compliment a cook for a meal you didn't eat?''

''You presume too much.'' Winer was teaching, which is what a rabbi does, and his tone indicated just that. ''You presume because someone does not eat, the food is not well prepared. It is a presumption against fact. There can be many reasons a person does not eat.

''In any case,'' the rabbi returned to his narrative, ''I stopped in the kitchen to compliment the cooks. They were so pleased, that nothing would do but that I meet everyone in that very well-kept kitchen.

"And that," he smiled, "is where I was when the shot was fired."

Benbow was taken aback. "You mean you had all those witnesses?"

Winer continued to smile.

"If you were so close to the dining room," Marie said thoughtfully, "you must have been in position to see who did it!"

Winer shook his head. "Reaction time. We were all so startled by the noise, nobody reacted immediately. Unfortunately, by the time we reached the dining room, whoever had done it was gone."

As anyone and everyone could deduce, that left Father Benbow and Sister Marie.

It was at that moment that Father Koesler decided to leave the room.

From the very beginning he had not been implicated since he had been with the two women. Not only was he not implicated, he had not contributed a word to this entire rehash of the crime. He surmised he would not be missed. And he was proven correct: No one seemed to note his departure or miss his presence.

This, Koesler had been thinking through the whole process, is ridiculous. There'd been a murder. The only sensible thing to do was to call the police. He had a hard time imagining that, of all the professional people here, he was the only one who thought of a police investigation. Could it be that the amateur detectives assembled thought it was their duty to solve the crime?

No matter. The police were needed, and he would make the call.

Ordinarily, in an emergency one dials 911. Koesler knew the procedure well enough: 911 would summon uniformed officers assigned to this precinct. Once satisfied there was a probable murder, they would notify Homicide. Particularly since so much time had already been wasted, he determined to cut through the red tape and get right to the heart of the matter.

Koesler did not need to look up the phone number for the Homicide Division of the Detroit Police Department. Inspector Walter Koznicki, head of Homicide, over the years had become a close friend. The two had occasion to phone each other from time to time. Thus Koesler's familiarity with the number.

Koesler had no expectation of finding Koznicki at headquarters. At this hour, especially on a Sunday evening, he very probably would be at home with Wanda, his wife, listening to classical music or reading. But there were a few officers with whom Koesler was familiar through previous dealings with Detroit's Homicide Division. Koesler breathed a quick prayer that somebody who knew him would be on duty.

On the third ring, a voice said, "Homicide, Sergeant Mangiapane."

The name rang a bell. Koesler knew the name; he tried to place Mangiapane, to recall which of the seven Homicide squads he was with. He had to decide quickly. He was aware that Homicide particularly did not suffer fools gladly. With one more quick prayer, he asked, "Is Lieutenant Tully available?"

"Just a minute."

Koesler was put on hold. That was progress of sorts. At least he wasn't informed that Tully was not in, or was "on the street." Such information could conceivably still be forthcoming. But so far—

"Lieutenant Tully," said a quiet, world-weary voice.

Koesler's hopes soared. Luck or Providence, it didn't matter; he'd reached someone with whom he was acquainted. "This is Father Koesler."

"Who?"

"Father Koesler."

Silence. Then, "Oh, yeah; Father Koesler. So, what's happenin'?"

Koesler could almost feel Tully's fatigue. He should be home in bed, Koesler thought. But he's not. My good fortune he's at work. "Lieutenant, there's been a murder."

"What?"

"A murder."

"Oh?"

"Yes."

"Don't you ever dabble in something simple like auto theft or bank robbery or check forgery?"

"I beg your pardon?"

Tully checked himself. This was no time for frivolity. Exhausted as he was, Tully found it funny—odd, at least—that this parish priest should with some regularity be involved in homicide matters. Given a few minutes to look it up, Tully could have come up with exact dates. It seemed barely a year ago that Koesler had been actively involved in an investigation.

"Forget it," Tully said. "Give me the details."

Koesler, relieved, gave him the basic information on what had happened at the college, leaving out the mutual interrogation carried on by the amateur sleuths.

Tully would be at the college in a few minutes. Koesler would wait for him at the front door of Madame Cadillac Hall.

8 TULLY PARKED—RATHER precisely, Koesler thought, for the sense of urgency he felt—in front of Madame Cadillac Hall in the space formerly occupied by Krieg's white stretch-limo.

Koesler had been pondering that parking space while waiting for Tully. Strangely, he hadn't adverted to the limousine or its absence, until Tully pulled into the vacated "no parking" zone. Vaguely, Koesler wondered how Guido Taliafero would react to his employer's death. Poor Guido, to beg he probably would be ashamed and to resume a professional football career he would undoubtedly be unable.

Tully and Mangiapane took the steps two at a time. Amazing, Koesler thought, what the stimulus of a murder investigation can do to regenerate dead-tired bodies and spirits.

Alonzo ("Zoo") Tully had been with the force more than twenty years. Black, of average build, with short-cropped graying hair, Tully, to the casual observer, was unprepossessing. On the other hand, the perceptive person noted Tully's eyes: While betraying a delightful sense of humor, they could be all business; active and intelligent, they were as magnetic as a black hole.

The bad guys had a habit of underestimating Tully. They

also had a habit of getting arrested by him and convicted by the evidence he brought to court. Unlike Rodney Danger-field, Tully had respect, the respect of his fellow officers as well as the grudging respect of the more discerning criminal element. For Tully, homicide was little more than a murder mystery, a puzzle that could and must be solved by sorting clues after culling red herrings and false leads. His record at solving these puzzles was enviable.

In Phil Mangiapane, Tully perceived a gifted sleuth in the rough. With Homicide only a few years, Mangiapane had made his share and more of mistakes. But in him Tully found the natural inquisitiveness and patience that with care and nurturing would produce a top-notch detective.

Mangiapane belonged to Tully's squad. As often as pos-sible Tully saw to it that they worked together. The arrange-ment was perfect as far as Mangiapane was concerned. Not only did he realize he could learn as yet unwritten knowledge from Tully; Mangiapane was genuinely fond of the senior officer.

Since he knew both men, Koesler was prepared for a somewhat effusive greeting. So too was Mangiapane, a faith-ful Sunday Mass Catholic.

Both were brought up sharply by Tully's unpreambled, "Where's the body?"

"In the dining room," Koesler responded. Then he clar-ified, "Actually, it's not the main dining room or even the cafeteria. It's a smaller, seldom used dining area. They're using it because there are so few of us here for this work-shop."

Without bothering to mask his impatience, Tully said, "Lead the way."

"Certainly." Koesler led the way down the main corridor.

He was silently angry at himself for being so garrulous. Of course they wanted to get to the scene of the crime. Whether it was a larger or smaller room made no difference. Not, at any rate, at this moment.

As they walked rapidly down the hallway, the three fell into a configured procession. Koesler and Mangiapane were roughly the same height, though the sergeant was much more mesomorphic. They flanked Tully like matched acolytes accompanying a priest—though in actuality, Tully, hardly a priest, wavered between agnosticism and atheism.

"The dead guy," Tully said, as they advanced, "his name's Klaus Krieg—the TV preacher?"

"Yes," Koesler answered. "He's also a publisher, which is what he was doing at this workshop. It's a writers' conference. Krieg wasn't a writer, but he published writers."

"But he was certainly more famous as a preacher, wasn't he?" Mangiapane asked.

"Oh, yes, absolutely," Koesler replied. "For one thing, anybody on television is bound to be more well known than anyone in the publishing business. But more than that, Krieg didn't publish mainline books; he worked exclusively with books of a religious theme."

"Oh?" Mangiapane said, "I don't think I ever heard of any of his books."

Tully spoke without looking at him. "When was the last time you read a book?"

Mangiapane grinned. "I look 'em over sometimes when we're in the supermarket."

Koesler nodded. "You'd know Krieg's by their racy covers."

"You mean the 'Romance' books?" Mangiapane said. "I thought you said they were religious."

"It turns out they're almost one and the same in Krieg's hands," Koesler said. "Actually, I think Krieg's books are racier than most of the 'Romances'—here we are." They had reached the dining room so quickly, their gait had been so fast that now that they'd arrived he was nearly out of breath.

The three entered the dining room.

"Over—" Koesler stopped abruptly. He was gesturing to the spot on the floor where Krieg's body had fallen. But there was no body. "I don't understand," he said. "It was right here. I don't know what happened to it." He turned almost imploringly to the two officers. "Honest."

The three approached the spot where, Koesler assured them, there had been a body. But there was no body, no blood, just a clean floor.

"There was a body," Koesler insisted.

Tully glanced around the room. "Didn't you say some others were here?"

"Yes," Koesler said, though he was so dumbfounded by the absence of Krieg's remains, he was beginning to feel as if he were in a dream. He knew none of the others would have moved the body; they would know better than to disturb the scene of a crime.

"Where are they—the others?"

"Upstairs. I left them in a room on the second floor. It's a learning clinic that's been converted to a classroom for this conference." There he went again: talking too much, giving extraneous explanations.

"They saw the body too?"

"Oh, yes."

"Would you find them and ask them to come down here?" Koesler left almost at a run.

Tully turned to Mangiapane. "Crazy! Why don't you look

around, Mangiapane? See if you can find somebody. Must be a kitchen around here someplace.''

''Right.'' Mangiapane began his search.

Left alone, Tully yawned elaborately. His bone-weariness was intensified by not finding the body where it was supposed to be. It had been a sluggish Sunday shift until Koesler's call—although Sunday or not, it was a rare day or night when Detroit let its Homicide Division off the hook by not killing any of its citizens.

Tully had been grateful. Business had been brisk lately and he was exhausted. But Koesler's call had started the juices boiling. Now wide-awake, alert and sharp, he had sped to Marygrove expecting to find a body and begin the investigation. He'd been prepared to meet the scene of the crime head-on and discover all the mysteries it held and its answers to questions as yet unasked. Now, no body. The fatigue returned.

Koesler returned, with the others in his wake. He was not quite as sheepish as he had been. If he were losing his marbles, at least he was not alone: The others had seemed as confused as he when he told them what hadn't been found in the dining room. As they entered the dining area they looked at the same empty spot on the floor. Each registered total amazement.

Mangiapane entered, the kitchen crew in tow. With the kitchen supervisor, cooks, assistants, waitresses, and KPs, along with the workshop faculty, there was a fair-sized crowd assembled.

No one risked being the first to speak.

''There was a body here,'' Tully said.

No one responded to the statement. But there seemed a general sense of affirmation.

"Where did it go?"

To Tully that seemed the logical next step.

Silence. They looked at one another.

Tully sighed. He dug out his badge from a back pocket, held it at arm's length so all could see it. "I'm Lieutenant Tully and this is Sergeant Mangiapane. We are with Homicide, Detroit Police Department, and I want an answer . . . now! Where did the body go?"

From out of the silence came a small voice. "He left."

"He left?" Tully repeated to be sure that's what he'd heard. "Who are you?"

"J . . . J . . . Julie," the small voice of a small waitress said.

"Okay Julie: He left. How did he manage that?"

"Well, he got up, and his chauffeur brushed him off, and then . . . they left."

"It wasn't supposed to happen this way. I'm so sorry. I'm so sorry and so very embarrassed." Sister Janet was quite obviously on the verge of tears.

Tully turned to her. "And you are . . . ?"

"Sister Janet, Janet Schultes. I'm responsible for this conference."

Aware that she was distraught, Tully tried to keep from his voice the frustration he felt. "Why don't you tell me what happened. What 'wasn't supposed to happen this way'?"

Janet fumbled a handkerchief from a pocket and dabbed at her eyes and nose. Her hand was trembling. "I didn't think it would work. He seemed so childish. But the agreement was made, and I couldn't get out of it."

As gently as possible, Tully waved his hand, cutting off her disjointed explanation. "Take your time, but start from the beginning. How did we come to get a corpse who gets up, is dusted off by his chauffeur, and walks away? The beginning, please.''

Janet reluctantly realized she was very definitely the center of attention and that the faculty of this workshop was every bit as eager to learn what had happened as were the police.

''You see,'' Janet began, ''this conference was set up almost a year ago. It was the brainchild of my predecessor, Jack Regan. Every conference or workshop of this sort must begin with a commitment from some major figure or celebrity that, you hope, will draw a significant enrollment. Jack began by extending an invitation to Klaus Krieg. Not a bad idea, all in all. . . .'' She glanced around at the faculty. ''Whatever your opinion of Reverend Krieg, he *is* in demand as a celebrity and he does fit the bill as someone who can draw a crowd.

''Jack told me he was surprised and delighted that Krieg accepted. But his acceptance was conditioned on two provisions. The first was that the other panelists be Sister Marie, Fathers Augustine and Benbow, and Rabbi Winer. He also insisted that Father Koesler attend as an expert resource person.

''It was a most unusual stipulation, but Jack wanted Reverend Krieg enough to agree to at least try to meet his demands.

''The second condition Reverend Krieg insisted upon is what has caused this trouble. He proposed we stage what he termed a psychodrama.''

''A psychodrama,'' Tully interrupted. Though a statement, it was a question.

''Yes, sort of an ad libitum play, a cinéma verité . . . a staged murder mystery. The idea was that this psychodrama was supposed to engage the creative processes of the faculty.

Reverend Krieg thought it would help set the stage for tomorrow's sessions if we were to stage a fake murder and then
encourage the amateur sleuths to try to solve the case.''

''And that's what happened?'' Tully asked.

''Pretty much, yes. The writers''—her gesture included
the four—''gathered here by late afternoon today. They had
not met previously, and things were a bit stiff. The faculty
did not much . . . uh . . . care for the Reverend's TV ministry or his publishing house. It seems that all of them had,
at one time or another, been offered a contract with P.G.
Press. But none had signed the contract.

''Then when Reverend Krieg arrived during dinner, everything seemed to galvanize around him. After dinner, when
the others had spread out through the building, we staged the
fake murder. But,'' and again she seemed on the verge of
breaking down, ''things got out of hand, as I feared they
might. Angry words were exchanged and, worst of all, we
never anticipated that the police would be called. I thought I
could keep everyone together in here until the setup was
consummated. If I had known anyone was about to call the
police, I would have called a halt to the whole thing.''

Suddenly Koesler felt guilty on two scores: He had called
the police without informing the others. As it turned out, if
he had mentioned it, Janet would have aborted the whole
thing. And secondly, his call to the police turned out to be a
false alarm.

''Janet!'' Marie spoke with incredulous anger. ''You
staged this whole thing! You let us accuse each other! You
staged this entire sorry scenario without telling us it was all
a piece of fiction. How could you!

''And when, for God's sake, were you going to tell us?''

That was all Janet needed. She burst into tears.

Martha hurried to her side and tried to console her.

"Oh, Janet," Marie said, "I'm sorry. You couldn't help it, I suppose. You had to live up to the agreement." She said it, but she wasn't sure she meant it.

Tully felt as if he had about one grain of adrenaline left and he wanted to expend it on the one who was responsible for this farce. And that surely was not the lady now dissolved in tears. "Just where is this Mr. Regan now?"

Janet mumbled something unintelligible into her handkerchief.

"What was that?" Tully asked.

"The University of California," Marie said. She had moved to join Martha in comforting Janet.

"Ahhh . . ." Tully said. It was as if the air were being let out of him and he were being slowly deflated. There, in far distant California, was the only one at whom Tully felt justified in venting his anger and frustration. The other lady was right: It wasn't this Janet's fault. She'd inherited the crazy scheme. This Krieg character wasn't really fair game either. It may have been his nutty idea, but all the Regan guy had to do was reject it and that would have been the end. The weariness returned with a vengeance.

"Zoo," Mangiapane said, "not only don't we have a body, we ain't got a murder either."

"Astute," Tully murmured under his breath. Then he said, "Let's go, Mang."

"Let me go to the door with you," Koesler said. Whatever else he might accomplish in the near future, he was intent on apologizing to the officers. Any number of times in his past Koesler had felt like a complete idiot, but never more than now.

The three men left the dining room, as did the kitchen and serving staff.

Remaining in the room were the unwitting and unwilling actors in the unfortunate psychodrama.

Janet sat at the table now cleared of dishes and accoutered with a fresh tablecloth and napkins. Marie and Martha flanked her. Winer and Benbow remained standing.

"It seems such a long time since we had dinner," Benbow said slowly.

Winer glanced at his watch. "Yes, it does. But it's only a couple of hours." No one else spoke. The silence was punctuated only by the soft sounds Janet made; her tears flowed less abundantly now.

"I must apologize, Sister," Benbow addressed Marie finally. "I'm afraid I said some pretty horrid things to you."

Marie tried to smile but did not quite succeed. "I guess I returned the favor. Our introduction to each other did not get off to an auspicious beginning."

Silence again.

"To be perfectly honest," Benbow said, "I don't know that we can return to point zero."

"Pardon?"

"I mean," Benbow continued, "just a few hours ago we were complete strangers to one another. And then in no time we were all but accusing one another of murder. After the bitterness of the things that were said, I don't know whether we can go back and patch up our relationship."

Silence.

"I'd like to think we could," Marie said thoughtfully, "but you may very well be right. Maybe it is too late to return to a neutral position and build our relationship on friendlier ground. Maybe we ought to call off this conference."

Janet looked at Marie in horror.

"No," Winer said with authority. "There are reasons—compelling reasons—why we must hold this workshop just as planned. For one thing, we have an obligation to those who signed up for it. They'll be coming in tomorrow. It's not their fault that things have gotten off to such a bad beginning."

Janet looked relieved.

"And . . . ?" Benbow prodded.

"And . . . what?" Winer said.

"Look, I agree with you completely," Benbow said. "We are honor bound to give the students their money's worth. No doubt about that. But you spoke in the plural. You said there were reasons why we had to go on."

Winer smiled briefly. "I, for one, want to find out what comes next."

"Next?" Marie said.

"Yes. Until Sister Janet spoke up a few minutes ago, I had no idea whatsoever why this particular group had been selected as the 'faculty' for this conference. And I assume the same could be said for the rest of you?" He looked around for a reaction.

"Well," Marie said, "we're all authors of mystery novels with a religious motif?"

"Yes," Winer agreed, "But we aren't the only ones doing that. Just as a matter of conjecture, I had been wondering why each individual here had been selected. I thought the core of the secret was revealed when, before dinner, we learned that each of us had been offered a contract by P.G. Press. And that each of us had turned said contract down.

"But now a new element has been added. Our would-be publisher insisted that we—specifically each one of us—be invited. He made this a condition of his acceptance. I find that both odd and intriguing.''

"So do I," Benbow said.

"And I," Marie agreed. "Not only did he, in effect, invite us, he wanted to play a game with us."

"Like marionettes on a string," Benbow added.

"And that's why," Winer said, "I especially want to stay for the next act. I can't think he had us invited just to play a trick on us. If we're going to discover the reason, we're going to have to play this out. Only now, I feel certain, we know something else is coming."

Marie shuddered. "But what? I feel as if I'm going in two directions at once. I want to leave and I want to stay. I distinctly don't want to play games with a madman."

"I have a feeling, Sister," Winer said, "that Krieg is not the sort of person who accepts no for an answer graciously. We've already rejected his proposal to join his publishing empire. Once again, it seems perfectly obvious he has something else in store for us. What's he really up to?"

"The rabbi has a point, Sister," Benbow said. "I'd rather face Krieg and get it over with. Besides, whatever he has in mind can't be that serious. Probably just something in very bad taste."

"Of course," Winer said, "all this hypothesis we've been bandying about is predicated on the fact that all the games we know about have been played." He purposefully focused on Janet. "There aren't any more games or plots—that you know about—are there, Sister? I mean, there weren't any more 'conditions' that Mr. Regan agreed to . . . are there?"

Janet shook her head vigorously. "No, no more conditions."

"By the way, Sister," Winer said, "just where *is* the man

of the hour, the erstwhile corpse? The Reverend Krieg is not staying with us?''

"Oh, dear," Janet said, "I forgot. There *was* one more stipulation. That was that he also have a room available for him off-campus. I remember Jack saying that the Reverend asked specifically about living conditions here. Jack said he tried to be as realistic as possible about the residence rooms. The Reverend asked Jack to book a room for him at the Westin.''

"In the Renaissance Center?" Marie asked.

"That's right," Janet said.

Marie pursed her lips. It was a prestigious riverfront hotel in that section of downtown Detroit that still worked.

Benbow whistled softly. "I think he's trying to tell us something. His own residence. His own liquor supply. His own food.''

"His own food?" Marie said.

"Didn't you see his henchman get him a dinner different than we had?" Benbow said. "I firmly believe he's trying to tell us something: that he not only is different from the rest of us, he's better—and merits better accommodations.''

"As long as we're dealing with comparisons," Marie said, "there's one area where he very definitely surpasses us: money.''

"No argument there, Sister," Benbow said.

Winer ran a hand through his trim beard. "Are we not forgetting someone?''

The others looked at him inquiringly.

"Father Augustine," Winer said. "Whatever happened to Father Augustine?''

Janet almost laughed aloud. "I confess I forgot about him

. . . or, at least stopped worrying about him the moment I heard the poor man snore.''

It was a much needed release of tension; they all roared with laughter.

''Then, Sister,'' Winer said, ''it is safe to assume that Father Augustine's plight, whatever it is, was not part of the psychodrama Reverend Krieg and Mr. Regan arranged.''

Janet was wiping her eyes, teared this time by laughing, not crying. ''No . . . no. I don't know what was wrong with the poor man. Jet lag, upset stomach, I have no idea. One thing I am quite sure of: He is being well cared for. The students who volunteered to help him are very responsible young people. They said they would call a doctor and I'm sure they have. They would have told us if it were serious. In this case, I'm sure, no news is good news.

''But, so that we'll all sleep well, I will check into the medical status of Father Augustine. I'll just slip the information under each of your doors.''

''Speaking of which,'' Martha glanced at her watch, ''it's still rather early, but I can't remember when I've been this tired. If there isn't anything more on the agenda—and for the life of me I can't think of what could possibly follow what we've been through—if we're done for the evening, I think I'll just retire.''

Winer looked at Sister Janet. ''I take it, Sister, that the visit to our classrooms that you announced after dinner was no more than a ploy to get us away from 'the scene of the crime,' and that there is really no need to go there before the sessions tomorrow.''

Janet nodded.

''Then,'' Winer said, ''I feel you have touched upon a consensus, Mrs. Benbow. It's off to bed we go.''

"Amen," Marie said.

Benbow stifled a yawn. "So much for our first exciting night in Dynamic Detroit."

And so, not one by one, but as a group, they left the dining room and its memories not of food but of surprises.

Meanwhile, between the dining room and the front door of the Madame Cadillac Building, Father Koesler had been talking virtually nonstop, apprising the two officers of all that had happened that evening.

The gathering of the writers; the gradual and mutual realization that each had been solicited by Krieg; the immediate sense of agreement that they would have prostituted their talent had they had the misfortune to sign with Krieg; the dramatic entry of Krieg partway through dinner; the departure of everyone but Krieg from the dining area; the gunshot; finding Krieg "dead"; the false alarm with Augustine; the confrontation between Winer, Benbow, and Marie as to which might have had the opportunity to murder Krieg; and finally, his call to Homicide.

Koesler was anxious that Tully and Mangiapane understand what had prompted him to summon them. He realized he undoubtedly would have saved them the trouble of coming out had he gone through the routine of calling 911. Surely an officer or two from the precinct could have observed the absence of a victim as easily as experts from Homicide.

Koesler felt about as sorry as anyone had ever felt about anything.

Throughout Koesler's detailed explanation, Tully paid only peripheral attention. He was just drained. It was really the end of his shift. With any luck, in a short while he could check out and go home. He would get a bit to eat, an extravagant hot shower and, again with any luck, a relaxing back rub. And so to sleep.

Not quite as tired, Mangiapane was relishing Koesler's tale.

After Koesler had expressed his contrition for the umpteenth time, Mangiapane said, "You don't have to feel so bad, Father."

"I don't?"

"This isn't the first time we got fooled by some kind of scam."

They had reached the exit. Tully was eager to leave and start the process that would, the sooner the better, free him to go home, get some tender loving care, and sleep—in that order.

Unfortunately, Mangiapane had begun a tale told out of school. Tully knew the story but he decided to endure it once again. He knew Mangiapane was telling the story for Koesler's benefit. And, well, what the hell, the priest had been through an ordeal himself this evening. Maybe learning that he was not alone in falling for a fictional mystery scam would make Koesler feel better. The priest might get some sleep tonight but it would not be preceded by any tender loving care. Too bad, Tully thought, but that's the way the collar buttons.

"This is a true story, Father," Mangiapane continued. "It started when a guy got a piece of mail, no return address, just a plain piece of paper with threatening words all over it—like 'murder,' 'kill,' 'an unsolved crime,' 'sudden death.' The words looked like they came from newspapers, magazines, other publications. Just these words cut out.

"The guy couldn't figure out why he got this threatening letter, but he was plenty scared. And he stayed scared, getting dead-bolt locks on his doors, double-checking the back seat of his car before getting in, parking near street lights at night, the whole thing.

"Then about ten days later, he gets another letter. Just like the first one, this has no return address. Just a plain envelope containing another plain piece of paper with threatening words cut out of various types of publications.

"By this time, the guy is scared enough to come to us. We took it pretty serious too. In fact we started an investigation. Sure enough, in another week, the guy gets another anonymous threatening letter. Now, none of these letters specifically threatens him personally; they're just filled with life-threatening words. And we keep adding to the file."

Koesler interrupted. "Did you put him under—what's it called?—protective custody?"

Mangiapane chuckled. "You mean like they do in the movies, where almost an entire police department stops everything they're doing and guards some potential victim for twenty-four-hour periods? So nobody can get close?"

The way Mangiapane rephrased the question, Koesler knew the answer was no.

"That just doesn't happen in real life, Father," Mangiapane said. "There's no possible way we can protect anybody who decides he's gonna do what he ordinarily does. If he's gonna go to work, walk outside, go out to eat, his regular routine—he's fair game.

"The only way we can protect somebody is if he agrees to retreat to a safe place. Say a hotel room or a jail cell. We've got to control the environment before we can offer secure protection.

"Anyway, this file we were keeping was filling out pretty good when, finally, he gets a piece of mail identical to the others, except this one promises the murder is gonna take place on Mackinac Island—at the Grand Hotel. And this time there's a return address—a travel agency in Royal Oak.

"Needless to say, the guys working this case hopped right over to the agency and really rattled their cage.

"The thing turned out to be a brand new enterprise for the agency. They were sponsoring a 'Mystery Weekend' at the Grand Hotel . . . not an awful lot different from your little psychodrama here. The agency was sending out fliers to likely customers. It turns out that this guy and we were the only ones who were taking it serious.

"When our guys were pinning this travel agent to the wall, all the poor guy could say was, 'But it was just promotion.' I can tell you one thing, Father: It'll be a long time before that guy tries another tricky promotion like that."

"And," Tully added, "it'll be a long time before we fall for another stunt like that. By the way, Father, that story was meant for your consolation—not for publication."

"I can keep a secret," Koesler assured.

"Yeah, you can, can't you," Tully replied.

"And," Koesler added, as the two detectives were leaving the building, "thanks."

Koesler returned to the dining area. Finding no one there, he assumed—correctly—that the others had retired for the night. He decided to do the same.

Before entering the room, he noticed a sign on the bulletin board advising that Mass would be at 8:00 A.M. in the chapel. On entering his room, he found a note from Sister Janet, asking him to say the morning Mass. The note had a postscript regarding the condition of Father Augustine: A doctor had pronounced him indisposed but very much alive.

It was only then that Koesler realized he had completely

forgotten Father Augustine. He had moved from reported death to a healthy snore to a normal prognosis. Koesler had been so distracted by other developments that, for all practical purposes, Augustine's condition had been blocked out. How soon they forget!

9 THE MASS, A reenactment of the Last Supper, is the core liturgical event of many Christian sects. In no religious expression is it more at the heart of everything than in Catholicism.

Catholics old enough to remember a time during and before the Second Vatican Council, will recall the expected routine of daily Mass. Virtually all priests offered Mass every day. Most parishes were staffed by more than one priest. Thus, most parishes had more than one scheduled Mass daily.

Nowadays it can be difficult to find parishes where Mass is offered daily. This reduction in the dependable frequency of Mass happened after—but not as a direct consequence of—Vatican II. The drastic and escalating shortage of priests, in no way foreseen by the Council, takes its toll on Daily Mass.

As challenging as it may be to find parishes with daily Mass, it is even more difficult locating parishes having more than one full-time parish priest. Parishes that traditionally had three, even four, assigned priests are now fortunate to have one.

People continue to get married and people continue to die. So weddings and funerals that used to be handled by a relative abundance of priests, now are the burden of the lonely pastor. Thus, to avoid being Massed to death, many pastors have cut back daily Mass to only a sprinkling of days in the typical week.

But there are a few holdouts still. Among these was Father Robert Koesler, who, no matter how many weddings and funerals accumulated, gleaned something special out of the sparsely attended early morning Mass. For him it was an appropriate time and an ideal way to commune with God.

It didn't matter that Sister Janet had asked him to offer the 8:00 A.M. Mass. He would have been there anyway if only to concelebrate with whichever priest happened to have the Mass. As it happened, Marygrove's chaplain had not yet returned from vacation; thus the invitation to Koesler.

At 7:30 he was kneeling in the ornate, vaulted chapel, gathering thoughts and prayers, taking stock of what yesterday had brought and what today might offer.

Last night he had been so relieved and grateful that the detectives were not angry at his blunder in calling them, and so exhausted from the Krieg-inspired psychodrama that he had drifted off to sleep earlier and slept even more soundly than was his custom at the rectory. So he felt extraordinarily refreshed as he prepared for Mass this morning.

Though distractions invaded his consciousness, he no longer fought them as he once had. By this time, they had become something with which one lived. Not infrequently they were welcomed in to become part of his prayer.

By any measurement, yesterday's high point had been the nonmurder of Klaus Krieg. In his memory, Koesler could see clearly that clump of flesh lying on the floor, blood all over its clothing. I wonder, he thought, what they used for blood. Clever having those rivulets of red from the mouth and nostrils.

A question kept recurring and as often as it surfaced he rejected it. The question was, ''Why?'' Why had Krieg insisted on a psychodrama whose central theme was his own murder? Koesler kept dismissing the question because he had no acceptable answer for it.

What a strange man! Did Krieg have to be in control of everything he touched? Surely he alone had been master of last evening's happening. The only other person who knew what really was happening was Sister Janet. Yet she was no more than playing a role in the drama. He alone directed the event.

And why would he stage his own murder? It was as if Krieg had been an invisible guest earlier when the others were expressing their strong feelings toward him. They certainly left no doubt that they disliked him intensely. Didn't one of them as much as say the world would be better off without him? And the others had seemed to agree. It required no great stretch of the imagination to extrapolate a death threat from such a vehement expression.

How could Krieg have known how strong their antipathy was? How could he know that they disliked him enough to wish him dead, if not murdered? Yet he had to be aware of all this. Having staged his own death, he had to have anticipated that, somehow or other, they would all become suspects in that death.

And finally, why did those otherwise godly people feel such animus toward Krieg?

Deliberately, Koesler had avoided the TV ministry of Reverend Krieg. On the other hand, Koesler eschewed all televangelists. Hearsay had it that Krieg was considerably lesser than Billy Graham—who was probably the most sincere of all—and only slightly above Swaggart. Yet no matter how greedy and/or dishonest Krieg's television program proved, nothing would explain the intensity of the animosity the members of this group held for him.

P.G. Press came closer to accounting for the hostility Koesler sensed in the group, and that only because, while the TV program could be avoided with a mere turn of the dial, the publishing house tried actively to recruit them. And P.G. Press might have snared one or another of them had they not had the good fortune to get good advice.

Even though this hypothesis did not seem a likely cause for the group's strong feeling toward Krieg, it was as close as Koesler could come to solving the puzzle.

It was the immoderate intensity of their feeling that confounded him. Krieg had given them adequate reason to dislike him. But, that much?

He checked his watch. Ten minutes to 8:00. Time to investigate an unfamiliar sacristy. While vestments and accouterments for Mass were roughly identical anywhere in the world, in an unfamiliar setting there was no telling where everything was kept.

On entering the sacristy he found, to his relief, that someone—Sister Janet?—had laid everything out for him— vestments, chalice, wine and water, altar breads, key to the tabernacle, lectionary—everything in place. Or, as Canon Law liked to put it, *omnia parata*.

He slipped the alb over his head, ran his arms through the sleeves and let the white garment fall, hoping it would reach the floor—or at least nearly. No luck; too short again. The sleeves ended about halfway between his wrists and elbows. The length was midway between ankles and knees. Why, he wondered for the zillionth time, why don't they make vestments—particularly the alb, which should cover the priest completely from neck to ankle—in large sizes? One can always roll up the sleeves or tuck up the surplus length over the cincture. But if it's too short . . .

There was still time to look for a more suitable alb. He began rummaging through the clothes press.

Gradually, he became aware that he was not alone. Startled, he turned from the armoire to see David Benbow standing there looking amused.

"Don't tell me," Benbow said. "You can't find an alb that's long enough."

Koesler returned the smile. "How'd you know?"

"I have the same problem when I go visiting."

The first thought occurring to Koesler was that, yes, Benbow would have that problem since he was only slightly shorter than Koesler. The second reflection was that Benbow was, indeed, a priest, an Episcopal priest. How religiously chauvinistic of him not to be cognizant of Benbow's priesthood.

Benbow broke the awkward silence. "I saw the notice upstairs about the Mass at 8:00. Martha and I decided to come down. I thought you might need some help. But I see somebody has set things up."

"Yes, everything but a decent sized alb. The most charitable thought that comes to mind is that whoever did this didn't know I was going to say the Mass. Either that, or she thinks one-size alb fits all."

"Er . . ." Benbow paused. ". . . you don't mind if Martha and I attend your Mass . . ."

"Of course not." Koesler felt foolish; it was such a modest request.

On Koesler's second thought, by some lights the request wasn't all that modest, after all. It was one thing to attend Mass. No law against that. Questions arose when Communion time arrived. There could be an awkward moment should either or both Benbows present themselves to receive Communion.

The program began when England's Henry VIII couldn't get a decree of nullity from the Catholic Church. Without the Church's declaration that his marriage to Catherine of Aragon was null and void, he was unable to contract a Church-sanctioned marriage with anyone else, more particularly in this case, Anne Boleyn. So, Henry split with Rome, declared himself head of the Church of England (which became the Anglican Church, of which the Episcopal Church in America is a branch), and bestowed on himself the desired nullity decree . . . and the desired marriage with Ms. Boleyn.

Shortly after Anglicanism had replaced Catholicism as the state religion of England, Rome pronounced that the line of apostolic succession had been broken. This was based on the premise that Jesus selected the Apostles as, in effect, the first bishops of the infant Christian Church. These apostle-bishops appointed others to function in this succeeding apostle-bishop role. Those who succeeded the Apostles in turn appointed others to exercise leadership and eventually to replace themselves. And so it went through the centuries. As far as the Church of Rome was concerned, two conditions were required for full membership in the One, Holy, Catholic and Apostolic Church: the bishops of said Church must be able to trace themselves in an unbroken line to the original Apostles. And second, said Church's bishops must subject themselves to the authority of the Pope.

A Church may refuse submission to the Pope while continuing to touch base with the apostolic line. In which case, Rome declares such a Church to be a schism or a schismatic church. Thus, for example, Rome recognizes the validity of the hierarchy, priests, and sacraments of all Orthodox churches. But the Orthodox are not joined to, or in communion with, Rome. Indeed, only recently did the Pope and the Patriarch of Constantinople rescind the excommunications they leveled at each other back on July 16, 1054.

In somewhat worse shape, at least from the perspective of Rome, are those Christian Churches that are not only out of communion with Rome but also have broken the apostolic line. Rome terms them heretical. Such is the case with all of Protestantism—at least according to Rome.

However, closest to Catholicism of all so-called Protestant Churches is Anglicanism. At one point in their history, Rome charges, the Anglicans radically changed the prescribed intent in their ordination ceremony and thus broke the apostolic succession requirement, becoming not only schismatic but heretical to boot. Yet in ceremony, vestment, hierarchical structure, and—since Rome approved vernacular liturgy—language, there is little if any visible difference between the two Churches.

Father Koesler did not need to recall this history in detail. Catholics are, or were, taught the differences between their "own true" Church and everyone else's very early in life and regularly thereafter.

Awareness of all this compelled Koesler to reexamine his response regarding Benbow's attending Mass. Episcopalians had no trouble whatsoever in permitting Catholics to receive Communion at an Episcopal Eucharist. Though Catholics, who had been carefully taught, seldom presented themselves at an Episcopal Communion railing. A matter of invalid sacraments and all that.

But, officially, only in specifically spelled-out circumstances, none of which, clearly, applied in the present moment, could a Catholic priest invite Protestants to receive Communion.

Would the Benbows present themselves to receive Communion at Koesler's Mass?

After giving the matter a solid thirty seconds of concentrated thought, Koesler concluded: Who cares?

The Pope cares. Various members of Church officialdom in Rome care. Most bishops would care, if only because they would be expected to care. Self-appointed Church vigilantes dedicated to keeping the Church holier than Christ established it would care. And Mark Boyle, Cardinal Archbishop of Detroit, if inescapably forced to face the issue, would have to care. Past practice would indicate that if Cardinal Boyle were forced to deal with the problem, he very well might establish a blue-ribbon commission to study the matter into eternity. It was one of many reasons why Koesler so admired Boyle: with the world falling down around our ears, whether or not sincere people could worship the same God together was of little importance.

Koesler realized that probably he was projecting his own feelings onto Benbow. Probably David Benbow felt no embarrassment in this situation. He might only have been observing some self-imposed protocol in asking if it would be permissible for him and his wife to attend Mass.

Be that as it may, Koesler felt the potential for embarrassment in the question. Koesler was at an unfair advantage. They were at a Catholic college, in a Catholic chapel. It was

Koesler's home field advantage and Benbow couldn't even compete.

All these considerations took only moments to flash across Koesler's mind.

He turned determinedly to Benbow. "I have a thought: How about concelebrating with me?"

Benbow was clearly startled. "Are you sure? I mean, are you sure you want to make this offer?"

"Believe me," Koesler said, "I am well aware of the complexities. But I don't think there'll be any problem. This is a small and tightknit group we have here. Like-minded people, I think. I really doubt there'll be any trouble. In fact, I think *I* would have had a problem if I *hadn't* invited you to celebrate the Eucharist with me."

"If you're sure?"

"I'm sure. How about it?"

"I think it would be grand. And I'm grateful."

"Then come on," Koesler said, "let's see if we can find a couple of decent-sized albs in here."

Rummaging through the vestment cases, they managed to uncover two large-sized albs. That was adequate for Benbow. Koesler needed an extra large, but by now he was convinced he wasn't going to find one. Large would have to do. It was, in any case, a significant improvement over the previous medium size.

They were nearly completely vested when the door to the sacristy opened and, somewhat breathlessly, Father Augustine entered, clad in Trappist habit.

"I hope I'm not too late to . . ." His voice trailed off. "What's this?" he asked, as he realized that both Koesler and Benbow were vested. "What's the meaning of this!"

"Welcome," said Koesler, warmly. "I wasn't expecting you. Feeling better?"

Augustine ignored the question. "I came down to concelebrate the holy sacrifice of the Mass."

The tone of voice and needless adjectives told Koesler here was trouble on a collision course. Nonetheless he chose to avoid a scene if at all possible. "And so you shall concelebrate. As soon as we find some vestments for you." If there was going to be any unpleasantness it would be of Augustine's doing.

Augustine readily accepted the challenge. "Father Koesler, is this some sort of joke? If so, it is in very poor taste."

Koesler, in turn, was quickly running out of bonhomie. "It's getting kind of late to start a canonical or theological disputation." He went to the door leading to the sanctuary and glanced into the chapel. "There are two nuns, Mrs. Benbow, and a couple of young ladies—students, I suppose—who are waiting for nothing more than a simple celebration of Mass. And we are, by this time, a couple of minutes late. Now, do you or do you not wish to concelebrate?"

"With whom? A heretic and someone who is violating the laws of God?"

"Now wait a minute!" Koesler was angered by Augustine's gratuitous use of the word heretic.

"There's no need for this," Benbow said apologetically. "I . . ." He began to remove the vestments he had donned.

"No, don't!" Koesler gestured, stopping Benbow. "Now look here, Augustine, there's no need for you to be so priggish."

"Priggish!" Augustine shot back. "Was Jesus being priggish when he cast out the moneychangers from the Temple?"

"Moneychangers! Are you kidding?"

"There is no justification whatsoever for you to concelebrate Mass with a representative of a heretical Church!"

"I assume you are allowed to read in the monastery, Father," Koesler said, "even if only ecclesial documents. If you've been reading, you know that the joint Catholic Anglican Commission has all but granted the validity of Anglican orders."

"I couldn't care less what some commission has 'all but' done."

"And I wish you'd stop throwing the word 'heretic' around."

"It's the proper word. Are you willing to admit that what you're doing is against the law?"

"I suppose is depends on what you mean by law."

"You know very well what I mean by law: God's law."

"When last I checked with my Bible, God's law was the law of love. At least that's what Jesus said: 'A new commandment I give you, that you love one another as I have loved you.' "

"You're hopeless."

Koesler began an inner battle against rising anger. "Look at it this way, Augustine: No one is forcing you to do anything. You may concelebrate this Mass with us, if you wish. After all, that's why you came down this morning. You can attend this Mass, if you prefer. Or you can go back to bed." Or, for all I care, he added silently, you can drop dead.

Self-righteousness radiated from Augustine the way Moses must have glowed when he descended from the mountain after his conversation with God. "None of the above," Augustine announced. "I will not concelebrate this farce. Nor will I even witness it. And, instead of going back to bed, I'm going to call your Chancery and tell them what's going on here."

With that, leaving neither time nor opportunity for further discussion, Augustine turned and stormed from the sacristy.

After a moment or two of embarrassed silence, Benbow spoke. "I'm going to solve this little problem." And he began to remove his vestments.

"You don't have to do that," Koesler protested. But he saw it was useless to argue the matter further.

"It was very kind of you to invite me to celebrate with you. And I sha'nt forget it. I should have just thanked you and declined your invitation. There'll always be an Augustine up on the battlements defending Mother Church."

"Yeah . . ." Koesler shook his head sadly, "or defending God. I've never figured out why God needs defending. For that matter, I don't know why Mother Church needs defending. Canon Law holds all the cards."

"And that was the law to which Augustine was referring."

"I know. I know."

"I hope you won't be forced to play cards with the Chancery."

"Why?" Koesler looked surprised. "Nothing happened . . . or, in the language of Canon Law, *nihil fit*."

"Doesn't the intention count in this diocese?"

Koesler snorted. "We've got enough problems staffing parishes without penalizing priests for what they're thinking. Besides, the buck on a thing like this stops at the desk of the archbishop. And, to stay with our metaphor, he doesn't like to play his hand unless he is forced into doing so."

Benbow had disrobed. "You're sure you'll be all right?"

"Certain."

"Then I'll just leave. I'll get Martha. Maybe they've started serving breakfast."

Koesler protested. "You don't have to leave entirely. When this thing started, your only request was to attend the Mass, and you certainly may do that."

"Don't know how to explain it, old man: The taste is gone." He smiled ruefully. "See you later."

The taste had faded for Koesler also. But he was not free to simply walk away from the scene. People—a few people anyway—were waiting for him to offer Mass. And he was late. Given his obsession with punctuality, this was an added vexation.

He was already vested, so he merely went to the altar and began setting things up for Mass. As he did so, visions of the ugly scene that had just transpired haunted him.

Things could have been so very satisfying. Along with, and as much as, many others, Koesler had long been unhappy and uneasy with the disunity, the divisiveness, the schisms within Christianity. On those occasions when he participated in gatherings that included members of various Christian sects, he was invariably troubled that this temporary, ad hoc harmonious fellowship could not be permanent.

What kept people of good will apart? Ancient arguments, disagreements, theological bickering, traditions of distrust, and people like Augustine, who, in Koesler's view, put Church laws and customs—all man-made—above the simple invitation of Christ to love as completely and encompassingly as He had.

Like most everything else in life, the offering of Mass could not be separated from the emotions of the moment. He had offered Masses that had been inspired, reflective, meditative, disrupted, distracted, disturbed. This Mass would be tainted by the angry words of Father Augustine. There was nothing Koesler could do about that. Just chalk it up to experience.

But it left him wondering about Father Augustine May, OSCO. Was there that much differentiating the mean-spirited May from the greedy, grubby Klaus Krieg? Did they deserve each other?

"In the name of the Father and of the Son and of the Holy Spirit. Amen.

"My brothers and sisters, in order to prepare ourselves to celebrate these sacred mysteries, let us call to mind our sins. . . ."

10

IT WAS MID-MORNING before Koesler again encountered Father Augustine.

Augustine got off the elevator at the first floor just as Koesler finished descending the stairs. Their paths merged as they turned to walk down the corridor. That was unfortunate as far as Koesler was concerned. Had they been going in opposite directions, a mere nod would have sufficed. Walking together in silence was awkward considering their contentious exchange a few hours earlier. Koesler felt distinctly uncomfortable.

Yet it was Koesler who spoke first. "Well, Father, did you call the Chancery?"

"Huh? What?" For all intents and purposes it appeared that Augustine had no idea what Koesler was referring to. "The Chancery? Oh, about that business of Mass this morning? Yes. Yes, I did. Uh-huh. Yes."

They proceeded a bit further in silence. "And?" Koesler asked.

"And it's damn hard finding the chancellor, a vice-chancellor, or an assistant chancellor on a Monday morning."

"But you did."

130

"What?"

"Find one."

"Eventually. One of the assistants."

"And?" Koesler could sympathize with dentists who had to pull teeth.

"He seemed bored by the whole business. Asked me if I knew whether you actually went through with the thing. Concelebrated. I told him I didn't stick around to find out, but I heard you hadn't."

"Then?"

"He thanked me for calling. Told me to call anytime."

Koesler couldn't help smiling. He could imagine the sort of day the Chancery priest had to look forward to. Maybe some pickets outside on Washington Boulevard protesting a Catholic school—or parish—closing. Maybe a priest getting arrested trying to invade the mayor's office to get him to close some crack cocaine house or tear down some of the vacant dangerous buildings wherein school children were being raped. Maybe a parish delegation angry at their pastor for trying to lead them back to the thirteenth century. Maybe a parish delegation angry at their pastor for trying to lead them on to the twenty-first century.

In any case, as he had anticipated, the Chancery wasn't about to get too concerned about an unauthorized ecumenical worship service. Especially when less than ten people were involved—no TV cameras, no reporters, no notoriety. Particularly when the bottom line was that it had been *celebratus interruptus*.

"You've got a funny diocese here, I must say, Father," Augustine added. "Nobody seems terribly interested in the niceties of Canon Law."

"Vatican II hit us hard."

"So I've always heard. Never experienced it until this morning. With all this going on I'm amazed that your archbishop was named a Cardinal."

"Had to be. He was the first elected president of the U.S. Bishops' Conference. Rome couldn't overlook that no matter how hard they tried."

"Maybe. Well, I guess so. Anyway, it doesn't matter much. I did what I had to do. Up to them now. I don't care what they do. No skin off my hide. But, if I were you, Father, I'd be careful. You can be rock-solid sure somebody, sometime, is going to bypass your rather laid-back Chancery and go directly to Rome."

"Well, good day." Augustine turned to go into Sister Janet's office, leaving Koesler alone in the corridor.

Strange, strange man, thought Koesler. After all those heated words in the sacristy, he had expected discomfiture, at least, in their relationship for the remainder of this workshop.

On the contrary, Father Augustine seemed to possess a most rare and uncanny ability to compartmentalize. Able to work himself into a sanctimonious frenzy then have almost no memory of it. Turn the outlaw in, to the authorities, immediately followed by washing his hands of the whole matter. Even slow to remember what it was all about.

Koesler chuckled. He'd met Augustine for the first time last evening. The very next day Augustine accuses Koesler of engaging in an unauthorized ecumenical service. The poor Trappist must think Koesler to be utterly without regard for Church law.

Nothing could be further from the truth. Koesler's life revolved around the Church. He read ecclesiastical periodicals voraciously and faithfully. In short, his grasp of theological trends and developments was easily as up-to-date as anyone's.

Thus, in the matter of concelebrating with an Episcopal priest, Koesler knew he was on arguably solid ground. Nothing now stood in the way of Rome's recognition of the validity of Anglican orders except what to do about women who wanted to be priests. It was seen as inappropriate to make the declaration of unity while the Anglican Church allowed women priests and the Episcopal Church had a female bishop. However, none of that had anything to do with historical accuracy and true doctrine.

The way Rome felt about women priests, let alone women bishops, it was not likely the current Pope would put his stamp of approval on the validity of Anglican orders, no matter how valid they really were.

In any case, the incident this morning between himself, Augustine, and Benbow was revealing.

Obviously Augustine was strongly wed to the letter of the law. Yet to be determined was whether he inflicted this tight interpretation, this legalistic rigidity, on himself as well. Over the years, Koesler had met any number of people eager to demand of others slavish obedience to rules and regulations. But when it came to themselves, they were much more understanding and permissive. Of course there were those whose legalism applied as equally to themselves as to others. In which camp was Augustine? Perhaps time would tell.

One thing about Augustine was certain: He could be cruel. And, indeed, this morning he had been brutal to David Benbow and, by extension, to Martha Benbow. Augustine had shown no sensitivity whatsoever in the delicate matter of liturgical practice.

As he strolled the manicured campus of Marygrove College, Koesler wondered about this mean streak revealed by the Trappist. How strong was it? To what extremes could it lead?

Last night, when the charade of Krieg's murder was played out, Augustine was the only character in the psychodrama who never became a suspect. That was due solely to his being very much under the weather. What if it had not been make-believe? What if Krieg actually had been murdered? What if Augustine had not been taken ill? Or had he really been ill?

Did anyone else on this "faculty" know about Augustine's quick temper and his churlishly cruel streak? If the others knew, would Augustine have been a prime suspect?

Interesting, if moot, questions. But purely hypothetical. As far as any of them knew, Krieg—who had not as yet this morning deigned to arrive on campus—was alive and well. There had been no murder. There were no suspects.

So, Koesler decided to forget about it. For all practical purposes, the incident was over and done with. Undoubtedly, the Benbows would not return to attend any future liturgies. They had been pretty effectively scared off.

Augustine thought he had learned something about Koesler. But the inductive reasoning process, arguing from one example to a general principle, would prove incorrect. Under ordinary circumstances, Koesler was anything but a lawbreaker.

On the other hand, Augustine was an interesting study.

Koesler had no first-hand knowledge of current monastic practices. He wondered if the monks still observed a "chapter of faults." For centuries, members of most religious orders, men and women, held a daily "chapter of faults," during which individuals openly and publicly accused themselves of violations of anything from the Ten Commandments to their monastic rule of life. And, as if that weren't enough humiliation, others in the community were invited, again openly and publicly, to add to the accusations any faults that the individual might have forgotten, overlooked, or been too ashamed to own up to.

If that practice was still in place, Koesler was grateful he was not a member of Augustine's community. Without doubt, Augustine would make certain there was hell to pay for everyone.

Father Koesler had no scheduled duties to perform in this workshop until early afternoon. He had toyed with the idea of returning to his parish, if only to go through the mail and get a few other chores finished—make it a little easier on himself when these five committed days were completed. But experience had taught that when one stepped into one's rectory office, one thing led to another. A whole day's work could snowball from a simple, innocent visit to the office to open the morning mail.

All in all, he decided to enjoy the gorgeous fall weather, walking through the cool shadows of Marygrove's acres of trees.

11

By anyone's standards, the schedule for the first day of this workshop was undemanding.

Apparently, whoever had set it up—Jack Regan?—realized that with a five-day conference, there was no great call to cram in nonstop events. The schedule provided ample time for students and faculty to get to know one another informally, for the faculty to have the leisure to fully develop their material, for the students to have every opportunity of tapping the faculty for all possible information, suggestions, guidance, and encouragement.

Morning was occupied largely with orientation-type activities: a tour of the campus, sale of books written by members of the faculty as well as some put out by P.G. Press. Sister Janet had the students gather in small group sessions for informal discussions on the nature of religious mystery novels.

All of this was punctuated with coffee and, at the earliest session, doughnuts.

There was only one major event in the afternoon. It was held in Alumni Hall. Since the group consisted of only 150 to 200 students, the large hall was shrunken by a room divider.

This event was the first and, until the final session, the only time the entire faculty would appear together. Each member of the faculty presented a synopsis of what he or she intended to teach and treat in the individual classes during the week.

Father Koesler, as the one and only "resource person," sat with the faculty on the platform. But, since he would not be formally teaching any classes, he was not expected to make a presentation. As far as he was concerned, he was auditing this session.

He found the present gathering fascinating due to the extraordinary interactions that had already gone on between the various members of the panel. Koesler had had the leisure to study the interplay since he was, in effect, a spectator.

This was the first any of them had seen of Klaus Krieg since supper last night. Koesler wondered if the students could detect the tension flowing back and forth across the stage. It was, at best, uneven, since Father Augustine had not played any role at all in Krieg's little psychodrama. Fortunately, in a sense, he'd been spared the emotional investment that make-believe fiasco had demanded. In all probability Augustine had been told what had happened. Still, that was in no way comparable to having gone through it.

On another level, there'd been the altercation between himself, Augustine, and Benbow this morning. Koesler had expected some leftover bad feeling from that. Seemingly there was none. At least Koesler could not detect any, and he was not only on the lookout for a sign of ill will, he was expecting it.

Since his brief conversation with Augustine after Mass, much of the anger he had felt was dissipated. Perhaps a similar type of meeting had diffused the hostility between Augustine and Benbow . . . though Koesler would have found it more difficult to forgive and forget had someone called *him* a heretic.

While Marie, Benbow, and Winer evidenced some tension—at least to the eye of one who was on the lookout for it—Krieg seemed untroubled and at ease. Well, thought Koesler, why not? Up to this point, Krieg had been in the driver's seat. So far, this had been Krieg's show. The feeling Koesler got, from the nuances that he was picking up from the victims of last night's charade, was that the tide was about to turn. Unless he was mistaken there were vibrations of a determination to exact some measure of revenge.

Rabbi Winer, the last of the faculty to deliver a prepared talk, was nearing the conclusion of his allocution.

Koesler dismissed further thought of the dynamics going on between those on the dais and began studying the students. One quick and easy conclusion he reached involved the predominant gender and median age of the group: decidedly female and, he guessed, in the forty-to-fifty age group.

It figured. Most men and women employed outside the home could not get away for a full week and probably would be unwilling to invest a vacation week on a writers' workshop. Though there were a few who looked as if they might have made this sacrifice.

Most of the students were women with gray hair and, judging from their bobbing heads, were wearing bifocals, maybe trifocals. There was also a sprinkling of young people, perhaps Marygrove students.

The group's reactions to the talks were interesting. Since Koesler did not recognize anyone in the crowd, his only means of deducing their purpose in attending was to note the manner in which they responded to the presentations. Still it was little more than a wild guess.

Some, perhaps the majority, seemed intent, eagerly sopping up the words, encouragement, explanations of the faculty. Koesler assumed these were novice writers, unpublished or insufficiently published. He could picture them at home, borrowing time from their daily chores to grind out the pages of their work in progress. He could visualize them sending in their manuscripts and anxiously awaiting each day's mail until the manuscript was returned with no more than a form letter rejection. If his scenario was correct, the major virtue of these people was perseverance. Disappointed but undaunted, they continued to mail in their submissions while hopefully learning more and continuing to write.

That's why they were at this conference: to learn. And that's what they were doing now: learning from some who lived the dream of earning a decent, if not substantial, income from writing.

It was unlikely that all these intent and intense students wrote mystery stories, let alone religious mysteries. That would have to be a rather narrow field. It was not that important what the faculty had written. What was of vital importance was that the faculty was published.

And, while he was ascribing motives to the students, Koesler reminded himself not to overlook the one member of the faculty who did not need to be published. He was a publisher. The horse's mouth, as it were.

If only they could put it all together. To pick up tips and learn that elusive secret of how to prepare a manuscript for publication and then to understand what it was publishers were looking for in submitted work. The magic formula. Put it all together and one day maybe the students would be faculty at one of these affairs.

There was another, much smaller, group in the audience;

those Koesler assumed, were simply fans of one or more of the authors, and/or the publisher. Instead of wearing the earnest, eager expressions of the writers, these simply smiled. They took no notes; just smiled. They seemed determined to enjoy these five days and so, by God, they would.

That pretty well took care of the students, with the exception of a very few who remained hard to pin down. Koesler put them on the back burner of his scrutiny. Because he could not figure them out, they piqued his interest.

Winer was finished and the formal presentations were concluded.

Sister Janet thanked the faculty and opened the floor to questions. At the outset, nothing was forthcoming. This did not surprise Koesler. It was a common reaction. Not that people didn't have questions. Many of them were embarrassed to volunteer a question, fearing that the others would think it stupid or inane.

Slowly, hesitantly at first, the questions began, until, encouraged that no one was going to pose the "definitive" question, hands were raised throughout the audience. In Koesler's experience, this was the classic way question-and-answer sessions developed. He began testing his theories on who was who by the nature of the question.

A smiling lady—no notepad at hand—directed a question to Sister Marie. How, the lady wanted to know, could Sister find time to write a book with all she had to do in Florida? (Very familiar with Sister's book. A fan, Koesler guessed.)

Marie's response was that writing full-time was, by far, the ideal way to do it. But that was a literary "Catch 22." One has to be successful at writing before one can afford to treat oneself to writing full-time. While pursuing that goal, there are few alternatives to working at a full-time paying job and writing concurrently.

Others on the panel contributed illustrations of how they managed their time. Coincidentally, each of all the writers held active religious vocations that made primary demands on their lives. Benbow attested that afternoons afforded the best opportunity to write. Marie traveled frequently; minutes squeezed out on trains, planes, and buses were most accessible for her writing. Winer's best times were early mornings and Sundays. The other three expressed doubts: Sundays were the busiest days for Christian ministers, priests, and in this case, a nun in charge of education that was emphasized on Sundays.

Good-naturedly, the three Christian authors chided Winer for working on Sunday. Just as affably, he reminded them that he was the only one among them observing the Sabbath—literally the seventh day of the week, Saturday.

Sister Janet appeared inclined to let the questions roll on. On most occasions such as this, there was a time limit for Q and A. But there was nothing more on the schedule until dinner. The arrangement was fine as far as Koesler was concerned. He had found the question period to almost always be the most lively and scintillating segment of this sort of program.

Without raising her hand, a youngish dark-haired woman shot a challenge at Winer. Didn't he think, she asked, that a rabbi's involvement with the world was too confined to make him the central character in a mystery novel?

In response, the smiling Winer explained some of the responsibilities and talents required of the average rabbi.

But, she persisted, what of the tendency of Jews to ghettoize themselves, to form their own tight-knit communities and become isolated from outsiders? What, she concluded, made Winer think the community at large would be interested in what this tiny handful of people did or thought?

Winer, holding himself under tight control, gave a brief synopsis of some of the major accomplishments of Jews through history, as well as a short review of Jews being driven by Gentiles into ghettos rather than choosing to isolate themselves. But Winer's presentation was strictly academic, almost devoid of passion or argumentation. The rabbi seemed convinced that there was no way he could enter this woman's closed mind, let alone change it.

Winer, Marie, Benbow, and Augustine were asked a representative number of questions mainly because the Q and A lasted so long. From the beginning, the most popular figure on the dais was Klaus Krieg. It was as if the students could not believe that they now had access to a genuine television personality. And it was obvious that many in the audience were very familiar with his telecasts.

To Koesler's observation, questions addressed to Krieg ranged from what seemed honest attempts to learn something about the publishing field, to the more celebrity-conscious queries regarding what life is really like in front of the lights and cameras and, most importantly, what Krieg's celebrity guests were really like off-camera.

It was toward what turned out to be the windup of the question-and-answer session that the blockbuster query came.

The question came from a mousy woman who seemed almost reluctant to ask it.

"Reverend Krieg," she began, "I've read a few of the books you've published, and there's one thing I've been wondering about: They always contain something extraneous to the religious storyline. What I mean is, there always seems to be an awful lot of . . . uh . . . oh . . . violence and . . . uh . . . sex in your books.'' She had not actually articulated a question. Yet the implication was clear.

Krieg did not immediately respond. Koesler had the impression he had fielded this or a similar question many times and was weighing his choice of approach.

Having decided, Krieg, adopting a more orotund tone, almost shouted, ''We are sinners, sister, each and every one! Violence prowls our streets. You good people from this area should be well acquainted with that!

''And sex!'' He passed the shadow of a glance toward his fellow panelists, but did not break cadence. ''Sex is everywhere. And we have fallen. We are fallen! Violence, sex, both are part of our lives, part of our fallen lives. I say again, we are sinners, sister! We are sinners. Violence and sex are part of our sinful selves. If it's part of our lives, it ought to be part of our reading. But, praise God, sisters and brothers! We have been saved. Washed in the blood of the Lamb! Praise God!''

Several in the audience repeated the doxology, ''Praise God,'' but somewhat self-consciously, as if unfamiliar with the participatory prayer of tent-preaching or the Black liturgy.

The dark-haired woman who had tried to pin Rabbi Winer spoke up, again without bothering to raise her hand. ''Wait a minute, Reverend. I haven't read everything all of the other panelists have written, but I've sampled something from each of them. You don't find that sort of thing in the books they write . . . at least not in the prurient way your books treat sex and violence.

''What about it, Reverend?''

Krieg's smile disappeared. This definitely was not the way

he'd anticipated the program would flow. When he replied, it was in a more subdued manner. "Well, sister, I don't know that I want to comment on the work of my distinguished colleagues. Comparisons are odious, as the poet says."

The dark-haired woman smiled a victor's smile. "Go ahead," she urged.

"Really," Sister Janet interrupted, "if Reverend Krieg does not wish to comment—"

"That's all right, Sister," Krieg broke in. "Praise God! If our sister out there wants to pursue the question, we'll do just that!" His tone changed subtly from that of the preacher to that of the lecturer, but nonetheless confident.

"The answer, sister," Krieg explained, "has something to do with the television ministry. Anyone here know how many people watch the Gospel of the Good News bein' preached over the Praise God Network?"

The heads that shook in negative response belonged to Marygrove students; actually none in the audience knew.

"On an average program," Krieg declared, "approximately sixty million souls!"

There was a shared gasp.

"Now, sisters and brothers," Krieg said, "all these millions of souls starvin' for the message of hope and salvation don't even know they're hungry! Praise God! Hungry for the Lord! Praise God!

"But they're not findin' Him in church. You take your average parish church—or synagogue, for that matter—of a Sunday or a Saturday. Attendance goin' down all the time. Then you take the Praise God Tabernacle. Climbin', everything's climbin'. I'm not just talkin' the souls occupyin' the pews of the Tabernacle. I'm talkin' viewers.

Besides the sixty million or so. Our message is broadcast in 143 countries.''

There was a quiet but definite audience reaction.

"Now I ask you, brothers and sisters, what's the difference? Why are we gainin' while they're losin'?" He paused to let the implications of the question sink in. Then he answered it himself. "Pizzazz!" Another pause. "That's right, brothers and sisters: pizzazz!"

His audience clearly was at sea.

"Lemmee give you an example. 'Member Fulton Sheen?" Krieg looked around, smiling benevolently. "Nah, you're too young to remember him . . .''

The majority, who did recall the popular radio and television prelate, appreciated the gift of years.

Krieg proceeded. "Fulton Sheen—monsignor, bishop—drew a good crowd. But I think it's clear he started with a premise, a hypothesis, an assumption. I think it's clear he started with the assumption that people weren't gonna watch him on TV, weren't gonna turn to his channel instead of watchin' Uncle Miltie just because he was a bishop. He had to give 'em somethin' extra.

"That voice! Could mesmerize you. But there was more. That getup! Full cassock, piping and all those buttons, cummerbund; shoulder cape; big cross on a gold chain. All that went with that magical voice. And extra added attraction: an 'angel' to erase his blackboard . . . 'member?''

"Well, now," Krieg continued, "that's just about the same thinkin' we did in the Praise God Tabernacle. We started out by askin' some questions. Like: Are people gonna turn us on instead of dialin' in Bill Cosby, '60 Minutes,' or NFL Football because they'd rather see a religion show?" He continued without pausing for any sort of response. " 'Course not. So we built us a temple the likes of which you ain't gonna find anywhere else. People see the Praise God Tabernacle, takes their breath away.

"Or, suppose we're gonna have a Crusade for Jesus—on the road, in a manner of speaking. Biggest stadium we can find. Beat the drums for weeks in advance. Make sure the house is full. That catch the eye of the viewer? Well, I should say!

"Then, how 'bout if we give 'em the best in country-western music? How 'bout we give 'em the biggest stars in Hollywood to entertain and give witness as well? How 'bout if we have experts to stage and pace all this? We're givin' 'em a show they want to see. And tucked in there kind of subtle-like is . . . religion. The Good News Gospel of the Lord, Praise God!"

"Praise God!" This time enthusiastically from the audience.

Koesler marveled at the ease with which Krieg could segue from preacher to teacher to apologist. There was no arguing the guy had a talent.

When dispassion returned, the dark-haired woman who had started all this said forcefully, "Reverend, the books . . . ?" She was smiling, seemingly amused at his performance.

"The books; yes, indeed, the books." Krieg, perceiving he'd won over the crowd, could afford to be amiable. "See, we at P.G. Press operate with an assumption. Just like Ol' Fulton Sheen assumed people weren't gonna tune him in just 'cause he was a bishop; just like our broadcast ministry assumes people aren't gonna tune us in 'cause they're in love with religious programming. Well, sister, this is it: we at P.G Press start with the assumption that religion is dull."

He paused for evident dramatic effect. Then, slowly,

as if carving the words in stone, "R-E-L-I-G-I-O-N I-S D-U-L-L."

That was it, indeed, thought Koesler. He'd been very carefully following the structured logic of Klaus Krieg. This is what the preacher had been building toward from the beginning. As far as Krieg was concerned, religion was dull. That explained Krieg's approach to evangelization—and everything flowed from that approach.

"You got a hard time with that," Krieg continued, "you just go in one of those religious bookstores. The kind that sells devotional stuff, books about the saints and the like. You're gonna see a store that don't sell many books. And you're gonna be lookin' at writers who don't make much money.

"P.G. books are religious enough with priests and nuns and monks and rabbis and bishops and here and there a pope. We simply ask people who write for us to . . . add a little somethin'. Somethin' that'll spice it up, attract readers. If that turns out to be a certain measure of sex or violence, well, so be it. Holy pizzazz! It's for the Lord. Praise God!"

This time, it was an unanswered doxology. Koesler wondered if Krieg had lost the crowd.

The evangelist may have harbored the same doubt, for he quickly added, "But I sense I have not been as clear as I might have been. When I say religion is dull and that it needs punchin' up, I'm talkin' 'bout the public at large. The souls we want to touch. Dear Lord, I'm not talkin' 'bout *us*. Why, I would not for a moment insult you by sayin' religion is dull for *you or me*. *We* don't have that problem. *They* do.

"Now, there's a place for the pious, devotional book— religion without a single frill. But that place is on a dusty shelf, where it's gonna sit from now until the comin' of the Kingdom.

"You can write a book that's gonna sell and reach all those souls who don't even know they're hungry. You can do that if you're willin' to follow the steps I'm gonna give you during this week. Steps that will help you sow the good word in an attractive package. Your book will feed the hungry, give drink to the thirsty, accomplish all this good whilst you earn yourself a pretty penny. And all for the Lord. Praise God!"

"Praise God!" the audience responded more confidently.

I'll be darned, thought Koesler, he got them back.

The dark-haired woman stood.

Troublemaking broad, thought Krieg.

"How about the other panelists?" she asked. "*Their* books are not gathering dust on a shelf." Her gaze turned to the others. "Maybe one of you would speak to this question. What about it? Is religion dull? Do you have to drag in sex and violence to sell books with a religious setting?"

Krieg shrugged, and with an alert and defiant look, took his seat.

Koesler studied the others on the panel. Benbow and Marie stared at the tabletop as if they were children hoping the teacher would not call on them. Augustine studied the ceiling as if seriously weighing Krieg's hypothesis. Winer seemed to be trying to restrain anger. Finally it was the rabbi who literally rose to the challenge.

"If my colleagues have no objection," Winer opened, glancing at the other writers on the dais, "I should like to comment on a couple of issues raised by Mr. Krieg."

Winer's dismissal of Krieg's title "Reverend" was noted by everyone. The other writers smiled at Winer. Did their smiles indicate permission for Winer to speak for them, or did they constitute silent agreement that Krieg warranted no religious title? Koesler didn't know, but it was interesting to speculate.

"My first comment," Winer proceeded, "is addressed to the presence of sex and violence in literature, specifically in books of a religious nature. Unfortunately, I have not yet read all the books written by all of my colleagues. Yet, having met them and in a short span of time gotten to know them surprisingly well, I feel it may be safe to speak in their behalf.

"All of us—Sister Marie, Father Augustine, Father Benbow, and myself—are writing in the mystery or detective fiction genre. To begin with, the fiction is also popularly known as 'murder' mystery stories. It may or may not come as a surprise to you that there exist rules and regulations for murder mysteries. One of these rules is that there must be at least one murder in each murder mystery. That having been said, I feel it safe to suggest that I cannot think of any murder that does not have an element of violence to it."

There were a few chuckles from the audience and smiles everywhere, save on Krieg's face.

"Thus," Winer continued, "it is not a question, I think, whether or not violence is compatible with religion. Good God, look at the Bible! It gets under way with fratricide—Cain killing Abel. And, in your so-called "New" Testament, it culminates with a most brutal death—the crucifixion of Jesus.

"What I propose is the consideration not of the presence or absence of violence as such, but rather whether the subject of violence is called for in the plot, and secondarily—and just as important—how it is treated.

"For instance, in one of my books there is a death of the

daughter of the president of the synagogue. It is pivotal to the essence of the story. I intended the book to be a murder mystery. Thus, there had to be a murder. And there was. The book was peopled with characters I hoped the reader would find interesting. The interaction of these characters hinged on their relationship to the dead girl. Who had the motive, the means, and the opportunity to do the poor girl in? There were quite a few suspects. As it turned out, only the rabbi was clever enough to figure it all out.''

Winer smiled self-consciously. The audience was appreciative of his humor.

''So we have an act of violence in a book with a very religious setting. Was it necessary? Did it fit? Oh, yes, I think so.

''The next question: How was the description of violence handled?''

''Rabbi,'' a student interrupted, ''aren't you just quibbling about taste? Good taste? Bad taste? Who's to tell?''

Winer considered the question for a moment. ''Ah, yes, my young man: taste. But good taste, bad taste, like morality and art, all depend on where one draws the line.

''For instance, in the case of violence—given in a murder mystery there is violence, given in life there is violence—one can write that so-and-so is shot or stabbed to death. Or, one can describe in lurid detail exactly how a person is tortured to death. All the agonies and terrors the torture victim suffers can be graphically depicted. More, one can dwell on the almost erotic pleasure the killer derives from the inflicting of torture.

''I would suggest that the first is an example of good taste, while the latter is in very poor taste.

''Sex. Sex is much like violence, a part of life. I think it almost impossible to write a book that has no reference to sex. If only to the stereotypical role of the sexes. There are traits considered feminine and those considered masculine; mannerisms, relationships that are inescapable in real life.

"When we come to intimate sexual behavior between people, once again we arrive at that line between good and bad taste. And here perhaps more than in any other situation it is difficult to know where to draw that line.

"People love each other sexually. They also manipulate and abuse one another sexually. And here it is not so much a question of description as it is minute detail. The word I'm searching for is 'pandering': what the Supreme Court likes to call 'appealing to a prurient interest.'

"We could go very far afield with examples. Suffice to say that I believe you will find in the books of the writers on this panel a very decided effort to express violence and sex in reasonable taste. And I also submit that in the books of P.G. Press you will find not just bad taste but execrable taste."

"Just a minute, Rabbi . . ." Krieg's seemingly perpetual beatific smile had almost completely disappeared. ". . . It is grossly unfair of you—"

"Please," Winer cut in, "allow me to finish. After that, the floor can be yours if you wish. We have many more days during which to thrash this out."

Krieg, who had half risen from his seat, fell back into the chair. Sister Janet leaned toward him and whispered something. He nodded, and tried with little success to reawaken the plastic smile.

"We will have ample time to discuss these issues," Winer said, "and I believe they are well worth an examination in depth. However, there is one more point I wish to speak to now. That is the statement Mr. Krieg made alleging that religion is, of its very nature, dull.''

Once again Winer's denial of Krieg's religious title was noted by all.

"For us, Jews and Christians," Winer continued, "the notion and subject of religion quite naturally takes us back to the Bible.

"Now, how can anyone in his right mind think that the Bible is dull? The stories of Abraham, Moses, David; the prophets; the remarkable women, Ruth, Esther. Fulton Oursler wrote a book about the Bible and called it *The Greatest Story Ever Told*. And that is what it is: the greatest story ever told. It needs no 'pizzazz.' It needs no hype. It needs nothing but understanding and communicating.

"And I will leave you with a question: If the Bible, the primary source of our religion, is the greatest story ever told, why would anyone suggest that it needed, desperately needed, 'pizzazz'? And I will suggest an answer to that question. The 'pizzazz' that allegedly is needed is brought out through gratuitous sex and violence in the most execrable taste imaginable.''

Krieg was on his feet, his complexion a preamble to a seizure. But before he could speak, a student broke in.

"Excuse me, Rabbi''—the student spoke loudly enough to override Krieg's first syllables—"this is a sort of delicate point, but 'the greatest story ever told' and 'execrable taste' are apples and oranges.

"The 'delicate point'?'' Winer inquired.

"P.G. Press books generally sell better than yours.''

The smile almost returned to Krieg's face.

Winer shrugged. "It is as the man said: No one ever went broke underestimating the taste of the American public.''

"For what it's worth, Rabbi," said the student, "I think that is a copout."

"Young man . . ." Sister Janet began a reproof in a tone familiar to many parochial students of yore.

"It's all right, Sister," Winer assured her, "let the young man speak his peace. We want this conference to be as open and honest as possible. You were saying, young man?"

For a moment, the student seemed impressed enough with Winer's forbearance to possibly withdraw his antagonistic comment. But his next thought was to make his point. "Whatever other reasons we've got for writing—altruistic maybe—we want to get published, we want to be circulated and read, we want to sell, we want to make money. I think P.G. Press has a pretty good track record doing just that."

"Yes," a hitherto silent student cut in. "Even if we want to communicate some sort of religious message or truth, we want to reach the maximum number of people. P.G. Press does that. I don't think you'd deny that, Rabbi."

Winer sighed deeply. "No, my dear young woman, no one could deny that some of the writers under contract to P.G. sell a lot of books—many more than any of the writers on this panel. Some of them appear more regularly on various so-called best-seller lists. What sort of effect they have on the reader is a question we must address in greater depth. Obviously, we have much to discuss in the coming days. It should make for an interesting conference."

Sister Janet glanced at Krieg to see if he wished to add anything at this time. Almost imperceptibly he shook his head. The beatific plastic smile had returned. No one else on the panel seemed inclined to further comment. Nor were any more hands raised in the audience.

Sister Janet thanked—with relief—everyone, and declared the session concluded.

She then noted that although the schedule called for a movie to be shown after dinner that evening, the name of the film hadn't been listed.

"Well," she said, "I think we have a treat for you, especially in light of the nature of this workshop. We have the 1954 British movie, *Father Brown*. This film stars Alec Guinness as G. K. Chesterton's very perceptive priest-detective, and Peter Finch as the thief, Flambeau. It also features Joan Greenwood. I think you will all enjoy it very much."

Judging from the smiles of most everyone in the room, Sister was guilty of understatement.

Koesler was pleased. He had seen the movie, but so very long ago he could scarcely remember it. Mostly he recalled having enjoyed it greatly.

He had read—or thought he had—all of Chesterton's stories about the adventures of Father Brown. They surely were among the most popular works of the great writer. Yet Chesterton himself had considered them merely avocational. An indication of how lightly he regarded the series was his treatment of the characters. In the first of the series, Flambeau was the villain. But Chesterton liked the character so much that in the sequel he brought Flambeau back as an ally of Father Brown.

Koesler was grateful to anticipate the movie. He was not all that keen about the prospects for dinner.

12 ON THE ONE hand, he was very hungry. On the other hand, his appetite diminished markedly when he considered partaking of nourishment with his fellow "faculty" members. The relationship between the writers and the publisher was akin to that of an impending tribal war. Scalps would be taken.

He had never before been on a panel quite like this. Of course he had experienced times when panelists disagreed with each other. That was to be expected, at least occasionally. The unique character of the present panel was that it had been preprogrammed as hopelessly irreconcilable.

And who was to blame? Regan, the absent host? In a way. He should have rejected Krieg's preconditions, even if it meant starting from scratch in setting up the workshop.

And yet, in the end, all roads led back to Krieg. He was the linchpin around whom this conference was built. The underlying question was why he had insisted on the presence of these specific writers.

So far it was evident that Krieg wanted these writers in his stable. It was also evident he had failed to corral them, at least up to the present. Was this a last-ditch effort? Did he

155

think that a face-to-face meeting would convince them to join them?

If so, that would contribute to the explanation of his response to those questions this afternoon. Was he trying to convince the writers that they were missing a very desirable larger readership by not signing with P.G. Press? If that was the case, thought Koesler, he had failed completely. Would there be still more overtures? Probably.

While he could make some sort of sense of Krieg's behavior in light of what he appeared to be trying to accomplish, the question that more deeply stumped Koesler was the unexpected intensity of hostility the writers exhibited toward Krieg.

So, all right, each of them had been courted by Krieg to sign with him. If anything, Koesler thought, the normal response to such an overture would be to feel flattered. However, after further thought and some helpful advice, each of them learns more about the intricacies of publishing and feels that he or she would be entrapped and, in a sense, enslaved with P.G. Press. At which point, they would be forced either to prostitute their talent or expend a lot of time and money getting out of the contract.

So each of the writers decides against signing with P.G. What's the big deal in that, Koesler wondered. Every day, millions of people routinely refuse invitations to join book clubs, accept another credit card, subscribe to an insurance policy, and so on, ad infinitum.

In like manner, the writers refuse Krieg's offer. Why does this upset them so? Each of these writers is a religious person. Each of them is a traditionally civil person. Why should they react so uncivilly to Krieg?

On second thought, Koesler recalled the hurtful words

flung at David Benbow by Augustine in the sacristy this morning. Not *all* the writers were paragons of civility.

Koesler had assumed that each of the writers was a kindly and understanding soul. Augustine had proved him in error. Could any of the others be masking a nasty disposition under the veneer of a religious title and/or habit?

The answers to these questions would possibly be revealed in time, Koesler concluded, as long as he remained alert, curious, receptive, attentive, thoughtful, and sober.

In keeping with that final condition, he declined Sister Janet's offer of a predinner cocktail. In this abstemious decision he was alone. From Sister Marie's innocuous white wine to Father Augustine's potent Scotch-on-the-rocks, the others seemed to feel they either needed or deserved a drink. And after this afternoon's session, Koesler thought they might very well need one.

Sipping at his tonic water and lime, Koesler studied the liquor tray. Same as yesterday, a meager selection of pedestrian brands.

He smiled when Rabbi Winer tried the cabinet door, behind which were ensconced Krieg's far more pricey labels, and found it locked.

Winer shrugged and, when he found the others observing what he'd done, he grinned self-consciously, half embarrassed, half amused. "The Reverend runs a tight ship," he commented. It was clear that Winer would use Krieg's religious title only sarcastically.

"I'm sorry," Sister Janet said. "We have a very limited budget. There is an extra key to that cabinet hanging in the pantry"—she pointed—"just through that door. The liquor does belong to Reverend Krieg, but I'm sure . . ."

Winer had not intended to disparage the liquor supplied

by the college. "Please, Sister," he hastily interrupted, "I intended no commentary on what you've offered. It's fine. As much as anything, I was interested in whether he'd had the cabinet locked."

"It was," Sister Janet began to explain, "part of the arrangement Reverend Krieg had with . . ."

". . . with Mr. Regan. We know," Benbow said.

"Strange," Sister Marie said, "for a person who hasn't been here for months to have such an impact on what we're doing."

"I guess Regan was the straight man in this scenario," Benbow said. "The one with all the punch lines is Krieg." He took the empty glass from his wife. "Here, dear, let me freshen this for you." He dropped a small ice cube in both his and his wife's empty glasses, nearly filled each glass with Mohawk Gin, then added vermouth as if he were using an eyedropper.

"Speaking of having all the lines," Marie said, "we haven't really had a chance to discuss that bizarre incident last night."

"Krieg's 'death.' The play within the play," Winer said.

Augustine was about to refill his glass but decided against it. He had entirely missed that episode. He had wanted to have the particulars explained to him but felt awkward in asking. This was his opportunity to be brought up to date and he didn't want to miss a word.

"I think Sister is absolutely right in referring to that matter as bizarre," Martha Benbow said. "I just can't imagine what the man had in mind."

"By the way," Benbow said, "just where is 'the man'? We couldn't be lucky enough to have had him leave town in a huff, could we?" His words belied his smile.

"He's upstairs in his room. He wanted to freshen up before dinner," Janet supplied. "As for last night, these acted-out mystery dramas are very popular now, you know. As I said, this had been all worked out between Jack Regan and Reverend Krieg."

"Mystery psychodramas may be popular," Marie said. "I don't doubt that for an instant. But I still say last night's charade was bizarre."

"The man has a strange mind," Benbow said. "I'm not sure what his real intention was in all that."

"If he was trying to plant a thought in our minds," Winer said, "he went to a lot of needless trouble. I daresay it was already there."

"Thought?" Martha asked. "What thought?"

Winer did not answer.

"His death?" Marie pursued.

"Why pussyfoot around it?" Benbow said. "The thought Rabbi Winer suggests—which we didn't need to be reminded of—is the Reverend Krieg's murder."

Martha gasped. "David!"

"Praise God!"

Krieg was in the doorway and in good voice and spirits. A couple of paces behind him was the considerable bulk of his bodyguard, Guido Taliafero.

Had Krieg overheard their conversation? Had he heard what David Benbow had just confessed? Krieg gave no indication.

At this point, the others couldn't help being in the same room with Krieg, but it was Sister Janet who effusively greeted and welcomed him.

Taliafero strode immediately to the cabinet, unlocked it, and proceeded to set out on the serving ledge a splendid array of spirits. He poured a couple of jiggers of whiskey neat and placed the glass in the hand of an inattentive Krieg in much the same way an operating room nurse slides a scalpel into a surgeon's hand. Taliafero then took his position near the door.

The others still had their original drinks, with the exception of Father Augustine, who, now that conversation about his previous lost evening had ceased, decided it was time for a refill of Scotch. Spontaneously he moved toward Krieg's superior supply, then hesitated.

"By all means, Father," Krieg said, "help yourself."

Feeling like a Judas, or an Esau who was selling his birthright for a high-class intoxicant, Augustine poured from Krieg's cache.

Almost immediately a sort of natural polarization took place and three groups formed. Krieg and Janet made up the first set. The three men—Augustine, Benbow, and Winer—composed the second cluster. They were joined by Benbow's wife, Martha. That left Koesler with Sister Marie. He didn't mind; he'd wanted to talk to her. He offered to refill her glass. She said she'd wait until dinner was served.

"Well, here we are," Koesler said. "One relic to another."

"Pardon?"

"There are not that many priests and nuns left. You and I are an endangered species."

"Don't I know." She gestured toward Sister Janet, who was busily listening to Krieg. "That woman is a reminder to me. We practically grew up together in the convent. But she is one of the last of my close friends who is still a nun. Most of the others are gone. Oh, I don't mean they've died—though a few have. No, the majority are 'in the world.' " She smiled.

"Odd how easily that expression comes to mind. 'In the world.' I can remember when that excluded all but us. We, in the convent, were *not* 'in the world.' Now even those of us who have remained nuns would have to admit we're 'in the world.' ''

"I guess. In charge of continuing education for an entire diocese and now author of a popular book. You've squeezed into 'the world.' But then, you're certainly not alone. We owe it all to Vatican II, *the* religious event of this century. From time to time I think of how drastically life has changed for priests as a result of the council. But, to be fair, priestly life has stood still compared with what's happened to convents.''

"I believe I will have a bit more wine." She smiled. "Dinner seems to be delayed.''

They moved to the tray the college had prepared; Koesler filled her glass. No point in his taking more tonic water; he was still nursing the ice cubes from his original drink.

Picking up their conversation, Marie said, "What's happened to converts is that there aren't any anymore. Or at least precious few. But I'm a bit surprised you're interested. Most priests nowadays are concerned almost exclusively with their own survival.

"Now I shouldn't have said that," she corrected herself. "I don't mean they are not giving service to their parishes or whatever their particular vocation calls for. I mean most priests don't think much about nuns—now that there's no chance of getting a passel of them for the parochial school.''

Koesler chuckled. "I used to be a regular confessor for nuns in parishes where there'd be anywhere from twenty to thirty or forty in a convent. That's where I learned the word 'promptitude.' Seems that's about the only sin nuns ever committed. They were late for things.''

Marie laughed. She had an engaging laugh. "Stop! You're bringing back memories. Memories that are treasured, but memories regardless. I would just as soon forget before they remind me too much of the grind we were in. Nuns as teenagers. The postulancy, the novitiate, first vows, perpetual vows. Then the parochial school and its unending routine. Up for early—and I do mean early—Mass, quick breakfast, Mass with the kiddies, school, lunch any time or way one could; afternoon classes, evening prayer, dinner, lesson plans, night prayers, and then to bed. Every day throughout the school year until summer break gave you a chance to finish one academic degree or begin another.'' Inwardly she winced at the memory.

"Is there any doubt that things have changed radically for you—for women religious?" Koesler said. "To my eyes, the biggest change has been the virtual end of communal life—those convents with all those nuns living so closely together.''

Marie grew serious. "You're right. There have been lots of changes: the habit; the rules that apportioned one's whole life; independent thought being discouraged. But most of all—you're absolutely right—there's no more community such as it was.''

"And that was, substantially, the reason for the founding of religious orders. So, although I've never asked anyone in your position—if you don't mind—why stay?"

"Why stay?''

"If you don't mind?''

"You first.''

Koesler chuckled. "Turned the tables on me, didn't you?

Well, I could claim inertia, but that would be facetious. I could say that something happens to a person after age fifty that discourages a midlife career change. And I suppose that could discourage even more anyone thinking of leaving a religious vocation.

"But, in reality, 'none of the above' to any significant degree compels me to stay in the priesthood. I suppose it's mostly the feeling Sancho Panza had about Don Quixote in *Man of La Mancha*—'I Like Him.' That's the way I feel about the priesthood. I like it. I've liked it ever since I was old enough to think about what I wanted to do as an adult.

"Of course, being a priest isn't the same as it was as we progress from one decade to another. The Council, of course, was the pivotal event. People no longer need the priest for just about everything, as they used to. Probably never should have been that dependent. But, I must admit, it was fun being that in demand. And the laity, who used to be called 'consultors,' on a diocesan level with the bishop or on the parochial level with the priest, really should have been called 'consenters.' Now, with parish councils, they come close, in many cases, to being arbiters.

"But that's okay. I like being with people as a priest. I prize the sacramental life of the Church and I've always felt honored being able to be a contributing part of that sacramental life. I enjoy trying to make the Gospel message practical in daily life through homilies.

"Oh, like many of my confreres, I am not nutty about some of the Church's present leaders and the gross amount of control they try to exercise over the people of God. In that respect, we're lucky to have Cardinal Boyle as our bishop. But, also like many of my confreres, I try to stay out of the hierarchical way and let my life revolve about the parish and the parishioners. And, on that level, I love it.

"Good enough reasons to hang in there?"

"Quite." Sister Marie had listened intently. By this time, she and Koesler were practically oblivious to the other two groups, who, in turn, were wrapped up in their own respective conversations.

"And now, Sister, your reasons," Koesler said. "Why are you still with us?"

Marie placed her glass on the table, apparently deciding not to have more wine, at least until dinner was served. "I've thought about it, of course, as you have."

"Haven't we all?"

"Yes, I suppose so. What with so many of our friends leaving the priesthood, religious life. Many of them good people. It has to make you wonder about yourself. That and all the changes. As you suggest, far more cataclysmic for us than for you. I've had to reevaluate my commitment more than once.

"I'm not the immature teenager I was when I entered some thirty years ago." Marie grew reflective, almost as if she were speaking to herself. "I guess I was running away from things—life—as much as entering with a gracious heart to serve Christ.

"Those early years, so filled with submission and dependence! Then the upheaval of the sixties and early seventies that tore apart structures and relationships and left only a remnant group.

"I don't know about everyone else, but some of us—myself in particular—had to find new—what?—virtues to rebuild our lives in religion. Instead of blind submission, maturity. And instead of dependence, interdependence."

"Interdependence?"

"Yes. We may not be living in actual convents anymore, but the Sisters depend on each other a lot for support and courage, for example. And that, of course, extends out to the laity. It's not the dependence we once felt for the rule and for our superiors. Janet, for example, depends on me. And I depend on her."

Koesler was about to say something, but changed his mind. Obviously, Marie had thought this out fully. Undoubtedly prayed over it. He knew he would profit from her conclusions. All he had to do was listen. Sometimes that was not easy.

She concluded her apologia as if she were announcing it to humanity in general rather than as a simple answer to Koesler's simple question: 'Why stay?'

"To me," Marie said, "the religious woman of today must be, fundamentally, what she has always needed to be: well educated and informed, compassionate, living her faith. Only she must be stronger, since much of the support she could once expect from her community, and the straight-forward demands made of her, are now gone. Before, she was supposed to feel compassion without expressing it. Now, she must not only feel distinctly womanly compassion, she must know intuitively how to share love without compromising the chaste life. Her faith must be stronger since she is no longer shielded to convent walls from a skeptical and agnostic world.

"She is also a challenge to the hierarchy since she obviously is qualified in every essential way to equal opportunity in the priesthood. Only the hierarchy's obstinate ignorance keeps her in a secondary subordinate role. Her very existence is a silent challenge the institutional Church must face. Free of family demands, she can be a persistent advocate for the powerless. She is a voice against injustice with a deep desire that oppression of everyone will cease.

"With the old structures left behind, new unlimited boundaries of every human need will be sufficient challenge in her service to Christ and humanity in and through her religious commitment."

She paused and Koesler remained silent. She was finished. It didn't seem there were any more words either of them could say that might add to her statement of purpose. Koesler found himself wishing there were some way her rationale could be published somewhere. In the climate of today's Catholicism, wherein too few could see any point to a religious vocation, hers was a voice that needed to be heard.

After a few moments during which they both reflected on what she had said, Koesler asked, "Before the convent, did you go to a parochial school?"

She smiled at the memory. "Yes. Grade school, high school, then off to Monroe and the convent."

"And IHM blue."

"Yes, and IHM blue."

"Were you like me? That you always wanted the vocation?"

"No, Father, not like that. I'm afraid my class would not have voted me the girl most likely to be a nun."

"Wild?" He was imagining the sort of behavior that would have been described as "wild" in a parochial setting of that era. By today's standards, it would not even be mentioned among minor sinners. He'd even smiled as he broached the word "wild."

But Marie didn't smile for a moment or two. Then a hesitant grin appeared. "Let's just say that conversion is good for the soul. Look what it did for Saint Augustine."

"That's true." For an instant he looked at her in a different light. Even in her middle years she was still most attractive. As a young woman she had undoubtedly been a knockout. It was like seeing actress Loretta Young all dressed up in the traditional nun's habit and regretting that all that beauty and charm was locked up inside countless yards of wool.

There was no time for further speculation in any case. The waitresses began wheeling in the food. Sister Janet invited all to dinner, and all responded eagerly.

Koesler reflected that just twenty-four hours ago, these had been the dramatis personae in Krieg's little psychodrama. The waitresses, the kitchen crew, Sister Janet—they'd all been in on it.

Krieg dead. Murdered. A consummation devoutly to be wished? Banish it from your mind, Koesler, he told himself. Certainly not Christian. Hardly humane. But, given all that had happened in just the last two days, a fairly reasonable conclusion.

Marie did not seem at all surprised when Janet invited her to lead the group in a blessing. Perhaps it had been prearranged.

"Blessed are you, God of all creation," Marie prayed. "Through your goodness we have this nourishment to share. May we share ourselves willingly and generously as You have shared yourself with us."

There was a pause. And everyone said, "Amen."

A nice ecumenical grace, Koesler thought. Yes, that must have been prearranged. No offense to Christian or Jew. Something for everyone.

He regarded the seating arrangement. The three women

again were seated consecutively. Then, clockwise, Winer, Koesler, Benbow, Augustine, and Krieg. Thus Krieg and Winer, this afternoon's adversaries, were seated opposite each other.

The fare was simple. A fruit salad in gelatin, beef broth, lamb, red potatoes, steamed vegetables. Simple but well prepared. Everyone partook of everything and all seemed to enjoy the food.

Conversation was not that enjoyable. Janet and Martha, mostly, attempted to introduce topics, but no verbal balloon stayed aloft. Awkward. It was awkward. But Koesler had expected little else.

Toward the end of the meal, Krieg spoke. "Praise God! You know," he said jovially, "there's one person here we've heard precious little from." Pause. "Father Koesler. Here we were, runnin' off at the mouth all afternoon, and there's the good Father just sittin' there takin' it all in."

If he had intended to embarrass Koesler by singling him out in this less-than-friendly atmosphere, Krieg was succeeding.

"After all," Krieg continued, "you are a bona fide member of this panel. So, Praise God! Let's hear it, Father. Your opinion of religion. Dull or not? I mean basically?" His very tone betrayed flippancy. It was as if the "father of the family" had taken the reins and the conversation was now well in hand.

Koesler, taken by surprise, swallowed injudiciously and started to cough. Winer and Benbow pounded his back. Benbow was about to apply the Heimlich maneuver but Koesler waved him off. Things were getting under control.

Koesler's complexion was florid. And he was embarrassed not only that he'd been singled out by Krieg like a child forced to recite, but also because he had almost choked to death.

"Sorry," he said, as his system returned to normal. "Something got stuck. I'm all right now."

"Well," Krieg declared, "that's a blessing. Praise God!"

"Yes. Well, to the point. When you introduced the supposition, the first thought I had was of all the dull homilies, sermons, religion classes I have been forced to sit through. And I was tempted to agree with your hypothesis. But I must confess, I didn't stay with that thought very long. I can't think of any book as worthy of study, reading, inspiration, or meditation as the Bible. To those of us for whom God is our beginning and our destiny, there isn't anything more exciting than religion.

"So I guess it comes down to what you mean by religion. If you mean religion secondhand, as it's communicated by very poor communicators, I suppose it can be—and is—pretty dreadful and painfully dull.

"Or think of it this way: There is no dull religion, just dull religious communicators."

Koesler expected Krieg to be peeved or at least annoyed. But Krieg was beaming. "Couldn't have said it better myself. Praise God!"

"But, this afternoon . . ." Koesler began.

"This afternoon," Krieg repeated, "this afternoon was salesmanship."

"Salesmanship!" Winer exclaimed.

"Indeed, salesmanship. You must have sensed it . . ." Krieg looked around the table at the others. "Each of us told the students, in the most gracious and benign manner, what we intended to cover during the coming week. We were so benevolent and ingratiating the audience was drifting off to sleep. They needed to be awakened, made eager to get into these workshops. That's the function I served. Woke 'em up.''

''Then you didn't really mean it? About religion being dull?'' Koesler asked.

'' 'Course not.'' Krieg smiled. ''Just like our friend the rabbi here said this afternoon. 'Greatest Story Ever Told!' ''

Did the man ever say what was really on his mind, Koesler wondered. Yet Krieg had just provided an autobiographical footnote. He was in essence a salesman. Probably missed his calling. Should have been a salesman, not an evangelist. On the other hand, Krieg probably wouldn't see a lot of difference between the two.

''Then,'' Koesler said, ''what about the topics of sex and violence and the like? Did you mean what you said about that?''

''Well, now that's another question. Lemmee take your own words, Padre, spoken just a moment ago. As I 'member, you said somethin' about, 'There is no dull religion, just dull religious commentators.' That about right?''

Koesler nodded. He was pretty sure where Krieg was headed.

''Well,'' Krieg said, ''some people were just born boring, poor souls. They're gonna be boring all their blessed lives. Nothin' for it. They're gonna be boring bus drivers or boring sewer workers. They're gonna be boring lovers, husbands, wives, parents. So we can forget them ever bein' a big success at anything, including evangelism.

''But even people with a knack for communication aren't successful just by rollin' out of bed each morning. The salesperson has to have a pitch, a tool—a way of making his service or product attractive to the buyer. And the tool, if it's gonna work, isn't necessarily something the *salesman* prizes.

It's something the *buyer* finds appealing, attractive, compelling, irresistible!"

Krieg paused. His glance moved from one to another of those present as if expecting someone to complete his premise.

Koesler tried supplying a conclusion. "And you believe that what the audience, the viewer, the reader finds compelling and irresistible is violence and sex."

"Graphic violence, explicit sex," Winer added.

Smiling broadly, Krieg turned both palms upward, indicating a self-evident truth. "What sells? Ladies and gentlemen, what does the American public shell out its cash for?"

"Not always," Marie protested, avoiding a direct answer to Krieg's almost rhetorical question. "The public appreciates things done tastefully."

"Such as . . . ?" Krieg challenged.

"In entertainment, information, education?" Winer said. "Lots of things. The classics. Music: Beethoven, Mozart, Brahms, Gershwin, Copland. They still fill concert halls and will till the end of time. The theater: Shakespeare, O'Neill, O'Casey, Miller. Literature: Chaucer, Cooper, Poe, Dickens, James, Wolfe. Television, for God's sake: some of the fine series produced by the BBC. You know the names as well as I. Not all of them lost in the mists of history either. Contemporaries. Lots of them."

It was doubtful that Winer had shaken Krieg. In any case, no one could tell from his continuing smile.

Nearly everyone had finished eating. Dishes were being cleared away. However, because he'd been talking steadily, Krieg was well behind the others. But when the waitress reached him, he indicated he was finished, and his dishes, still containing considerable food, were removed. Dessert and coffee were then served. All the women, none of the men, accepted the apple pie. Only Janet took cream with her coffee.

"You're quite right, Rabbi . . ." Krieg, stirring his coffee in an attempt to cool it, returned to the fray. "I do know the familiar names. But I'm not talking about literature or art that lasts forever. We are dealing with a pop culture." His expression altered to one of sympathy. "Sad as it is to say, still, realistically, we cannot hope that all the books you have written are going to be on people's shelves as long as, say, Shakespeare." A small, consoling chuckle.

"We all know," Krieg continued, "the Bible is the all-time best-seller in the history of the world. I dare say it would be difficult to find an American home—almost impossible to find a hotel room—without one." One more chuckle for the Gideon Society. "And in all these homes and rooms, how many of these Bibles are read?" He left that truly rhetorical question hanging.

"Meanwhile," he went on, "what sort of book does the great unwashed American public buy? Ever see people selecting a book in a supermarket, book chain, airport newsstand? Not *War and Peace*.

"Ever notice the general run of covers publishers put on paperbacks, the type of dustjacket on hardcovers?" Pause— a dramatic pause.

"It all tells us something," he continued. "And we all, deep down, know what it tells us. These are the books publishers count on selling. And this is the packaging they hope will sell them. And that's the market P.G. Press is in, friends. Praise God!"

There was no echo from his listeners.

"And as you four know by this time, I'm sure," Krieg's

tone became almost conspiratorial, "it's the market I've invited each and every one of you to join me in."

Marie gasped as if she'd been trapped by Krieg's discourse. Benbow and Augustine seemed embarrassed.

It was Winer who spoke, and spoke calmly, forcefully and personally. As if, of a sudden, he and Krieg were alone in the room.

"That's right. We've already discovered that each of us was offered a contract with you. And that each of us, after mature consideration and professional advice, has decided not to be associated with you. Our connection with each other, aside from the fact that we share a clerical or religious calling, is that each of us has been approached by you and each of us has rejected your offer.

"It requires no genius to guess this is the reason why you stipulated as a condition of your acceptance that each of us be invited to this workshop. What you have in mind isn't completely clear. But you've got something in mind. Of that there can be little doubt. If I had to guess, it would be that you are going to make one last effort to change our minds and sign us up with you.

"How am I doing?"

Krieg chuckled, and stroked his chin. "Well, Rabbi, you certainly don't write mystery stories for nothing. The only problem is, you make it seem this whole thing was my idea. Not so. I was planning nothing of the sort. No thought of this at all.

"Out of the blue, a man I'd never met, never heard of before, phoned me. Jack Regan had this idea for a writers' conference, a very specialized workshop in mystery novels with a religious setting. Was it so extraordinary, unexpected, that you four should come to mind? Praise God! It was a heaven-sent opportunity to meet you in person and—what else?—give it one more shot. And when heaven sends me an opportunity, I assure you, I take it.

"Now, fortunately, Mr. Regan was very strong on having me participate in this conference. So set on me was he that I was able to establish a few prerequisites. The first, and nonnegotiable, condition was that he secure your presence. And, praise God, he did. And, praise God, here you all are."

Koesler studied the four writers. Something was going on between them and Krieg. Some sort of perceptible bad chemistry. What could it be?

Krieg spread his hands, palms up, on the tabletop. "But there's no harm in this. It's what the American business world labels 'the bottom line.' It's a free country. You don't have to sign with me."

"Right," Winer said. "A free country. We don't have to sign with you. And that's what we've told you. We are not— let me speak as forcefully as I can for one—I am not signing with P.G. Press. How much more clear can I be?"

The smile lost none of its self-assurance. "It's a free country, all right. You have the right to decline, but I have the right to give it another go. Who knows . . ." Krieg spoke slowly and softly, emphasizing each word as he enunciated it. "Who knows? I may just make each of you an offer you cannot refuse!"

There was a protracted, electric silence as the writers and the publisher studied each other. Koesler sensed that Krieg had just thrown down a challenge that the writers at least understood, whether or not they would accept it.

Who would break the silence?

It was David Benbow who spoke through clenched teeth. "I'll see you dead and in—"

"David!" Martha Benbow almost shrieked his name. Her tone not only interrupted, but silenced her husband.

But everyone in the room well understood what was left unsaid. What David Benbow had been going to say was that he would see Krieg dead and in hell before ever signing a contract with Krieg's empire.

Koesler took stock. Krieg's smile had disappeared. In its place was a look of shocked surprise, even, oddly, fear. None of the writers had backed down. Each seemed tacitly to be in general agreement with Benbow. Martha, Janet, and, Koesler presumed, Benbow himself, were deeply shaken.

The silence that followed Benbow's cut-off statement seemed as if it would never be broken. It was as if a gauntlet in the form of a threat had been thrown and it simply lay there with no one willing to either accept or retract the challenge.

Then Martha, clearly mortified, said, "I'm sure . . . I'm certain David did not mean that. He would never . . . could never . . . oh, dear . . ." She was near tears.

Janet cleared her throat. "This has been a long day. There's been a lot of tension . . ." (*A lot of tension I did not anticipate or expect*, she added to herself. *And why should I have to carry this load? I didn't arrange for any of this to happen.*) "I think we just need some time to calm down," she continued. She glanced at her watch. "It's almost time for the movie. I'm sorry, but there seems to be no time for after-dinner drinks. The students will be gathering about now. Why don't we go and relax a bit? That should help us wind down. Tomorrow we can start fresh."

She was grateful there were no general sessions scheduled for tomorrow. The faculty would not convene except for meals. She resolved to be on her guard lest another altercation break out during mealtime. Maybe she'd be able to enlist

Marie's help in peacemaking. But after this evening she could not be certain. About anything.

There was no immediate response to Janet's invitation that they take in the movie.

Then Martha, somewhat more composed, said, "I think that's a fine idea, Sister. Come on, David, let's go see the film."

Benbow shook his head. "Not in the mood, I'm afraid, dear. You go ahead. I think I'll take a bit of a walk. I'll see you in our room later."

"Reverend?" Janet addressed Krieg.

"What?" Krieg had been lost in his own thoughts.

"The movie. Would you like to join us at the movie?" Janet explained.

"Oh, no, I think not. I'll just wander up to my room. A bit tired. Suddenly a bit tired."

"Up to your room?" Janet repeated. "You're not returning to the hotel for the night?"

"Think not. Not worth the trouble. I'll stay here tonight. But no, no movie. Thanks just the same."

"Father?" Janet addressed Augustine.

"Not tonight. I'm sort of sleepy."

"Rabbi?"

"I want to go over my notes for tomorrow's classes. I'd better do that before I get too tired."

"Marie?" Janet had hoped that she could get at least a few to join her. She knew the students would be pleased if the faculty were to join in some of the extracurricular events.

"I've got some correspondence I've got to catch up on, Jan. Sorry."

"Father?" With Koesler, Janet was down to her last chance.

"Matter of fact I'd like that. It's almost time, isn't it?"

Koesler glanced at his watch. "Why don't you and Mrs. Benbow go ahead? I'd like to finish my coffee. Would that be all right?"

"Certainly, Father." Janet was grateful for some company no matter the delay. "Martha, why don't we go now? Father Koesler can join us in a few minutes."

With that the group went its separate ways. Left seated at the table, while the waitresses cleared dishes, were Koesler and Krieg. Each had about half a cup of coffee left.

Koesler went to the hot plate where the pot of coffee was kept. He brought the pot to the table, filled his cup, and gestured toward Krieg, who nodded; Koesler filled the other cup as well.

"That was a bit of a surprise," Koesler said.

"Father Benbow? I'm sure he spoke only in the heat of the moment. I'm sure he didn't mean what he said literally."

"I'm glad you're taking it that way," Koesler said. "I agree: He didn't mean it."

"I must confess he surprised me though . . . I mean, an Episcopal priest!"

"Violence!" Koesler said.

"Hmmm?" Krieg missed the point.

"Religion, violence, sex." Koesler could not suppress a grin.

Krieg smiled in return. It was the first time Koesler had seen a genuine, as opposed to a plastic, smile from Krieg.

"Ah, yes," Krieg said. "Religion, violence, sex. Seems there's been a lot of talk about that lately."

"For some reason, I hate to say this, but I kind of anticipated that would be a prominent topic of conversation. Having read one of the books you published and then reading up on stories about you and your philosophy of publishing, I just guessed, what with the writers who were invited, I guessed we'd be talking a bit about the subject.''

''Perceptive,'' Krieg commented.

Koesler removed from a jacket pocket a newspaper clipping much the worse for wear. ''Since I thought the subject would inevitably come up sometime during the week, I brought this along with me.''

Krieg seemed amused. ''Does that clipping go back to the invention of the printing press?''

''Only to March 1989, from *The New York Times*,'' Koesler said.

''It's not holding its age very well. Looks like it's about to give up the ghost, as it were.''

''That's because I've used it in some homilies and talks. I think it's going to be very relevant during this workshop. I didn't want to spring it on you with no warning. Mind if I read part of it to you now?''

Krieg shrugged, took a sip of coffee, and waited. Clearly, permission had been granted.

''The occasion,'' Koesler began, ''was the American Film Institute's seventeenth annual Life Achievement Award presentation to Gregory Peck. What I'm going to quote is one of the remarks he made. All right with you?''

Krieg's smile reverted to plastic.

''Well,'' Koesler said, ''the article noted that the actor, in his acceptance speech, went beyond the usual gratitude and platitudes. It quotes him as saying''—here Koesler read from the clipping—''There has been a lot of glamorous financial news in the papers lately. Multimedia conglomerates . . .

'' 'If these Mount Everests of the financial world are going to labor and bring forth still more pictures with people being blown to bits with bazookas and automatic assault rifles, with no gory detail left unexploited; if they are going to encourage anxious, ambitious actors, directors, writers and producers to continue their assault on the English language by reducing the vocabularies of their characters to half a dozen words, with one colorful but overused Anglo-Saxon verb and one unbeautiful Anglo-Saxon noun covering just about every situation, then I would like to suggest that they stop and think about this: Millions is not the whole ball game, fellows. Pride of workmanship is worth more. Artistry is worth more.' "

Koesler carefully refolded the relic and returned it to his pocket.

"That's it?" Krieg said.

"Didn't you find that a rather impressive statement?"

"Gregory Peck is a great actor. He is a larger-than-life presence."

Koesler seemed puzzled. "I agree. So, don't you consider that an impressive statement? And, more to the point, isn't that a refutation of your stand?"

"I think not, good Father. As time goes on, it seems we are never going to see eye to eye, which is all right. As someone said earlier this evening, it's a free country."

Koesler was bewildered. "But, how . . . how do you respond to the challenge in Gregory Peck's concluding words?" Koesler did not need to refer to the clipping again; from repeated readings he knew the words by heart. " '. . . stop and think about this: Millions is not the whole ball game, fellows. Pride of workmanship is worth more. Artistry is worth more.' "

Krieg finished his coffee and returned the cup to the saucer in a gesture of finality. "Father, good Father, did you ever notice how frequently it happens that the one who tells you that money isn't important, has already made his?" Krieg paused to make certain his point was taken. "Now, I wouldn't argue that artistry and pride aren't desirable. But tell that to Mozart. One of the greatest artists of all time. Who starved, was penniless, and whose bones lie—God knows where—in a pauper's grave."

"Yes, but—"

"Excuse me, good Father. By and large, the writers under contract to P.G. Press are not Hemingways or Fitzgeralds. They'd like to be but they never will be. And, truth be known, I'm getting a bit tired of being cast as the heavy in this scenario. Granted, the writers at this conference are a cut above the majority we have under contract. What's more, they carry the ring of authenticity. And that is not unimportant baggage. But were they to sign with us, with our promotional machinery, they would increase—double—their sales."

"But they would have to conform to your . . . style—no?"

Krieg spread his hands. "We would deliver sales such as they've only dreamed about."

Koesler tried his coffee. It was lukewarm. He nudged cup and saucer toward a waitress. This was the last of the waitresses and these were the last of the dishes to be removed.

"Then," Koesler said, "I take it nothing would dissuade you from continuing to leave no gory detail unexploited, no unhappy Anglo-Saxonism unused, no intimate erotic detail undescribed?"

Krieg shrugged. "As I have said, it sells."

"Well," Koesler rose, "I guess we agree on one point anyway."

"Uh?"

"We're not going to see eye to eye."

As Koesler left the dining room, Krieg gave him the benefit of one last large plastic smile.

* * *

A classic, Koesler reminded himself, was enduring. Of course there were other qualifications, but, among other things, classics lasted.

Certainly Chesterton's writings endured. And, although he considered it an avocation, his "Father Brown" series certainly proved to be his most popular work. As far as Koesler was concerned, the "Father Brown" movie he'd just seen pretty well captured the spirit of the original. A tribute to the artistry of Alec Guinness.

It brought to mind anew Gregory Peck's words: "Artistry is worth more. Pride of workmanship is worth more. Millions is not the whole ball game, fellows."

The more he thought about it, the more Koesler admired the resolution of the four writers at this conference. The bottom line, rationale for just about everything in today's world, was that both the writers and Krieg were on the mark.

Krieg was right, in that there was a market for sleaze in America. Try as they might, authorities would never totally eliminate a travesty such as pornography. There was a market for it. Trash remains popular on television and in the movies. There was a market for it.

How much of a market was another question. In much of the Western world, at least, markets were established through packaging and merchandising. Was popular taste that bad? Was there an inherent attraction to garbage? Or were those who package and market the product merely uncommonly adept at selling? Moot questions?

Koesler was convinced that Klaus Krieg was indeed a superior salesman. He had packaged and marketed Christianity, to his own immense profit. He had packaged and marketed religious literature, to his own considerable profit.

Koesler strongly believed that it wasn't so much that there was a natural market for exploitive violence and sex as there were skilled salespeople who created and promoted that market. But there *was*, unquestionably, a market out there. To that extent, Krieg was correct.

On the other hand, the writers were correct. There was a market for artistry and pride of workmanship. Granted, it was not nearly as easy to reach that market. But it was there. Carefully crafted music, theater, literature, television, art; works of dedication lasted. Even contemporary art proved the point. As long as civilization endured, the music of Gershwin, Porter, Rodgers, Kern would be played and sung. Forever, companies would perform *South Pacific, Oklahoma!, My Fair Lady*, and the like. Acid rock would fade to an obsolete and forgotten phenomenon of the second half of the twentieth century.

The writers were to be admired in their resistance to the salesmanship of Klaus Krieg. The question was: Could they persevere? Could they continue to resist Krieg's considerable prowess?

The weather was growing brisk. It was becoming a typical nippy Michigan autumn evening, Koesler had decided on the walk through Marygrove's campus. Without a topcoat, he was getting a chill.

As he entered the Cadillac building, Koesler realized he had not seen David Benbow during the walk. But it had been hours since Benbow had proposed taking an after-dinner walk. He must have returned to his room by now. Probably retired for the night.

Contemplating bed himself, Koesler decided to see if he could get a nightcap. He headed down the empty corridor to the dining room. Strange how threatening a large institution can seem when it's empty.

Koesler entered the dining room and turned on the light. He was vaguely aware something was amiss. But what? Nothing. Surely nothing.

It was an after-dinner drink he wanted. There was no hint of a liqueur in the cache supplied by the college. He needed access to Krieg's supply. But that was under lock and key.

Wait . . . He glanced at the cupboard holding Krieg's private stock. The cabinet door was ajar. Odd.

Something was wrong, very wrong. He looked around the room. Cloths covered all the tables except the one the faculty had used; that had no tablecloth. The linen should have been laid preparatory to tomorrow's breakfast.

He moved toward the bare table. The tablecloth was on the floor, together with the flatware, some shattered china, and a body.

Another game? Another little psychodrama?

Koesler thought not.

He bent down for a closer look. He could detect no blood. There also was no pulse.

Now he knew what it was he had sensed on entering the room. In his priestly duties, Koesler had become familiar with the distinctive odor. It was the odor of death.

This time there would be no mistakes. He would go right to the top and call his friend, Inspector Walter Koznicki.

The question that baffled Koesler as he rang up was, if this was indeed a murder, why would anyone want to kill Rabbi Irving Winer?

13

TECHNICIANS WERE ALL over the place. To the unpracticed eye, it seemed to be chaos. But, as in an ant colony, there was a distinct and definite purpose to everything. Lights popped as photographers captured the scenes that the detectives wanted preserved on film. Measurements were taken, samples gathered, and people interrogated. Questions! Endless questions!

Standing to one side, conversing as they observed the preservation and enshrining of the scene of the crime, were Father Koesler and Inspector Koznicki.

Koesler was bringing Koznicki up-to-date on what had preceded the death.

"Then, when you came into the dining room tonight, you found the body of Rabbi Winer. And you were the first to find the body, Father?" Koznicki asked.

"That's right," Koesler said. "At least I presume I was first. If I hadn't decided I could do with a nightcap, probably nobody would have discovered the poor man until tomorrow morning."

"And you went to Reverend Krieg's private supply?"

"I didn't really think about that until I got to the dining room. As I told you, Inspector, the college put in a wet bar with most of the standard liquors: gin, whiskey, Scotch, vermouth, beer—but no cordials. What I had in mind was a touch of cognac or Benedictine.

"Well, I was at the door of the dining room when it occurred to me that only Krieg had the liqueurs and he kept his private stock under lock and key. That's why I was surprised to see the door of Krieg's cabinet open."

"The cabinet belonged to Reverend Krieg?"

"Not really. It, along with all the furnishings, belongs to the college. But Krieg had appropriated it. It appears to be the only cabinet in the room that can be locked."

"I see." Koznicki briefly answered a question from one of the officers. "Then someone left the cabinet unlocked?"

"Not necessarily," Koesler said. "Before dinner this evening—before Krieg showed up—Rabbi Winer tried the door of the cabinet, to see if it had been left unlocked. It hadn't. But Sister Janet told us—and everyone was present to hear her—that an extra key to the cabinet was kept"—Koesler pointed—"just inside that door. And it must have been that key that was used; after I called you, I checked it and it wasn't on its hook. And your men found a key under the rabbi's body."

Furrows appeared in Koznicki's forehead. "But . . . but what could have been the purpose of locking the cabinet when another key was readily available?"

"Games, Inspector, games. We have been playing lots of games ever since this group assembled. It has everything to do with what I told you about how Krieg wanted these four writers in his stable. I think it is certain that that is the principal purpose for this writers' conference."

"Oh?"

"Yes. Ostensibly four successful writers and one successful publisher assemble for a workshop. One should naturally conclude that the purpose is to help amateur writers to get published to their heart's content. But in this instance, seeing as how Krieg in effect set the whole thing up, the purpose of the conference is to give Krieg one last shot at getting writers he wants under contract to him. Thus we had games: the psychodrama; Krieg's having a suite downtown as well as a room here, his own menu when he doesn't want to eat the food we're eating, his own liquor supply—that sort of thing. I think the Reverend Krieg has been trying to impress these four people that he is in control of everything, including, by inference, them.''

"Interesting."

"Yes. And I've told you of the writers' reaction to all this. Extreme hostility! To a degree that has surprised me."

"Indeed." Koznicki answered another whispered question, then turned back to Koesler. "One would think that if a writer did not wish to sign a contract, that would be it. Even if the publisher were to be more persistent—as Reverend Krieg evidently has been—still, there should not be all this tension and talk of murder."

Koesler shook his head. "But, that, Inspector, is what has indeed happened."

At that moment, Sergeant Phil Mangiapane approached Koznicki. "Doc Moellmann thinks it was cyanide, Inspector."

One eyebrow raised slightly. "Unusual for the medical examiner to give an opinion so quickly," said Koznicki.

"He didn't say for sure it was cyanide. He thinks it is. But if you ask me, he's pretty damn sure—uh, 'scuse me, Father. The M.E.'s got this glint in his eye and he's giggling a little bit. If I had a bottom dollar, I'd put it on cyanide."

Koznicki suppressed a grin. Obviously, Mangiapane had grown accustomed to Moellmann's many eccentricities. If the M.E. was relishing this, he was, indeed, pretty sure.

"What happened," Mangiapane continued, "was that the rabbi was sitting at the table when he took the drink. The Doc says he must have gone into instant convulsions . . ." The detective referred to his notes. "Then he probably clutched the table and the cloth was dragged off the table when he slipped off the chair and onto the floor. Doc says he was dead within four or five minutes."

"What was the rabbi drinking?" Koznicki asked.

"Frangelico," Mangiapane said, and immediately returned to his notes. "Doc says whoever put the stuff in picked the right kind of booze: Both the Frangelico and the cyanide have an almond odor. So the guy wouldn't think anything odd about the aroma of the Frangelico as he opened it and poured it. "Oh"—he began reading his notes verbatim— "and Doc says the condition of the body also suggests cyanide. He says the lividity is the clue. The guy looks all red. Doc says the poison paralyzes the enzymes in the body that allow the transfer of oxygen from the blood to the cells. The body is full of oxygen, but the oxygen is unused." Mangiapane looked particularly pleased with himself.

"Is there any chance any of the other bottles have been poisoned?" Koznicki asked.

"Doc doesn't think so. There's no special odor to any of the rest of the booze. But he's takin' it all downtown for tests. And, of course, he'll do the autopsy on the rabbi. But, like I say, he's pretty sure."

"Hmmm," Koznicki said, "I wonder—if Dr. Moellmann is correct—I wonder how the killer knew to tamper with just the Frangelico specifically."

"I have an idea," Koesler said. "Last night after dinner, Krieg offered each of us a drink from his supply. Of all the choices possible—and I think he's got one of everything and probably back-up bottles of each—"

"He's right, Inspector," Mangiapane interjected, "not only one of everything but the best of everything."

"Yes," Koesler agreed. "Well, Winer chose Frangelico. And, now that I think of it, he was followed by the Reverend Krieg. So, even anyone who hadn't known beforehand, could, if he or she paid any attention last night, have noted that Winer and Krieg favored the Frangelico. It just so happened that I was standing off to one side, and since I was not conversing with anyone, I was able to observe what everyone else was drinking."

"Excuse me, Father," Mangiapane said, "but Krieg wasn't the one who was murdered; Winer was."

"The supposition at this moment, Sergeant," Koznicki said, "is that the Reverend Krieg was the intended victim and that Rabbi Winer was simply at the wrong place at the wrong time drinking the wrong liqueur."

"Oh . . ." Mangiapane felt foolish.

Koesler wanted to explain and, at the same time dispel, Mangiapane's embarrassment. "You weren't here, Sergeant, when I was telling the Inspector what's been going on here over the past couple of days."

For Mangiapane's benefit, Koesler recounted in some detail the interaction that had taken place, omitting only that which Tully and Mangiapane had learned when they had responded to the false alarm last night.

"So, you see, Sergeant," Koesler summed up, "while there has been a great deal of animosity shown by the writers to Krieg, it has been Krieg's overt aim to get any or all of the writers under contract to his publishing house.

"Although I can't really envision any of these religious people actually committing the sin of murder, from everything that's been said, a plausible case could be made that one or another of them might actually try to kill Krieg.

"And, as for the possibility that Krieg might be involved, the last thing in this world that he would do would be to kill one of the writers he was trying to sign."

Mangiapane had followed the discussion attentively; he now proceeded to summarize. "So," he said, "the idea is that someone put the poison in the Frangelico thinking that Krieg would drink it—based on the fact that that was his liqueur of choice last night. But, before Krieg gets to the bottle, Winer takes a drink, and that's all she wrote." He seemed content.

"It was not a bad plan, as I see it," Koznicki said. "The killer might think that he had a fail-safe scheme. After he— or she—poisoned the Frangelico, he—let us simplify things— would figure that he would be present after meals when one would expect liqueur to be served. If anyone other than Reverend Krieg approached or accepted the Frangelico, the killer would be able to take some action—drop the bottle, or 'accidentally' spill the contents of the glass or some such. But, as you said, no after-dinner drinks were offered due to the argument. Then, if it so happened that the Reverend Krieg would stop off for a nightcap alone and drink the poison"— Koznicki spread his hands—"so much the better. But what the killer did not foresee was that someone else would drop in unexpectedly, use the extra key and, unfortunately take the fatal drink."

"And that," Koesler said, "is what must have happened.

Rabbi Winer must have come back downstairs from his room later in the evening. I can well imagine that he might have had trouble getting to sleep. Of all of us, he undoubtedly had the most hectic day. He probably thought that a drink or two would calm him down and help him get some sleep.''

"So," Mangiapane continued the scenario, "he comes in. He's the one who checked before dinner to see whether the cabinet was unlocked. He's the one who was specifically told about the whereabouts of the duplicate key. So he goes directly to the key, unlocks the cabinet, pours himself a small glass of Frangelico, sits at the table, and . . .

"He probably downed the glass in a gulp, went into convulsions, clutched at the cloth, and pulled it with him as he fell to the floor. And that's how we found him.''

"And," Koznicki concluded with a tone of regret, "the one who poisoned the liqueur was not there to intervene.''

"And so he became a murderer," Mangiapane said.

Koznicki looked up as from a reverie. "He or she was a murderer from the outset. Except that the real victim was not the intended victim. Which means, of course . . .'' He gave no indiction of completing the remark.

Koesler completed it. ". . . the intended victim—Krieg—still lives. Will the killer try again? Or, now that everyone has been alerted, will the deed be aborted or postponed?''

"Good and relevant questions, Father," Koznicki said. "I do not think the person we are dealing with is the type to be permanently dissuaded because of one failure. There must have been sufficient motivation. It required too much deliberation—courage, if you will—to dare the deed in the first place. I think there will be another attempt. We must be vigilant.''

"Excuse me," Mangiapane said, "I've got to get back to Zoo."

Koznicki and Koesler were left alone with their private thoughts.

"I specifically wanted Lieutenant Tully on this case," Koznicki said finally.

"He's your best, isn't he," Koesler said.

"There are many fine officers in the Homicide Division."

Koesler smiled. "But he is your best, isn't he?"

Koznicki smiled back. "Yes."

"Do you anticipate this case being that difficult to solve?"

"I have no idea. Only time will provide that answer. It is not the difficulty in itself that will be the problem. It is the victim. It is," Koznicki made a small but encompassing gesture, "the setting."

"I'm afraid I don't understand."

"There may be a great number of murders in the city of Detroit, but we do not as a rule kill members of the clergy."

Koesler's eyes widened in understanding. "The image!"

"Precisely. The city administration will be most eager to have this case closed as quickly as possible. The media will have a field day with this story. A visiting rabbi murdered in a Catholic college at a workshop given to the study of religious murder mysteries!"

"Of course. Put those ingredients together and the story almost writes itself. So that's why you assigned the case to Lieutenant Tully."

Koznicki nodded. "He will have all the help he needs or wants."

"This is sort of like that case years ago, when we first met, isn't it? Remember: when those priests and nuns were being murdered by that demented man who left a rosary as his calling card.''

Koznicki grimaced. "How could any of us forget that? But, yes, there is a similarity. Again it was a case of who was being killed—priests, nuns, save the mark! Then as now, the city's reaction was to do everything possible to expedite a solution. And, again, Father, due to the nature of this case, I would very much appreciate it if you would give us the benefit of your observations—in a most unofficial capacity of course. If that is not asking too much?''

"Of course, Inspector. But I don't know that I'll be of much help.''

"Nonetheless, if you please?''

"Certainly.''

Koznicki was not playing a hunch. Over the years he had come to rely on Father Koesler in cases such as this. Whenever Catholicism was introduced into a murder investigation, Koznicki could depend on Koesler to provide a unique contribution toward the solution.

Koesler had the background. He'd been a Detroit priest for the past thirty-five years. He had ties to and easy familiarity with most of the priests and many of the nuns of the Archdiocese of Detroit. He was at home in the old Church as well as the new. He kept up with theological developments. Thus, when there was an understandable gap in the knowledge of things Catholic on the part of the police, Koesler was able to fill in that gap nicely.

Beyond that, Koznicki had learned that, despite the priest's demurrers, Koesler had an uncommonly keen eye for detail. His observance of Krieg's choice of Frangelico as an after-dinner drink was an excellent example. Koesler's powers of observation had been demonstrated in any number of investigations over the past several years.

Besides these very good reasons, Koznicki wanted Koesler in the inner circle of this case for the simple fact that the two enjoyed each other's company.

Mangiapane returned. "Father, Zoo . . . er . . . Lieutenant Tully wants—uh, would like you—in the room across the hall—uh, now."

"Okay," Koesler glanced at Koznicki.

"I will just come along too," said the Inspector.

Tully had not requested Koznicki's presence. But Mangiapane well knew the department's pecking order. "Yes, sir!" he said fearlessly.

14

OF THOSE WHO'D been invited, Koesler was the last to arrive.

The room held himself, Koznicki, Mangiapane, Tully, Janet, Marie, David, and Martha Benbow, Augustine, and Krieg. This was the first Koesler had seen of Krieg since the murder. His appearance left little doubt that he'd been badly shaken.

Koznicki immediately motioned Tully into the corridor, although not out of Koesler's line of vision. He could see that the Inspector was addressing Tully in what, for Koznicki, was an animated manner. Koesler guessed the two detectives were bringing each other up-to-date on what they had discovered to this moment.

While they conversed, Koesler, affecting nonchalance, studied the others in the room. To a person, everyone appeared to be very struck, as well they all might be, at the murder of a confrere, even though they had known him but briefly. The silence was total and strained.

By far, Krieg seemed the most affected of all. He was so pallid he looked as if he might faint at any moment. And gone, completely gone, was any vestige of the patented smile. The smart money had it that Krieg had just escaped a sudden and unexpected death. And his escape was no more than an accident, a fluke. If Rabbi Winer had not known there was an alternate key to the cabinet, if he had not suddenly gotten a thirst for a nightcap, the Reverend Klaus ("Blitz") Krieg would now be headed downtown. Not to the Westin Hotel but to the morgue. It was enough to give any person pause. And it certainly had reached Krieg.

Out of the corner of his eye, Koesler noticed movement; Koznicki and Tully reentered the room. Their expressions gave inscrutability new definition. Koznicki remained in the background. Tully seated himself on an undraped table. Although this, another comparatively small dining room, was filled with tables and chairs, there was no sign it had been used for dining—or any other purpose—for a long while.

"Ladies and gentlemen," Tully began, "what appears to have happened is that a bottle of Frangelico liqueur was poisoned. The substance used appears to be cyanide. There can be no doubt that whoever poisoned the liqueur intended to kill someone. We believe the intended victim was Reverend Krieg."

At the mention of his name, Krieg's complexion grew even more ashen. Koesler had not thought this possible.

"We don't know," Tully continued, "exactly when the liqueur was poisoned, but we can narrow it down a bit. Since two of your group—Reverend Krieg and Rabbi Winer—drank from that bottle last evening, we know there was nothing wrong with the liqueur at that time."

"Excuse me, Lieutenant," Benbow said, "but how do you know that? Is there a hidden camera someplace in that room?"

For a moment Tully enjoyed the luxury of wishing that room *had* been outfitted with a hidden camera. It would make this a much easier investigation if all the police had to do was run the film and watch the murderer poison the liqueur. But life, particularly a policeman's life, was tougher than that. Besides, Tully was in no hurry for a society where Big Brother watched everything everyone did at all times.

"We have the testimony of an eyewitness, reliable, who saw Krieg and Winer pour and consume drinks from that bottle. There may have been others who saw the same. The point is, one survivor is all we need to know that, at least at that time, the bottle was free of poison."

"Just a minute, Lieutenant," Augustine said. "What about the possibility that an amount of the poison insufficient to cause immediate death was used? That way it could have a cumulative effect. The rabbi might have gotten a small amount of cyanide last night. Then tonight, the second drink—or maybe he had several—would have killed him. If that were the case, the liqueur might have been poisoned even before last night." Augustine seemed inordinately proud of the point.

Tully, expressionless, regarded the monk for a few moments. "I know of no way anyone can measure a dose of cyanide that will kill only on the second drink—or not on the first. You're probably thinking of cases where arsenic has been added to food in very small quantities over a considerable period of time.

"Anyway, we will be testing the liqueur to see how much poison was in it. Judging from the coloration of the body, it was a healthy dose. Although"—Tully almost but not quite smiled at his inadvertent use of the word "healthy" to describe a fatal dose of poison—"a little cyanide goes a long way."

Augustine seemed to physically retreat within himself.

"That brings us to tonight. Sometime between last night's dinner and late this evening someone poisoned the liqueur. It was not unrealistic to expect that later last evening, or after dinner this evening, or surely sometime during this week, Reverend Krieg would have another drink of his favorite liqueur. If someone else were to reach for the Frangelico as an after-dinner liqueur, whoever poisoned it would be able to block its use—by 'accidentally' spilling the contents or dropping the bottle, for instance. Obviously, no one, least of all the killer, anticipated that anyone besides Krieg would return at night and, in effect, break into the cabinet."

"Just a minute, Lieutenant . . ." The interruption this time came from Janet. "You seem to be saying . . . you're implying that one of us here is the guilty party. And I resent that. I deeply resent that!"

"Somebody put poison in a drink. It had to be someone with motive, capability, and opportunity."

"Yes," Janet replied, "but we are not alone on campus. There are many students boarding here temporarily during the conference."

"We know that," Tully said. "They're in . . ." He checked his notes. ". . . the Florent Gillet Student Residence. But of the six campus security guards, two were assigned to this building, Cadillac Hall, and three were at the Student Residence. And all of them agree that no one left the residence this evening. And no one entered Cadillac Hall tonight except Reverend Benbow, who took a walk and then returned. No one left the campus after Krieg's assistant drove out in the limo, presumably after the Reverend dismissed him."

Krieg nodded weakly.

"Besides, we're also looking for motive. And from what's

been said among yourselves over the past couple of days, it seems as if there might be plenty of motive right here in this room."

Tully might have added that he did not fathom the intensity of the writers' animosity toward Krieg. But he was going to make it his business to damn well understand what was at the core of it just as quickly as possible.

"Now," Tully continued, "the Medical Examiner tells us that Rabbi Winer died sometime between 8:00 and 10:00 this evening. I would appreciate it if each of you could tell me where you were between those hours. Let's start with Father Koesler."

"Me!" Koesler was clearly startled. "But you know—"

"For the record, Father. Everyone."

"Well, I was . . . I was at the movie."

"From beginning to end?"

"From beginning to end. That's right."

"Anyone see you there?"

Koesler almost laughed. "I'd say so. Sister Janet was strong about making our presence known to the students so they could see that at least part of the faculty would be with them even when not required to be. So the three of us sat together at the front of the auditorium."

"The three of you?"

"Mrs. Benbow, Sister Janet, and I."

"None of you left the theater at any time?"

"No."

"Father Augustine?"

"I went to my room right after dinner and stayed there until I was called down here after they found the body."

"Anyone who can corroborate that?"

"I was in my room, alone. No, no one can verify . . . but
I resent—"

"Reverend Benbow?"

"Well, as you've already mentioned, I took a walk after
dinner. And then I returned to this building and went up to
my . . . uh . . . our room."

"Anyone see you?"

"The guards. They saw me leave and then return."

"It was a short walk. No more than half an hour at most.
That leaves plenty of time you were in the building. All that
time you were by yourself?"

"I'm afraid so. Martha was at the movie."

"I see. Sister Marie?"

"Lieutenant, I don't see the purpose of this. Let's say your
hypothesis is true and that the liqueur was poisoned sometime after dinner last evening. That leaves all of that time—
from after dinner yesterday until sometime between 8:00 and
10:00 tonight—for the murderer to act. That's what . . . better than twenty-four hours. Why, then, are you so eager to
know what we were doing for a few hours tonight?"

"Narrowing it down, Sister. You'll remember that after
dinner last night you went through the psychodrama that
Reverend Krieg arranged. Krieg and the kitchen attendants
were in the dining room constantly until you returned to
'view the body.' Then you all were together in one of the
classrooms until I came. After which you all retired. And,
because of all the commotion, the head of the campus security force called five of the six guards into this building.
They say there was no further movement throughout the
building the rest of last night.

"Then during the day today, people have been in and out
of the kitchen and dining room all day long. It's not likely

someone who had to get a key from an adjacent room, open a cabinet, find the specific bottle, and then carefully pour in the poison—it's not likely the killer would have chanced being seen doing this by all the people who were milling about this area through the day.

"No, the best opportunity the killer had was after dinner this evening. All the excitement of last night was over. Things were very quiet and, as we are learning, no one will admit to being in this area. On top of that, after dinner everyone announced where they planned to spend the evening. Three of you to the movie, one for a walk, and the rest of you to your rooms. It was the perfect time for one of you to return and pour the poison."

Tully paused, but Marie appeared to have nothing further to say.

"So," Tully said, "Sister Marie, your whereabouts from 8:00 to 10:00 this evening?"

Marie seemed to sigh, but it was inaudible. "I'm afraid my case is a carbon copy of Father Augustine's evening. I went to my room and stayed there . . . catching up on some correspondence." She brightened. "I have the letters I wrote if you want to see them."

Tully shook his head. "You could be a fast writer. You could have written them anytime. Any outside verification?"

Marie lowered her eyes and shook her head.

Tully nodded once, concluding one phase and beginning another.

"I think it would be good," Tully addressed Janet, "if you would continue with this workshop."

"Lieutenant," Janet said, "as the resident host of this conference there's nothing I'd like better than to proceed. But what about Reverend Krieg? We can't let anything happen to him. And from what you've said I have to assume that his life is still threatened.''

"That depends," Tully said. "The only way we can create a safe environment for you, Reverend Krieg, is to keep you under lock and key in a safe place with police presence and protection.''

"I'd have to stay in my room?" The mere fact someone had addressed him personally seemed to have awakened something within Krieg. His color began to return.

"Something very much like that, yes," Tully replied.

Krieg pondered that for a moment. "No, I won't do that. Out of the question.''

"Then we'll do our best, but it can't be perfect. Now, about continuing the conference. Are you all willing?''

"Funny," Benbow said, "we had this same choice last night when we wondered whether to continue the conference after some heated words had been exchanged. And the odd thing is that it was Rabbi Winer who said something about having to go on. To see how this would end. And now, this is how it ended for him: He's gone.''

Tully gave them a few moments to consider their choice.

"Reverend Krieg is the one at risk," Marie said. "If he's willing, I'm sure the rest of us will go along.''

Another pause. Tully would wait as long as necessary for them to decide.

"I'm willing," Krieg said, quietly.

"Then so am I," Marie.

"And I," Benbow.

"All right," Augustine.

"Good," Tully. "Then the next order of business is that each of you will be interviewed by one of our officers.''

"Now?" Janet said. "Lieutenant, it's late, and these people will have to work tomorrow in an extremely trying atmosphere. Couldn't we—"

"Sister," Tully interrupted, "this is a homicide investigation. The investigation has top priority. We'll ask you all to cooperate and give your statements now." There was something about the way he emphasized, "now," that made it clear that the time frame was non-negotiable.

There were no further objections.

"One thing more," Tully said, "we will want to search your rooms. All of you."

"No you don't! No you don't!" Augustine was vehement. "That's going a bit far. We know better. You can't do that without a search warrant."

Tully regarded him, then said, "If you insist on one, we'll get one."

"You'll have to show probable cause before a judge will issue one," Marie said.

"After all that's been said here, the things you've said to each other in the presence of witnesses, the threats," Tully said, "it shouldn't be difficult at all to convince a judge."

Tully waited, but there were no further arguments. "Of course we'll have to wonder why you are so reluctant to have a police search. But that's up to you. You can give us permission to search or you can tough it out. Up to you."

After a few moments, Marie said, "Very well."

Benbow, with a glance, checked to see if his wife had any objection. Seeing none, he said, "You have our permission."

Augustine seemed to be fighting the issue within himself. "Oh, all right. But you can be sure the people back in Massachusetts are going to hear about what a police state you have here in Detroit."

Tully ignored the virtually undeliverable threat. "Good. Now, please, all of you stay where you are. The officers will be here very shortly to take your statements."

Tully did not leave a happy group behind him. But as he, Koznicki, and Koesler left the room Tully felt the emotional charge of commencing the investigation. It was off the ground. The chase was on to discover whodunit.

He quickly dispatched officers, some to interrogate the faculty, some to search their rooms.

"It was fortunate they backed away from their insistence on a warrant," said Koznicki.

"Yes," Tully said. "That could have taken some time. I'm sure we wouldn't have any trouble getting one. But we'd have had to limit ourselves to whatever areas we listed in the warrants. Now we can bring to light anything we happen to find."

"What did you think of the session with them just now?" Koznicki asked.

"Interesting," Tully said. "They're amateurs, of course, but they are familiar with police procedure. Probably done their research well. But one thing puzzles me."

"And that?" Koznicki asked.

"They're not turning on each other."

"Not turning on each other?" Koesler said.

"Sister Janet just doesn't figure in that group. Martha Benbow might be a stronger suspect if only on behalf of her husband. But, then, she was at the movie during the 8:00 to 10:00 time of death.

"That leaves Benbow, Augustine, and Marie. Each of them seems to have some kind of grudge against Krieg. Only we don't know why. It's gotta be more, lots more, than that they just don't want to write for him. Hell, all they've got to do is say 'no.' Even if they have to say it more than once. God, it's a free country. Krieg can ask them pretty please as often as he wants. And they can say, 'Get lost, creep,' as often as they want.

"I think, first thing, we gotta find out what's the kicker. Why are they so sore-assed about it?

"But the most puzzling thing is that they're not going after each other. I gave them every chance to jump on each other. Augustine could say Marie or Benbow did this or that, which makes them more likely suspects. Or Benbow could say Augustine or Marie did such and so, which turns the spotlight on them. But no; they stuck together. When one agrees to be interrogated, they all agree. When one agrees to a search, they all agree. It doesn't make a hell of a lot of sense. But it will," he added, "it will."

"The statements they made, the questions they asked," Koesler said, "didn't you find them rather unusual?"

"Unusual?" Koznicki repeated.

"For one thing," Koesler said, "I know that without their consent you wouldn't have been able to search their rooms without a warrant. But I didn't know about 'probable cause'— that you wouldn't be able to get a judge to issue a warrant without convincing him that there was reason to believe they could be guilty of a crime and that the search was necessary."

"Yeah," Tully said. "Well, like I said, they're amateurs. They've done their homework; probably learned a lot from research. That's good news and bad news. Maybe they can be helpful if they pay attention and let us know what they think, what they suspect, what they see and hear. On the other hand, they are just as likely to get in the way."

"And one thing we must never overlook," Koznicki said. "One of them killed a man."

"Yeah," Tully agreed.

"If you don't mind," said Koesler, "I have one more question."

Tully said nothing, but he came close to minding. What he'd said about the others in this ersatz faculty also applied to Koesler. The others wrote murder mysteries. Granted Koesler had been involved in actual homicide investigations. And, to be fair, he had made few mistakes, and had actually been very helpful on occasion. But they all were amateurs and while they could prove useful, they could even more probably get in the way.

Plus—and this was more like the bottom line—there was the awareness that Koesler was a close friend of Walt Koznicki. And Koznicki, although he needn't and didn't throw his considerable weight around, was still the boss.

It was with all that in mind that Tully accepted another question.

"The thing that kept bothering me in there was how narrow the scope of this investigation is. Now I know I'm not a detective and I'm not a real part of this investigation—nor should I be.

"But you seem to be insisting that the crime had to be committed this evening between 8:00 and 10:00. That the liqueur had to be poisoned during that time. And that it had to be done by either Dave Benbow, Augustine, or Marie.

"Isn't that a bit restrictive? I know that people have been in and out and around the dining area all day long. But isn't it just possible that somebody, somehow, managed to get into the dining room, into the cabinet and poison the drink sometime during the day, long before dinner?

"And if that is possible, isn't it also possible that almost anyone could have done it?"

Tully nodded. "Sure, everything's possible. Thing is, we got a hot potato goin' on here. People downtown are gonna want this thing closed yesterday, which gives us an advantage we don't ordinarily get: We'll get lots of help. With all that help, we'll be lookin' into everything. All the things you mentioned and more, Padre. The students, the kitchen people, the security guards—everybody's being checked and interrogated. When we get done with the initial phase of this investigation, we will pretty well know what everybody has been doing nearly minute by minute all day today."

"Well," Koesler said, "I must say that's reassuring. I'm sorry I raised the question. No," he corrected himself, "I'm glad I asked, because it puts my mind at ease. But then . . ."

"But then," Tully picked up, "if all that's goin' on, why am I concentrating on Benbow, Marie, and Augustine?"

"Well, yes."

"It could be anybody, Padre, like you say. But if it isn't Benbow, Marie, or Augustine or any combination thereof, I'll swallow my badge. They make up the list of the likely perps. That's why with everybody else covering everybody else, I and a few others are gonna zero in on those three."

15

"FATHER KOESLER!"

The priest spun around. The greeting had been delivered so unaffectedly and enthusiastically that it had taken him by complete surprise.

It was a woman with an uncommonly pronounced smile. Dark hair styled in bangs, no glasses, hazel eyes, about five-feet-six, comfortably filled out; she looked like someone's idea of the stereotypical homemaker.

Who was she?

It happened all the time. Priests meet so very many people. Especially priests who move from parish to parish during their extensive tours of duty. Inevitably, no matter where he happens to be, people will accost a priest with something like, "Father so-and-so! Remember me?"

More often than not the answer had to be, "Not really."

Which usually was followed by, "You married me!" Or, "You baptized me!"

A priest Koesler's age will have witnessed the marriage of hundreds of couples, most of them fading into one unrecognizable mélange. Ditto baptisms, first Communions, and school plays.

So he tried to be as pleased about this chance meeting as

was the young woman who had greeted him. But his hesitation communicated his failure to place her.

"Angie Moore," she supplied. "Sergeant Angie Moore. We worked together briefly last year on an arrest . . ."

Aha! That was it. "Of course . . . Sergeant Moore."

It all came flooding back. "The last time I saw you you were sitting on the floor and you were cut . . . bleeding. How are you now?"

She laughed. An infectious, musical laugh. "That was a year ago, Father. I'm fine. I would've lost more blood if I'd given to the Red Cross."

"Good, good." Now what? "So, what are you doing here, Sergeant?"

"There's been a murder, Father. I work in Homicide, remember?"

Damn! "Of course. How stupid of me."

"Did you see her, Angie?" Tully was tiring of this reunion.

"Yeah, Zoo. I saw her. And learned a lot."

Tully explained to Koznicki and, necessarily, Koesler also. "I asked Angie to get in touch with Mrs. Winer, the rabbi's wife . . . widow. So you saw her. How did it go?"

The transformation was instantaneous. It was as if her happy surprise at meeting Koesler hadn't happened. Angie Moore was all business.

"It was rough," Moore said, "real rough. I guess they must have been real close. One of those exceptions, a long and happy marriage. I thought I was gonna lose her right after I gave her the news. I mean, I thought she was gonna faint. But she didn't. She hung on. She wanted so much to know what happened she must have forced herself to hold on."

"And then?" Tully prodded.

"And then she wanted to know how it happened. Wait a minute . . ." She took her notepad out of her purse and consulted it.

"I told her," Moore said, "that it had been a mistake—the result of a fluke, an accident. That someone had intended to kill Klaus Krieg, but that her husband had accidentally been poisoned with a drink intended for Krieg.

"At first she didn't say anything. Then she said, 'What a waste! What a waste!' "

"Strange," Koznicki commented.

"That's what I thought," Moore said. "But I got the impression she wanted to open up to me. So I just kind of kept quiet and waited. And then, she did.

"She said, 'What a waste! Irv went to that workshop to have it out with Krieg once and for all. And that Irv should die in Krieg's place—I can't believe it!'

"I agreed with her. Then I asked what she meant by her husband 'having it out' with Krieg.

"She didn't respond immediately. Like she was debating with herself whether to open up or not. Finally, she said, 'You see, my husband was in a Nazi concentration camp . . .' " Moore looked at Tully. "Did you know that?"

"Yeah," Tully said. "He had a number tattooed on his arm." Tully shrugged. "He was Jewish."

"Well," Moore continued, "I asked her what her husband being in a concentration camp had to do with Krieg. She didn't say anything for several minutes, just sat looking off into the distance. Finally, I guess everything overflowed. She started to talk, so slowly and quietly at first that I could barely hear her.

"She said, 'It was near the end, just before the camp was

liberated. Irv had suffered the pains of the damned for seven years. He lasted longer than just about anyone else condemned to that hell on earth. Then something happened.' She stopped for a moment . . . as if she was struggling with herself. Finally, she seemed to come to a decision—sort of as if she had decided to trust me. Actually,'' Angie looked a little ill at the memory, ''I think she was so close to breaking down that she had to overflow—you know, confide in another human being. And I guess 'cause it was another woman, it was easier for her.

''Anyway, she said, 'He became an informer, a traitor to his own people, a collaborator with the Nazis.'

''Then she broke down crying. She was sobbing so hard I put my arms around her and just held her. Finally, she pulled herself together. And she said, 'Irv didn't know I knew. It was the one thing, the only thing he never told me. I found out when I started researching his genealogy. He was so proud of his heritage, I wanted to get a family tree put together for him. I went to a lot of trouble, writing, getting names of his friends, his family.

'' 'It was one of his friends—well, actually a distant relative—who still lives in Germany. He told me. He said Irv didn't know that quite a few people knew what he'd done in the camp. He wanted Irv to know that the Jews who knew about it bore him no ill will. They understood. They had been there. You did what you had to. You stayed alive.' She shook her head, and added, 'He was just a boy.'

''Then she looked at me and she said, 'I never told Irv. What good would it have done? It didn't matter if they forgave him or understood. I know him. I know he never could forgive himself. So I didn't let on I knew his secret. If he didn't tell me, he didn't want me to know. I couldn't let him know that I'd found out, even if it was by accident.'

"That seemed to be all she wanted to tell me. I waited, but nothing more came. So I asked her what all that had to do with having it out with Krieg here at the conference.

"She said, 'It had everything to do with it. Because Krieg had found out. Oh, it wasn't that difficult. It wasn't that difficult for me to find out, and I don't begin to have the money, the power, the resources that Klaus Krieg has. It just wasn't as difficult as Irv probably thought it was.

" 'See, one of the times Krieg called, Irv wasn't in. So Krieg talked to me. I guess Krieg assumed Irv had told me what had happened in the camp. Of course, Irv hadn't told me. And if I hadn't found out on my own, it would've been a terrible way to find out—from Krieg. But if I hadn't already known about it and if Krieg had discovered that I didn't, he would have threatened Irv that he would tell me about it too.'

"I said, 'Too'?"

Tully exhaled so audibly it sounded almost like a whistle. "Blackmail! Krieg was blackmailing Winer. *That's* what it's all about."

"That would explain why the rabbi was so upset at Reverend Krieg's repeated efforts to sign the rabbi to a contract," Koznicki said.

"That's it," Moore said. "Mrs. Winer said that Krieg, after he got done using every legitimate means to get her husband to sign, had threatened and finally issued an ultimatum that if Winer still refused to sign, Krieg would get the story out in the open."

"Could it have hurt that much?" Koesler asked.

The others looked at him as if he'd dropped out of the sky. They had nearly forgotten he was there.

Their reaction slightly embarrassed Koesler. Nonetheless, having surfaced, he proceeded. "I mean, it happened so long ago. In the context of where and how it happened, it is so understandable. And, according to his wife, everyone who knows about it has forgiven him."

"I asked her the same question," Marie said. "But she said that at the very least he would lose his credibility, and very possibly the president of the synagogue would move to have him dismissed. And they'd probably do it. She was convinced that if that had happened his life both as a rabbi and a writer would end. But most of all, if it had become public, her belief was that he would just have disintegrated."

Silence.

"So," Tully said, "Winer came here to have it out once and for all with Krieg."

"Do you think it possible the rabbi intended murder as a last resort?" Koznicki asked.

"Sure sounds like it," Tully replied.

"Father Koesler has told us of his surprise at the hostility toward Krieg not only on the rabbi's part, but from all the other writers," Koznicki said. "Is it possible . . . ?"

Tully nodded. "Angie, go get Krieg. He's in the dining room."

Shortly, Moore returned with Krieg.

"Reverend," Tully said, "Sergeant Moore here just got done talking with Rabbi Winer's widow."

"Praise God! Poor woman."

"Yeah. Mrs. Winer said you know about a . . . uh . . . a very compromising situation in the rabbi's past and that you were blackmailing him, threatening to reveal his secret, unless he signed a contract with you."

Krieg smiled in plastic benevolence.

"True?" Tully's tone betrayed there was little fuse left.

"Whyever would a minister of the Gospel do a thing like that?"

"You deny it, then?"

"What's to deny? Are there letters? Documents? Tape recordings of any such threat I might have made to the good rabbi, Lord rest his soul?"

Tully glanced at Moore, who shook her head.

"No hard evidence, Reverend, of any threat; just your word against the widow's," Tully said. "But what we've learned from Mrs. Winer explains a lot. So this is off the record. Rabbi Winer stood to lose everything. He came here allegedly to settle things with you. His plans might have included murder."

"He was a man of God!" Krieg protested.

"So are you," Tully shot back. "So are all the others in this crazy conference." Tully slipped into a more conciliatory attitude. "Reverend, it's been observed that you are not much liked by the writers here. Some of us have been wondering why that is. Mrs. Winer gave us an excellent reason—at least as far as her husband was concerned."

"But I—"

"Hold on just a moment, Reverend," Tully said. "We are not officially accusing you of anything like blackmail. And you don't have to deny or answer to anything. Right now, anyway," he added. "But let's just suppose—for the sake of argument—that Mrs. Winer was on to something. Suppose her husband did have a skeleton in his closet. Suppose you knew about it. Suppose you told him you would pull that skeleton out of the closet if he didn't sign a contract with your publishing company. Something he very much didn't want to do. Suppose that was the reason he showed such hostility toward you.

"Now, as far as the casual observer was concerned, the high degree of hostility Winer had for you was excessive, inappropriate—improbable, to say the least. But not if you throw in blackmail.

"With blackmail thrown into the pot, it all makes sense. In fact, it would be a credible reason why Winer might want to kill you—absent some lesser way to get you off his back.

"But, instead of making an attempt on your life, Winer is murdered, with a poisoned drink meant for you. His mistake inadvertently saved your life.

"Now, who besides Winer would hate you enough to attempt to kill you? Well, for openers, how about the remaining three writers on this panel? There doesn't seem to be much difference in the way any of them feel about you.

"Why would they show feelings toward you just like Winer's? Could it be for the same reason Winer had?

"Whatever their reasons, I think you know why they don't particularly care for you. And there's one thing you'd better remember: Whoever tried to kill you missed. We haven't caught that person yet, so he or she is still out there and still hates you enough to try to kill you.

"If I were you, I would be awfully, awfully careful. And, think about it, Reverend: You may just want to talk to us. It would give us a leg up if we knew what this person's motive was.

"Now we can't force you to talk to us, but if you think about it carefully enough, you might just want to."

During Tully's admonition to Krieg, Koesler studied the televangelist closely. It was interesting to watch the smile slide almost imperceptibly from plastic to rubber.

Strange man, Koesler concluded. He'd seemed more annoyed than shocked when he had learned of Rabbi Winer's death. Not unlike an investor learning the market had suffered through a very bearish day. Which simile probably wasn't far from the truth in this case.

For one reason or another, Krieg seemed to have had every expectation that he could persuade the rabbi to sign with P.G. Press. Blackmail? So, with Winer's demise, Krieg had lost an investment. One surely would expect considerably more from the minister. But . . .

And then, when it became clear that Winer had died from a poison meant for him, Krieg had looked as though he were close to death from mere shock.

Yet when Tully began talking to Krieg just now, the Reverend appeared to have put the incident out of his mind. As if it had never happened. But it was obvious all along that the murderer was still free. Free to try again. Did Krieg think that, having failed, the killer would give up?

Whatever Krieg may have thought, Tully's lecture had brought the preacher back to earth with a thud.

Would Krieg now break down and confide in the police? Koesler guessed that the secret of what was going on between Krieg and the writers hid something that was translatable into a lot of money in the coffers of P.G. Press. A great deal of money on one side of the scale; human life—perhaps Krieg's own—on the other side.

Koesler was reminded of the routine of the late comedian Jack Benny, in which a thief approaches Benny and says, "Your money or your life." An extended silence follows. The thief exasperatedly repeats, "Your money or your life!" And Benny replies, "I'm thinking! I'm thinking!"

That must be what Krieg was doing now: thinking about

either protecting his life or possibly adding significantly to his fortune.

Koesler had time to develop all these thoughts because Tully tolerated a lengthy silence during which one could almost perceive wheels turning in Krieg's mind. In the end, it became apparent Krieg was not going to cooperate.

"All right," Tully said, "we're going back into the dining room. Angie, I want you to tell the others what you told us about our conversation with Mrs. Winer."

The others, being interviewed in various parts of the dining room, one on one with police officers, seemed startled at the sight of Koznicki, Tully, Moore, Krieg, and Koesler entering. The interviews were put on hold while Tully introduced Moore.

In a more concise fashion than she had in the corridor, Moore recounted her conversation with Mrs. Winer. Tully noted the writers' reactions carefully. So did Koesler. They all seemed genuinely moved with pity for the rabbi's widow and absorbed by the rabbi's concentration camp ordeal.

At a signal from Tully, Moore stopped short of explicit mention of blackmail. The conclusion was left to the listeners to draw. To a person, they seemed to make the connection and arrive at the inevitable conclusion.

As Moore ended her narrative, Tully asked for questions. None.

Did anyone have any comment?

No one. Everyone seemed determined to tough it out.

Very well, then. Tully directed the detectives to resume their interviews.

In a low voice, Tully directed Moore to commence a supplementary investigation into the backgrounds of the three remaining writers. "Just in case there's something to this blackmail thing,'' he said, ''dig around. See what turns up. Take two or three from our squad. If you need more help, see me.''

Things were frozen in a status quo that Koesler did not find at all auspicious. He prayed that something would break, something would happen, before another life would be forfeited.

16

As soon as Sergeant Moore had begun talking about Rabbi Winer's life in the concentration camp, David Benbow was fairly sure of how it would conclude. When she told of Winer's turning informer, Benbow knew exactly what the conclusion had to be.

Winer was being blackmailed by Krieg. Benbow could be sure of it since the same thing was happening to him. Until now, he hadn't known about the rabbi's predicament. Winer's unfortunate experience caused Benbow to reexamine his own dilemma. Though, even after all this time, he still couldn't decide whether his own experience was fortunate or unfortunate. And, God knows, Benbow had rehashed the situation countless times, without resolving it.

It was about to happen once more, God help him. Benbow didn't want to go over it again, but he was going to. He recognized the signs.

He found himself paying less attention to the detective who was interviewing him. That was dangerous. Most of the questions were routine, background information; but, at any moment, the cop could slip in a trick question. That's what cops were supposed to do. That's what they did in Benbow's books. The clever cop versus the clever crook. The cop always won in the end. That, of course, was fiction.

Because this question session could prove to be important, possibly crucial, Benbow wanted to pay attention. He simply was unable to do so. Memory was taking over. He was grateful that he'd been through this reminiscence so often that it was like seeing the same movie for the umpteenth time. He could play the tape, all the while paying minimal attention to the interview. He would have to rely on his instincts, which remained sharp, to alert him to any hazard the interview might generate.

Every age of man has its own peculiar problems. For purposes of this excursion, Benbow's thoughts returned to his final year at Northwestern University.

How tortured and indecisive he'd been in the face of the choice between the ministry and a career in law. His family had a proud history in the legal profession. Going back to his great-grandfather there were attorneys and judges sprinkled through the legal and judicial system, from the practice of civil and criminal law to the Supreme Court of Illinois, to the Circuit Court of Appeals. His family quite naturally took it for granted that young David would take his place—and it promised to be a prominent place—as a barrister. One with a promising future.

Clouding this assured picture was the magnetic pull of the priesthood of the Anglican Church.

What attracts a young person to the ministry? Lots of things, increasing as one matures. With David it began when, as a small boy, he was taken to services by his parents on a regular basis. He was not the sort who had to be dragged to church. He was naturally fascinated by the ritual, the vestments, the music, and the unique ambience when all of that was mingled with the distinctive use of incense. Only occasionally was he attentive to a sermon. In time, he came to realize that nearly everyone shared that attitude toward sermons. And that, while ritual had enjoyed centuries to develop and ripen, sermons were only as good as a preacher's weekly ruminations.

In his more mature years, deeper, more substantial realities of the priesthood beckoned.

Priests did all the engaging things David as a child had found compelling. They ministered to the sacramental life, they presided over Eucharist, they wore impressive costumes, they were shown respect quite universally.

But they also had entreé into people's deepest psyches. They instructed, they counseled. Priests were well advised to expand their psychology skills to be able to field more and more complex cases before needing to refer a client to a professional psychotherapist.

The more David considered a religious vocation, the more natural it seemed to be his life's vehicle. He made his decision.

His family greeted his determination with varying degrees of opposition, resistance, and contravention. He was throwing aside a career in law that was made for him and he for it. He was sacrificing meaningful financial security to the detriment of a family that would one day depend on him. He was proving a deep disappointment to his father, his grandfather, many of his uncles, and their country club cronies. If he insisted on being so goddam charitable there were plenty of pro bono cases out there he could tackle. What was so goddam demeaning about a career in law anyway? It got nasty.

Through it all, he remained steadfast. Eventually, led by the gracious persistence of his mother, the family came around. It was not so much the acceptance of his chosen calling as it was the reluctant resignation to the inevitable. Trying to make the best of a most unhappy situation, his father, followed by uncles, aunts, and cousins, had to admit that the life of a clergyman was not as bad as many another, such as, say, a tennis bum or similar sort of derelict.

Then came Martha Clarke. She was by no means David's first girlfriend. Not even the first about whom he was serious. He was a most attractive and desirable young man. Tall and blond, with classic features; well built, though not athletically gifted enough to make any of the varsity teams, he attended many of their games and was a standout participant in many intramural sports, especially tennis and golf.

Above and beyond this physical charm and magnetism, there was the special appeal his future promised. It was no secret on campus that his family was larded with jurists, all with impressively lucrative careers.

Photos of various Benbows appeared regularly in the newspapers and local magazines. They qualified as visits with the rich and famous. In these "quality of life" sections of the daily press, in society columns that noted who attended which social function, it was rare that one or another of the Benbow names was not prominent in boldface.

And all of this one day would be David's. And his wife's. The line of those who yearned to be young Benbow's wife-elect was extensive and cosmopolitan.

However, as David confided his hitherto secret desire to enter the ministry, one after another of these ladies-in-waiting bade him fond adieu. By the time it became fairly common knowledge that he was not going to become an attorney but a clergyman, as far as those Northwestern coeds who had been vying for him, he might just as well have been inducted into a celibate priesthood.

Enter Martha Clarke.

Martha was a slow bloomer. Unlike many another young lady on campus, she was serious. Serious about social concerns, serious about religion, serious about commitment, and, above all, serious about her studies. She was serious about nearly everything before David became serious about almost anything.

Thus, as David zeroed in on his religious vocation, became a more mature young man, and watched his friendships change both in quantity and quality, he was, without design, moving into Martha's circle.

Years, even months, before they met, the chemistry would have been all wrong for David and Martha. Now it was near perfect. She could not imagine a husband more ideal than one who was serious about the truly important things in life and who was willing to pledge his future by entering the ministry.

They were together as often as possible, and they talked incessantly about their future. It was Martha's decision, after some typically deep thought and prayer, to abandon her pursuit of a degree and get a job to support them while David was in the seminary.

At first, David vehemently opposed her sacrifice. In the end, he had to capitulate. While his family was beginning to tolerate the notion of his clerical ambition, their indulgence did not extend to supporting him—let alone his wife—while he pursued his goal. The seminary would require his total investment of time and energy. There seemed no alternative to Martha's plan. She would work, he would study.

She chose real estate, principally because, irrespective of gender, there was virtually no ceiling on one's prospects in that field. There was no perceived limit on how many houses one could sell if one worked at it in a dedicated manner. And dedication was mother's milk to Martha.

So they were married.

Since Martha's parents were dead, David's father bent far enough to provide a splashy wedding for them. But shortly thereafter, cold reality set in. She worked, he studied. Both played their roles diligently. In time, David was ordained and assigned to an upper-middle-class parish on the outskirts of Chicago. At this point, it became possible for Martha to withdraw from the business world and become a home-maker. Something she would of course have done with dedication.

But it was a little too late for that.

Martha's diligence had begun to pay off handsomely and literally. She was earning David's salary many times over. And it did come in handy—although, as often as he allowed himself to think of it, it did tarnish his self-image.

Professionals in their chosen fields, they began to take on inflexible routines. His work week focused toward the week-end when he would conduct formal services. Meanwhile there was plenty to keep him busy Monday through Friday with meetings, classes, instructions, and counseling.

Martha evaluated, showed, and sold houses morning, noon, and night, weekdays and weekends.

In time almost everything in their lives became subject to scheduling. When they might balance their checkbooks, when they might eat together, when they were able to squeeze in some precious quality time, when they might enjoy sex.

Sexual expression had had a playful, spontaneous character for only a few months after they were first married. They did not engage in intercourse before marriage. Their honeymoon was all either of them could have expected. Soon thereafter scheduling became a limiting and controlling factor. Regulating so natural an expression of their love so early in their marriage exacted a price. The price—a rigid formality plus the sublimation of powerful instincts—they were willing to pay in exchange for the financial security they were building. Somehow, Martha seemed more willing to sublimate than David, though it was not easy for either and led to arguments—which grew less frequent as time proved them futile.

Enter Pamela Richardson.

Pam Richardson was one of many parishioners who came to David regularly for instruction or counseling or both. In Pam's case it was counseling.

Pam had been an orphan, adopted at age five by a couple who should not have been allowed to adopt anyone. It wasn't physical abuse, it was psychological deprivation. Her adoptive parents withheld love, approval, and encouragement. She became very withdrawn at an age when she could not absorb so radical a privation.

As an external manifestation of her inner insecurity, Pam developed a facial tic that affected only the left side of her face. So, when she experienced almost any emotion—happiness, for instance—only the right side of her face reacted. This produced an admittedly grotesque abnormality.

The man she learned to call ''father'' laughed and ridiculed her. The woman she learned to call ''mother'' wasn't any help. She saw it her duty to be supportive of her husband. Pam came in a distant second.

However, mother did take the little girl to a doctor who,

by testing, ruled out any physical cause for the abnormality. For no obvious reason, the doctor predicted that the little girl would recover from this psychosomatic illness when she reached her fifteenth birthday.

Whether he had the insight of the psychic, was extraordinarily inspired—or lucky—or whether it was the power of suggestion that made it a self-fulfilling prophecy, at her fifteenth birthday Pam's tic vanished, never to reappear. But her depression continued, even intensifying, as she no longer had the external defense mechanism of the tic as an escape hatch.

It was in a state of deep depression that Pamela first visited Father David Benbow. So deep was her depression it bordered on despair. David came very close to referring her to a specialist immediately. He probably would have had he not been taking a course in pastoral psychology at the time. As part of the course, he was assigned a professional psychologist who monitored the cases he was then handling. Thus, through him, Pamela in effect had the benefit of professional care without paying for it.

In the beginning, David's monitor was equally apprehensive about Pamela's condition. David was advised to try supportive therapy in massive doses to try to generate some sort of positive self-image, which seemed to be totally lacking.

So it began.

David could not have imagined a plainer young woman. Pamela never wore any sort of makeup. She always appeared tired, virtually exhausted. This she attributed to a recurring nightmare that made her reluctant to fall asleep.

In the repetitive dream, she was backstage in a large auditorium that was filled with strangers. She was, very reluctantly, competing in some sort of pageant. The other candidates (for what, it was never clear) were beautiful, intelligent women her own age. She dreaded going on stage where she was certain to be humiliated.

Eventually it would be her turn. She didn't even know what she was supposed to do when she stepped through the curtains. She never entered onto the stage willingly. She was pushed out. Once on stage, people began to laugh at her. One in particular, a strange half-man, half-animal that resembled a hyena, laughed her to scorn. (Her father, David wondered, who, by his constant, brutal ridicule, had ravaged her fragile ego strength like a scavenger?) At this point, she would waken in a cold sweat and fight off sleep for the remainder of the night.

David and his monitor studied this nightmare in great detail. Its manifest content seemed unmistakable. It was her father, more than anyone else, who subverted her self-confidence. As an orphan, she needed to be warmly accepted by someone very special. Instead, she was rejected by a "mother and father," the very people one would expect to be most nurturing and loving.

She was, then, the ugly duckling in unfair competition with others with whom she ought to be able to compete fairly. She wanted to stay secluded from everyone—backstage—but society kept demanding that she mount the stage of the workaday world.

She couldn't escape. Not in the real world, not even in sleep.

One more item: On the rare occasion David could get her to laugh, she would reflexively cover the left side of her mouth as if the early tic were still present. It wasn't, of course, but subliminally did she imagine it was?

It was slow, painstaking therapy. David at times felt as if

he were monkey-in-the-middle between his monitor and his client. Gradually, however, his nonjudgmental acceptance and encouragement began having an effect.

The first sign was so subtle, David almost missed it.

For the very first time—in his contact with her, and, in fact, in many years—she wore the softest hint of lipstick. But, thank God, he did recognize what for her was a sizable, if tentative step. He complimented her effusively. She smiled broadly, covering the left side of her face.

Thereafter, she wore makeup regularly and charmingly. David never failed to notice and compliment her on her appearance. Next she began wearing more attractive clothing. David was amazed at the external transformation. She was really quite an attractive woman. Not a ravishing beauty, but one who would catch the eye of the discerning man.

Progress came more rapidly now. The day she laughed openly without even an attempt to cover her face, David and his monitor celebrated later with a toast of an inexpensive wine.

Finally, she vanquished the nightmare. She was unsure at first that it was gone permanently. But night after night of peaceful sleep convinced her it was over.

With no regression in sight, it seemed safe to declare her cured. A psychoanalyst might have kept her in therapy for years more. But in the school of psychology to which David and his monitor belonged, the sessions were over. He agreed with his monitor that it was over.

But it wasn't.

She kept making appointments with him. He kept scheduling her appointments. They always found something to talk about. The forty-five-minute hours became fifty-minute hours. Then a full, honest sixty-minute hour.

Her transformation had been slow, inchmeal. Something
like those hair color formulas that supposedly darken gray
hair so imperceptibly that no one notices that the user is
"peeling years away." Nonetheless, Pamela's transformation had taken place and was continuing. Since she had begun using makeup stylishly and wearing flattering clothes,
she had very definitely changed from a plain, all but invisible
person to an appealing young woman.

Being noticed and being asked out by men was a new
experience. She was unsure how to handle it. She decided,
and made it a routine decision, to turn down all invitations
to dates. She did this out of loyalty to David. But she would
not have been able to explain her reasons. He was a priest,
moreover, a married man. He was her counselor/therapist.

Transference was running wild. David Benbow had become her father figure, her older brother, her friend and con-
fidant, her secret lover, "pure and chaste from afar," as the
song had it.

David was familiar with transference. He had studied it as
part of his psychology course. He had experienced it many
times with clients. He knew—or was pretty sure he knew—
what Pam was undergoing. He did little to control or channel
her strong and chaotic emotions.

Some three months after counseling therapeutically and
theoretically had ended, Pam invited David to dinner at her
apartment. Technically, the invitation was for the Reverend
and Mrs. Benbow. But Martha never saw the invitation. The
evening in question Martha was scheduled to be in charge of
the real estate office. It figured that she would be babysitting
the office, showing houses, or contracting to sell. She was
driven.

Pam expressed regrets she did not feel upon learning that

Mrs. Benbow would not be able to attend. It was only when David arrived, presenting a bottle of medium grade wine (all he could afford without Martha's knowing of the unscheduled purchase) that Pam learned that Martha had no idea where David was that night.

It was an innocent evening, with a satisfactory dinner and pleasant conversation. David helped with the dishes. It ended at the door with a brief, modest embrace. He kissed her cheek. She kissed the air. And yet . . . and yet each felt some surge of excitement. Nothing of any consequence had occurred, but she felt slightly incestuous and he felt a bit adulterous. It had everything to do with his thinking he was called to a higher life than average men, her being virginal, their previous therapeutic relationship.

In the face of all that, they continued to meet for dinner at her apartment at least once every other week. Familiarity, like everything else in their relationship, grew gradually, slowly. Rather than remaining seated at table after eating, they sat on the couch—a sofabed—frequently holding hands. At parting, they kissed on the lips, but as brother and sister might.

It happened, as it most certainly had to happen. One evening he talked freely and openly about his marriage, painting it as considerably less intimate than it actually was. Her heart went out to him in his self-described isolation. They kissed passionately. She invited him to disrobe her. He protested that he did not know how he could stop at that point. The invitation was not withdrawn.

All he could think of was what a waste it had been to cover that body with so much clothing for so many years. He had never even imagined breasts being such perfectly molded mounds of flesh.

He was right: He could not stop.

The barrier had fallen, never again to be rebuilt. They felt guilt, deep and abiding guilt. But, simply, their passion far outweighed the guilt.

They met no more frequently than they had before. But now there was no pretense that the evenings were mere dinner parties with small talk. They were trysts pure and simple. David had his cake and ate it too. Pamela joyfully anticipated their times together. Yet both knew that for her this was a dead-end trip. David made it clear that for both personal and career considerations, he could not, would not, leave Martha. Pamela insisted she understood.

But how happy can anyone be traveling an avenue that leads nowhere?

Pamela's plight added guilt to David's still sensitive conscience. When enough guilt accumulated, he phoned for an appointment to see Father Alfred Massey, a universally respected older clergyman who had been one of David's seminary instructors.

After a substantial dinner prepared and served by Mrs. Massey, the two clergymen retired into the rector's study where they would not be interrupted.

"Well, my boy," Massey opened as he filled his pipe, "what's on your mind?"

"It's been a long time since I visited with you and Sara." Benbow was beginning to feel ill at ease.

Massey chuckled noiselessly. "Since you were a student. Yes, I'd say that qualified as a long time. And I'd say there's something on your mind."

Benbow tried to smile but it wouldn't come. "What I . . . we . . . say tonight, it will be held confidential?"

Massey nodded. "Of course, if that's the way you want it. I'm not the type that runs off at the mouth in any case. Now, what is it, my boy?"

David told the tale: the therapy sessions monitored by an instructor; the friendship that grew from and extended beyond the professional relationship; finally, the affair that continued to this moment.

When he finished, he felt a decided sense of relief. He hadn't anticipated the sensation but he should have. From his own experience of listening to the problems of others, in and out of the confessional, he'd experienced at least vicariously the miracle of the talking cure. But now he circled his emotional defenses closer, waiting for the unknown, namely Canon Massey's reaction to an open-and-shut case of adultery.

Massey relit his pipe, puffing until his head nearly disappeared in the clouds of smoke. "How's Martha?"

The question clearly surprised Benbow. "She's . . . fine. Working hard as a realtor."

"Yes, she always was a hard worker . . . put you through school, if memory serves . . . no?"

"Yes."

"Does working hard mean what I think it means? That you seldom see each other?"

Benbow nodded.

"I see. May I ask, in general, about your marital relationship?"

Benbow would not lie, as he did with Pamela. Not now, not to Massey. "If you overlook the fact that we have to schedule almost all our intimate times together, it is not bad. Not bad at all.''

Massey's eyes narrowed as if trying to see through the smoke, to understand. ''Well, I know that you and Martha are still young, and that spontaneity in marriage is important at your stage. But if your sexual activity with her is as satisfactory as you indicate, then why . . . ?''

Benbow pulled at his earlobe, turning his head from direct eye contact. ''I'm not sure. I haven't actually faced that question until just this moment. Maybe it's man's hunger for variety.''

''But surely more . . . ?''

''Before we were married?'' Benbow smiled. ''Before I married Martha, there was no one, no wild oats. We were both virgins when we married. I've come to think that's both good and bad news. Good news on the virtue scale. Saving oneself for one's life companion. No sins of fornication or adultery, and all that. But bad news in the long run, I fear. Always the curiosity about what it might be like with someone else. Whether the experience could be different, better, more exciting.''

''And . . . ?''

''And?''

''Did you find it all that much different? Better? More exciting with . . . ?''

''Pamela.''

''Yes, Pamela?''

Benbow thought for several moments. ''Yes, as a matter of fact. If I can state this without embarrassing either of us. It's a difference—a vast difference as it turns out—in personalities.''

In spite of himself and despite the gravity of the matter,

Benbow couldn't help smiling. "Martha surprised me from the start. I thought all women were like this. She had no experience. She acted instinctively. The same sort of drive, of get-up-and-go that has brought her so much success in real estate . . . well . . . it's the same in everything, including bed." He looked thoughtful. "In marriage counseling, a problem frequently arises because the husband doesn't bother satisfying his wife. That's never been a consideration with Martha. Sometimes she gets concerned about whether I'm having a satisfactory orgasm. She . . . has no problem in that area.

"Pamela . . . well . . . Pam was—is—different. The two are diametrically opposed personalities. Martha does. Pam is done to. She's utterly, completely passive. I find that attractive, stimulating, erotic, a turn-on."

"You could get one of those life-sized dolls," Massey muttered.

"I beg your pardon. What was that?"

"Nothing." Massey tapped the dottle out of his pipe, selected a fresh pipe from the rack, and began the ritual anew. "Well, David, we are now faced with a number of predictable, hypothetical, rhetorical questions. I don't feel we need to get into it too deeply. You know what you must do."

It was a rhetorical question in the form of a statement. Yet David was unsure of his response. Still, he couldn't help being frank. Not now. Not after he'd opened himself so candidly to his respected colleague. "Not really," he said. "It seems there are at least two, maybe three alternatives. I could maintain the status quo. Martha is not aware of anything. I'm slightly more than fulfilled with two women almost programmed to fit my moods."

Massey's mouth was a tight line. "David! I want to remain as nonjudgmental as possible. But really . . . !"

"No, no, I understand," David interrupted. "I know in my heart that's not a viable alternative. It's completely unfair to Pamela. And I feel guilty as hell about it. That's why I'm here. But even though it's not going to solve anything, I had to mention it as an alternative.

"Then there's breaking up with Pam. It would tear me apart. Her too. But that's the obvious, 'moral' choice no matter how much pain is involved, isn't it?"

Massey continued to puff wordlessly.

"But there's a third possibility. What if I confessed the affair to Martha and offered her the choice of divorcing me? Uncontested. That would let me marry Pam and we'd be happy. Of course, it would shatter Martha. But, I think, only for the moment. She would promptly get so reinvolved with her real estate, that after a short while she'd wonder who was that person who once shared her life.

"So, Father, I don't find the future as cut and dried, as rhetorical, as it might seem."

Massey removed the pipe from his mouth and shook his head. "David, David . . . the alternatives to what you correctly called the 'moral' situation don't exist for you."

"Don't exist?"

"Maintaining the status quo, continuing your adulterous relationship with Pamela will drive you mad. I've seen it happen to too many good men. Your conscience will never let you rest. The guilt has forced you to seek me out. It's clear from your own lips that you know it can't continue as it has.

"Besides, you risk losing everything if you continue this

clandestine affair. Just as you also risk everything should you divorce Martha and 'make an honest woman' of Pamela.''

"Lose everything? I don't . . .''

"David, there are two grounds for deposing a priest.''

"Yes: in the case of faith or morals. I know.''

"You're not in the process of denying any of the doctrines of the Church. You aren't making heretical statements. The matter of faith is clear-cut and fairly easy to judge. The area of morals is a horse of a different color. There are gray patches. But a priest's adulterous relationship qualifies nicely.

"Just how do you suppose your congregation would feel toward you if they knew you had engaged in adultery with a vulnerable woman who was your dependent client in therapy?''

It was the word "vulnerable" that reached him. It burned his soul like a brand. It was true. She was very vulnerable and he had taken advantage of her vulnerability.

"I think,'' Massey continued, "there is no question that you would not survive a morals challenge. And it makes no difference whether you keep Pamela as your paramour or divorce Martha and marry Pamela.''

"No difference!''

"No difference. In the eyes of your people, nor, I assure you, as far as the bishop is concerned: You will have betrayed the professional ethics of the therapist-client relationship. It is bound to come out that you were romancing someone who had come to you trusting that she would receive professional help.''

"But that's not true! Pam's therapy was concluded before—a long time before—we became lovers!''

"Try to convince others of that. Besides, even if you could convince anyone, the next charge that would be brought would be that you were setting her up for the later affair. One is just as bad as the other.''

Benbow considered his position as Massey had outlined the probabilities.

Massey could surmise what the younger clergyman was thinking. ''That's not all,'' he added.

Benbow met Massey's eyes evenly.

''You are the author of a book, a novel that, I understand, sold rather well.''

Benbow nodded.

''It's a good book, I think,'' Massey said. ''I read it. Enjoyed it. Going to write more?''

''Uh-huh.''

''Thought as much. The formula was good, good enough to bear repeating. The Episcopal Church played a big role in your book, David. You brought an authentic touch to it. The reader could tell that right off. What if by the time you get around to writing the next book, what if you are a deposed clergyman, disgraced in the eyes of your Church as well as in the psychology profession?''

Massey paused to let the full impact of that possibility pervade David's mind.

''Under those circumstances,'' Massey continued, ''think your reading public would be as enthusiastic about a writer who's been held up to ridicule and scorn by two respected professions? Think the publisher would risk 'taking a bath,' I believe they call it, by publishing a writer with so uncertain a future?''

David was speechless. It seemed that Massey had finally stumbled upon a few genuinely rhetorical questions.

''That's a pretty bleak picture'' Benbow said at length. ''Think that would really happen?''

"Don't you?"

"I suppose so. If it got out. After all, I have no intention of publicizing my relationship with Pamela, professional or romantic."

Massey tipped his head forward and studied Benbow as if looking over the top of glasses, which, in reality, were non-existent. "David, you must know that in this day and age it is difficult to hide such things. What you've told me this evening did not come as a total shock or a complete surprise."

"It didn't?"

"You know how clerical gossip is. Oh, there's been nothing of a documented nature that I'm aware of. But your habits have changed. You're probably not even aware of that. Just subtle things. Like being away from the rectory on given evenings. Now and again someone would ask Martha about it. She'd quite innocently give the excuse you gave her. Presbytery meetings, confirmations, other events that Martha accepted at face value, but which the inquiring clergy knew had never taken place, or that if they had you were not present.

"Now I don't want to unnecessarily distress you. I don't think anyone has guessed what's really going on. But they're not far from the truth. David, you are on extremely thin ice. If you don't do something about this, you're going to fall in. And if you do, you'll likely drown."

Benbow was pensive for a few minutes. Finally, he said, slowly, heavily, "There doesn't seem to be much choice then."

"It took longer to reach that conclusion than I would have expected. But, no, I think there is not much choice."

After a few more moments' silence, David said, "This is

going to be tough, probably the hardest thing I've ever done. I don't think I'll make it without God's grace. I wonder, would you mind if we had the rite of reconciliation?''

''Confession? If you wish. Certainly.''

Benbow made his confession of sin, which did not much differ from the prior conversation. Before granting him absolution, Massey told him, as a penance, to meditate on the 51st Psalm, which begs so eloquently for God's infinite and ready mercy.

David Benbow left Father Massey's rectory that evening clean and determined to walk the straight and narrow.

17

AND SO HE did. For a while.

It did not take the Reverend David Benbow long to start the arduous journey back to a morally upstanding life. The very week of his confession and purpose of amendment before the Reverend Alfred Massey, David kept his date with Pamela Richardson. She did not answer the door clad only in mesh stockings and apron as propounded by *The Total Woman*. But it was almost that skimpy.

Pamela had no way of knowing this was to be a momentous evening during which her life was to be disrupted and her heart broken.

David had steeled himself against his own weakness and her desirability. She sensed something was amiss when he did not return her kiss. To arouse him, though he regularly needed little seduction, she had worn very little and what there was was easily removable. Somehow, as he seated himself in a distant, solitary chair and projected his awkwardness, she felt cheap and indecent.

He told her nothing she did not know. That their relationship was unfair to Martha. That their relationship was sinful in the eyes of God and the Church. That their relationship threatened his standing in the Church. She knew it was coming before he got to the part where he stated firmly that their relationship, for all of these reasons and more, must end.

She said nothing. There was nothing to say. She would not bring herself to beg or plead. The few tears that tracked erratically down her cheeks were the overflow of those she could not withhold. It was an embarrassing scene for him, a humiliating moment for her. After his tortured explanation of his inescapable decision, and with no spoken response from her, David left her apartment for, he felt sure, the final time.

It did not take the Reverend David Benbow long to rekindle his affair with Pamela Richardson.

There had been no change in David's relationship with his wife. How could there have been? As far as Martha was concerned, all had been well, all was well, all would be well. She was unaware of any failure in their marriage. There was no way she could know her husband had found a gap and filled it with Pamela Richardson. Martha charged ahead as a realtor. The more successful she became, the more involved she became and the more time she devoted to work.

David tried to fill the empty spaces with work and various professional involvements. Much of it was merely busy "make work." He daydreamed a lot, and all of it involved Pamela. There were so many memories—every one of them pleasant if not rapturous.

Life during the separation was, if anything, worse for Pamela. She did not even have the temporary relief of other involvements to distract her. So she was more than primed when the phone call came.

It was mid-evening Tuesday. Martha had not been home for supper. She'd phoned and told David not to expect her until quite late. They had planned to spend this evening together. They had scheduled dinner followed by a relaxing evening of leisurely foreplay and lovemaking.

It was the fact that the evening had been programmed. David had an easy time convincing himself of that. It wasn't that he was weak. God knew how good he'd been, how hard he'd tried. But Lord love a duck, she could at least honor their appointment for an amorous evening.

David sat by the phone, staring at it until he was nearly mesmerized. At last he picked up the receiver and dialed the familiar number.

"Hello?" Her tone was tentative.

"Lonesome?" he asked gently.

Instantly, she melted. "For months," she said.

"I'll be right over."

"I'll be ready."

So it began again. The same clandestine air; the same doubts, worry, concern, and above all, the same guilt.

David could not bring himself to return to Alf Massey. It would be too reproachable. He had promised, as part of the rite of reconciliation, save the mark. In time, David made an appointment to see a priest whom he had never met in a neighboring city, but whose prolific sectarian writings David had long admired.

The two spent a pleasant evening together at the elder clergyman's home, talking mostly about their separate and different writing careers. Finally, David was forced to speak of the real reason he had come. He told the whole story, including his evening with Alf Massey, the ensuing virtuous interlude, and his recidivism.

"So," the priest said, "what do you plan on doing about this situation?"

"I've come to seek your advice." David leaned forward

in his chair, his gaze intense. "This is not merely an immoral liaison. I have grown through my relationship with this wonderful woman. I am far more understanding with my parishioners, not so quick to condemn as I once was. I think it may be good for clergymen—at least some of us—to be in the state of sin, or what an unenlightened Church might consider the state of sin. Otherwise we too easily become sanctimonious bastards, condemning others whose temptations and failures we cannot understand.

"Besides," David continued, "my love for and with Diane"—he would not use her real name—"has made me a better writer . . . added a dimension to my work that was not there before.

"Well, what do you think?"

"I think," the priest said, "you are trying to theologize a swollen prick."

That pretty well did it. What could anyone say to so insensitive a clergyman? For the first time, David began to reevaluate the man's religious writings. This time around David found the writings, formerly so admired, shallow and lacking in Scriptural depth.

Enough of advice. David was forced to admit that he was avant-garde, well ahead of his time. He thought of all the deadly dull sermons he'd heard preached by ninnies who were not conscious of any deliberate sin. Clergypersons who spoke down to the poor miserable sinners cowering in their pews. Better for those shepherds if they had sinned. Better for their congregations, their parishioners.

Well, he was sinning with considerable gusto. Not only was he sinning against Martha and with Pamela, he was lying more and more outrageously to Martha. And, he was convinced, he was becoming better. Not morally better, perhaps. But, somehow, curiously, he was becoming a better priest. More patient with those who claimed his time. More receptive to those who confessed their sins in shame and embarrassment. He was rather proud of that.

Nor was that all. He was becoming a better writer. More knowledgeable about the baser passions that motivated the Common Man.

It showed in the publisher's appreciation of his third and latest manuscript. It showed in the book's reviews and sales. This was only David's third novel. Yet through it he moved up from bare survival to respectable sales.

As is customary, his publisher sent him copies of reviews of his book clipped from various newspapers and periodicals. His favorite came from a Boston paper. Among other things, the reviewer wrote: "Benbow exhibits remarkable insight into the mind of a woman bent on seduction. Inviting her victim into her web of intrigue, then suddenly turning from pursuer to pursued, from active manipulation to passive submission, Sarah proves herself the most effective seductress since Salome.

"Father Benbow must have heard some interesting confessions over the years!"

David had laughed as he showed that review and many others to Pamela. She, in turn, appreciated the pleasure of her anonymous debut in literature.

The ointment was not without its fly, however. David noticed a subtle change in the way some of his parishioners related to him, even some of the clergy as well. All were well aware of his literary accomplishments, of course. Most were proud of the honors bestowed on their pastor and/or friend. That wasn't the problem.

Actually, David could not pinpoint the problem. It had

something to do with his ability to describe illicit affairs with such evident authenticity. The same observation as that made in his favorite review. How could he know so much? Did he actually possess so vivid an imagination that he could transcend inexperience? Was he drawing from professional confidences? If so, was he careful to mask them sufficiently to avoid revealing real identities? Or could he possibly be projecting his own experiences? And if that were true, was he not chancing deposition?

To further complicate matters, David could not be certain he was not imagining it all. Guilty consciences frequently played tricks like this. David knew that to be so. And he was guilty, about that there was no doubt whatever. But it was this very guilt that was making him a better man, a better priest, a better writer.

In the end he leaned toward the theory that it was all in his mind. This was by far the more comfortable supposition. To speculate otherwise was to admit that his affair with Pamela threatened to bring him down, write finis to his ecclesial profession, his literary career, his marriage, to a most satisfying life that was getting better by the day.

Nonetheless, doubts lingered, sometimes haunting his waking hours, occasionally invading his dreams.

Enter Klaus Krieg.

At first blush, David was flattered. It is one thing—and a marvelously wonderful thing—to be accepted by a publishing house. It is an even more heady experience to be sought after by a publishing house. And, beyond doubt, P.G. Press wanted him. Nor was P.G. Enterprises unknown to David.

He had watched the televised Reverend Krieg more than once. It was a professional interest. While David had no inclination to indulge in an Elmer Gantry-like fire-and-brimstone ministry, he was fascinated by Krieg's ability to manipulate a diversified crowd.

David might never have paid any attention to the publications arm of P.G. Enterprises had it not been for that television ministry. As it was, he was barely aware that Krieg published books of a religious nature. Occasionally he'd seen some in bookstores and markets, but the garish covers had discouraged investigation.

When the contractual overture came from Krieg, David began looking into P.G. Press. He had been around long enough and had enough worldly experience to know about the nonexistence of the free lunch.

Among his upwardly mobile parishioners were representatives of many diverse professions. One in particular was a sales representative for a large commercial publishing house. David talked with this gentleman about the P.G. offer and was strongly advised against signing the contract. So he sent Krieg a brief, cordial, one-man-of-religion-to-another letter declining the offer without stating any reason for the rejection.

And that, David thought, was that.

But it wasn't.

Evidently Krieg had some sort of inability to take no for an answer. Periodically, he would write David, always finding a fresh angle on which to hang another invitation. David began deliberately postponing a response to such proposals, hoping Krieg would get discouraged or resign, or lose interest, or experience any reaction that would cause him to cease and desist. But nothing seemed to work.

Things got even more intense after the publication of David's third and latest book nearly a year ago. *Father Emrich and the Reluctant Convert* received nearly unanimous favorable criticism in the periodicals that deigned to review it. And, though sales were only slightly better than that of his previous work, that was satisfactory.

David's continued success triggered an increased effort by Krieg to sign him. But oddly, the Reverend's communications no longer called for a formal reply. In fact, Krieg's missives now consisted almost entirely of propaganda highlighting P.G. Press's achievements. Krieg made quite clear what manner of success he envisioned for David once he were to enter the fold. His overtures required no reply; they merely overflowed with information about the rosy future beckoning David.

Under the weight of all this literature, and freed of the necessity to respond, David read all or most of what he was sent from P.G. Press, then filed it all in the wastebasket. But he had to wonder where all this was leading.

The other shoe had dropped some six months ago with an invitation to the Reverend and Mrs. Benbow to visit P.G. Enterprises just outside Mission Viejo, California.

Martha said it was quite out of the question for her. She had several major closings scheduled, and trusted no one else to handle them. But she strongly encouraged him to go. It would be a nice break for him; he needed one; no sense waiting for her to have time for a vacation, not with sales doing so well.

Finally, with many misgivings, David accepted the invitation. All that Martha said was true. He needed the refreshment of some time off and away. And in truth, he was curious to see for himself the complex institution that was P.G. Enterprises. The compelling argument he gave himself was that the visit might end Krieg's full-court press to sign him to a contract. David had said no to the proposition in every possible way but face to face.

It was at the end of March—not a bad time to trade Illinois weather for that of Southern California—that David Benbow visited P.G. Enterprises, all expenses paid.

On arrival, David was given a complete tour of the vast complex. He was properly impressed. He had no reason to doubt Krieg's characterization of the television studios as state-of-the-art. The cathedral itself was a gigantic atrium that ascended endlessly toward heaven.

During that extended weekend, David was ushered about by interchangeably bright, mostly blond, young men and women, who seemed never to stop smiling. His quarters were flawless. His every want was seen to, in many cases anticipated.

Friday and Saturday evenings he dined with the Reverend and Mrs. Klaus Krieg. Mrs. Krieg—"just call me Betsy"— seemed to dote on every word that fell from anyone's lips, but especially those of her husband. As far as David could determine, Betsy had no original thoughts—nor, for that matter, many thoughts at all. But she was gorgeous and well kept. David quickly learned to enjoy looking at her and to expect nothing of substance from her. Betsy and her husband appeared to get on wonderfully. He treasured her and she appreciated him and all he provided for her.

Sunday night, David's final evening in this lavish complex, was memorable. He sensed it would be even before he learned he would be dining alone with the Reverend Krieg.

If everything, particularly the meals, during these three days had been without flaw, tonight's dinner was as close to perfection as one could come this side of heaven. It seemed that Krieg had somehow researched Benbow's eating habits.

Nearly all David's favorites were served: vichyssoise, Caesar salad, lamb (medium-rare), new red potatoes, asparagus with hollandaise sauce, red fruit gelatin, double chocolate cake.

The preludial white wine gave way to a fine red with the meat. Coffee was served, and a bottle of cognac placed on the table.

Krieg lit a cigar and contentedly exhaled a thick cloud of aromatic smoke. As far as Benbow was able to tell, Krieg smoked cigars at every opportunity except when someone present would be offended. Although he was not a smoker, David enjoyed the aroma of both pipe and cigar. Krieg apparently knew that. Not once did he ask David; somehow he knew.

Krieg seemed to examine the cigar as he spoke. "Have you enjoyed the weekend?"

David smiled. "That has to be a rhetorical question."

Krieg returned the smile. "Good, good. I was hoping it would be restful. It pays to get away from the grind from time to time."

"How about yourself, Klaus?" They had been on a first-name basis from the moment David arrived. He knew some referred to Krieg as "Blitz" but this privilege of so addressing him had not been extended.

"Me?"

"Yes, there's no sign that you ever take a break."

"This . . ." Krieg's expansive gesture seemed to encompass the entire P.G. kingdom, ". . . this is my vacation. It's all I wanted. All I ever aimed for."

If this is the whole ball of wax, David thought; *if this is everything you want, why have you been bugging me to work for you?* But, to remain the gracious visitor, he said only,

"Well, it does seem to have just about everything a man could want." He drained his coffee cup.

"More?" Krieg leaned toward the coffee pot.

"No, that's plenty. What a marvelous dinner!"

"Yes, it was good, wasn't it?" Without asking, Krieg filled the bottom curve of two snifters with cognac and offered one to Benbow. "Come . . ." Krieg stood. "Let's go to the gallery."

Taking their glasses with them, the two moved out onto an arcaded balcony three stories above the grounds. P.G. Enterprises was built on elevated terrain. From this vantage, they could easily view the countryside. The evening lights of Mission Viejo, largely residential, were beginning to go on.

It was a cool, pleasant evening; the view was tranquil, a perfect dinner was being serenely digested; the cognac generated an agreeable burning sensation in his throat. "God's in His heaven; all's right with the world," came to mind. But somehow, God seemed to have very little to do with any of this. Strange; the place was named for Him. P.G.: Praise God. Ostensibly, God's work was being done here. The two standing on this balcony were men of God. But there was no denying David's conviction that God was at best a secondary figure in P.G. Enterprises.

After a prolonged silence, Krieg spoke. "It's not the panorama of Chicago—your country—or for that matter the hills of San Francisco, or the skyline of New York, but it is restful, peaceful . . . don't you think?"

Benbow nodded wordlessly.

"You know, David," Krieg went on, "there is one thing that hasn't been mentioned once during your stay here."

Benbow very well knew what had been missing: the point

of it all—his signing a contract to write for P.G. Press. However, he kept silent.

"This is a beautiful site," Krieg went on, "in a beautiful corner of the world, where the weather is always beautiful. Don't you feel it, David? Isn't this a bit of heaven on earth?"

Benbow gave this a few moments' thought, then said, "I'd have to agree: It's all you say it is."

"Then you can understand why we want to share it with everyone we can. It's like wanting every human soul to be admitted to the eternal presence of God in that heavenly land where there are many mansions."

Benbow recognized the familiar tone that he'd heard so often while watching the messianic presence of the Reverend Klaus Krieg on television. Does he turn himself on, David wondered. Is it a self-fulfilling wish? "Wait a minute, Klaus. I thought we were only indulging in figures of speech. This place may be 'a bit of heaven on earth' metaphorically, but it's not literally heaven. We've got to go some before we get there. And I'm confident that the real heaven will be beyond the wildest dreams of even P.G. Enterprises."

Krieg guffawed. "Of course, David . . . of course. You gotta pardon an old war-horse who's never quite left tent revival meetings behind him. Bit of an exaggeration there, I'm afraid.

"But seriously, you know, if you were to become a member of the team, so to speak, this would be a second home to you. We'd put it right in the contract." His expansive gesture included everything within the horizon, the greensward, the sky, Mission Viejo with its twinkling fairytale lights and superb climate. "All of this, David—all of this would be yours." Pause. "Praise God!"

Krieg's words struck a resounding chord in Benbow's

memory. Didn't he know, David wondered; wasn't he aware of what he'd just said? It was right out of the Synoptic Gospels. The classic scene of the devil tempting Jesus. David had used the text so often he knew it verbatim: "Again, the devil taketh him up into an exceeding high mountain, and sheweth him all the kingdoms of the world, and the glory of them; and saith unto him, 'All these things will I give thee, if thou wilt fall down and worship me.' "

The parallel was so striking, at least to David, that he thought it incredible that it might not have occurred to Krieg. Krieg promising him all of Mission Viejo and a slice of P.G. Enterprises if David would fall off his high horse and sign the blasted contract. He felt like borrowing the words of Scripture: "Get these hence, Satan: for it is written, 'Thou shalt worship the Lord thy God, and Him only shalt thou serve.' "

Benbow regarded Krieg intently. Apparently, he was oblivious to the similarity of his statement to that famous passage of the Gospel. Still, David harbored doubts. Krieg, after all, was a preacher. Who should be more familiar with Scripture? Did he have some sort of defense mechanism that blocked any comparison between him and Satan? David thought the latter supposition more probable.

Neither of them had spoken for nearly five minutes. While David pondered this singular proposition, Krieg appeared simply to be enjoying the evening: the food, the drink, the weather; the comfort and security of his P.G. empire.

"Well?" Krieg said at length.

David responded with a wordless, quizzical look.

"See here, David," Krieg said, "P.G. Press has been romancin' you for quite a spell now. You had to know that's what this weekend was all about. We want you. I want you. When you gonna sign that contract?''

David's quizzical look turned to one of wonderment. ''But Klaus, I've given you my answer—many times more than once.''

''You haven't given the right answer yet.''

''It's the only answer I've got.''

''You got somethin' against money, wealth?''

''Of course not, Klaus. I'm a priest. I know what it is to stretch a meager salary. But we're doing all right now, between Martha's income and my salary . . . and, of course, the books.''

''You could make more with me, a lot more.''

''Maybe''—a noticeably more resolute tone crept in— ''maybe not. Maybe I would not be able to deliver what you would demand of me.''

''What makes you think that?''

''Advice from a friend.''

''Sales reps don't know everything there is to know about the publishing business. They're just out there beatin' the pavement and talkin' to bookstore owners and the chains.''

''How did you—?'' David didn't complete the question. He wouldn't have said anything if he hadn't been so startled: How did Krieg know the advice came from a sales representative in his parish?

Quickly, David recovered. ''Look, Klaus, I happen to believe the advice, and I respect the person who gave it to me. I simply don't want to chance signing with you. If you want me to say I am flattered you want me so badly, I'll gladly say it. Just about any author would be pleased, complimented beyond measure, to be courted as perseveringly as you have me, especially with this lavish weekend. But it doesn't matter what you say, Klaus; my answer is no."

"It might matter what I say."

"What do you mean?"

Krieg swirled the last sip of cognac around the bottom of the snifter. "There's Pam."

"What!"

"Pamela Richardson."

Her full name! God! How did he know? How did he know what food was David's favorite? How did he know who had given him the advice to steer clear of P.G. Press? How did he know about Pam? How in hell did he know!

"Right about now, you're probably wondering how I know."

Was he clairvoyant?

"Now look, David, when I want something I get it. It's happened just about all my life. 'Course I don't get a fix on just anything. I make sure I really want it 'fore I go after it. But, then, when I decide this is what I want, why I just go out and get it."

Impossible! No one can do that, get whatever he wants. On second thought, he'd have to amend that: No one *he* knew could do that. But then he didn't intimately know anyone in Krieg's income bracket. Oh, there were his wealthy relatives, of course. But he hadn't had any contact with them in years. Maybe it was true; maybe if money was no object, maybe you could get whatever you wanted.

But Krieg was not going to get David Benbow by default. Maybe there was a bluff to call somewhere here.

"Pamela Richardson," David said. "Someone I'm supposed to know?"

Krieg burst out laughing. "I'd say so—even in the Biblical

sense. You've had carnal knowledge of her lots and lots of times.'' He took a black notepad from his jacket pocket and began leafing through it. "Would you like some dates?''

Could he still be bluffing?

"So, you have dates in a notebook. That means nothing. It's no more than your word against mine.''

From the corner of the balcony railing, Krieg picked up a large manila envelope. It had been there all the while, but David had not noticed it.

Krieg removed the envelope's contents and fingered through a series of 8×10 glossy photos. He handed them to David, who looked at them one by one. They were black-and-white shots of him and Pam—almost everywhere: walking arm-in-arm down a tree-lined street, picnicking on the grass of a public park, dining in a restaurant. All very innocuous—yet pictures of almost every time in recent memory that they had chanced being together publicly. He had expected the stereotypical sleazy bedroom shots. He was greatly relieved.

"So? I have been in the company of a young lady a few times. Is there any law against that? God or man's?''

"David, David . . .'' Krieg shook his head. "You must have caught on by this time. C'mon, you're a smart kid. I know more about you than anyone—your mother, your wife, your mistress, anybody. I just showed you the tip of the iceberg. I thought you'd be impressed that I knew who touted you out of signing my contract. Then there's knowing every blessed thing you like to eat, that you don't mind cigar smoke—pipes, for that matter—the name of your mistress. Weren't those fine, clear shots of you and Pamela?

"We could go on, David, but I wanted to spare you the tapped phone conversations, the tapes of all those amorous affairs that took place in her apartment—we erased the small talk, gossip, and things like that, and concentrated on the sexy sounds and sweet nothings. Do you really want me to trot out all that . . . really?''

David slumped, figuratively and literally. He had to admit that it was feasible that Krieg, immorally and technically, had procured all he claimed to. Benbow had never been so embarrassed. Not even as a child. Someone had shredded his privacy and recorded his most secret words and intimate actions. He gave hardly any thought to begging Krieg for mercy. The man had made it crystal clear that he got what he wanted. And he wanted David.

Shame gave way to an intense anger. ''Klaus, this is blackmail!''

Krieg smiled ruefully and shrugged.

''It's blackmail!'' David repeated. ''And you, a Christian minister! Have you no shame!''

''Me? I didn't sneak around to a young lady's apartment— a *vulnerable* young lady . . .''

Vulnerable. It was the word used by the Reverend Massey that had so affected Benbow. Had Krieg bugged that conversation too? By now, David would have put nothing past the man.

''I didn't sneak around to a vulnerable young lady's apartment,'' Krieg repeated, ''to seduce her and carry on an adulterous relationship after having been advised to break it off not once but twice! And you think *I* should be ashamed!''

''All right, all right,'' David said. ''I've sinned. I won't excuse myself. But I failed. I was weak. Your sin is coldly deliberate. Your sin is full of malice. And you won't get away with it. How is it going to look for a minister of the Gospel to admit that he's been no better than a peeping Tom? You're going to degrade yourself. You may even destroy yourself.''

"Oh, I wouldn't think so, Father Benbow. If you recall, it was a fellow minister who turned in Jimmy Swaggart, and he suffered no ill for it. But that isn't part of my plan. You see, I have numerous friends in the fourth estate. There are ways of leaking information. Why, Father, I wouldn't even be involved. Somebody else. And, far from destroying myself, I know for a certainty that the news media will be grateful. Indeed—grateful.''

David felt a strong urge to pitch Krieg off the balcony. The impulse was brief. Later, on reliving the scene, Benbow had to admit to himself that the real reason he hadn't done it was that the fall probably wouldn't have killed the bastard. David was deeply ashamed to realize that the very moral consideration of murder had had nothing to do with his holding back.

At this point, at least all the cards were on the table. David now knew clearly what the stakes were. And Krieg seemed to hold all the aces. Yet David was not quite ready to throw in his hand.

But first he had to buy some time.

Benbow did his best to introduce a tone of surrender, submission, entreaty to his voice, as he stated that this could, indeed, be an unrefusable offer, but that these revelations had come unexpectedly, that he'd need time to consider all the ramifications of signing with P.G.

Krieg countered that Benbow had had plenty of time— years—to weigh every possible consequence. This was decision time.

Benbow, affecting to try to be as reasonable as possible, acknowledged that Krieg was, of course, free to act now, spread the slander, and ruin Benbow's careers, marriage, life. But, he said, it was clear Krieg had not gone to all that trouble and expense for the purpose of defamation of character, but rather as a most impressive bargaining chip, in order to force Benbow's signing with P.G. Since Krieg had already waited years, as he himself had admitted, what was so difficult about giving him just a little more time? After all, Krieg wanted Benbow's signature on a contract, not his head on a pike. The head was destined for hanging only if the signature was not forthcoming.

With some reluctance, yet with the acknowledgment that basically Benbow's point was well taken, Krieg agreed to wait a bit longer. But, he warned, his patience had worn thin; an affirmative response had better damn well be forthcoming, or . . .

Finally, in a pretense of some sort of conciliation, Krieg assured that the destruction of David's reputation was the furthest thing from his intention. So there need be no fear of a premature revelation. On the other hand, David must know the consequences of an ultimate rejection of the contract. There could and should be no doubt that Krieg was ready and able to make public David's secrets. To reckon otherwise would be to risk certain destruction.

The Reverend Father David Benbow returned to his rectory a sober and worried man. Martha detected the mood but could not pierce the curtain David had drawn about himself.

Martha was not the only one puzzled by David's uncharacteristic transformation. Pamela had never seen her lover in such an unremittingly dark frame of mind. It affected their total relationship. They barely spoke, and on those occasions when they did, he would become lost in thought at any point in a conversation. She took special pains with dinners; he scarcely touched them.

And, as a unique event, he had become impotent, at least with respect to her. She had no means of knowing he remained sexually active with his wife.

Pamela was convinced by the evidence that overwhelmed her that her affair with David Benbow was over, presently and permanently. She scarcely paid attention to the words David used to tell her.

He knew what was wrong, of course. Krieg's threat was so imminent and far-reaching that it exacerbated Benbow's guilt. If it were not for his affair with Pamela, Krieg would have nothing, no hold on him whatever.

There was no way of eradicating the affair retroactively. No way, in the face of all Krieg's evidence, that David could claim that it had never happened. It got so that every time he was in the presence of, or saw, Pamela his fatal folly was brought home to him ever more forcefully. She became the personification of his downfall. Not that he thought for a moment that the entire mess was Pam's fault. No, the fault lay in David's groin. But he could not amputate any of his organs. His sole recourse for any measure of personal peace was to end the affair and see Pam no more.

He did not take too kindly the fact that, after their breakup, she took up with several young men of promise, according to all reports. She seemed to be having a marvelous time while he wavered between helpless hatred for Krieg and the no-win situation of his dilemma. Should he sign and risk his career or refuse and risk his career? And what of his soul?

Like Professor Henry Higgins, he was indignant that his erstwhile protege was using the devices and maneuvers he'd taught her. Under his guidance she had grown from being an ugly duckling with a distracting and disconcerting nervous tic to become a Carmen-like seductress. In quick order, Pam narrowed the field, singling out a promising bank executive several years her junior. After a brief engagement, they were married—not by the Reverend David Benbow.

Her marriage threw David into an even deeper funk. It was as if his love affair had not only been pronounced dead; it had been entombed.

And for all of this he had Klaus Krieg to thank—overlooking, for the moment, his own culpability for initiating the affair with Pam. For a while, David had been so obsessed with Pam and her happiness in the face of his misery that he had virtually lost sight of Krieg's ultimatum.

With Pam's marriage and the ultimate end of their relationship, David recalled with horror that there was some sort of time limit to the ultimatum. Although he hadn't set any specific date, Krieg had made it clear that David was running out of time.

However, with no recent contact from Krieg, David decided to let bad enough alone. Unless he were blessed by some unforeseen circumstance that would free him from Krieg's clutches, Benbow would have to sign. It would take no more than a moment or two to sign the stupid contract. So why not wait until there was utterly no more room for maneuvering? Meanwhile, who could tell; something might happen.

Then the invitation arrived. In effect, it was a command performance from Krieg to attend a writers' workshop at Marygrove College in Detroit.

The invitation was innocent enough. Not unlike many another invitation he'd received, as had other published authors. The difference was the small paragraph explaining the role of Krieg in this conference. It would be meaningless except to someone obligated to Krieg.

David knew. It was time. Unless . . .

David's attention focused on the other three proposed faculty members. He had heard of them. Two of them were first-time authors, but all had garnered good notices.

David studied their names. He had no way of knowing. But, supposing . . . just supposing they were in the same or a similar boat as he. It was not inconceivable. Supposing all, or one or another, were being sought by Krieg for his stable. Supposing there was a kindred soul in that group. Could something be worked out? What? Strength in numbers? Together might they not be able to effect the "miracle" that would eliminate Krieg as their tormentor?

Contact with them would have to be discreetly handled.

He couldn't write or call any of them now. Not without betraying his humiliating situation. Contact would have to be made in person—and even then only circumspectly.

He would have to wait until they had assembled at the college. He would consider it indicative if all the invited accepted. Difficult to think that all would have schedules that permitted attendance at the same workshop. If every one of them accepted and was present, that would indicate the possibility that they were united in a reluctant bond to Klaus Krieg.

Sound them out as judiciously as possible. Who could tell what might transpire? Maybe, just maybe, this dilemma might find a satisfactory conclusion. Maybe God would not have to intervene. Maybe they could do it themselves. Praise God!

18

EVEN DURING A school term, with a full complement of students, Marygrove's campus was rarely this busy.

Particularly bustling was Madame Cadillac Hall, overflowing with police, the media—print, radio, and television—as well as the students who had signed up for the writers' workshop. Gawkers and the curious lined the iron fences that surrounded the grounds. Police were stationed at regular intervals to keep bystanders off campus.

The story of the murdered rabbi had broken last night, reported on the late TV and radio newscasts and the early morning editions of the *News* and the *Free Press*. The city of Detroit, which routinely absorbs multiple murders daily, was shaken by the bizarre event of the killing of a visiting rabbi on an otherwise peaceful Catholic campus. The city might burn down around it, but Marygrove traditionally was spared this sort of notoriety. Yet now it had happened, and the city was stunned.

Inspector Walter Koznicki did not need a directive from Mayor Cobb to clean up this mess forthwith. He got one anyway. Lieutenant Alonzo Tully didn't need a similar directive from his boss; he didn't get one. Just the promise of

all the police manpower he needed. Everyone in authority
wanted this one locked up as quickly as possible.

There had been police task forces on the local scene before, lots of them. And Tully had participated in several. This
was the first time he had been in command of one. It was a
singular feeling. He had never been in charge of hundreds of
soldiers in war either. But he surmised the two experiences
were not all that different. On this field and in the heat of
battle, he found he was not bad as a modern major general.

His troops were being efficiently utilized and he had done
a credible job at delegating complementary responsibilities.
Some of the officers were interrogating the workshop students, both those living on and off campus. Others were
combing nearly every inch of Madame Cadillac Hall with
deliberation and meticulousness. Still others were going over
the scene of the crime: the dining room used by the workshop's faculty. What remained of the faculty, minus the de-
ceased Rabbi Winer, had been interrogated at length and in
great detail last night. The panel members remained under
a loosely structured surveillance—with the exception of the
Reverend Klaus Krieg. Because he refused to stay in one
securable place, he could not be protected in any absolute
way. But in the number and quality of officers used, the police approached perfection.

Tully, through his delegates, was keeping abreast of what
was going on in all areas of this investigation. In his mind,
the most important detail, headed by Sergeant Angie Moore,
was the group inquiring into the backgrounds of Augustine, Benbow, and Sister Marie. Due to the questionably un-
warranted bitterness they exhibited toward Krieg, these three
had to be the prime suspects at this point in the case.

It was natural, then, for Tully to feel a particular anticipation when he spied Angie Moore hurrying down the corridor toward him. Her haste telegraphed the message that her squad had uncovered something of moment.

With Tully was Father Koesler. His presence in the inner circle of this investigation was due, in part, to Inspector Koznicki's invitation.

"Got somethin'?" Tully greeted Moore.

Moore nodded perfunctorily at Koesler. Under more casual circumstances she would have greeted him warmly. Now she was strictly business. "Yeah. We started calling people last night, till it got too late. Then we started again early this morning."

"And?"

"And Benbow's got—or at least had—one on the side."

"A mistress?" Tully wasn't sure Koesler understood what Moore meant, and he wanted to make sure there was no communication breakdown.

"Uh-huh."

"How long's it been going on?"

"Years."

"How notorious?"

"Hard to tell. The first several calls we came up dry. Phoned some of his friends, a few parishioners whose names he gave us. Nobody knew anything except they were concerned about his being involved in any way in an act of violence. Then we got a break. One of the parishioners—I think her type used to be called 'a pillar of the Church' "—she glanced at Koesler.

"They still are," he said.

"Anyway," Moore continued, "this gal was hesitant at first. It was her hesitation that gave us the idea that she knew something. So we dug a bit and she finally opened up. Actually, she was just dying to tell us.

"This involves a gal Benbow was counseling. From there it turned into an affair."

"Before," Tully said, "you said Benbow 'had' this affair. It's over?"

"Apparently. See, it was this lady who led us to another and another and another—all gossipy types—who filled in some details. Seems Benbow tried to keep it under wraps, took precautions, hardly ever appeared with her in public. But snoops who want to know generally find out. That's what happened here. That's why we think it's not widely known. My guess is most—almost all—of his friends and parishioners are in the dark on this one. But those few who do know are sure of themselves. One of the informants claimed it was all over, that it ended abruptly after Benbow took a trip. From another person who knew nothing of the affair, we learned that that trip was to P.G. Enterprises in California."

A restrained smile spread over Tully's face. "So, Krieg found out and threatened to reveal Benbow's affair—scared him enough to make him end it."

"That's what we figure. It's the only way it makes sense. Shortly after that trip, Benbow stopped visiting the woman completely. Then, for the first time, other men began seeing her, taking her out, visiting her. A little while back, she married one of them."

"With Krieg's connections," Tully said, "he undoubtedly could have found out with his own resources alone. But if that many people knew, it certainly would have been easy for him. So what kind of stick did Krieg hold over him?"

"We figure," Moore said, "that pulling this out of the closet probably would have ended or seriously compromised

Benbow's writing career . . . at least as far as the religious aspect of it was concerned. Probably the Episcopal Church is not as quick with penalties as the Catholic Church, but I doubt they would look the other way when it comes to notorious adultery.''

"Hmmm, the whole ball of wax," Tully said. "How about his wife?"

"Always the last to know, Zoo," Moore said. "Far as we can tell, she still doesn't know. Or, if she does, according to all accounts, she gives no indication she does." Pause. "So, what do you want to do with this one?"

After a moment's reflection, Tully said, "Nothin' just now. There's no point in it. We already know how Krieg would react. The same way he did when we confronted him with Rabbi Winer's secret past: 'Who, me?' But the pattern is holding true. Two for two. It looks like Krieg was blackmailing these writers to get them to sign a contract with him.

"As far as that theory goes, so far so good. Both Winer and Benbow had secrets that could ruin them if anyone revealed them. I think Krieg threatened both of them. It's the only thing we know of so far that would explain why they hated him. Now, if we find something similar in the past of the monk and the nun, it's gonna be a little tight for Krieg to deny the whole thing. And we will have four people with enough motive to commit murder. Any luck with the other two, Angie?"

"Not yet, Zoo. I've got a team working on each one. We're in touch with Augustine's monastery, going through the various monks and the abbot, of course. Nothing of any significance so far. Before he joined the monastery he worked in a New York ad agency—one of the big ones. But there aren't too many left there who remember him. It was a long time ago. Lots of the people who worked with him are either retired or dead. But we're staying with it.

"The nun is a little tougher. She's been all over the place. Taught at something like twelve schools in this area. Chicago too. Took postgraduate courses at different colleges. Again, all over the place. Now she's got that job in Florida."

"The thing is, Angie," Tully said, "with what you found out about Benbow, the odds go up fast that there's something in the backgrounds of the other two. There's gotta be something. If Krieg could find it, by damn we ought to be able to. So, hang in there, Angie, and keep me plugged in. Need any more help?"

"I don't think so, Zoo. We're getting the knack. The team's sort of in the groove; they're doing a great job. We're gonna break this one, I just feel it." With that, Moore hurried back to her troop.

Tully turned to leave and check the progress of the others on his team. Before he could go, Koesler spoke.

"One thing puzzles me, Lieutenant."

Tully stopped, one eyebrow raised.

"It would seem to me," Koesler said, "that Reverend Krieg would be the most cooperative person in this whole investigation. After all, it's his life that's being threatened. In fact, if it hadn't been for an unforeseeable fluke, he'd be dead now. Yet he seems to be more an obstacle than a help."

Tully thought for a moment. "It's odd, but it's not unique. You'd naturally expect somebody whose life is on the line to be scared sh . . . uh, stiff." Apparently Tully discarded one word and chose another in its stead. "Ordinarily that's the way it is. Now somebody's trying to kill Krieg. You'd assume he'd want to leave town. Or, better, so we'd have a chance to catch his assailant, to at least hole up in his apartment with security while we investigate the case and come up with the perp. You'd assume he'd be the most scared and cooperative guy possible.

"But it doesn't always work out that way. Sometimes it's macho bravado. The guy doesn't want to admit that anything could scare him. I think there's a little of that here. That might explain what's goin' on, at least to some extent."

"Yes," Koesler said, "that could explain it. Just in the short time I've known him, he strikes me as one who would not want to admit to any weakness or fear. It would compromise his professed confidence in God and God's alleged commitment to protect him. It might wipe that perpetual grin off his face. It would compromise. And . . ." he grew more thoughtful, "something that occurred to me while you were explaining this. I've met a few people over the years who never give up. When they want something, nothing stands in their way. They simply don't understand 'no' and won't take it for an answer."

"Sounds good," Tully said.

"Applying that theory," Koesler continued, "Reverend Krieg probably considers Rabbi Winer a lost commodity rather than a murdered human being. And even if one of the three remaining writers wants him dead, he's probably still counting on signing the other two. Probably he is constitutionally incapable of conceiving that he could be killed along the way.

"As I say, I've met his type before." Koesler shook his head. "But I still can't comprehend such bullheadedness, especially in the face of betting one's life on the outcome—" He looked startled. "Well, speak of the . . ."

A small entourage was making its way down the corridor. At its center was Klaus Krieg. In his retinue were a few

steely-eyed men and women, who, Koesler correctly surmised, were police officers. The others were students.
Though he didn't know their names, Koesler recognized their
faces.

The company passed Tully and Koesler seemingly without
noticing them. The police were on the lookout specifically
for any danger. The students were hanging on each of Krieg's
words. And Krieg, a smile on his lips, was happily pontifi-
cating. As he passed, he exclaimed, "Praise God!"

In their wake, Koesler sniffed. "Cigars?"

"Krieg," Tully said. "Didn't you get the odor in the residence hall?"

"Yes, now that you mention it. But I didn't know who was
smoking. Now that I think of it, the odor wasn't there yesterday, but it was there strongly this morning. And the only
difference was that Reverend Krieg stayed here last night
while he spent the previous night downtown at the Westin.

"Funny," Koesler added, "I haven't seen the Reverend
smoke. Not in the classroom or the dining room."

"Somebody said he doesn't smoke when there's a chance
anybody'd be offended by it."

"Not a common virtue, that bit of abstinence." Koesler
was impressed—for the very first time—by Krieg's apparent
thoughtfulness.

"Gotta see how the troops are doing." Tully turned
abruptly and left.

Koesler stood for several moments reflecting on all he'd
just heard. Then he remembered it was time for the scheduled morning Mass. Celebrating it remained Koesler's responsibility. He had offered the service to Father Augustine,
who declined with little civility. Apparently, he was carrying

a grudge from the altercation he himself had caused in the sacristy yesterday morning.

No one else was in the sacristy. By now Koesler knew where everything was, so he vested quickly. Even at that he was a few minutes late. Pretty good crowd, he thought as he entered the sanctuary to begin Mass. The congregation by no means filled the large chapel, but it was substantially more numerous than yesterday's skeleton group. He wondered if all these pious souls would have been in attendance were it not for what had happened. There are no atheists in a Catholic college; especially with a murder investigation going on, he thought, and almost chuckled.

Mass began. Buried in one of the clusters in the congregation was Father Augustine. In black trousers and an open-neck white shirt instead of his religious habit, he went largely unrecognized. He seemed deep in thought as Koesler began the opening prayers.

Mechanically, Augustine joined the others in prayer: *"I confess to Almighty God, and to you my brothers and sisters, that I have sinned through my own fault . . ."* For some reason, these words returned him to the present, then, like a springboard, their meaning drew him back into the past.

No longer was he a sixty-year-old man, fully formed, with most of his life behind him. In recollection, he was a young man whose future seemed limitless.

19

HE WAS IN college. If anyone had told him then that one day he would become a Trappist monk, he would have laughed himself silly.

His name was Harold May. He was the son of a career Army man, so his family had lived in many, many places, on military bases throughout the United States and many other countries. So far, it had been an interesting life, filled with excitement and adventure.

As he grew up, he watched his father climb the military ladder and he listened as his father explained to his mother, and sometimes to him privately, the carefully made plans for advancement.

Harold admired his father and was terribly proud of his accomplishments. Harold loved the dress uniforms, the decorations, each more splendid than the previous with each new promotion. Harold was determined to follow in his father's footsteps. But not in the military. It would be a major disappointment to the father, but the son wanted wider horizons than the military could offer.

And that was why Harold May was at UCLA, achieving. He was heavily into various Liberal Arts courses, with great emphasis on Journalism and English. His goal was advertising, but not the bottom nor even the comfortable middle rungs of the business. He knew where he wanted to go and he knew what it would take.

He also knew enough not to waste time in pursuits that would prove to be dead ends. Thus, slight of build and not particularly well coordinated, he participated in no organized sports. Oh, he fooled a bit with pick-up games of softball and touch football. But his interest in these was no more than social and, worse than being no good at them, he was likely to be injured playing them. He found he could socialize as well or better on the sidelines. For recreation, wisely, he walked, often, far, and rapidly.

There was no way he could know it then, but this era during which he was attending college would later be known as "The Golden Age of Television." And he happened to be where the action was.

Harold was among the first to realize what television would mean to the advertising world. That TV would turn the ad business upside down and inside out.

A very quick study, he required minimum time hitting the books. He also cut as many classes as he could get away with. A good part of the time he appropriated from studies he spent at the TV studios doing anything and everything he could on the technical side of the lights. So many of the young people who worked with him planned careers in television, but not in the coolie labor demanded of them now. They were going to be dramatic or comedy stars or directors or producers, or in charge of one or another of the technical facets of the business. One day they'd have a shelf full of Emmys. Or so they dreamed. Actually, few of them would achieve any measure of success in an industry where many were called but few chosen.

Harold, on the other hand, was utterly uninterested in television as such. Although the term ''commercial television'' was not yet prevalent, that was precisely the designation he foresaw. In this, he was prescient.

Until the fifties, advertising was pretty well confined to the print medium: newspapers, magazines, fliers, unless one wished to count movie previews, which, then as now, were teasers luring moviegoers to a forthcoming film. And if one wished to count coming attractions as ads, they were ads created by the film industry.

Hollywood, for all practical purposes, had cornered the market in film-making. That industry knew how to make moving pictures for the big screen. It was a short step from that science to making moving pictures for a little screen. Hollywood had the skills and techniques to blend moving pictures and sound, even animation. And New York's ad community did not. At least not in the beginning.

And there lay Harold's genius. He knew that the two—movies and advertising—were destined to meet. Indeed, at that moment they were on a collision course. The ad community was about to be caught in an embarrassment of ignorance. Not only did they not understand the techniques of film-making, they did not even know the jargon.

That was why young Harold May spent every possible spare moment on, in, and around the sound stages of Hollywood. He fully intended to combine all that he was learning behind the camera, in the cutting rooms, in the production offices, with his university courses.

Even with this singleminded dedication to his chosen career, Harold managed to squeeze in a not inconsiderable social life. And this brought to light another of Harold's talents that surprised him, and amazed many of his friends.

Harold could drink.

Harold could not only drink prodigious amounts of alcohol, he had an astounding ability to hold it and not become intoxicated while all about him were drinking far less yet getting falling-down drunk.

This talent did not go uncelebrated. Several of his friends, both intimate and casual, were heard to say in one way or another, ''God, I wish I could drink like Harold!''

Decades before safety experts urged groups of drinkers out for a night on the town to designate a nondrinking driver, Harold was the designated drinking driver.

Actually, he was not only proud of this talent, he was even grateful to God for it. Naturally, he had heard those stories of three-martini lunches for which ad people were notorious. He knew it was no mean trick to float through liquid lunches, be a hail-fellow-well-met, and still conduct business soberly.

It was not unlike a man with a mesomorphic body excelling at a sport such as football. God had gifted such a person with an unlikely body, steroid-free, and the athlete made good use of his gift. So it was with Harold. He believed that, for His own good reasons, God had granted unto him all those special gifts that were aiding him in the preparation for a life of upward mobility in the advertising business. But was it God doing all this? In the end, that was anyone's guess. However, Harold was a very religious young man. His mother, as often as possible, attended daily Mass. His father, and commandant, enrolled him in parochial school—or, if there were no Catholic school on the base, catechism classes.

As is often the case in such circumstances, little Harold kept learning the same religious lessons over and over. His formation in morality was shallow but absorbed. Hopscotching from one military base to another, he had the opportunity to meet a vast mix of people his own age, but not necessarily of his religious persuasion. It was a practical if raw course in comparative religion. From conversations and discussions, he learned that many Protestants believed drinking and gambling were immoral. While Catholics were more cautious: There was nothing wrong with drinking as long as one did not become theologically drunk, which happened when one's face hit the floor. Likewise with wagering: Nothing wrong with that as long as one did not lose the farm. All was well unless one indulged excessively. Moderation, in all things moderation.

Except with regard to sex. His Protestant buddies were not nearly as restricted in sexual matters as Harold.

Harold was taught that sexual expression had two purposes. The primary purpose was the procreation and education of children. The secondary purpose was the legitimate relief of concupiscence. He learned that at least once every year. That old devil concupiscence! He didn't even know what concupiscence was until about his eighth or ninth year—which was when he learned about the purposes of sex.

So there the matter stood. Catholics, especially, it was believed, if they were Irish, drank like camels. They also bet on each pitch in a baseball game. Protestants couldn't wear makeup, play cards, or have more than a rare glass of wine at dinner. But they did fool around.

None of these religious differences seemed odd to Harold because he had been taught and did believe that the one, holy, Catholic and Apostolic Church was the one, true Church of Jesus Christ. And that pretty well put all the others in their place.

Oh, yes, Harold was religious. And as far as he was concerned, his life was in sync with God's will. He would have done more wagering—perhaps a virtue rather than a vice—but that he had little scratch with which to place a decent bet. He dated, but he never went further than necking and petting—worth from five to ten "Our Fathers" and "Hail Marys," depending on the confessor. Basically, God had given Harold all the tools he needed to score big in the advertising world, his chosen profession. And, as if he needed any further sign in that delicate arena of the multi-martini lunch, he could hold his own and then some. Could anything God did be more a sign of Divine Providence!

Harold graduated.

He selected the William J. Doran Agency, one of New York's largest, most innovative ad firms. For years, in his imagination, usually just before sleep at night, he had been drafting a clever query letter to go along with a catchy resume. He sent them to Robert L. Begin, creative supervisor at the Doran Agency.

The tactic worked. The letter and resume won Harold an interview luncheon with Begin.

They met at "21," one of New York's posher restaurants. It was a pivotal luncheon that would determine, to a large extent, Harold's professional future. Begin was relaxed about it. And why should he not be? He was in the driver's seat. It was Harold's future that was at stake. And it was Begin's prerogative to recommend the hiring or rejection of this young man.

The pressure was on Harold. He was on the spot. But no one would ever have known it. The way he saw it, this was the moment for which he'd been born. It was, as they used to say in the Crusades, God's will.

After introductions, the two were seated at a preferred

table near the rear of the dining area. The waiter acknowledged and deferred to Begin. Harold noticed.

To Harold, Begin seemed the embodiment of the company man: attired in a light gray suit—appropriate for a warm June day—he wore rimless glasses—bifocals—and expensive cuff links and a trendy wristwatch. His thinning graying hair lent an aristocratic appearance.

The waiter took their orders. A Manhattan for Begin; a martini, up, for Harold.

Begin began to explain the make-up of the Doran Agency. Although Harold had researched it thoroughly, the novice listened with an absorbed expression.

There were, Begin spelled out, drawing barely perceptible lines on the tablecloth with the prongs of his fork, five departments in the company.

"The account management division," Begin said, "provides liaison to the client with regard to current as well as new business. The creative department, which, I take it, is your primary interest, Harold—"

You betcha, thought Harold.

". . . the creative department contains both the art department and the copywriters. Then there's the production department, the people who put the ad on the printed page. The media department decides where the ad will run: paper; magazines; which papers and when; which magazines. Finally, there's the research department, which develops strategy for the target audience and tests the advertising concept.

"The important thing, Harold, is that all this describes the team effort that advertising very much is. To paraphrase, 'No department is an island.' "

Begin was interrupted by the waiter inquiring whether they were ready to order. They were. Begin would have the catch of the day. Harold would have the Caesar salad and another martini, up. Begin took note.

Begin took Harold through much of the ad business history, then focused on the Doran Agency and its six prime accounts. Of course Harold knew who the accounts were, but, again, he didn't interrupt. They were: a major pharmaceutical company; a national brewery; a brand tobacco firm; a cosmetics business; an airline; and International Motors, presently striving to become one of the Big Four auto companies.

Begin noted the flicker of desire in Harold's eyes at the mention of International Motors.

It was a subtle reaction, but Begin had trained himself to be alert to such small signs. He wondered if Harold May had a future with Doran. Judging from his credentials alone, probably yes. Then Begin wondered if Harold had a future in the International Motors account. Likely not for a long while. The level at which Harold would enter the company was light years away from such an important account.

By the time they had all but finished their lunch, Begin had just about completed his guided tour through advertising in general and Doran in particular. The waiter returned to ask if they wanted coffee. They did. And Harold ordered his third martini. Begin took note. Then he opened the conversation to Harold.

It was the moment for which Harold had patiently waited.

While not derogating from anything Begin had said, Harold launched into a flood of knowledge acquired over the years. When he felt that Begin was sufficiently impressed, Harold played trump: Los Angeles, Hollywood, television. "There's always going to be a place for print advertising, of course, Mr. Begin . . ."

"Bob, please."

"Thank you. Bob. It's just that, to be effective, print has to have longevity and consistency."

"You're right, Harold. And that's the way we project at Doran. The client has to be sold on the woodpecker theory."

"Woodpecker?" Harold didn't think he'd missed a term, but this was unfamiliar.

"The woodpecker, hitting the same spot over and over again, just the same way!"

"Of course," Harold agreed. "But something different happens when you get to TV advertising, don't you think? I mean television imposes itself on its audience—where print gives you the option of looking or not looking."

"Keen observation," Begin commented. "But you mentioned Hollywood, television. I'd be interested in your views of TV as it relates to advertising." He tried to affect a casual tone.

Harold caught Begin's heightened interest. He was not surprised. He'd expected it.

"From what I've been able to put together," Harold said, "effective TV advertising is going to have emotion, humor, and fancy production."

"And print ads don't?"

"Not really. The TV medium is, by its very nature, more flamboyant, more flashy than print. The emotion is right on the surface. It can fool with humor in a way that print can't afford to. Pratfalls, clips of old Mac Sennett comedies, dancing cigarette packs, things like that. And when it comes to fancy production, the print medium simply can't compete. You're going from a single picture per page to production numbers staged maybe in Busby Berkeley style."

Begin could not hide his excitement. He urged Harold

to tell him all he knew about this monster that threatened to skyrocket the ad industry. While Harold still had much to learn, he was not the complete innocent when it came to hoarding bargaining chips.

So, in sketchiest detail, Harold told of his experience behind the camera, building sets, staging, cutting and editing film, even a bout or two in the director's chair—albeit in extremely small productions. Nonetheless, the sum total of all this hands-on experience gave him a very distinct advantage over the garden-variety creative ad person. A conclusion with which Bob Begin concurred.

The waiter presented the check. Begin, accepting it, asked Harold if he wanted another drink—one for the road. Harold declined. Begin took note. Three martinis, par for the course. And Harold showed not one ill effect. This one might be a winner.

In short order, at the recommendation of Robert Begin, Harold was hired by the William J. Doran agency.

Harold was assigned to the bullpen. The bullpen was christened such by the copywriters who had occupied that position, paid their dues, and eventually escaped it.

It did not take Harold long to figure out that the bullpen separated the floaters from the self-motivators. Junior copywriters essentially were unassigned. The go-getters would find projects. The others would contemplate the ever-changing universe. There was no doubt that Harold intended to work—and to climb. But no one offered him a project, and he couldn't find the rope.

So, in the beginning, Harold spent much more time looking for work than actually working. Timing his entrances carefully so it would not be apparent that he was, in effect, begging for work, he wandered from office to office, asking, "Anything I can help you with?"

That was how he got his first assignment. It as an "on pack." One of the agency's toothpaste accounts was offering a sample-size tube of toothpaste along with a small toothbrush. It was a travel package. All that was needed was filler body copy for the enclosed ad. Harold wrote the copy in about the time it would have taken to dash off a memo. He hadn't invested all this preparation just to write filler copy.

But it was a learning experience.

One does not climb quickly by wandering about offering one's services. The next most logical step was to seize the ball and run with it. He planned that step more carefully.

Weeks passed before he completed and introduced his next venture. He approached Fred Ruhman, an associate creative director in charge of the team that handled the Kingbrew account.

"Fred," Harold began, "I had a hell of a lot of trouble getting to sleep last night. But just before I drifted off, I got this idea for a Kingbrew Beer presentation. The video possibilities knocked me cold."

"No kidding. C'mon into my office and let's talk about it."

Once they were ensconced in Fred's office, Ruhman gave a great performance as one who was politely interested in an underling's idea, amateurish as it might be, and who would out of kindness hear the subordinate out.

Harold knew that, in reality, Ruhman was well up the creek with no paddle. The Kingbrew people expected a presentation for a major TV ad campaign in a couple of days. And Ruhman's team hadn't been able to get off the dime.

Ruhman listened patiently, showed little emotional response, and ended by thanking Harold and urging him to feel free to come in for a consultation anytime.

Harold did not have long to wait. Shortly after the meeting with the Kingbrew execs, word spread rapidly throughout the agency. It was a winner. Kingbrew bought the entire concept. They were thrilled with the presentation. Everything was coming up roses at the William J. Doran Agency. And it was all due to the fertile imagination of Fred Ruhman.

Fred Ruhman!

It was another learning experience.

There was no possible way Harold could claim credit for his pilfered concept! If push came to shove, it certainly would be Ruhman's word against his. And Harold knew whose word would prevail. Although it would be a cold day in hell before Ruhman arrived at a similar campaign on his own.

Go for the jugular.

Harold plotted.

It took another several weeks—during which he wrote filler copy and found pretexts not to attend meetings, lunches, dinners, or have contact of any sort with Fred Ruhman—for him to perfect his next presentation.

This time he went above Ruhman's level to the creative supervisor, namely, Bob Begin, who, it turned out, was more than willing to become Harold's protector.

Begin listened to Harold's presentation, his graphics plan, his proposal to combine live actors with animated cartoon characters, his imaginative use of International Motors vehicles. International Motors. Begin recalled their luncheon and that flicker of naked desire in Harold's eyes at the mention of International Motors.

So, Harold was closing in on the quarry. Well, more power to him.

The presentation was good—no, superior. Better than anything the Doran Agency—or any other, for that matter—had done heretofore. If this proposal were given an appropriate setting, worthy of its intrinsic importance, International Motors would belong to Doran for the foreseeable future, if not forever. And Harold's star would go into orbit.

Another, in Begin's position, might have feared helping a subordinate to, in effect, leapfrog over himself. There was a natural tendency to keep subordinates subordinate and to use them as stepping stones on one's own trip to the top.

Begin had a larger vision, which was not without an altruistic element.

On the one hand—the beau geste—he liked Harold, and wanted to see him succeed. But few people do anything for one reason alone. Thus, on the other, more self-interested, hand, Begin was inclined to hitch his wagon to Harold's star.

Both Begin and May understood the path frequently taken toward, and to, the top in the ad industry. One tended to be wed to one's clients. If one got a stranglehold on a most important client, one tended to rise in the company; if the client was deemed irreplaceable the ascendancy could be to the presidential suite. In the Doran Agency, International Motors was such an invaluable customer.

Begin knew that even with all his talent, experience, and expertise he personally would never hold a most important client such as International Motors in the palm of his hand. Whereas Harold just might. With his fertile imagination and singular specialized experience, it was conceivable that Harold one day might be able to demand a presidential position with the ultimatum that otherwise he would walk to the agency down the street, taking his International Motors with him. And at such time he might well be able to carry out such a threat. On that glorious day when Harold advanced into the presidential suite, he, Bob Begin, wanted to be at the winner's side.

So Bob Begin put all his eggs in Harold May's basket. It was risky, but, as Begin saw it, the odds favored the bet.

Thus, Begin pulled all the necessary strings and set up the presentation. William J. Doran himself sat in—though not without trepidation—that day. It was a double-header! Not only was Harold's head on the block, so was Begin's.

Success!

The collective noses of just about everyone below the level of creative supervisor were bent. Harold, in short order and with few stops in between, rose from the bullpen to the post of associate creative director on the strength of—what else— the International Motors account.

Harold was not yet "there." But he was getting there.

He was being sought out. No longer was he the one who wandered the halls looking for something to do, searching for a break. Deferentially, people came to him. Nor was he standoffish. He treated others generously, even those who had treated him patronizingly during his apprenticeship in the bullpen.

Lunches—with his peers, superiors, clients—became elongated. Harold found that food was becoming less and less important. It didn't really matter whether he had a salad, a meat, or a fish dish; all that counted was the quality of the martinis. He joked that lunch time was his attitude adjustment period of the day. He never ceased to be amused when in the company of anyone being exposed to hard liquor for the first time. The pinched face, the shudder, as if the neophyte were tasting poison. Harold had never experienced a single negative reaction to booze. From his very first drink, it had been as mother's milk to him. Some were born to drink, others not, he concluded.

Years passed. Harold's position in the agency grew ever more secure. Everyone was given to know that, for all intents and purposes, the International Motors account was his baby. But his sphere of influence spread well beyond that single account no matter how important it was to the agency. He had been given several bonuses and merit increases. He was being openly touted as the next creative director, a position that would put him virtually a heartbeat away from the presidency.

But something was happening to Harold and his favorite pastime—lunch. It had to do with his "attitude adjustment" period. The triple martini no longer sufficed to adjust his attitude. He was developing an ever higher tolerance. It happened by gradations. Gradually, he became aware that the pleasurable floating feeling was eluding him. He missed the sensation, but would not admit, even to himself, that he felt desperate about the loss.

He had become celebrated for his daily luncheon procession of martinis. Two before solid food, one during the meal. He did not want to adjust his routine. He did not allow himself to reflect on the fact that he needed, really needed, more.

Initially, he solved his problem by having a martini alone in his office before going out to lunch. It worked for a while. Then he found that four wasn't doing the trick. As far as he was concerned, this indicated nothing more than that his storied ability to hold his liquor had built up. The only obvious problem was how he could add enough booze to adjust his attitude without revealing this need to others. They would never understand.

The solution was easy enough. He heavily stocked the wet

bar in his ample office, and instructed his secretary to schedule no appointments after 4:30 P.M. By that time he would have had enough to drink that he wouldn't remember any business that he'd discussed.

Sobriety of sorts would return to Harold early in the evening. It was a state he learned to try to avoid. So he drank through the evening hours until he slipped into a dreamless, nonrefreshing sleep. He continued to get to work at approximately 9:00 in the mornings, but wasn't able to accomplish much until near noon when he had his single preliminary-to-lunch martini. This preluncheon drink was always the first of Harold's day; he convinced himself that as long as he didn't drink any liquor before 11:30 A.M. he remained in control.

Of course his altered behavior became obvious to just about everyone in the agency. All the subterfuges he thought hid his nipping at the bottle couldn't possibly do the trick. He became the subject of disrespectful jokes. Among the younger employees he became known as ''42'' because he visited the ''21'' restaurant twice a day.

Somehow, perhaps because he had organized his affairs so well before he tobogganed into what everyone else knew as his problem drinking, his work did not unduly suffer. During his increasingly rare clear-headed intervals, he was still able to be creative, sometimes brilliant. And, because he was still productive, his peers and superiors could wink at his self-destructive behavior, which, left unchecked, would probably one day be the cause of his downfall.

Ironically, many years later, a smashingly successful television ad campaign would be built around a pirate-eyed dog who would drink but always ''remain in control.''

All were willing to look the other way except Bob Begin,

his original guardian angel. Again, Bob's motives were mixed. On the one hand, Harold's present course very definitely was not leading to the presidency, which track Begin had been depending on for his own future security. On the other hand, a talented person was throwing his life away. For both reasons, Begin decided to get involved. It took every last ounce of emotional and psychic strength he possessed, but eventually he prevailed upon Harold to attend a few meetings of Alcoholics Anonymous.

At first, Harold resisted all efforts to get him to realistically assess his personal condition. He was willing to admit that AA was not all bad for those who needed it. He didn't need it. He was still steadfast in his resolve not to drink before 11:30 in the morning.

Harold was blessed that Begin continued to urge him to be faithful to the meetings and that several members of that group were tenacious in their invitations to join them. Gradually—very deliberately—Harold began to see himself in the admissions of the others.

He learned that the natural ease with which he first adapted to liquor, far from indicating immunity from addiction, suggested an alcoholic tendency. The others' repeated confessions of loss of control brought home to him the helpless feeling he habitually denied. Alcoholic after alcoholic admitted, "When I start drinking, I have no idea, I can't predict, what the outcome might be."

The final nail of self-revelation came when others confessed their dependency: "I need booze just like other people need food and water."

The recovering alcoholics listened patiently as Harold pleaded his nonaddiction—since he was able to abstain until

11:30 every morning—although they scarcely could control their laughter at his naiveté.

In time he became a full-fledged member of Alcoholics Anonymous. The easiest of the famous twelve steps for Harold was admitting the existence of a power greater than himself. If Harold believed in anything, he believed in God. Indeed, it was his belief in God that sustained him through the agony of withdrawal, in and out of the William J. Doran Advertising Agency, and led him into the Order of Cistercians of the Strict Observance, or Trappists.

He chose the Trappists for several reasons. He felt he needed plenty of penance, and the Trappists, at least when he first joined them, were rigorous: prayer and work and little else. The renowned Thomas Merton had just made the order popular if not illustrious. And entering the Trappists was an excellent way of disappearing into a community where, save Merton, there was little if any individuality. Harold was, among other things, trying to lose his notoriety.

However, it was not long after he had met ''Father Louis'' (Merton), and shortly after the famous priest's weird death, that Harold decided he was destined to become the next Merton.

Meanwhile, back on Madison Avenue, the fate of Harold May was the subject of animated conversation and debate in advertising circles and over leisurely lunches until, after a reasonable interval, the advertising career of Harold May and its possibilities was laid to rest.

Requiescat in pace.

Only in one person's mind did the memory of Harold May not fade. Robert Begin never forgot Harold. Begin felt somewhat like the young Catholic woman engaged to a young agnostic man. She desperately wanted unity of religion in her marriage. To humor her, he took instructions in the Catholic faith—and was so influenced by them he became a priest.

Similarly, Begin had introduced Harold to Alcoholics Anonymous with the hope that the group could help him off the road to self-destruction and back on the path to the presidency with its perks for both of them. But, along the way, Begin lost Harold to God.

Harold—first Brother, then Father, Augustine—threw himself wholeheartedly into the religious life. He did well as a Trappist. That he was a gifted writer had been proven in his secular life, and his abbot knew it. So Augustine soon was assigned the duties of a scribe. He meticulously researched, then wrote treatises that were published in academic journals. Because they appeared in such scholarly publications, no one expected Augustine's pieces to be so interestingly and imaginatively written. So, few readers recognized that he was several cuts above the ordinary.

In addition to this writing ability, Harold's ease and skill in allocution in the monastery also were soon noted. That marked the beginning of Harold's "outreach" assignment; to spend weekends outside the monastery helping in nearby parishes, thus creating a greater sense of presence and opportunity for recruitment for the order.

At first, Harold was reluctant to leave the monastery and its shelter from the world. After all, he hadn't left the world only to return to it. Then he began to enjoy the camaraderie of the parish priests he met on these assignments.

Parish priests, in turn, generally enjoyed entertaining visiting priests, and did well in offering quality bed and board, especially board. While the visitor's accommodations might be spartan—frequently an afterthought in the rectory's architecture—food and drink were usually topflight.

Harold was to learn that he hadn't learned much. He'd never bought the AA maxim, "Once an alcoholic, always an alcoholic." He held himself to a couple of drinks before dinner on Saturday parish assignments, but it was extremely difficult.

After evening confessions, he drank himself into oblivion. If Sunday morning duties had not been so strictly routine, he would never have been able to carry them off. After his final Mass on Sunday, he would demonstrate once again that AA saying, "One is too many and a thousand are not enough."

This led to quite a few altercations with Massachusetts Highway police except on those Sunday afternoons and evenings when he was lucky enough to get back to the monastery safely without encountering the law. In all his run-ins with road cops, one thing and one thing only saved him from a ticket, the drunk tank, a trial, probation, or imprisonment: He was a priest—and police were notoriously slow to ticket the clergy.

Then came the book.

The plot came to him in dribs and drabs, mostly during private prayer. At first, he thought he was undergoing a chronic failure in his prayer life: distractions. He confessed them as such—until he was able to see the gold at the end of the rainbow.

It was a believable plot, with three-dimensional characters, complete with a surprise ending. Conscientiously, he brought his new project to the abbot, who at first was cool to the notion of a contemplative dabbling at a mystery novel. But, persevering, Augustine finally convinced Father Abbot of the good that could accrue to the order, and the potential added income for the monastery.

The book was written in what was—if anyone kept statistics on how long it took to write a novel in a monastic setting—probably record time. Everyone in the monastery was impressed, especially when it was accepted for publication on the very first submission.

There was an author's tour, agreed to most reluctantly by the abbot—*"Ad majorem Ordinis gloriam"* ("for the greater glory of the Order"—and the monastery). At least Augustine thought there had been a tour. Being outside the monastery with liquor readily available, he largely lost those weeks to memory. Augustine himself would have been literally lost had he been on his own. Fortunately for all, his publisher had arranged for a driver in each city, who shepherded him from one interview to the next.

Augustine was assured that in most of these interviews he had performed admirably. That he had to take on faith. Most of the time, he was deeply, gravely under the influence.

But never before 11:30 in the morning.

It was after returning to his monastic routine and enforced sobriety that the first invitation from Klaus Krieg came to join P.G. Press. And then a second and a third. Each offering something more than the previous offer.

Then came Augustine's conversation with his former colleague at the agency, and his conversation with his abbot. There followed Augustine's final rejection of any possible offer Krieg might make.

At least Augustine considered his rejection final.

It was not long ago—Augustine would never forget the day—when Krieg visited the monastery and made a proposition he felt sure could not be rejected.

In a former day, Krieg would have experienced great difficulty getting permission to visit one of the monks. With the strict rules regarding silence and cloister, Augustine might have been well beyond Krieg's ability to reach. Now, with more relaxed rules, it was relatively easy for the two to meet. It was made even easier since Augustine did not object to Krieg's request for a meeting. Augustine began to regret that decision as soon as Krieg started spelling out the terms of what was actually an ultimatum.

Quite simply, Krieg knew all there was to know about Augustine's drinking problem. From his college days—when no one seemed to sense any problem at all—to the ad agency, to AA, to the weekends away from the monastery, to the book tour—Krieg knew it all. And, quite simply, everyone would know it all unless Augustine signed with P.G. Press.

Augustine was not stupid. He knew immediately what such a revelation would do to his present and future life. There was the distinct possibility that he might be expelled from his treasured monastic life. But even if not, his freedom to go and come, the weekend respites he so enjoyed, all would come to an end. Perhaps the greatest blow, his dream of becoming the second Merton would disintegrate into a nightmare. The most dissolute sinner could become a saint by, at some point, reforming his life and turning to virtue. As was the case with—among many—the original Saint Augustine. Indeed, Merton had sown his wild oats before becoming the saintly monk. The reverse procedure was not allowed. Father Augustine, outside of drinking, had sown few wild oats. The drinking, however, qualified as vice enough.

Now he was supposed to be beyond vice and embarked on a life of unmitigated virtue. It just wouldn't work. Exposure of his past—and especially his present—drinking bouts would send crashing every hope he had.

A dilemma! But one that was not immediately pressed by Krieg. He left the monastery that day without exacting a commitment from Augustine. The ultimatum was there, without doubt. But it was not dated. Krieg had given Augustine time to stew and fret. Augustine was unsure if it was not kinder to a condemned man to just take him out and shoot him rather than keeping him on death row for an unspecified time.

Then the invitation came to participate in this writers' seminar at Marygrove. Immediately he saw Krieg's name and the description of his role in the workshop, Augustine recognized that this was not an invitation. It was a summons. A summons he could not refuse to an offer he could see no way to refuse.

In the weeks between the mandatory acceptance of this invitation and the start of the workshop, Augustine thought of little else but his position between a rock and a hard place.

In Augustine's mind, this was a desperate problem. Reluctantly, he concluded that any possible solution would require desperate means. For the very first time in his life he was forced to consider the ultimate act of violence. He surprised himself with how naturally, logically, and practically he was able to consider doing great harm to another person. Was it the compelling predicament in which he found himself? Was it his new familiarity with the murder mystery genre? Was it the gross evilness of Klaus Krieg?

Slowly, Augustine came to believe that the world would be better without this impostor, this gross creature who debased the nature of religion.

Gradually, Augustine began to form a plan. The methodology was not far different from the way he had formed the plot for his novel: distractions during prayer—in both instances most practical distractions. It was a simple plan, based mainly on a few traits and habits he'd noticed in Krieg during their visit together.

By the time he arrived in Michigan for the workshop, Augustine's plan had been refined to the utmost degree. His only question was whether he possessed—what was it: sufficient courage or malevolence?—to pull it off. For reinforcement, he brought with him some liquor. He fully expected that to carry out his plan, he would need a gigantic "attitude adjustment."

Then came interference from that foolish David Benbow.

Just after his arrival at Marygrove, Augustine found a cryptic note slipped beneath his door. It was from Benbow. It contained a subtle suggestion that it would be beneficial to meet. The wording of the note was veiled. If one did not know what Klaus Krieg was up to, it would have been impossible to make any sense of the communication. However—and this was the single touch of brilliance to the note—if one knew what was on Krieg's mind, the message was clear enough.

Thus, Augustine, whose signature on a book contract Krieg coveted, was able to recognize that Benbow was in the same fix. And from the wording, that, perhaps, so were the rabbi and the nun. In any case, if Winer and Marie were not among Krieg's coveted few, the note would be harmless if unintelligible gobbledygook.

Absently, Augustine wondered whether Winer or Marie would rendezvous with Benbow. It didn't much matter to Augustine. Benbow, as far as Augustine was concerned, was a fool. Conspiracies were like planned obsolescence. They had moving parts and so were destined to break down. It was better to work alone. But then he thought wryly that if anyone besides himself was out to stop Krieg, so much the better. It didn't matter who stopped Krieg as long as Krieg was stopped.

Ah, but that was as of Sunday.

Monday evening, last night, saw the tragic death of Rabbi Winer. Now things had changed. It was a good thing, thought Augustine, that he had come prepared with more than one plan. There was more than one way to skin a cat. And more than one way to make sure that, like the third monkey, Krieg spoke no evil.

20

"THE MASS IS ended. Go in peace to love and serve the Lord."

"Thanks be to God."

Koesler concluded Mass. Most of the crowd immediately filed out of the chapel, chattering to each other. A few stayed behind to peacefully meditate for a few minutes while the ruckus dissipated down the corridors.

Koesler returned the vestments and sacred vessels to their appointed places. Since boyhood he had always found something special in daily Mass. From the first grade in parochial school through the final year in the seminary—twenty years—daily Mass had been compulsory. So it was difficult to know whether he actually appreciated what he was obliged to do. But he had survived all those years with a special treasuring intact. In fact, Mass meant more to him now than ever before. If anything, morning Mass had become the focal point of each day.

And so it had been this morning. As he recited the so-familiar prayers, his personal prayer turned to the bizarre events of the past couple of days. All these talented people he had met for the first time—just hours ago, it seemed. Now, one of them was dead—a murder victim. A case of the mistaken victim, to boot. The intended victim: a charlatan or a genuine minister of the Gospel?

It was not clear yet in Koesler's mind that three people of religion, an Episcopal priest, a Catholic monk, and a nun, were suspects!

None of his questions had been resolved during this morning's Mass. But Koesler felt that contented quiet of the soul that he always did as he concluded the liturgy.

His soul did not remain unrumpled for long. In addition to the ruckus in the corridor, there was a young woman looking for him. Barely able to be heard over the noise, she was calling his name.

As he emerged from the chapel, she approached him directly. "Father Koesler?"

He nodded.

"The police want you," she said, somewhat breathlessly.

"Wanted by the police," he reflected. "I guess it had to happen one day."

She missed the attempt at humor altogether. "Oh, no, Father. They just want to talk to you, I think. They're in the private dining room."

"Thank you." For a moment he enjoyed a sense of self-importance in being needed by the police, as if they couldn't do their jobs without his expert contributions. It was only momentary. He knew he had been included in this investigation only at the invitation of his friend, Inspector Koznicki. And the only possible contribution he might make would be in clarifying some religious question the police couldn't be expected to understand fully. So it was with renewed humility that he hastened toward the meeting.

"Ah, here you are!" Koznicki greeted him expansively.

"Good of you to come, Father. The case has developed a bit and we wanted you to be informed."

Koesler was quite certain the Inspector's "we" was a sort of editorial—maybe Papal—plural, and that the others were not that eager to include this outsider.

The others were Lieutenant Tully and Sergeants Moore and Mangiapane.

It was Tully who spoke. "We think we've found the secret that Krieg's been blackmailing the monk with."

"Oh?"

"Augustine's been hitting the bottle hard for a long time."

Koesler was not particularly shocked. By no means was it a problem of epic proportion, but he'd met his share of problem drinkers in the priesthood. "How bad is it?"

"Didn't show up, it seems," Tully replied, "until his later years at an ad agency"—he consulted his notes—"the William J. Doran Agency. Seems he got hung up on boozy lunches, and it went from there. Got so bad he was losing days at a time."

"Was he fired?"

Tully smiled briefly. "Uh-uh. Seems no one cared as long as he brought in the business. And he brought it in pretty good. Well," he backtracked, "someone cared: one of the other guys at the agency. We talked to him. Retired now, but remembers it like yesterday. Took pity on Augustine— Harold May then—and got him into AA.

"Then we got lucky. This source, a Robert Begin, volunteered that, funny thing, somebody from P.G. Enterprises had contacted him a while back. Wanted to know all about Harold May. Said they were researching for a tribute to prominent people who had conquered alcohol."

"This is interesting," Koesler said. "But what's wrong

with that? I should think somebody with a drinking problem ought to be issued a medal for joining AA. And then becoming a Trappist! Maybe P.G. Enterprises wasn't kidding when they claimed they were going to honor him.''

''Could be. But it didn't end there. This is a story that doesn't have a happy ending.''

''Oh?''

''I'll let Mangiapane take it from here. He's the one who dug this up.''

The big officer reddened. ''Well, not all by myself, Zoo. I mean, the team was workin' on it.''

''Tell him.''

''Okay, sure. Well, Father, it seems that Father Augustine is sort of famous—make that notorious—with the Massachusetts State Police. They've got citations on him for DWI—that's Driving While Intoxicated—long as your arm. And those are only the times he was written up. Most of them warned him, read him the riot act. Cops are sometimes reluctant to write up a priest. And the ones who did just saw the tickets squashed someplace up the line.

''Now, as far as we were able to tell, he's pretty clean while he's in the monastery. I guess the opportunity isn't there. But we got a list of parishes from the . . . uh . . . procurator of the monastery. There are nearby places where he helps out on weekends.'' Mangiapane looked at Koesler brightly. ''That was my idea—checking into the possibility of weekend help.'' He seemed quite pleased with his knowledge that weekend ministry was a phenomenon of Catholic ecclesial life.

''Anyway, some of the priests in these parishes were not at all helpful. I'd say almost hostile. But most of them were cooperative, and admitted that, 'Father did tend to drink a bit Saturday nights, sometimes Sunday afternoons. But not so's it would interfere with his ministry.' See, Father, just like when he was in the agency: blotto, but somehow bringing in the business.''

Koesler shook his head. ''And this problem is current?''

''The most recent road citation is within the past month,'' Mangiapane replied.

Koesler thought back to Sunday evening, when Augustine had missed all the excitement of Krieg's little game of whodunit. The monk hadn't been ill; he'd been dead drunk.

''But Lieutenant,'' Koesler addressed Tully, ''I believe you said you were pretty sure Augustine's drinking was the reason Krieg was able to blackmail him. There's more?''

''We don't know,'' Tully admitted. ''There may be more. The point is, this is for sure. The guy has a serious drinking problem. And the other point is, it's enough. There's no telling how messed up he'd be if this gets public. For one thing, the cops'd stop letting him off the hook. The courts would have to treat him like any other drunk and, with his history, which would be dragged into it, he could be in the slammer for a long, long time or, at very least, have to submit to court-ordered treatment.''

''And if all this came out,'' Koesler reflected, ''his history of alcoholism, his drunk driving, the favors he's gotten from the authorities in Massachusetts''—he shook his head—''he might be able to get published by P.G. Press, but probably any legitimate publisher would hesitate to take a chance on him.''

''That's about it,'' said Tully. ''Krieg has him over a barrel, just like Benbow and the late rabbi. See how it's all coming together? We almost don't need the nun. We could almost presume the four writers are a matched team. Almost.

But we're investigating her too. I'll bet there's somethin' in her past that's bad enough that, just like the others, she couldn't say no to Krieg and make it stick. When we find what the nun's hiding, we're gonna start playing hardball with the other three. One or more of them are gonna have a lot of explaining to do.''

As Tully was completing this statement, Koesler grew aware of a disturbance just outside the dining room. The noise was no sharper than the hubbub already produced by the crowd; yet it had a different, more urgent tenor.

Two men—police officers, as it turned out—burst into the room. They belonged to Tully's squad, so they reported to him rather than to Koznicki. ''Zoo,'' one of them, nearly out of breath, said, ''Come on! It's Krieg!''

Tully followed the two detectives at a dead run. He was followed in turn by Mangiapane, Moore, Koesler, and Koznicki. The latter two were in no physical condition to move this fast, but the excitement of the moment gave them unexpected impetus.

No thought was given to the slow elevator; the group took the stairs. Three floors up, then down the corridor to the private rooms assigned to the workshop faculty. All, especially Koznicki and Koesler, arrived winded. Other uniformed officers had sealed off the staircase as soon as the first contingent left the main floor. Thus, none but the police and Koesler were now on the third floor. Suddenly, Koesler caught sight of an ashen-faced Krieg sitting on a chair in the hallway. An unlit cigar hung from loose fingers; he seemed close to shock.

Koesler was as puzzled as he had ever been.

From what the detectives had said, and the dispatch with which they'd taken the stairs, he'd thought Krieg must have been found dead. But here he was, looking like death warmed over, but not moribund. Not yet.

"What happened?" Tully's tone and bearing suggested that one or another of his officers might have blown an assignment and exposed Krieg to danger.

"Nothin', Zoo," said one of the uniformed officers. "But plenty might have."

"Well?" Without doubt, Tully wanted a complete exaplanation, and quickly.

The same uniformed cop replied. "We've been with Reverend Krieg all morning, Zoo. Nothin' happened until we all came up here to his room after breakfast, just a few minutes ago. When we got to his room we were about to go in and he was about to light up that cigar there . . ." He gestured toward the cigar, which Krieg continued to hold loosely. "Freddy here caught it first and knocked the lighter out of his hand, or we all coulda been fried."

Tully turned to the first officer's companion, evidently Freddy.

"Gas, Zoo . . . couldn't be anything else," Freddy said. "Somebody must have saturated Krieg's room. If he had lit that lighter, the fumes would have caught it and we woulda had one hell of an explosion." Freddy spoke casually enough but there was a slight tremor in his voice. Clearly, he knew just how close he and the others in that entourage had come to a sudden, fiery death.

"Okay," Tully said. "You done good, Fred. Cordon off this area and get the 'techs up here for prints, pics, and whatever. By the way, did you check: Are Augustine, Benbow, or Sister Marie in their rooms?"

The first officer answered. "We checked, Zoo. Nobody else is up here. Not the monk, the nun, Benbow, or his wife.

We would have been the only ones to get it and none of us would be talkin' to you now.''

The hint of a smile crossed Tully's lips. "Nobody here. Isn't that interesting. It would have told us one thing if only one of them wasn't here. But none of them! That tells us a different story completely. Okay," he said to the officers, "get crackin'."

Tully and Koznicki went directly to Krieg. They spoke to him, not loudly, but audibly enough for Koesler to overhear.

"Reverend," Koznicki said, "this is the second attempt on your life in two days. Is it not time you cooperated with us?"

Nothing about Krieg changed. He remained in a stupor state. It appeared that he hadn't heard the Inspector.

"How many times," Tully rephrased, "do you have to come close to getting killed before you get worried about it?"

"What?" Krieg seemed to be coming out of his trance.

But the detectives were sure Krieg had heard at least Tully's question, so they did not ask a third time. They merely waited.

Finally, Krieg spoke. "Tragic, tragic, but . . . accidental, I'm sure."

"The only accident," Koznicki said, "happened when Rabbi Winer drank a poison intended for you."

"And," Tully added, "nobody tripped and spilled gasoline inside your room. Somebody who knew that you smoked a lot—and that would include everybody who shares this corner of the building with you, the cigar smell was that strong—planned to let you blow yourself to kingdom come."

Krieg opened and closed his eyes several times as if trying to regain focus. "I find that very hard to believe."

"Believe!" Tully said forcefully.

"We know what is going on, Reverend," Koznicki said.

"What's going on?"

"Yes. We know that you very badly wanted these four authors to sign contracts with your publishing company," Koznicki said. "You tried every legitimate way you knew to get them. They all refused. Somehow you were able to discover embarrassing secrets in their lives. Then you began in effect to blackmail them with these secret events—threatening to reveal them if the writers would not sign. Now it seems obvious that one or more of these writers is trying to silence you. On consecutive days there have been two attempts to kill you. Does this not frighten you? Anger you?"

"You know these so-called secrets?" Krieg challenged.

"Uh-huh," Tully said.

"All four?"

"Three. But we'll know the fourth before long," Tully said.

"It seems to me, then," Krieg said, "that you know as much or more than you claim I know. With all that alleged information, you should be able to solve this case. If someone is trying to kill me—a hypothesis I deny—then you have all you need to catch the person. That is your job, isn't it?"

If he had tried to anger two detectives he was succeeding.

"You refuse to cooperate, then?" Koznicki asked.

"Cooperate? In what? Your fantasy?"

"Are you so avaricious—or so stupid—that you would risk your life?" Koznicki said incredulously.

Krieg merely shrugged.

At that moment, Sister Marie appeared in the corridor. She seemed appropriately startled at all the commotion. By now, the area inside and outside Reverend Krieg's room was awash with police personnel taking pictures, measuring, taking notes. She moved directly to Krieg and the two detectives.

"What's going on here?" she demanded almost as if she were addressing an unruly second grader.

"Maybe you could tell us," said Tully. The response drew a sharp glance from Koznicki, whose parochial school background made it difficult to relate to nuns with anything but deference.

Marie ignored the insinuation. "What is that?" She sniffed. "It smells like gasoline."

"It is," Tully said. He fished a paper from an inside pocket and studied it for a moment. "What are you doing up here, Sister? You're scheduled for a class now."

"I . . . I forgot and left my notes in my room. I was just coming up to get them."

Or, thought Tully, *you came up here to see if your plan worked and Krieg was out of your way.* At the same time, he knew he was getting ahead of himself. As far as the record was concerned, they had not as yet found anything in Marie's past, the revelation of which could motivate her toward homicide. However, a well-honed instinct told him at least all three remaining writers were solid suspects.

"Well," Tully said, "luckily you'll find your papers intact. If we hadn't stopped the Reverend from lighting his cigar, this gasoline could have become a lethal bomb."

Marie shuddered. "Again? This was another attempt on his life?"

Tully nodded. "Uh-huh. By the way, Sister, did you know Krieg smoked?"

"Did I?" She crinkled her nose as if catching a foul odor. "Of course. How could anyone live in these quarters and not smell the cigar smoke? It was not here yesterday morning—but then neither was the Reverend Krieg. He was staying at a hotel. But he stayed with us last night and this morning the odor permeated everything. Of course I knew he smoked. So did everyone else who stayed in this section of the building.'' She paused in thought a moment. "Lieutenant, what sort of question was that? Are you accusing me of something? Of trying to murder Reverend Krieg?"

Tully regarded her coolly. "Sister, you will know without a doubt if I accuse you of anything. This is a homicide investigation and we're going to pursue it. Along the way, we're gonna ask questions. Some of them may sound offensive. If you take offense, that's your problem." His voice softened only slightly. "If it helps any, you are definitely not the only one who is going to be questioned before this is over."

Tully and Koznicki moved to one side. They consulted with each other, checked on the progress of the investigation of Krieg's room, and agreed on a statement that would be released to the press.

Meanwhile, Sister Marie remained where she had been standing. She felt shaken. She also felt guilty. The guilt began tugging at her memory, calling her back to another era.

Then she noticed that Father Koesler had been standing nearby all this time. She approached him. "I wonder," she said, "if you would be kind enough to take the class I'm supposed to have now?"

"Really," he began to protest, "I'm not . . ."

"I think you can handle it quite nicely, Father. It just has to do with the use of real police in researching a mystery novel. I know this is your forte. You've done a lot of that, or so I've heard. I mean, you've had lots of contact with the police. Even now . . ." She didn't complete the thought.

"You're upset, Sister. That's understandable. But I guess I can wing it with some hints about getting the cooperation of the police—even if it's for a novel. They really are very helpful to writers by and large."

"Thank you very much. I appreciate it." Marie pinched her forehead. The headache was pronounced. She slowly descended the stairs to the main floor, and worked her way through the crowded corridor. She entered the now empty chapel and knelt in the rear pew.

The Gothic interior of the chapel was so traditional, even with the altar placed just inside the sanctuary instead of at the rear wall. Religious statues and paintings abounded. It put her in mind of her home parish in Detroit. She had spent a lot of time there, too.

She was eighteen again, in church, and feeling guilty.

21

THURSDAY BEFORE FIRST Friday. How often had she done this? Marie Monahan had plenty of time before it was her turn to go to confession. Let's see, approximately eight times each scholastic year for, since she'd begun going to confession in the second grade, eleven years. So, eighty-eight times.

As far as she could recollect, it was Saint Margaret Mary who had the vision during which Jesus promised grand spiritual rewards to those who "made" the first Fridays.

The idea was to go to Communion on nine consecutive first Fridays and all the promises Jesus made to Saint Margaret Mary were yours. Somehow, someone must have dismissed the magical number nine, for she, Marie Monahan, and her classmates had completed nine consecutives long ago. Like so many Catholic devotions, the first Fridays had become a quasi superstition. If nine first Fridays were good, a limitless number of first Fridays was infinitely better.

The confessions, of course, were necessitated by the Communions. No one in the world could have foretold then, in 1960, what would be accomplished by the Second Vatican Council, to begin the following year. One of Vatican II's achievements would be the divorcing of confession from

307

Communion. Catholics would be advised that they could go to Communion without first going to confession practically forever as long as they did not commit a mortal sin. Just when they got used to going to confession only infrequently, if ever, a later Pope would emphasize the necessity of individual frequent confession, and put confession and Communion back together again. After Vatican II, the casual Catholic was frequently confused.

The eighty-eight confessions Marie had just carefully computed by no means approached the total number of times she'd been to confession to date. Sometimes she would confess every week or every other week. And always, always, the same thing: disobedience, angry thoughts, inattentiveness in school, gossip. Venial sins, imperfections.

There were times when she suspected she might find some other sins if she examined her conscience when she was in the second grade. Never having been given an update, she retained a child's approach to confession. In this she was not unlike many, if not most, adult Catholics.

The inside joke to all this was that by her peers she was considered to be "wild."

"Wildness" meant something considerably different in a parochial school of 1960 and prior than it would some thirty years later. Marie was a starter on the girls' basketball and softball teams. She was a cheerleader. She was a tomboy. Her tight-knit circle of girlfriends tended to be boisterous. Worse, they were forever testing the dress code limits of "Mary-like" modesty. As often as they could get away with it, they'd be mischievous and roll their waistbands until their school uniform skirts hung well above the knee. Or they'd "forget" to fasten the top buttons on their blouses, leaving a fraction of a bra exposed. Around them at all times the vigilance of the nuns was ever required.

Marie Monahan was never in the running as the sodalist selected to crown the Blessed Mother's statue on May Day.

And yet, with all of that, to her knowledge, she had never in her life committed a mortal sin.

Probably the simplest mortal sin possible to a Catholic would be the deliberate missing of Sunday Mass. The next most commonplace would be a grand dinner of meat on a Friday. After that, things got complicated. Stealing an article of significant value or lots of money would do it. Or killing someone, of course.

Possibly the classic mortal sin—and this was far more the venue of males—was almost any sexual sin anyone could imagine.

The gravity of sin, in those days, was measured by three criteria: the matter, the intention, and the circumstances. Matter: the difference, say, between ten cents and ten dollars. Intention: inadvertence, force, or fear could limit responsibility. Circumstances: participation in a "just war" justified killing. Sexual sins did not admit parvity of matter. Thus whatever the intention or circumstance, one embarked on a sin of sexual nature with serious, grave, mortal matter.

But Marie Monahan had never committed a sexual sin.

That fact was not a commentary on her natural attractiveness. She had neither a good nor an accurate self-image. She considered herself quite plain. Actually, she had a natural beauty that came close to perfection. The boys in her school were well aware that Marie Monahan was amply endowed and that, under that bulky school uniform, there were sensuous adult curves just begging to be fondled. All such male thoughts and vulgar references were confessed with religious regularity.

It was her turn. She'd been waiting to go to confession for more than half an hour, inching forward as each student ahead of her was shriven. All this time wasted, when she should have been examining her conscience. All she'd done was to entertain distractions.

She knelt on the unpadded bench, rested her folded hands on the little shelf. Directly in front of her was a dark and seldom-if-ever-cleaned cloth behind which was a wooden door that made a terrible racket when the priest slid it open or shut. It was dark in there. Neither priest nor penitent could see each other even when the little door was open. The cloth and darkness saw to that.

Slide . . . Bang!

"Oh," she whispered, "bless me, Father, for I have sinned. My last confession was about two weeks ago."

Snort, cough, growl. The priest cleared his respiratory passages.

"Since then," she whispered, "I disobeyed my mother four times and my father twice. I gossiped a bit, nothing very serious. And," remembering a few minutes ago, "I had distractions in church. And that's about it.

"I'm sorry for these and all the sins of my past life, especially for disobedience."

She thought that a representative confession. It had been serving her, with slight variations, for the past eleven years.

"For your penance," the priest's voice sounded tired and bored, "say three Our Fathers and three Hail Marys. And now, make a good Act of Contrition." She could not have guessed how bored—almost terminally—he was. He'd been hearing practically the same humdrum story for the past six hours, beginning with the third graders and marching upward through the classes. The sole salvation of his sanity was that the present—final—penitents were high school seniors. Purgatory was about to end.

Marie mumbled the Act of Contrition while the priest mumbled an absolution in Latin. That they were speaking in different languages simultaneously, neither paying any attention whatsoever to the other, did not bother them.

It did not take Marie long to forget that confession and, indeed, school in general. Christmas vacation was about to begin and that was on everybody's front burner.

Marie had been invited to the season teen club dance by none other than the captain of the football team. It was such a natural: a three-year letter man in football, basketball, and baseball—and team captain in football—dating the school's outstanding female athlete and captain of the cheerleaders. The wonder was that it had taken them so long to get together.

It took so long because, on the one hand, with her poor self-image it never occurred to Marie that the school's prime catch knew she was alive. While, on the other hand, she was regarded as the unapproachable—the virgin queen, above and beyond accepting casual dates, and probably frigid to boot.

She shared her excitement, as she shared everything, with Alice, her best friend in all the world. Together, they began planning and preparing for the magic evening. Alice, too, had a date. And not a loser by any means, but not the captain of the football team and an all-state pick in three sports.

At long last, December 21 arrived, and it was perfect. The evening was brisk and clear. A dusting of snow made it seem as if clusters of tiny diamonds had fallen on earth.

When Marie walked into the decorated gym on the arm of Bucko Cassidy there was almost a collective gasp from the assembled crowd. They were perfect together. Young, brimming with good health, tight skin perfectly formed, a blooming couple who easily could have stepped out of the advertisement pages of any popular magazine.

Bucko and Marie felt everyone's gaze on them. It was exhilarating.

The evening went as well as could be expected. Marie and Alice were able to steal a little time together to compare notes. By and large, Alice was having the better time of the two. Her date had interests that transcended sports. Bucko Cassidy, on the other hand, was limited conversationally not only to the sports world but more parochially to his own considerable athletic accomplishments and his bright professional future.

Bucko's only departure from his totally egocentric monologue was when he turned to Marie and said, "But what about you, Marie: Which sport do you think I should pick for a pro career?"

It was all she could do to keep from laughing out loud. "I don't know, Bucko," she said in restrained self-control. "You're so good in all of them. But don't you think you'd last longer in baseball?"

"Last longer?"

"Yes. What's the average football career? Less than ten years—twelve if you're lucky. Basketball? All that constant running takes it out of your legs. But baseball, now there's a career that could bring you a big paycheck for lots of years . . . don't you think?"

"Geez, Marie, I think you're right."

"But all that has to wait until the scouts make their offers and you see the whites of their contracts."

"Neat, Marie, neat!"

Marie could scarcely wait to closet with Alice and bring her up to date on Bucko's greatest problem in all the world.

It was toward the end of a pleasant evening with no surprises that Bucko popped his surprise: the postparty party.

Marie begged off. She had a curfew. Bucko protested she could phone her parents and tell them she'd be a little late. Besides, they wouldn't stay long.

They argued. They discussed. Marie weakened. She talked it over with Alice, who advised against it. Marie talked it over with herself. She thought of all those deadly dull confessions. She'd never even had necking or petting to confess. If her confidantes were truthful, she must be the only senior who never did anything even vaguely naughty.

She agreed to go.

Bucko was happier about her decision than he had any right to be. She remembered that later.

At first, all went well. Her parents agreed, reluctantly, but they agreed. Her mother would wait up for her. There was an abundant crowd of seniors at the party—another reassuring sign.

But there were no adults. The owners of the house had gone on a skiing holiday in Northern Michigan and their son had opened their bountiful liquor supply.

About half an hour after they arrived, Bucko suggested they go upstairs. The downstairs was already too crowded and getting more so by the minute. Marie knew what he had in mind. Finally she was going to find out what it was like to engage in some serious necking.

They found an empty bedroom. There were several layers

of coats on the bed. A sweep of Bucko's athletic arm solved that problem. The coats were on the floor and he and she were on the bed.

Things began happening too fast. Bucko was all over her. She pushed him away and sat up. "Bucko! I'm not a baseball. You don't have to rub the cover off me!"

Bucko considered the situation. "You're right," he admitted, "We're too keyed up from the dance and all. Let's go back with the gang."

It was Bucko's finest thespian moment. He had no intention of calling off this carnal intimacy.

Back to the dull confessions. After a moment's thought, "We don't need to do that, Bucko. Just go slower, can't you?"

"Sure. Wait a minute." He located his coat on the floor and drew a flask from a pocket. "Let's have a shot of this. It'll relax us."

"I don't know . . . what's in it?"

"It's just a little booze. It'll help. Come on . . . here."

She looked doubtful. But, she had to admit, she could use something to relax. She was tighter than a drum. Well, one doesn't commit one's first deliberate mortal sin lightly. "You first," she said.

"Okay." He took a sip and handed the flask to her.

She sampled one mouthful, then another. Then, straightaway, she collapsed on the bed. Bucko stepped into the bathroom and emptied his mouth. Even so, he was somewhat affected by the knockout drops he'd put in the liquor.

When Marie regained consciousness, she was in Bucko's car. She did not feel at all well. She looked at Bucko behind the wheel, but saw him in a confused haze. "What time is it?"

He checked his watch as they passed a street light. "One-thirty."

Half an hour past her extended curfew. Not good, but not tragic. What was definitely not good was how she felt. "Stop the car, Bucko!"

"We're almost at your house," he protested.

"You're gonna have an awful mess to clean up."

He stopped as abruptly as he could on the slippery street. She leaned out of the car. Bucko was glad he'd stopped.

She said no more. She was using every ounce of her young and normally healthy constitution to regain self-possession.

With a determined effort Marie survived her mother's concerned scrutiny. She made it upstairs to her room by putting one foot in front of the other and telling herself over and over, "It isn't that far." She was glad her stomach had emptied outside. There was no way she could have done that quietly in the bathroom. Without removing her clothing she fell into bed and was in a dreamless sleep immediately.

She woke abruptly about 10:00 A.M. She felt terrible. Her mouth felt as if it were coated for the winter. She tried to remember, but all she could recall was the dance, going to Freddy's house with Bucko, the bedroom, and then, vaguely, coming home.

Something was missing. The bedroom. She tried harder to remember. Bucko brushing the coats off the bed. The beginning of a wrestling match. The drink. *The drink.* Why had she reacted so violently to a drink? She'd had alcohol before, in small measures of course. But she'd had only a couple of mouthfuls last night. Could the drink have been drugged? But why? Why would he do such a rotten thing? Unless . . .

Her mind was clearing. There was something peculiar about her clothing. It didn't seem to fit her correctly—tight where it should have been loose and vice versa. She began removing it. Her gown was slightly off center. Ditto her bra. Someone had dressed her hurriedly. *And where were her panties?* She could not know that Bucko had won a ten-dollar bet by displaying those earlier this morning.

There were flecks of blood on the inside of her thighs. She checked herself more carefully with a small hand mirror. She found the sticky white matter. It had to be semen. She'd read about that.

She'd been raped. Drugged, then raped.

Marie was overwhelmed by a flood of emotions, all of them negative: anguish, shame, horror, humiliation, outrage, great fear—and guilt, guilt, guilt. For the first time she understood how one person could seriously contemplate murdering another person. She would know the feeling once again when, many years later, a televangelist/publisher would threaten to reveal something more than this secret.

Marie managed to get to confession before Christmas. She confessed that she'd had intercourse, which was probably not technically correct. Bucko had raped her. But she confessed it just to be on the safe side. She did not want to die and have God tell her, "You should have confessed the whole thing. You know what you were taught about being the near occasion of sin and all." This time she didn't get just a few Our Fathers and Hail Marys. For a penance she got five rosaries and the Stations of the Cross and a hellfire-and-brimstone lecture.

After much deliberation, she concluded there was no way

to retaliate against Bucko Cassidy. There was nothing she could do except to act as if he didn't exist. Which didn't seem to bother him. Nothing bothered him as long as his athletic body stayed in one fit piece.

The real and deadly serious problem arose a month later when the normally regular Marie was two weeks overdue for her period. And she had begun to feel, not unwell, but peculiar. As if something deep inside her was changing.

She was pregnant. She'd never been before, of course, and she hadn't passed or failed any pregnancy test, but she knew it. She knew she was pregnant. Her emotional response escalated to terror and panic. There was only one person in whom she could confide. Not her mother, father, a priest or nun. Alice. Outside of the priest in the confessional, which was protected by its anonymity, Alice was the only one who knew what had happened to Marie at Freddy's. Now Alice alone knew about the pregnancy.

Alice's eyes were wider than they had ever been. "What are you going to do, Marie?"

"Oh, Alice, I don't know. I've thought of everything: keeping the baby, giving it out for adoption. But either way I'd have to tell my parents. I can't, I just can't do that. Which leads to thinking about the Ambassador Bridge and a short winter swim in the Detroit River." Marie could speak calmly, almost dispassionately, because by now she was drained, physically, emotionally, and tearfully.

"Suicide! Marie, that's impossible! I won't let you do it. I'll stay with you twenty-four hours a day!"

"Alice . . ." Marie would have laughed, had not laughter also been gone from her life. "Alice, don't be silly."

Neither of them spoke for quite a long while.

"There's one other possibility." Alice spoke softly, guardedly.

Marie studied her friend. "Alice! Abortion?"

"I know, I know; it's out of the question," Alice said. "I've heard everything in religion class you have. But, think about it. Just think about it," Pause. "You can't commit suicide. That's worse than abortion. Not only would you kill the fetus, if there's one there, but you'd kill yourself. You can't tell your folks. I can understand. I couldn't do that either. What's left?

"It would be a blessing—don't get me wrong now—but it would be a blessing if you miscarried. It could happen. I read that happens sometimes just because it's a first pregnancy. Maybe we could look at an abortion like that—as a planned miscarriage." Alice looked intently at Marie.

Marie twisted her handkerchief between restless hands. "I don't know. I don't know. Besides, how could I get one? Where would I go? Not only is it a sin, it's against the law. I don't know. I just don't know."

Alice, hesitantly, "I have a friend . . ."

"Alice!"

". . . who has a friend who does this. Right out of her home."

"Her home?"

"Uh-huh. How much money can you get hold of?"

"Babysitting, odd jobs, I've got about $50 in savings."

"And I've got about $40."

"Alice! I couldn't let you—"

"My friend says this woman charges between $100 and $150. Maybe she'd do it for $90."

"Alice!"

But the decision had been made. Both Marie and Alice—

especially Marie—felt strongly conflicting emotions. Neither of them believed in or wanted abortion. But there seemed no alternative, no alternative whatever.

The abortionist, after considerable haggling, finally agreed to the $90 fee. Alice accompanied Marie to the modest neighborhood home. Marie accompanied the woman into the bedroom. It occurred to her that nothing seemed to be sterile or even very clean. But she was too frightened and defensive to complain or question.

The procedure was simplicity itself. A long plastic stirrer was inserted roughly through the vagina and planted firmly in the cervix. Marie screamed. Alice ran to the bedroom door, but it was locked. The woman instructed Marie to leave the stirrer in place. Over the next two or three days the stirrer—and the fetus—would be expelled. So—words that held no meaning—there was nothing to worry about.

Alice saw Marie home. She would have stayed with her, but Marie was too sick to tolerate company. Her mother bought the explanation that it was the flu. That gave Marie the opportunity to go to bed and stay there.

Inside Marie foreign things were happening. The mucous plug had been pierced and a serious infection had begun. The irritation had opened the cervix. It was only a matter of time, two days in fact, before the stirrer was expelled, followed by the ravaged fetus.

Marie was in misery such as she had never before known. She had a high temperature, fever, spasms, chills, and hemorrhaging. She was rushed to the hospital, where the doctor in emergency convinced her he'd be able to help much more efficiently if she told him all she could. He performed a D and C and administered massive doses of antibiotics.

She was lucky. The infection had been checked. Two things

became certain: She would live, and she would feel more guilty than she ever had or ever would again.

The doctor, as he was required by law, reported the illegal abortion. Marie's parents, hesitant at first, now, miraculously, supported her. They contacted an attorney, who advised her, and answered her questions. Apprised of her right to remain silent, she refused to tell the police the name of anyone involved in the abortion, including the abortionist, and especially Alice. With no testamentary evidence, the police had no recourse but to file the case away with the hundreds of other unsolved abortion crimes.

All loose ends were now tied, except for the sorry state of her immortal soul. For the first time, she was deathly afraid of going to confession. But, as a Catholic, there was no alternative. Not if she wished to regain the state of Sanctifying Grace.

She confessed having an abortion. She was dumbfounded when the voice of the unseen priest asked if she knew there was a special penalty attached to this grave sin. She knew of no extra penalty; wasn't one of the worst of all possible mortal sins enough? Since she had not known that the penalty of automatic excommunication was attached to those who have, procure, perform, or assist at abortions, she did not now incur the sanction. It was one of those rare cases when ignorance was a shield.

She had expected this confession to be torturous; the confessor did not disappoint her. After excoriating her, he imposed as penance that she recite the rosary every day for a month. Before absolving her, however, he had one more admonition. He said, and she would never forget his words: "Young lady, I cannot make this part of your penance, but if I could I would. You should go off to a convent and become a nun. You should give up forever every pleasure of the flesh, legitimate or not. You should expiate this terrible sin for the rest of your life.''

Only then did he absolve her. She was so shocked by his admonition, she didn't even remember reciting the Act of Contrition.

She talked that one over with Alice. It was Alice's opinion that, with all due reverence, her confessor was an ass.

But his words had touched something deep inside her, something she had never before consciously considered. It was difficult for her to understand, let alone explain. It was as if she were destined to be a concert artist but had never taken a piano lesson.

The priest had advised her to become a nun to do penance for her sin—a completely negative motivation. But seriously considering the vocation for the first time, she found herself more and more naturally called to it.

There was one special nun who had taught Marie in that particularly difficult senior year, to whom she felt very close. They talked frequently now and at great length. Alone among all the Sisters who had taught her, Sister Marian Joseph, IHM, had seen beneath and beyond the ''wildness'' that was so natural to Marie, the especial qualities, the potential for an intense spiritual life. Sister Marian Joseph deeply believed that Marie would make an excellent religious. In fact, Sister was convinced that if Marie did not become a nun, she would have completely missed her genuine life's vehicle.

In one of their final conversations before Marie graduated, Sister Marian Joseph said, ''Marie, this is the perfect time for you to enter. There's a new breed postulant now who thinks, evaluates, and exercises more common sense than we dared to. And you'd fit right in.''

"New breed? I'm not sure . . ."

"Let me put it this way, Marie. When we entered, we wanted—most of us desperately wanted—to become nuns so badly, we'd do anything we were told or expected to do to reach the goal. So some odd things—odd now in retrospect—happened."

"Odd?"

"I can remember, though it was a long time ago, lots of things that happened in the mother house in Monroe that were weird—by today's lights."

"Such as?"

"Oh, in the refectory—the dining hall—we had 'virtue boxes.' "

"Huh? Boxes with virtues in them?"

"I told you this was odd. No, boxes that held small pieces of paper on which were written virtuous deeds or actions. When you entered the refectory, you took one of the slips from the box and carried out whatever virtuous action was written on it."

"I still don't get it."

"Oh, for instance, you might pull out a slip that said, 'Abstain from meat during this meal.' "

"And you wouldn't eat meat? But what if that were the only main course?"

"Then you went hungry—or ate a lot of potatoes. But we were young and some of us were mischievous—not unlike yourself, Marie. I remember one time some of us 'loaded' the virtue boxes so that all the slips read, 'Take your supper on the floor.' "

Marie began to giggle. "And the refectory was filled with nuns sitting on the floor, eating?"

Sister Marian laughed at the memory. "Then we had responsibilities—we called them 'charges.' One time my charge was to clean the lower cloister with its tile floor and brick walls. And I was cleaning it, sweeping the floor, when an older nun was passing through. She took the broom from me and said, 'Why are you sweeping it that way? You must sweep it this way.' And so, without another word, I did it her way.

"I wanted to be a nun so badly that I didn't want to make waves. It was easier, a more direct route to becoming a professed sister, to bury your intelligence, your common sense and go along than to challenge the system. And if you stepped out of line, exercised your own personality, you were likely to hear from a superior, 'Did you come to join the convent or to change it?'

"Marie, we're right on the verge of the Second Vatican Council. I feel certain there will be radical changes. I can't foretell what they'll be, but they're coming. The Sisters of today and tomorrow are in the best position to react to these changes. I've watched you carefully, Marie. You are perfect for the changing religious life. That's why I was so delighted when you came to me to talk about it."

This was what she wanted to hear. Not the negative denunciation in the confessional, but the positive recognition and motivation from a nun she respected.

So Marie made application to the Sisters, Servants of the Immaculate Heart of Mary. She mentioned to neither Sister Marian Joseph nor the screening board in Monroe the tragedy of her abortion. The hearty and undiluted recommendation of Sister Marian Joseph, a Sister well respected in the community, won Marie admission as a postulant.

She found convent life much as Sister Marian had described it, except for community life. No one could have adequately described that. It had to be experienced. As dear and complete as had been her friendship with Alice, that was now only a most pleasant memory. Her religious Sisters became her real sisters.

She went through her postulancy, her novitiate, took her interim vows, then final vows. Then came the various "missions," one of which was to Marygrove, where she and Sister Janet, whom she had known at the mother house, were again classmates.

Sister Marian Joseph also proved to be a prophet. Yet even she could not have foreseen all the accomplishments of Vatican II. But she was correct in assuming the Council would shake things up in a virtually unprecedented way. And, of all groups in the Catholic Church, nuns were foremost in studying and making practical the documents of the Council. No sooner did the bishops assembled in Rome publish a document than it was devoured by the Sisters. And among the forefront of these was Sister Mary Ambrose, the former Marie Monahan. Mary Ambrose was the religious name Marie had chosen. However, a few years later and as one result of the Council, many of the nuns reverted to their original names. By the time she had entered the religious education field and written her book, she long had been known as Sister Marie Monahan, IHM.

After the considerable success of *Behind the Veil*, Marie received the first of a series of invitations to sign with P.G. Press. She was tempted neither by the promises of significantly more money nor wider exposure to readers. The mystery novel was an avocation to her. She was immensely pleased and proud of being a published author, but she had no inclination to capitalize on every potential gain. Besides, from the outset, the Reverend Krieg's importunate overtures struck her as phony. And a little research into P.G.'s backlist

put the proof to that impression. She had no intention whatever of writing the sort of book P.G. published.

From time to time, though less and less frequently as the
years passed, she would relive the abortion. Whenever it
came to mind, always unbidden, she would wince and reex-
perience her grief that it had ever happened, but also the guilt
that would never completely leave her at peace despite having
been absolved.

At least no one else—with the exception of Alice, Marie's
family, and those close to the investigation—knew about it.

Or so she thought until the Reverend Krieg made her the
offer he was sure she could not refuse. After her initial shock,
she wondered how Krieg had ever unearthed her secret. She
never learned that one of Krieg's private investigators, while
talking with her former classmates, tripped upon the rumors
that had circulated about what happened that night. Rumors
began by Cassidy's bragging. Armed with that information,
the operator checked a number of possibilities, including the
possibility of pregnancy, and a subsequent adoption or abortion. Police records, for which the operator paid a nominal
sum, revealed the abortion. Krieg had his weapon.

When Marie recovered from the shock of this discovery,
she was as furious as she had been when Bucko Cassidy had
raped her. But it was an impotent fury that she directed at
Krieg. There was nothing she could do but sign with him or
risk the chance that he would actually expose her secret. If
he were to do that, she knew her shame and disgrace would
be so great she would not feel comfortable again until she
had shriveled into a cloistered place of hiding.

Once she received the invitation to participate in this writers' workshop and realized that Klaus Krieg would be here
too, she knew this was the time of decision. She had returned

to Marygrove as guardedly despondent as she had ever been. Realistically, she felt that when push came to shove she would sign. Even after considerable prayer and thought, she had arrived at no viable alternative to giving in to Krieg.

Then, her first evening at the college, she had received an enigmatic note from the Reverend David Benbow. From the tone of the note rather than its literal content, she recognized that, for some reason he did not disclose, he was in the same predicament as she. She accepted his invitation to meet, which they did the following night—at about the time of Rabbi Winer's death.

As Benbow had no intention of revealing what it was Krieg held over him as blackmail, he made no attempt to discover Marie's secret. They operated only with the tacit understanding that both were in a career-threatening bind and that Krieg held the whip hand that promised to devastate their lives.

Cautiously at first, then boldly, Benbow suggested a plan at once subtle yet promising. It was a scheme born of the desperate corner into which they'd been forced by Krieg. It was clear as they plotted together that neither felt comfortable with what Benbow proposed. Yet neither could conceive of an alternative solution.

It was agreed that Benbow's plan would require at least two people to carry it out. Actually, it would have been more practical if more had been involved. At that point, Benbow admitted that he had sent invitations identical to Marie's to Rabbi Winer and the monk. They had obviously chosen not to accept Benbow's invitation, either because they were not threatened by Krieg as were David and Marie, or—and this seemed more likely to Benbow—they were in the same boat but, for their own reasons, simply preferred not to meet.

Finally, David and Marie agreed they must and would act.

They would use Benbow's carefully constructed plan. They would act when Benbow gave the agreed-upon signal.

The only remaining question was when to put their plan into motion. And that question was crucial.

After considerable discussion, they agreed that the wisest course would be to defer action as long as possible, rather than seizing the present moment. For one thing, they had no way of knowing Krieg's timetable. At some point during the workshop's five days Krieg would undoubtedly drop the other shoe, as it were, and impose his ultimatum. Timing, then, was of the essence. They had to act before Krieg, and forestall his exposing them.

Yet it was perfectly possible that either or both Winer and Augustine had a plan to thwart Krieg. Since neither Benbow nor Marie wanted to resort to violence—radical fear alone allowed them to even contemplate it—there was the possibility that Winer and/or Augustine might make it unnecessary for them to put their plan into action by striking first.

The point then, as Benbow explained to Marie, was to allow just enough time for one or both of the others to take care of Krieg. Failing that, David and Marie must act.

It was their final agreement, then, that the crucial factor of timing would be left in Benbow's hands. He would give the signal if it were needed. And then they would put a stop to Klaus Krieg.

Talk about God's will! Praise God!

22

WAS IT SOMETHING in his genes, his training, his nature? What was it that so regularly prompted Koesler to agree to requests, often without proper reflection? He wondered.

From considerable experience, he knew that it was akin to academic suicide to walk into any classroom as a teacher without having done his homework. Yet, when Sister Marie asked him to take her class, he had agreed. She had tossed off the subject as something in which he had more than adequate experience. After all, he had had an unusual amount of contact with the police. How many priests had been involved in actual homicide investigations? Thus, according to Sister Marie, all he had to do was walk into a classroom cold, and field eager and reasonable questions on the subject. So, despite his experience, he had agreed to her request. And he had paid for it.

Though it was a lovely, cool morning, Koesler was perspiring beneath his black clerical suit and Roman collar.

One does not just walk into a classroom relying on some miraculous *dabitur vobis*. He realized that the moment he walked in and confronted the eager faces. One does not begin a class by inviting questions. Questions follow a presentation—sometimes. They certainly do not precede a presentation. Somehow he had managed to carry it off this morning—at least he hoped he had. But he had paid the price in emotional investment. No blood or tears, but there had been plenty of sweat.

As he hurriedly exited the classroom, he almost literally ran into Sergeant Angela Moore, who'd been scurrying down the corridor. He apologized.

"That's okay, Father. This'll save time in trying to find you. They'll want you there for this." She managed to sweep him along with her.

"They'll want me?" Koesler fell in step with her. "Some new information?"

"Uh-huh." She said no more, but led the way to the modest dining room that had become a makeshift headquarters for the police.

Koznicki and Tully were standing near the center of the room. Various other officers were occupied in other parts of the room.

Tully took one look at Moore's face. "You found it, didn't you?"

"Uh-huh." Koesler now noticed Moore's flushed excitement. "Yeah," she said. "This has got to be what Krieg found and the nun didn't want to get out."

Koesler fought a sudden urge to leave. He felt as if he were eavesdropping. He had developed a liking and respect for Sister Marie. And Sergeant Moore was about to reveal the secret Marie so desperately wanted kept hidden. Hers was, after all, the one remaining confidential matter to be exposed. But he knew that Inspector Koznicki wanted him there. Koesler steeled himself to hear the worst.

"It was an abortion," Moore said, rather more forcefully than necessary.

"An abortion!" Koesler's involuntary reaction was so unexpected that it startled the others. However, their surprise was momentary.

"When'd it happen?" Tully asked.

"She was a senior in high school."

"A senior in high school!" Ordinarily Koesler would be listening to the experts and contributing nothing at this point. But he felt that someone should be standing up for this good woman. "High school!" he repeated. "That must be . . . some thirty years ago!"

"That's about right." Moore turned slightly to face Koesler. He had entered this matter actively and neither of her superior officers was curbing him in any way. So she felt free to address his concern.

"How . . . how could you uncover such a thing? I mean . . . thirty years!" Koesler said.

"A fluke, mostly," Moore admitted. "Although we might have uncovered it ourselves, given time. But, I don't know . . ." She seemed to drift off in speculation.

"How did you uncover it?" Koznicki brought her back to the present.

"Oh, Stewart found it," Moore said.

"Stewart?"

"Uh, Patrolman Stewart, Judith." Moore located the officer's name on the report she was holding. "She's a rookie. Hasn't got anything to do with this investigation. She's stationed in the First Precinct. She was reading about our case and she thought the name sounded familiar. Marie Monahan. So, she thought about it until the bell rang. She thought she'd seen the name in one of the old abortion files."

"Isn't that a bit contrived, Sergeant?" Koesler broke in. He was surprising himself that he was so actively responding to this charge against Sister Marie's reputation. He couldn't help himself. It didn't seem right that a good person's reputation could be so easily trashed. "Doesn't the coincidence stretch credibility?"

Moore didn't know whether to engage this outsider in a pedantic debate when there was the serious business of a homicide investigation going on. She glanced around and caught the affirmative if slight nod given by Inspector Koznicki.

"It's not all that odd, Father," Moore explained. "Our newer people especially like to visit the basement at headquarters where all these old records are kept."

"Why would they do that?" Koesler asked.

"It's just fascinating reading," Moore said. "We don't write up reports this way any more. It's the terminology as much as anything else. Often as not, they use terms like 'thug' instead of 'criminal' or 'perpetrator.' They're very . . . uh . . . emotionally written. They're fun to read. Sort of like an old Batman strip. So, especially the newer people, when they find where these records are kept, well, it's not uncommon for them to spend a little spare time browsing through them.

"That's what Stewart was doing recently, see? She was going through the records—just recreational reading—when she got into the abortion files. And today when she saw the name of the nun mentioned as part of our investigation— well, as I said, it rang a bell. She says she remembered it because it was so Irish. Stewart figured that back then, with a name like that, abortion would have been not only a crime, but a sin."

"I still find it hard to understand why you would keep records that old," Koesler said.

Koznicki had been quietly studying the police record of Marie's abortion that Moore had handed him. "You see, Father," he explained, "with the frequency of criminal appeals of cases, the police tend to hold on to all records, just in case. Just in case a civil lawsuit is filed, we will not be caught short. We throw nothing away. It makes for a cluttered basement, but it also insures that we will not be caught needing a record that has been discarded.

"This record, for example," Koznicki continued, "of an abortion performed on one Marie Monahan, gives the name of the doctor who repaired the damage caused by an obvious amateur, who, it seems, almost killed Miss Monahan. So there is a complete medical record. But no name of the person who botched the original abortion. Apparently, Marie Monahan refused to cooperate with the investigating officer—which, I should mention, was not uncommon. That is why there are so many old records of abortion investigations in these files. Very, very infrequently did the victim of an illegal abortion agree to testify. And without the victim's testimony, there was no case."

Koesler said nothing. Seemingly, he had run out of questions and challenges.

"Well, that ties it," Tully said. He seemed satisfied that they would be delayed no more by Koesler. "That's a full house," Tully continued. "Each of these writers has something in his or her past that they didn't want revealed. Desperately didn't want revealed. The rabbi had betrayed his own people. The monk is an alcoholic. The priest was an adulterer. And the nun had an abortion."

Somehow, stated so flatly, so abruptly, these sins—if such

they were—seemed to Koesler to be best kept buried as they had been prior to this police investigation. Then he recalled that the police were only reacting to what had already been ferreted out by Klaus Krieg.

"And," Tully continued, "Krieg discovered every one of their secrets and threatened to publicize them unless they signed contracts with him."

"How do you suppose he dug up all these secrets, Zoo?" Moore asked.

"Right now, I don't know. But with his money, just about anything is possible. I got the feeling we're getting down to the bottom line. It feels right."

"Just one more question, please," Father Koesler said. "Doesn't it seem peculiar to anyone but me that we suddenly know so much about everyone connected with this workshop with the exception of the Reverend Krieg? I mean, all of a sudden we know some of the deepest, darkest secrets of four very dedicated religious—secrets we wouldn't even have guessed existed except that Krieg found out about them and because of him the police investigated and found them out. But Klaus Krieg—the one who started all this—Klaus Krieg remains in the shadows. Doesn't this seem odd?"

In the silence that followed Koesler's question, it seemed the detectives were quietly passing around the responsibility of answering. Sergeant Moore fumbled through the sheaf of papers she was holding. She extracted three of them from the file and handed them to Koesler.

"I guess we assumed that you knew Krieg's background," she said. "What we've got on him is no secret. Nor, with what we've got, is there room for many secrets. We weren't trying to keep anything from you, Father. In fact, you know as much about this case as any of us. That's the way Inspector

Koznicki wanted it. But these," referring to the background papers she had just handed Koesler, "should bring you completely up to date."

Once again Koesler felt embarrassed. In the context of what Moore had just said, his complaint about Krieg sounded to Koesler himself petulant and pushy.

In mutual awkwardness the group was about to break up when Sergeant Mangiapane hurried into the room. Everyone could tell from the expression on his face and his abrupt manner that he had important new information. "We just got done searching their rooms—the three writers—"

Moore interrupted. "Did you get their permission again?"

"We got a warrant," Mangiapane said.

"So soon?" Moore pressed.

"This morning," Tully replied. "Remember, the mayor wants this one cleaned up in record time." He turned back to Mangiapane. "What did you find?"

The beatific look returned to Mangiapane's face. "In Benbow's room, a gallon can with some gasoline still in the bottom. In Sister Marie's room, several gas-soaked cloths."

Tully looked thoughtful. "Maybe they got careless. Maybe one of them planted the evidence. Either way we get them together now and lay it on the line—the bottom line."

"They're already together, Zoo," Mangiapane said. "We got 'em in a classroom on the second floor."

The detectives left for the classroom without another thought about or word from Koesler. The priest was left in the dining room, holding, if not the bag, several papers outlining the life and career of the Reverend Klaus Krieg.

Koesler lacked the stomach to watch what was undoubtedly going to be an intense grilling of Augustine, Marie, and Benbow, perhaps Mrs. Benbow as well. He sat at a table and spread the papers out before him. The first page was a publicity release; the other two, the summary of what the police had discovered.

Born in 1950, Krieg was now forty years old. That surprised Koesler. He would have guessed Krieg to be somewhat older. Not that he looked or acted particularly ancient, but that he had accomplished so much, built so much, raised so much funding in a relatively brief time.

Koesler's second major surprise was the fact—the boast, as Krieg put it—that the preacher had at one time been a Catholic. It was from the chains of authoritarian Catholicism that the minister had freed himself by being born again in the Spirit. A freedom from the bonds of sectarianism and sin that he offered to all who would join him in the baptism of the Spirit. However, make no mistake, the freedom P.G. Enterprises offered did not come cheap. The ''initiation fee'' was closely followed by special projects fundings, followed by good old-fashioned obligatory tithing.

Another surprise. He was born in Imlay City, Michigan. This from the police report.

Koesler had simply assumed that Krieg was a native Californian. Or, that if his origin were elsewhere, then certainly New York or Chicago. The assumption was based on the size of Krieg's empire. How could such volume spring from little Imlay City?

Then, Koesler was reminded of Jesus Christ's extremely modest home town. So modest, indeed, that the more sarcastic of Jesus' contemporaries remarked, ''Can anything good come out of Nazareth!'' So, why not? Koesler wondered whether inhabitants of Imlay City realized that the famous Klaus Krieg, multimillionaire and television personality, had once walked their streets.

Koesler was familiar with Imlay City. It was, roughly, at
the knuckle of the thumb. Since the state, at least the lower
peninsula, was in the shape of a hand geographically, Mich-
iganders tended to pinpoint areas in the state according to
their position in the "hand." Nowhere was that habit more
prevalent than when the locale was in the "thumb" area, as
was Imlay City, about halfway between Flint and Port
Huron.

In addition, it was within the boundaries of the Archdiocese of Detroit, and the pastor of Imlay City's one and only
Catholic church, Sacred Heart, had been one of Koesler's
classmates. Which more than likely explained how Koesler
happened to know its exact location.

Interesting, Koesler mused as he succumbed to a day-
dream. Klaus Krieg born a Catholic in the Archdiocese of
Detroit. He found religion so vitally important in his life that
he apostasized from Catholicism and formed his own sect.
What if he hadn't done that? What if whatever had moved
him to discard the Catholic Church hadn't happened? Would
that appreciation of religion have led him into the Catholic
clergy? What would he be like as a priest today?

A preacher of no little note, undoubtedly. Whatever else
anyone might want to say about him, he could be a spell-
binding orator. Another Charlie Coughlin?

Or Billy Sunday?

Or Elmer Gantry?

Koesler found himself reviewing what little he knew about
the Reverend Krieg from firsthand knowledge. While he was
familiar with Krieg's reputation as a televangelist, Koesler
had never seen him on television, nor, for that matter, in any
other way. So his first impression was formed when, just days
earlier, Krieg had burst onto the Marygrove scene with the

expected fanfare and his own private chauffeur and general factotum.

Koesler allowed his reliable memory to wander through recollections of the past few days. To be frank, he was looking for telltale remnants of a former Catholic faith. Former Catholics regularly betray habits—most of them not consciously—of Catholic customs, practices, traditions, even superstitions.

In their liturgies, Catholics make the sign of the cross so habitually the habit often carries over to completely unrelated events. At the conclusion of anything—a movie, a stage play, a concert, a lecture, whatever—it is not unknown that a practicing Catholic, or a one-time Catholic, might make the sign of the cross. The same could be said of genuflecting before entering an auditorium or theater row, or—in a situation where spontaneous prayer is called for—coming up with a distinctly Catholic prayer.

Thanks to television, millions have seen a singular gesture usually made by an athlete with a Catholic background. The gesture consists of an abbreviated and hurried sign of the cross that does not quite reach forehead, navel, and the extremity of either shoulder. It is, if only because it could be nothing else, a sign of the cross, but it ends with the boxer, ballplayer, athlete, kissing his right thumb.

As far as Koesler knew, no one had done a definitive study of that peculiar sign; indeed he was convinced that even those who make the gesture probably don't advert to the reason they kiss their thumb. The closest Koesler could come to a rationale rested on a practice popular among those who frequently and piously recite the rosary. It is common for those who pray the rosary to begin by holding the crucifix in their right hand—with which they make the sign of the cross—

and, on completing the sign of the cross, kissing the crucifix. It was Koesler's hypothesis that those athletes who indulge in what has become for them a superstition don't consciously think of what they're doing. Why, after all, would anyone kiss his own thumb?

What has happened is that they grew up watching mother pray the rosary. They've seen her over and over again make the sign of the cross, and end by kissing the crucifix. But to the youthful observer it might not have been clear just what was being kissed.

So, today's boxer, football, basketball, baseball player makes the sign of the cross—for luck, most probably—kisses the finger that would be holding a crucifix if one were present, and then goes out to beat hell out of the other guy or die trying.

Koesler almost smiled at the memory of uncounted hockey players going over the boards, making the sign of the cross, kissing the thumb, then whacking an opponent with the hockey stick. He almost smiled. But he did not. Instead he grew serious.

What was it? Something he had just been thinking of. They grew up watching mother pray the rosary. *They grew up watching mother pray the rosary.*

Thoughts tumbled into his mind. Unbidden, the thoughts came in no particular order. It was as if he had dropped the pieces of a jigsaw puzzle in the center of his brain with the accompanying urge to put them together so that the puzzle would make sense.

Klaus Krieg grew up watching his mother say the rosary? No, that wasn't it. But something like that. What had the little boy watched his mother do?

Before Koesler could answer that, other pieces needed placement.

Instead of trying to find vestiges of Catholicism in what he'd seen of Krieg, Koesler tried to simply take an objective view of what he'd actually seen and heard Krieg do and say.

Gradually the jigsaw picture began to take shape. It revealed quite a different image than anyone had been looking at up to this time.

The question facing Koesler now: Would this picture hold up in the face of strong arguments against it? And he was not kidding himself: He was sure that even if he could join these fragments together so that they constituted a brand new theory of what had been going on here, he would face determined opposition. Indeed, opposition from the police who had been investigating the case. Opposition from the experts.

Koesler quite nearly quit at this point. Who was he kidding? He was no expert at solving crimes. The experts were upstairs now, questioning, challenging, solving the crime. And they were not even considering the scenario he'd seen with his mind's eye as he put his own peculiar jigsaw puzzle together.

The trouble he faced now was that he was hesitant to test his theory. It seemed to him almost as if the theory were his baby, and he was afraid the baby was about to be declared ugly. But he could envision only two alternatives. One: swallow it; forget it. The police knew—or thought they knew—they were in the home stretch: They were homing in on the guilty party. They had hard evidence now that they'd found the remnants of the gasoline that, on the surface of it, was meant to blow Klaus Krieg sky-high. The temptation was strong to sit back and do nothing. It would be interesting to watch the remainder of this drama much like attending a movie. It seemed that the police were mere minutes away from a solution. But was it *the* solution?

Interesting question: Could it be possible for the police to solve this case incorrectly? What possible reason could there be for the police to be mistaken?

Two: The second alternative was to play out his hand as far as it would reach. The reason: It was probable the police lacked the insight he had as a Catholic priest and one who was interested in all aspects of religion. He owed it to his friend Walt Koznicki to test his hypothesis. He owed it to justice for the innocent as well as the guilty.

With any luck, it would require no more than a few phone calls. With a lot of luck, one call would do it.

Koesler walked to the general office. As he expected, Marygrove had a Catholic Directory of the Archdiocese of Detroit.

If nothing else, it had been a long time since he'd talked to his classmate, Father John Dunn. It would be pleasant to chat with him. And chat they would; John never used one word when he could think of two or three.

Koesler dialed 1-724-1135. *Please God, let John be there and let this be the only call I have to make.*

"You have reached Sacred Heart parish. This is the real-life Father John Dunn speaking . . ."

"It's Bob Koesler, John—"

"Bobby! It's so nice for us out in the boondocks when one of you big city slickers remembers us."

"John, though we seldom write, we never forget. But, as it is, I'm in a bit of a hurry. Can we get down to business?"

"Ah, 'twas ever so."

"John, I need some information you may have in your

records about an individual—maybe a family. It should be a baptismal record, maybe a marriage record.''

"Are you going to take care of the bill for all this?''

"Quit kidding.''

"All right, what's the name?''

"Krieg.''

Silence. Then: "What is this, a run on that family this week?''

"What do you mean?''

"This is the second call I got this week on the Kriegs.''

It was Koesler's turn to be taken aback. "Who else?''

"I forget the priest's name. Said he was with the tribunal in Windsor.''

Koesler did not know what to make of this. It was completely unexpected—and was certain to require more phone calls. But, sufficient for the moment the mystery thereof. "Well, John," he said, "let's get with this before it's time for the World Series.''

"Say, Bob, what about those Tigers? Things look pretty bleak for them this time around. Puts one in mind of 'The score stood six to five for the Mudville Nine that day . . .' ''

Casey at the Bat! Well, it was small enough price to pay for finding Father Dunn at home and able to take nourishment.

23 WHEN FATHER KOESLER reached the classroom that was being used for the interrogation, he found it cordoned off by uniformed Detroit police. Evidently they had been instructed to allow him entrée because, even as he hesitated, they opened a path for him.

He halted at the door of the classroom. A large two-way glass in the door permitted him to see into the room even if he could not hear what was being said. Whatever was going on must have been deadly serious judging from the expressions of those whose faces he could see. Sister Marie and Martha Benbow seemed to be in tears. The men looked as if they would be if it had been socially acceptable. He had arrived none too soon.

His knock at the door caused a look of surprise to supplant the intense grim expression everyone had been wearing. Lieutenant Tully appeared annoyed at the interruption. It was Inspector Koznicki who opened the door to Koesler.

"I'm so sorry to interrupt your proceedings," Koesler said.

"Quite all right, Father," Koznicki said. "I fear we forgot you in the rush to begin this interrogation. Come right in." He stepped back to let Koesler enter.

342

"If it's all right with you, Inspector, instead of my coming in, I'd like to invite you to come out."

Koznicki was clearly startled. "Come out? You want me to leave this interrogation?"

Koesler took a deep breath, then forged on. *Damn the torpedoes, full speed ahead.* "Yes, Inspector, you, Lieutenant Tully, perhaps Sergeants Mangiapane and Moore. And . . . the Reverend Krieg."

This select subcast of characters did consent—after some hesitation—to assemble in the office opposite the classroom. The police guards would ensure that the others, suspects all, would remain in their present classroom.

There was an air of expectancy in the office. Tully, Moore, and Mangiapane, as well as Koznicki, had, to a greater or lesser extent, worked with Koesler before. All knew that it was not like him to go out on a limb without good reason. It had better be considerably stronger than merely good to justify interrupting an interrogation that could and should close this investigation. Or so, at least, Tully thought.

Koesler easily dismissed the temptation to open with, "Well, I suppose you're wondering why I've called you here." Instead . . .

"Something occurred to me," the priest said, "that may make a considerable impact on this situation. It happened when you"—he nodded at Moore—"gave me Reverend Krieg's—what shall I call it?—his curriculum vitae, as it were."

Krieg, to this point, had appeared politely interested, even amused. Now, for just a split second, a look of apprehension crossed his face. The expression was noted by both Koznicki and Tully.

"Allow me to recapitulate," Koesler said, "not because

any of us is unaware of what's happened, but because, to suit my purpose, I have to separate the facts—what we know happened—from an interpretation of those facts.''

Tully, particularly, felt this unnecessary, but said nothing. He had gone this far in including the priest in this investigation; he could see no reason not to humor him one more time.

''We began,'' Koesler proceeded, ''with four writers and a publisher invited as an ad hoc faculty for this workshop. The writers specialize in mystery novels cast in a religious setting. The protagonist in their books, in each case, is an extension of the author of each one: an Episcopal priest, a rabbi, a Trappist monk, a religious Sister. The publisher specializes in religious books. All five of these people are successful, in varying degrees in this general field.

''Now, it's been established that Reverend Krieg wants— covets might be a better word—these four writers for his stable. And, to this end, he has offered each of them a contract to be published by P.G. Press . . . all right so far?''

No one had any objection.

''I can well imagine,'' Koesler continued, ''that it would be flattering for a writer to be pursued by a publisher. But it's a free country, and in keeping with that truth, there is nothing that says a writer must sign a contract with any specific publisher. All one need do is say no. Which, we are told, each and every one of these writers said to P.G. Press.

''On the other hand, it is nowhere written that a publisher need take no for an answer. And this, we are told, also happened. P.G. Press hounded—I think that's the word—all four writers.

''Still, nothing terribly unusual going on. We've all had the experience of being pestered by salespeople who simply won't give up. In fact, what we consider 'pestering' to the dedicated salesperson is just a good salesperson doing his or her job.

"In this case, P.G. can say please. The writer can say no. P.G. can say pretty please. The writer can say a thousand times no. To some extent, just about everyone in this country has gone through this sort of verbal exchange at one time or another in one context or another.

"What started every one of us on the outside looking in on this cross-fire between writers and publisher was the vehemence of the writers in rejecting the publisher, and their evident antipathy—one might even say loathing or hatred—toward Reverend Krieg.

"Why, was the obvious question—why was everyone so emotionally riveted in his or her refusal to sign with P.G.? We are, after all, dealing with rational, dedicated religious people: a monk, a rabbi, a nun, and a priest. Here are people whom we should suppose have much more than average patience at their command. Here are people we would expect to be capable of politely refusing an offer—even if that offer were repeated too frequently. Yet even if we were to encounter one or another of the writers who might be lacking in a sustained ability to refuse politely ad infinitum we would not be terribly surprised. But, all of them? *All of them?* Each and every one of the writers was furious at P.G. Press and the Reverend Krieg. Why would that be?

"Then we learned that each of these writers had at least one deeply embarrassing episode in life that could spell ruin for career and/or vocation if the secret were to be revealed. You police suspected the existence of such skeletons. Your investigation uncovered these embarrassing secrets. It was then you discovered why the writers were so angry and why they were having such difficulty in making their rejections of P.G.'s overtures stick. The Reverend Krieg had uncovered these secrets and was threatening to reveal them unless the writers signed. He was making them an offer they could not refuse: blackmail.''

"Now, just one minute, Father Koesler," Krieg said. "Praise God! Blackmail is a strong word. You can't prove—"

"Hear him out, Krieg," Tully cut in. "I think he's getting to the good part."

"I surely hope so," Koesler said. "Anyway, we now have the reason why the writers are so angry with P.G. Press in general and Klaus Krieg in particular. But, angry enough for one of them to kill him?"

"Well, one of them tried," Moore said. "One of them tried and got Rabbi Winer by mistake. And that's what we're trying to figure out now. Which one—or ones—tried to kill Krieg and got Winer by mistake." She did not try to conceal her impatience.

"Yes, Sergeant," Koesler said, "but before the event you describe, something else happened that I think was related. Remember the psychodrama? Reverend Krieg set up this play within a play, as it were, in which he was murdered—ostensibly by one of the writers. The staging was so realistic that I called the police, and Lieutenant Tully and Sergeant Mangiapane came here to investigate a murder that hadn't happened."

Mangiapane smiled. "That's okay, Father. It happens. Like I told you then, this was not the first false alarm we ever answered."

"And it was very kind of you, Sergeant, to let me off the hook. But the question that's never been answered to my satisfaction is why the Reverend went to all that trouble. It was explained away as a kind of game. But I've always thought it was more than that."

Krieg was smiling broadly. "I think that explanation is sufficient. But, Praise God, if you've got to look for something more, you have only to look at my state of mind. After all, I am not insensitive. What it boils down to is that, yes, I want these writers under contract. It will be beneficial to them and to P.G. Press. All right, for our mutual good, I may have pursued this matter a bit further than the average publisher might. But, Praise God, I'm only doing it for their own good. Can I help it if they develop an antipathy toward me to the point where I fear for my life? Maybe I did have more than one reason for staging that psychodrama. Maybe I wanted them to face realistically what evil consequences would follow if I were to be murdered. And just maybe I wanted the police to be alerted as well. Is there some sort of crime in this? I mean, really! Praise God!"

It was Koesler's turn to smile. "That's it exactly, Reverend Krieg. You *did* want the police in on this as early as possible.

"The reason is obvious. You had to know you were assembling four very angry people—four very threatened people—at this conference. Despite their religious station, it was well within the realm of possibility that one or more of them, pushed to the wall, might try to harm you—maybe even threaten your life. You brought your own bodyguard with you. But I can see where you would value having police protection as well.

"In fact, I think that's why you stipulated that I be invited to take part in this workshop: because I have a history, limited though it might be, of having been involved in homicide investigations in the past. You figured that with your cleverly staged murder, there was a good chance I would get the police involved. And I did.''

Krieg still smiled, but not as broadly. "Now why would I do a fool thing like that?"

"A very good question," Koesler said. "It didn't even occur to me until just a short time ago, when I started to think of things in a different light. It all began when I learned that you were once a Catholic."

Krieg's voice had a touch of challenge to it. "You're not going to hold that against me, are you?"

"No, Reverend, not that. But when I discovered you'd been a Catholic, I began to look for telltale traits that might be vestiges of your Catholic upbringing. Call it an avocation, but I am so deeply into Catholicism that I tend to value those little habits and superstitions that most of us Catholics share.

"Except . . . except that I didn't find any such signs in your behavior. None at all."

Krieg was clearly annoyed. "Really? Really! Hasn't this gone on far enough? Inspector . . . Lieutenant . . . isn't it about time we go back across the hall and get on with the investigation? I mean, Praise God, are we here to discuss homey little Catholic practices?"

"Sort of," Koesler said. "But, as Lieutenant Tully said, we may be getting to the good part.

"After I looked for, but did not find, any distinctly Catholic idiosyncracies in your mannerisms, it occurred to me that I might be going about this business backwards—something I've done lots more than once. So I just reviewed what I had observed about you in the few days I've known you.

"The very first thing that came to my mind when I tried

to remember what you'd done that drew my attention was food.''

"Food!"

"Yes, food. I remembered our first dinner together on Sunday evening.''

"What of it?" Krieg was challenging. "I came late for dinner. As I remember, the food was cold.''

"Do you recall what you had to eat?"

"Of course not. It was of no consequence.''

"I wouldn't have thought so at the time. But I noticed anyway.''

"And now you're going to tell everyone what I had to eat for Sunday dinner." Krieg was contemptuous. "Really, Inspector, how long is this going to go on? What earthly difference can it make *what* I ate?''

Koznicki, his expression of thoughtful interest unchanged, continued to gaze at Koesler. Tully looked as if he were withholding judgment. Moore and Mangiapane were kids watching "Sesame Street."

"Actually," Koesler replied, "it wasn't so much *what* you ate as what you didn't. The main course was beef Stroganoff. And I noticed that Rabbi Winer ate everything else that was served that night except the Stroganoff. He just toyed with that. Didn't eat a bit of it.''

Krieg sighed noisily, signifying a boredom he was being forced to endure.

"When you arrived, Reverend, everyone else was just about finished with dinner.''

"That's what I said. Or, if this is some sort of kangaroo court, perhaps I'd better phrase it, 'I stipulated to that.' ''

"But, Reverend, the dinner had not been served in common dishes. Each person was given an individual serving—a plate with the food already on it.''

"So!"

"So, it wasn't a case of the food's being cold. It wasn't cooling in a common dish all the while we ate. Your meal, Reverend, was undoubtedly being kept warm since you were expected for dinner. But you looked at the remains of what had been served and decided to have something different than the rest of us.''

"That's a crime?''

"Impolite, perhaps. Unmannerly, maybe. Not a crime. Not yet.''

"And what is that supposed to mean?''

"You had what the rest of us had as far as the salad and vegetables were concerned. But as the main course, you had an omelet. And you had milk, followed by coffee with cream.''

"I did?''

"The kitchen staff undoubtedly could corroborate that.''

"Marvelous, Father Koesler; you have a unique memory. I can't imagine anyone else who would—or would want to—recall everything I have to eat.''

"Oh, it didn't make all that great an impression at the time. It was only later that I began to wonder about it, without even knowing I was wondering, in fact. And I began wondering the very next evening when we had dinner together again.''

"What did I eat, good Father?''

Koesler smiled. "We were served a fruit salad, beef broth, lamb, and red potatoes.''

"And I suppose the kitchen people could corroborate that again. Inspector, must I sit here and listen to this drivel?''

"For the moment I would do so if I were you," Koznicki said. "Father Koesler is not in the habit of wasting anyone's time."

Krieg's countenance hardened. "All right, Father. We had salad, broth, lamb, and—what?—potatoes."

"And coffee," Koesler said.

"And coffee," Krieg repeated.

"Except that this time I noticed that only Sister Janet took cream in her coffee. I passed the cream to her and noticed that no one else asked for any."

"Meaning I didn't have cream in my coffee. Well, that should do it . . . whatever 'it' is." Krieg dripped sarcasm.

" 'It,' Reverend Krieg, is dietary laws. It occurred to me when I was thinking of your growing up as a Catholic child learning Catholic habits, idiosyncracies, superstitions, whatever, from your mother."

"My mother!" There was a decided change in Krieg's attitude. At mention of his mother, he became perceptibly aggressive. "What does my mother have to do with any of this?"

"Just about everything," Koesler replied. "I was thinking of you in terms of myself. Two Catholic kids growing up in a Catholic environment. I was thinking of you learning about the rosary as I did, watching as Mother recited it regularly and fervently. Then it occurred to me: Maybe you were without any discernible Catholic mannerisms because you didn't really grow up in a Catholic atmosphere. You didn't learn the rosary from your mother. But you did learn that you should never mix dairy and meat products in the same meal."

"This is an outrage!" Krieg erupted. "My mother is a saint! How dare you drag her into this sordid affair!"

"I think you're right, Reverend: It is a rather wretched

affair and your sainted mother doesn't belong in it. It's just that she taught you dietary customs. She taught you so well, you observe them without even thinking. That's not odd. Catholics follow Church rules, regulations, and laws out of pure habit. There are any number of Catholics who still do not eat meat on Fridays. Outside of a certain few Fridays, it's not even a matter of law any more. But many Catholics continue to exclude meat from their Friday menu. It's a matter of ingrained habit.

"When you saw the remnants of beef Stroganoff on the plates, instinctively you knew you could not eat that dish because it contained both meat—the beef—and a dairy product—sour cream. A sign to your chauffeur and he ordered a different dinner for you. I noticed him being very insistent with the waitress.

"So instead of Stroganoff you had an omelet. No meat in that, nor in the salad or vegetable—both of which you ate. Keeping the meal clear for dairy products, you added a glass of milk, and cream in your coffee."

'I don't—'' Krieg began.

"Just give me one more moment," Koesler broke in. "The following evening, if you'll recall, we were served fruit salad, consomme, lámb, and potatoes. No dairy product. After dinner, you had coffee without cream. Remember? Sister Janet was the only one who took cream. People who drink coffee take it black, or with cream, or with cream and sugar, or with sugar. And that's the way they drink it all the time. Once you notice how a person takes coffee, you know how to serve it from that time on to that individual. Unless . . . unless the person is consciously or unconsciously observing some dietary restriction, such as one that does not permit meat and dairy products at the same meal."

There followed a few moments of silence.

Then Krieg said quietly. "And where are you going with this line of reasoning, Father Koesler?"

It was the unspoken question on the minds of everyone else in the room.

Instead of directly addressing Krieg's question, Koesler said, "All I've really been doing, Reverend, is putting together building blocks that seem to fit. For instance, Rabbi Winer was the only other person who did not eat the Stroganoff."

"So two people out of eight don't care for Stroganoff. That seems normal enough."

"And the first word I heard you say was a Yiddish one. The rabbi was telling his story at dinner Sunday night. You happened to reach the dining room just as he got to the punch line. Only you were the one who said it, 'Gevalt!' "

"Oh, come now, Father—Officers—isn't this getting a bit thin? English-language dictionaries are filled with foreign words that are so popular and common that they are accepted in ordinary English usage. 'Gevalt!' is just one of many foreign words that are understood by almost everyone. I just have no idea what you're driving at. Does anyone?" Krieg looked at the others but got no reaction. The police were busy absorbing, weighing, and evaluating the interchange between the priest and the minister.

"Reverend," Koesler said with some solemnity, "I think you know, I really think you know very well where I'm heading. Although at this point as I was mulling over these facts just a few minutes ago, I was hesitant to take the hypothesis I was forming any further. Then I decided I owed it to too many people not to follow through to whatever end it might lead."

Tully noticed a change in Krieg's eyes. They began darting about the room, as if things were closing in, as if he were being pressed into a corner.

"I noticed," Koesler continued, "that the information sheets that Sergeant Moore gave me state that you were born here in Michigan, within the Detroit Archdiocese, in fact, in Imlay City. There is only one Catholic parish in that city," Koesler added parenthetically, smiling at the memory of his classmate giving him much more information than required. "Sacred Heart parish was established as a mission in 1874 and as a parish in 1928. Anyway, it's been there much more than long enough to have served you and your parents.

"By the way, I could just as easily have gotten like information from any Catholic parish in the world. But it was convenient checking things out with the pastor there who happens to be my classmate.

"First, I asked him to check the baptismal record. He found your record easily from the alphabetical listing. We already knew the year of your birth, and figured, correctly, that you would have been baptized shortly thereafter. That's the custom among Catholics.

"There was your name, date of birth, date of baptism, names of godparents, and your parents' names. Your father, Helmut Krieg, and your mother, Rebecca Weissman. And next to your mother's name, the letters 'AC'—*Acatholica*—non-Catholic.

"Then, I asked the pastor to see if he could locate a marriage record for your parents. He did. They were married at Sacred Heart parish just a year before you were born. The form included spaces for the name of the priest who witnessed the ceremony, the two witnesses, the date of marriage, your parents' parents' names—your mother's parents were Asa Weissman and Sarah Blum—your parents' names, their residences, and their place of baptism. Your father was baptized in a Cleveland Catholic Church. Your mother was never baptized. She was Jewish. And a dispensation from the impediment of disparity of cult was granted, so your father, a Catholic, could validly marry your mother, a Jew, who would remain a Jew.

"Since your mother was Jewish, it confirmed the hypothesis I had formed without this verification; that, by Jewish law, you are a Jew."

An extended silence followed.

"This," Koesler said finally, "may be why you were so familiar with the rabbi's Jewish joke. This is why neither the rabbi nor you would eat the meat-and-dairy-mixed Stroganoff. This is why you stayed with a meatless meal on Sunday and, when meat was the main dish on Monday's menu, you passed on all dairy products—even to not taking cream in your coffee. You didn't learn the rosary from your mother. Instead, you learned the customs of Judaism, chief among which are the very strict dietary laws for which Jews are known."

Another significant pause. Tully beckoned Mangiapane to him. He whispered to Mangiapane, who nodded and left the room. Koesler didn't know what that was about, but, he reflected, it was not the first time someone had walked out on one of his sermons.

At length, Krieg looked at Koesler and spoke. "So Jews would consider me to be Jewish. So what?"

"No," Koesler said, "I think you'll find that if the Jews accept you as one of them—and they have very strict laws governing who is Jewish—the rest of the world will agree with them.

"But back to the building blocks. Once we establish the fact that you grew up being Jewish, lots of other details fall into place. The first, and most important, of these blocks is that your situation is precisely the same as the four writers you were blackmailing. You could not afford—any more than they—to have your secret revealed.

"How would it look for one of the world's leading Christian evangelists to be Jewish? Your considerable following may or may not be sympathetic to the cause of Israel as a state. But how would they, as fundamentalist Christians, react to being led by a Jew? If your ancestry were revealed, you stand to lose everything. Not unlike the nun, the monk, the rabbi, and the priest, eh?

"So, then I ask myself, what if one of the writers discovered your secret? What would happen if one of them found out you were Jewish? If *I* could discover this secret, surely someone else could. The problem would be in arriving at the initial suspicion that you might have Jewish ancestry. Who would be in a position to suspect such a thing?

"Maybe Marie, Augustine, or David Benbow would search for some flaw in your background to use as a bargaining chip. But where would they look? To your private life? To your corporate affairs? They would not find anything, would they?

"But of course there was another person of Jewish heritage in our group: Rabbi Winer.

"A few moments ago I told you I called Sacred Heart parish in Imlay City. I neglected to mention that when I asked for your record of baptism and your parents' record of marriage, my classmate commented that mine was the second call this week for those very same records. I asked who had called for them and he said an official with the Windsor tribunal. Now, isn't that an odd coincidence?''

Judging by the reaction of everyone in the room, including Krieg, the consensus was, yes, that was an extremely odd coincidence.

"Well," Koesler continued, "that somewhat complicated my line of thought. And I do not relish complications. I had to find out who else was interested in these documents.''

"I've been in situations similar to Father Dunn's, when a call will come from a chancery or tribunal in some other diocese for one record or another. There's nothing particularly secret about such information. The presumption is that another diocese has need of the record, so you give the information readily, without question. It was the coincidence—that our neighboring diocese in Canada and I should want the same information at roughly the same time.

"So I phoned the Windsor tribunal and found—not to my great surprise, really— that no one there had called for such information.

"Then I checked with the college's switchboard for outgoing long distance calls from Rabbi Winer's room. And what do you suppose? There was a call to Imlay City. Clever of the rabbi to masquerade as a tribunal official. But why did he do it?

"I don't know what Rabbi Winer may have observed before we assembled here at Marygrove. P.G. may have published a specialized treatment of rabbis or Judaism, I don't know. But I do know that Rabbi Winer saw the same things I saw on Sunday evening. It was his joke whose punch line you stole, Reverend. He might have wondered how you would be familiar with the Yiddish word for ultimate frustration or agony. But, I understand that many non-Jews, especially those who've been in the military service, or those who've heard Myron Cohen's act, or those who have Jewish friends, may well be familiar with either that specific joke and/or that specific word.

"And, having toyed with—but not touched—his serving of beef Stroganoff, he saw you order a special dinner that began and ended with dairy products and not meat. That, in itself, of course, would not have been nearly enough for the rabbi to arrive at any hard conclusion. Except that he, like the others, was looking for something, anything. And he would have been much more sensitized to Jewish dietary laws than a Gentile. Apparently, it was enough to trigger his inquisitiveness. He had access to the same press release I saw. He knew you were born in Imlay City and that you had been a Catholic. Proof was only a phone call away—for him as well as for me.

"Once he learned that you were officially Jewish, he saw his magic bargaining chip. And it was evident in his behavior. Before his discovery he meekly agreed to appear at this convocation and was submissive to you at dinner.

"And then came the remarkable transition. Rabbi Winer challenged you among ourselves, and before the students. Indeed, the rabbi was the only one of this faculty who dared oppose you publicly.

"You know, I've always thought one of the strongest proofs for the resurrection of Jesus was the transformation of the Apostles. From the first time we meet them as Jesus calls them to follow Him, the Apostles never come off as particularly admirable or courageous men. And that includes their deserting Jesus when he was crucified. Then, something very definitely happened. Something had to have happened for these ordinary men, who very justly could have been termed cowards, to change so dramatically. One day they are cowering behind locked doors, hiding from their enemies. Then, suddenly, they become fearless. They are transformed, in an instant, into true, brave, and courageous followers of Jesus.

"Something had to have happened. I believe it had to be the resurrection of Jesus—his triumph over death—just as they claimed.

"Well, to a lesser degree, something had to have happened in the life of Irving Winer. One day he meekly comes to this assembly when summoned. The next day he becomes the one and only fearless opponent of Reverend Krieg. Something had to have happened. I believe, Reverend, it was the discovery of your Jewish heritage. He knew. He *knew*.

"He must have told you on Monday what he had discovered. You probably denied it, but he had the proof.

"You saw that your only hope was in getting rid of the only one who knew your secret. You didn't have much time but you used it well. He knew your secret and you knew his. It was a Mexican stand-off. You had to find a way of upsetting that balance in your favor.

"And that, Reverend, is why you killed him."

"Now, wait!"

But Krieg's voice no longer snapped with a commanding tone.

"After dinner on Sunday," Koesler continued, "you offered us drinks from your impressive supply. We each selected a liqueur. As the polite host naturally you chose last. You chose the Frangelico—which happened to be the same bottle Rabbi Winer had selected. Later, you took advantage of that coincidence. Then, when the rabbi was found dead from drinking the poisoned Frangelico, we reached the conclusion you were leading us to.

"And, maybe—now that I think of it—we may just have uncovered another reason why you wanted the police in on this and why you made sure I'd be here and, you hoped, would summon the police.

"As far as Marie, Augustine, and Benbow were concerned, you held all the cards. The possibility that you might have had a secret past likely would never have occurred to any of them. But Rabbi Winer shared your Jewish heritage, at least in part. If any one of your victims might have stumbled upon your secret it surely would have been the Rabbi. You must have had good reason to fear that something—some unconscious habit, some quirk of behavior—might give the Rabbi cause to delve into your background and ferret out the truth you feared might be discovered. And, indeed, it seems he did.

"In such an eventuality, should it occur, you had to have an alternate plan. One that would do away with the Rabbi while making it appear that you had been the real target and that it was your life that had been—and continued to be—threatened. And for this scenario, you, of course, needed the police. And I got them for you."

At this point Mangiapane hurried back into the room, whispered animatedly with Tully, then left the room again. Mangiapane was perturbed or excited, Koesler couldn't tell which. In either case, he wanted to conclude his narrative.

"In any case, when Rabbi Winer was found poisoned from drinking the Frangelico you both favored, the conclusion everyone reached was exactly what you wanted: Someone had attempted to kill you by poisoning your liquor. Whoever that someone was, he or she had to get in line. But, by mistake, Rabbi Winer drank the poison intended for you. That had to be the case since quite a few people had motivation to kill you. And no one wanted to kill the rabbi.

"No one but yourself.

"After dinner, everyone left the dining area. Some of us went to a movie, others took a walk or retired to their rooms. The dining room, once it was cleared, would be empty. You invited Rabbi Winer to join you. You probably intimated you'd work everything out with him.

"Maybe you had several options. But the way it worked out you were left undisturbed. You offered him the Frangelico. He drank it and died almost instantaneously. Then you left. You didn't even have to worry about fingerprints, since your prints as well as Winer's were already on the bottle that we all saw both of you use earlier."

"You didn't even have to worry about being seen coming out of the dining room; had you been, all you would have had to do was pretend that you had just found the rabbi's body and were going for help. But that wasn't necessary. Your luck held; nobody saw you. Your luck held . . ." he repeated, ". . . until now."

Krieg summoned his last ounce of bravado. "Father Koesler, you don't have a shred of proof for all the false accusations you've made. You've created a pleasant story without any foundation whatsoever. And besides the fact that you have no proof, if it is not my life that has been threatened throughout this workshop, then how do you explain the latest attempt to kill me just a little while ago when someone tried to arrange it that I would blow myself to kingdom come? Are you going to suggest that I did that to myself? How could I when I was being guarded, protected by a detail of Detroit police officers all morning?"

A triumphant tone crept into Krieg's voice as he concluded what had to be his ultimate defense.

"That's true," Sergeant Moore attested. "We had some of our people with him all morning. Even if he'd wanted to, he couldn't have dumped that gasoline in his room."

Tully spoke. "I may have the explanation. A few minutes ago I was pretty sure where you were going with your explanation, Father. So I tried to anticipate you. Krieg could have carried the whole thing off with the exception of the gasoline attempt on his life. But if he'd done the whole thing—and I have to agree with you, he did do it—and the explosive gas was another attempt to convince us someone out there was still after him, then he had to have help."

"Guido Taliafero," Koesler almost whispered. He'd forgotten all about Krieg's "shadow."

"Uh-huh," Tully affirmed. "I sent Mangiapane out to find him and start asking him some hard questions. Mangiapane came back to tell me that Taliafero is one scared hombre. He's startin' to sing pretty good. And the subject of his song is you, Krieg."

"Reverend Krieg . . ." Koznicki spoke with the solemnity of an Inquisitor General. "I place you under arrest for the murder of Rabbi Irving Winer. Sergeant Moore will now inform you of your rights."

24

THE KOZNICKIS' HOME had that special lived-in atmosphere that comes from having and raising a family in it over a great number of years. The rooms seemed to echo with childish voices; the floors seemed to creak and groan under pounding young feet. The voices and the feet belonged to the active children who were now grown and gone and raising their own families.

The den belonged to Walt Koznicki. It was a man's room. It was a police officer's room. Citations and trophies vied for space with books and with photos of Koznicki as a beat cop, in various stages of advancement, with notables—Detroiters and visiting firemen. The little remaining space held several heavy chairs and a small desk, leaving barely enough room to navigate.

The weather on this, the second Sunday in September, was dreary. Rain beat down in body-seeking torrents, and the added forecast of thunderstorms made staying inside seem even cozier.

Walt and Wanda Koznicki had invited Father Koesler to dinner, which was over now. Wanda would join them in the den as soon as she had put away the leftovers and loaded the dishwasher. Koznicki and Koesler sat quietly, satisfied and comfortable, watching the steady rain beat against the window.

Both were lost in thoughts, which were interrupted when Wanda entered the room carrying a tray.

"Ah," Koznicki said, "you will join us now?"

"As soon as everything's done in the kitchen," Wanda said. "I just brought you some fresh coffee." She placed a full cup on a small stand next to Koesler's chair. "You take yours black, don't you, Father?"

Koesler smiled. "Every single time," he said.

Wanda glanced at him. It was an odd response. She thought he might elaborate. But since the priest said no more, she put the other cup near her husband and left the room.

Koznicki was smiling broadly. He had caught the allusion of Koesler's words. "That was the beginning, was it not?"

"I guess it was." Koesler savored the aroma of Wanda's coffee. For a woman who liked coffee as much as she, he wondered why she never seemed to want any when she made it. "Krieg was right. I was not at all surprised when he was familiar with a Yiddish word. Myron Cohen could have told that joke; maybe he did. When he got to the punch line, the very context would have defined 'Gevalt!' And once you heard it you'd remember it.

"But I did wonder about Krieg's diet. It wasn't too surprising when he preferred an omelet to the Stroganoff. It was a little odd, though, that he didn't eat what was served. Most people do at sit-down dinners. It's the rare bird who insists on an entirely different main dish. It was just out of the ordinary enough to attract my attention so that I took note of what else he ate at that first dinner we shared."

"I am surprised," Koznicki said, "that Sister Janet, or

whoever planned the menu, didn't take into account the Jewish dietary laws—in honor of Rabbi Winer's presence.''

Koesler smiled. ''It's just as well she didn't—or I never would've latched on to the discrepancy . . . there wouldn't have been anything for me to pick up on.'' He shook his head. ''That's the interesting thing about the Gentiles' perception of Jews. We tend to think of the Jews as abstaining from pork. So we make sure not to insult our Jewish guests by including pork on the menu. We don't stop to consider the rest of the Old Testament injunction, 'Thou shalt not boil a kid in its mother's milk.'

''In any case, I didn't really pay that much attention to the dinner Monday evening until we were served coffee. Sister Janet took cream. I guess it was subconscious, but I was waiting for Krieg to ask that the cream be passed to him. When he took his coffee black, it dawned on me why I was waiting for him to ask for the cream. It was because he had taken cream the night before.

''Of course there was no reason to draw any sort of inference at all. It was just odd and it stuck in my mind. Actually, to be honest, I bought the whole thing about some sort of plot to kill Krieg. First, there was that seemingly unreasonable animosity the writers had for Krieg. Then, after what appeared to be the botched effort to murder Krieg that ended in the death of Winer, I was sure that one of the remaining three was guilty—or that possibly there was a conspiracy. It just made me sad. I didn't want to suspect any of these people. But it seemed unavoidable.''

Koznicki sipped gingerly at the still hot coffee. ''And so it might have been. Sister Marie admitted that she and David Benbow did discuss a plan to do away with Krieg. But it came to no more than that: a meeting that concluded with their admitting to each other that they simply were incapable of murder.

"Then David Benbow was forced by Sister Marie's confession to admit that he had surreptitiously extended a similar invitation to Augustine and Winer. Of course we know now that the rabbi was the only one of the four writers who knew exactly what he was doing. He held the key to the one chink in Krieg's armor. And Augustine had his own plan for Krieg, which, likewise, he had to abandon because he was incapable of killing anyone."

"Unlike Krieg," Koznicki added.

"Unlike Krieg," Koesler concurred. "It wasn't until I stood looking at that press release and the fact sheets your people worked up that everything began falling into place. To borrow the words of Father Augustine, it was the whole damn thing. That there was no Catholic vestige at all visible in Krieg made him seem to be not quite what he was supposed to be. Then the dominos began to fall. I remembered quite vividly how Rabbi Winer alone seemed able to stand up to him. And there were the dietary peculiarities. Then even 'Gevalt!' fell into place.

"And then," he said, "Lieutenant Tully and I talked about how odd it was that Krieg wasn't scared, didn't seem concerned or fearful for his safety. Well, of course he wouldn't be, since his life was not actually at stake."

"The ironic thing," Koesler mused, "is that even though Rabbi Winer discovered Krieg's secret, I'm sure it wasn't necessary for Krieg to kill him. Let's face it: It was truly a stand-off. Sure, Winer knew about Krieg. But Krieg knew about Winer. And that reciprocal knowledge was the best defense for each of the two. But Krieg panicked. All he could think of was getting rid of the one person who had the power to destroy him and his empire. And, when it came right down to it, having panicked he did fairly well at thinking on his feet. He took advantage of the coincidence that he and Winer shared the same drink preference. He took advantage of his own psychodrama 'murder'—it fell right into his spur of the moment plot. Unless . . .'' Koesler hesitated. ''Unless, of course, the alternate hypothesis was true: that Krieg had this whole plot formed well in advance.

''In either case,'' he concluded, ''it was Krieg who killed Winer.''

''How sad,'' said Koznicki. ''It was all so unnecessary. Most assuredly, the rabbi would have kept Krieg's secret, using the knowledge only to make Krieg back off and desist hounding him and the other three writers. And''—he spoke increasingly slowly and thoughtfully—''we will never know, of course, but one wonders whether another factor, no matter how slight, was that, having betrayed fellow Jews almost a half-century before and having suffered the intense long-term guilt over it, one wonders whether Rabbi Winer would have held back due to the thought of again informing on a fellow Jew—even though undoubtedly neither Krieg nor the rabbi would have considered Krieg truly Jewish.

''Or is it,'' he looked at Koesler, ''something like, 'Once a Catholic always a Catholic,' . . . or, 'Once a priest always a priest'?''

Koesler smiled and shrugged. He seemed lost in thought, ''Strange . . .'' he said, finally.

Koznicki waited, but when nothing more was said, he asked, ''Strange? What is strange?''

''Oh . . .'' Koesler stirred himself from reflection. ''I was just thinking about Krieg and Rabbi Winer—how similar their situations were.''

"Similar?"

"Yes. Each had a secret—and a deep-seated fear that he would be ruined if that closet skeleton were to be revealed. That fear haunted both Krieg and Winer, and, sadly, motivated Krieg in his fatal decision to murder the rabbi."

"Hmmm . . ." Koznicki murmured, ". . . and yet we learned that a few of the rabbi's fellow Jews did find out what had happened in the concentration camp and they had been understanding—forgiving even." He looked at Koesler questioningly. "Could that not have been the case with Reverend Krieg? Might his followers have been unconcerned about his Jewish heritage?"

Koesler shook his head. "I don't know, Inspector. I don't think anyone can tell for sure. The rabbi's forced collaboration with the Nazis was certainly not common knowledge. A rare few discovered it and those few loved and admired him enough to understand the impossible pressure he'd had to endure at Dachau. Would his entire congregation have been as understanding? Would his literary fans have found it easy to overlook, or to forgive and forget?

"The same thing with Krieg. We don't know that anyone knew his secret. I guess we'd just have to assume that he concealed his mother's ethnicity and religion.

"But what would have been the effect on his congregation, his millions of TV viewers, had they known? Would they have continued to support him and his ministry in the lavish manner to which he'd become accustomed?

"It would be nice to think," Koesler warmed to his speculation, "that the rabbi's congregation as well as his readers would have put themselves in his shoes. My Lord, he was only a kid! But, congregations do fire their rabbis—as well as their ministers.'' He smiled. ''Fortunately, it doesn't work that way with Catholic parish priests.

''But''—he grew serious again—''people can be fickle. By and large, they want their men of the cloth to be without blemish. If they find a chink in the armor, they can become disenchanted quickly—and cruelly. Besides, Rabbi Winer guarded that secret so carefully he didn't even confide in his wife. He must have been deeply ashamed. So, quite independent of any practical consequence to his ministry or his career as a writer, he feared his secret being revealed for more personal reasons.

''And the threat may have been more intense for Krieg.''

''Oh?'' Koznicki invited further comment.

''I think so. No television preacher can forget what happened a couple of years ago. Oral Roberts said God would call him if he didn't meet fund-raising goals. And he became a laughing stock. Jimmy Swaggart bought some private voyeurism and lost more than half his flock. Jim Bakker's sexual episode with a church secretary stung him badly and opened the door to a financial investigation that ruined him. Ever since those disasters, preachers have had to be extremely careful not to muddy the waters.

''Of course, Krieg broke no law. But, then neither did Oral Roberts. He just made himself play the fool. Krieg had to weigh the possibility that vast numbers of contributing Christians would be uncomfortable, to say the least, at being led by someone who—technically but indeed in fact—was a Jew.

''Now, I know you're going to say, 'But Jesus was a Jew.' Of course he was—but few Christians think of Him in that light. Obviously, it is rare, if not unique, that a Jew would become a Christian evangelist as popular and influential as Klaus Krieg. And obviously, Krieg thought it a serious problem or he wouldn't have guarded the secret as he did. Could his ministry have survived the revelation that he was Jewish?

"Remembering the thin ice Roberts, Swaggart, and Bakker found themselves skating on, I think it a good bet to speculate that Krieg might well have not survived. In any event, the possibility that he would have been ruined was strong enough to make him plot and carry out a murder.

"So, there we are." Koesler looked at Koznicki thoughtfully. "Would Krieg and Winer—or Sister Marie, David Benbow, and Augustine, for that matter—have lost their reputations, their vocations, their careers, had their secrets been disclosed? We don't know for sure. What we do know is that that's the way they perceived it. They believed in the worst-case scenario. And, in the end, that's what counted: Each and every one believed that he or she would be ruined. Each and every one was so embarrassed over the events of their past that they reacted in fear and dread.

"In the end, that's what counted," Koesler repeated. "They believed they would be ruined. Whether or not that actually would have happened doesn't matter as much as the fact that they believed it would."

"And now," Koznicki said, "the Reverend Krieg has been arrested and charged with murder in the first degree. Although I think it would be much more difficult to prove had Lieutenant Tully not thought of the chauffeur. And if Mr. Taliafero had been more intelligent, we might have had to work on him longer than we did. When we noted that his gloves reeked of gasoline, his excuse was that those were his work gloves and that they always smelled of gas and/or oil. But when we found the vial of cyanide in the limousine's glove compartment," he shook his head, "the end was not far off."

The Inspector grew more thoughtful. "The biggest complication the Reverend Krieg faced was time. Time to plan his strategy and time to carry it off. Actually, given those limitations, in very truth, he did quite well. It is not all that easy to find and purchase cyanide. I think Taliafero would never have found it, left to his own devices. It was Krieg who steered him toward a jewelry repair shop. That direction, plus all the money necessary to make an illegal purchase, was all he needed." Koznicki chuckled. "For their sake, it is a pity Krieg took it for granted that Taliafero would dispose of the remainder of the cyanide after poisoning the Frangelico." He looked a bit more thoughtful. "I wonder if he planned to use it on the Reverend himself eventually . . ."

"And, refresh me, Inspector; he was promised . . . ?"

"In exchange for agreeing to testify against Krieg—who had planned and plotted the entire affair—the chauffeur will be allowed to plead to second-degree murder. He will face a sentence of from ten to fifteen years. Otherwise, he would face the same sentence as Krieg: life in prison with no parole."

Koesler felt a slight shiver. He didn't know whether it was the chill weather or the prospect of a man like Krieg being behind bars without hope for the rest of his life. "There is no hope for Krieg? None at all?"

"In his sentence? Michigan is firm in life without parole for murder one. His only hope would be a pardon either from the governor or the president."

"Now that you mention that," Koesler said, "I wonder whether he might pull it off. Did you see him on the local and national newscasts the other night? His tears would make Jeremiah envious. If anyone is looking for a contrite sinner, he need look no further. What difference does it make that it's all an act? There are few politicians who do not highly value and carefully practice the art of acting.

"You know," he said, pensively, "at one time Klaus Krieg had everything he needed to lead an exemplary life. His father cared enough to go through all the rules and regulations and conquer all the obstacles for a Catholic marriage. His mother showed her love and devotion for her Jewish heritage as she taught him to respect noble Jewish traditions. He had the best of two great faiths. He became a respected religious leader. But none of that made him a good or holy person. Greed became his god.

"Oh, and that brings up one last question I meant to ask: What about Marie and David and Augustine? What about the skeletons in their closets?"

Koznicki hesitated for a moment. "I think they will be safe. Yes, I think they will. The writers and their secrets are no longer of any value whatsoever to Krieg.

"And perhaps—just perhaps—he may feel that his holding back might carry some needed weight when and if he applies for his hoped-for pardon. As we know—and the writers found out—his kind never stops manipulating—and never gives up."

"And," Koesler pressed, "was what he did to them—the blackmail—a crime? I heard one of your officers mention that if they hadn't nailed him for murder, at least they could have gotten him for extortion. And all the time, I thought money had to be involved in such cases."

"The officer was correct, at least technically. The crime of extortion is one of compulsion. The victim is compelled to do something he or she would not ordinarily do because of the threat made. It is a felony punishable by up to five years in prison. But it is easy to understand why the crime is

MURDER, MYSTERY and MORE!

from
William X. Kienzle

not frequently prosecuted. In this case, which of these writers would have felt strongly enough about the blackmail to voluntarily reveal the secret in order to prosecute the case?''

There was another brief silence.

''Well,'' Koznicki observed finally, ''it was a short week.''

Koesler nodded. ''Not quite two full days. Marygrove refunded the students' tuition. Which I thought was more than generous, seeing the students got more instruction and information from the real-life events than they ever would have gotten from all the classes we might have conducted.''

Wanda reentered the den, carrying a tray with three small glasses and an attractive bottle of liqueur. ''Anyone care for an after-dinner drink?''

Both Koznicki and Koesler were caught off-guard. For a few seconds they were frozen. Then they began to laugh.

''Sorry,'' Wanda said, joining in their laughter, ''but all we seem to have in the house is this Frangelico.'' She poured three drinks. ''I do read the papers, you know!''

Koznicki and Koesler raised their glasses to toast Wanda and each other. Simultaneously, they saluted, ''Praise God!''